"Woman's Need calls me, as Woman's Need made me. Her Need will I answer as my maker bade me."

The mage chanted furiously, in some language Kero didn't recognize. She somehow knew that the *sword* did, though; for the first time she felt something from it—a strange, slow anger, hot as a forge, and heavy as iron.

Kero *wanted* to run, but the sword wouldn't let her. She could only stand there, an easy target. The mage sneered, and raised his hands. They glowed for a moment, a sickly red, then the glow brightened and a spark arced between them.

The blade's anger rose to consume her, and she shifted her grip from the hilt to the sword-blade itself. She balanced her sword for a moment that way, as if it was, impossibly, nothing more than a giant throwing knife. It didn't seem to weigh any more than her dagger had at that moment.

Her arm came back, and she threw it, like a spear.

It flashed across the space between herself and the mage, arrow-straight and point-first. . . .

NOVELS BY MERCEDES LACKEY
available from DAW Books

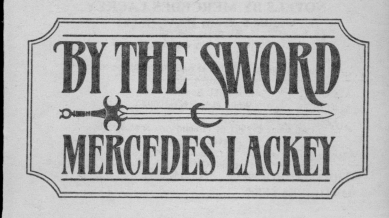

BY THE SWORD

MERCEDES LACKEY

DAW BOOKS, INC.

DONALD A. WOLLHEIM, FOUNDER

375 Hudson Street, New York, NY 10014

ELIZABETH R. WOLLHEIM
SHEILA E. GILBERT
PUBLISHERS

DAW Book Collectors No. 840.

First Printing, February 1991

6   7   8   9

DAW TRADEMARK REGISTERED
U.S. PAT. OFF. AND FOREIGN COUNTRIES
—MARCA REGISTRADA,
HECHO EN U.S.A.

Printed in the U.S.A.

Dedicated to the memory of
Stan Rogers
Singer, Songwriter, Inspiration
Whose words and music
gave me heart and courage
when I needed them most.

OFFICIAL TIMELINE FOR THE

by *Mercedes Lackey*

1000 BF   0   750 AF   798 AF

Founding of Valdemar

Prehistory
The Mage Wars:
Era of the Black Gryphon

Reign of Elspeth
the Peacemaker

THE LAST HERALD-
MAGE TRILOGY
Magic's Pawn

Reign of Randale

THE LAST HERALD-
MAGE TRILOGY
Magic's Promise
Magic's Price

BF   Before the Founding
AF   After the Founding

HERALDS OF VALDEMAR SERIES

Sequence of events by Valdemar reckoning

| 1270 AF | 1315 AF | 1355 AF | 1376 AF |

Reign of Roald

Reign of Sendar

Reign of Co-consorts Arden & Leesa

VOWS AND HONOR DUOLOGY
The Oathbound
Oathbreakers

Reign of Selenay

THE HERALDS OF VALDEMAR TRILOGY
Arrows of the Queen
Arrow's Flight
Arrow's Fall

BY THE SWORD

THE MAGE WINDS TRILOGY
Winds of Fate
Winds of Change
Winds of Fury

BOOK ONE

Kerowyn's Ride

One

"Blessed—look *out!*"

Everyone turned and stared; at Kero, and at the boy about to lose the towering platter of bread. The racket of pots and voices stopped, and Kerowyn's voice rang out in the silence like a trumpet call, but no one answered *this* call to arms. They all seemed confused or frozen with indecision. The scullion staggered two more steps forward; the edible sculpture, two clumsy, obese bread-deer (a stag and a reclining doe), began sliding from the oversized serving dish he was attempting to carry alone.

Idiots! Kerowyn swore again, this time with an oath her mother would have blanched to hear, but it seemed as if she was the only one with the will or brains to act. She sprinted across the slickly damp floor of the kitchen, and caught the edge of the platter just as the enormous subtlety of sweet, egg-glazed dough started to head for the flagstones.

The lumpy mountain stopped just short of the carved display plate's edge. She held it steady while young Derk, sweating profusely, regained his breath and his balance, and took the burden of twenty pounds of sweet, raisin-studded bread back from her.

He got the thing properly settled on his shoulder and headed for the Great Hall to place it before the wedding party. Kero listened for a moment, then heard the shouts and applause from beyond the kitchen door as the bread sculpture appeared. The clamor in the kitchen resumed.

Kero licked sweat from her upper lip, and sighed. She would have *liked* to have staggered backward and leaned against the wall to catch her breath, but she didn't dare take the time, not at this point in the serving. The moment she paused there would undoubtedly be three more near disasters; if she took her attention away from the preparations, the tightly-planned schedule would fall apart.

She knew very well she really shouldn't be here. She probably *should* have been out there with the rest of the guests, playing Keep Lady; that was what would have been "proper."

To the six hells with "proper." If Father wants this feast to be a success, I have to be in here, not playing the lady.

The kitchen was as hot as any one of the six hells, and crowded with twice the number of people it was intended to hold. The cook, an immense man with the build of a wrestler, and his young helpers were all squeezed in behind one side of a huge table running the entire length of the kitchen. Normally they worked on both sides, but tonight the servers were running relay with platters and bowls on the other side, and may the gods help anyone in the way.

Kero chivvied her recruited corps of horse-grooms out the door. They were a lot more used to being served from the beer pitchers they were carrying than doing the serving themselves. Then she spotted something out of the corner of her eye and paused long enough to snatch up a wooden spoon. She used it to reach across the expanse of scarred wooden tabletop and whack one of the pages on the knuckles. She got him to rights, too, trying to steal a fingerful of icing from the wedding cake standing in magnificent isolation on the end of the table butted up against the wall. The boy yelped and jumped back, colliding with one of the cook's helpers and earning himself a black look and another whack with a spoon.

"Leave that be, Perry!" she scolded, brandishing the spoon at him. "That's for after the ceremony, and don't you forget it! You can eat yourself sick on the scraps tomorrow for all *I* care, but you leave it alone tonight, or more than your knuckles will be hurting, I promise you."

The shock-haired boy whined a halfhearted apology and started to sulk; to stave off a sullen fit she shoved a handful of trencher slabs across the table at him and told him to go see that the minstrels were fed.

Some day . . . spoiled brat. I wish Father'd send him back to his doting mama. A cat's more use than he is, especially when everybody's too busy to keep an eye on him.

Fortunately, all Perry had to do was show up with the slabs of trencher bread and the minstrels would see to their own feeding. Kero hadn't met a songster yet that didn't know how to help himself at a feast.

The first meat course was over; time for the vegetable pies, and the dishes straw-haired Ami had been plunging into her tub with frantic haste were done *just* in time. Kero sent the next lot in, laden with heavy pies and stacks of bowls, just as the remains of the venison and the poor, hacked up bits of the bread-deer came in.

It's a good thing that monstrosity didn't hit the ground, she reflected soberly, snagging Perry as he slouched in behind the servers and sending him back out again with towels for the wedding guests to wipe their greasy fingers. *What with Dierna's family device being the red deer and all, her people would have taken that as a bad omen for sure.* There was no subtlety for this course, thank all the gods and goddesses—

Not that Father didn't want *one. More dough sculpture, this time a rampant stag—as a testament to my darling brother's virility, no doubt. It's a good thing Cook had a fit over all the nonsense that was* already *going to wind up being crammed into the oven!*

There was a momentary lull, as the last of the emptied dishes arrived and the last of the servers staggered out; and everyone in the kitchen took a moment to sag over a table or against the wall, fanning overheated faces. Kero thought longingly of the cool night air just beyond the thick planks of the door at her back. But her father's Seneschal poked his nose in the doorway, and she pushed away from the worn wood with a suppressed sigh.

"Any complaints so far?" she asked him, her voice clear and carrying above the murmur of the helpers and the roar of the fire under the ovens.

"Just that the service is slow," Seneschal Wendar replied, mopping his bald head with his sleeve. "Audria's Teeth, child, how do you stand it in here? You could bake the next course on the counters!"

Kero shrugged. *Because I don't have a choice.* "I'm used to it, I suppose, I've been here since before dawn. Anyway, you know I've supervised everything since before Mother died.'' The simple words only called up a dull ache now; that priest had been right—

Damn him.

—time did make sorrow fade, at least it had for her. Time, and being too busy to breathe.

"I'm sorry I can't do much about the service," she continued, keeping an ear cocked for the sounds of the servers returning. "There's only so much stableboys and hire-swords can learn about the server's art in a couple of candlemarks.''

"I know that, my dear." The Seneschal, a thin, tired-looking man who had been the scribe and accountant with Rathgar's old mercenary company, laid a fatherly hand on her arm, and she resisted the urge to shrug it off. "I think you're doing remarkably well, better than *I* would have, and I mean that sincerely. I can't imagine how you've managed all this with as little help as you've had."

Because Father was too tightfisted to hire extra help for me, and too full of pride to settle for anything less than a princely wedding feast. Lord Orsen Brodey consented to this marriage; Lord Orsen Brodey must be shown that we're no jumped-up barbarians . . . even if Rathgar's daughter has to spend the entire feast in the kitchen with the hirelings. . . .

She felt her cheeks and ears flush with anger. It wasn't fair, it wasn't—not that she really wanted to be out in the Great Hall either, showing off for potential suitors and their lord-fathers. Bad enough that Rathgar never thought of her; worse that he'd think of her only in terms of being marriage bait.

Which he would, if he ever thought past Lordan's marriage . . . Lordan's *far* more important marriage. After all, *he* was the male and the heir . . . Kero was only a girl.

Kero set her jaw and tried to look cheerful, or at least indifferent, but something of her resentment must have penetrated the careful mask of calm and competence she was trying to cultivate. Wendar patted her arm again and looked distressed.

"I wish I could help," he said unhappily. "I told your father three years ago, when—when—"

"When Mother died," Kero said shortly.

He coughed. "Uh, indeed. I told him that you needed a housekeeper, but he wouldn't hear of it. He said you were already doing very well, and you didn't need any help."

Kero clenched her teeth, then relaxed with an effort. "Somehow that doesn't surprise me. Father—" She clamped her lips tight on what she was going to say; it wouldn't do any good, it wouldn't change anything.

But the sentence went on inside her head. *Father never really notices anything about me so long as I stay out of sight, his dinner arrives on time, and the Keep doesn't smell like a stable. I suppose if anyone had mentioned that a fourteen-year-old girl shouldn't be forced into the job of Keep Lady alone, he'd have said that the girls in his village were married and mothers by fourteen. Never mind that the most any of them had to manage alone was a two-room cottage and a flock of sheep, and usually didn't like even that. . . .*

She sighed, and finished her sentence in a way that wouldn't put more strain on Wendar than he was already coping with. "Father had other things to worry about. And so do you, Wendar. You've got a hall full of guests out there, and no one keeping an eye on the servitors."

Wendar swore, and hurried back toward the door into the Great Hall, just as the wave of servants returned with the dirty dishes from the last course. Wendar sidestepped the rush, and dodged between two of them and through the doorway.

Stuffed pigeons were next; a course that required nothing more than the bread trenchers. That would give the kitchen staff enough time to clean the platters now being brought in before the fish course of eel pies was served.

A full High Feast, and who was it had to figure out how our little backwoods Keep could come up with enough courses to satisfy the requirements? Me, of course. Tubs full of eel in the garden for days, the moat stocked with fish in a net-pen, crates of pigeons and hens driving us all crazy . . . let's not talk about the rest of the livestock. Kero rubbed her arms, and rerolled the sleeves of her flour-covered, homespun shirt a little higher. *Damn these skirts. Breeches would be easier. The helpers get to wear breeches, so why can't I?* She wondered if Dierna had any notion of how much work a High

Feast was. She ought to; she'd been trained by the Sisters of Agnetha—in fact she'd been sent to the Sisters' cloister at the ripe age of eight, so she ought to have had time to learn the "womanly arts."

Dierna ought to have had *proper* instruction in those womanly arts too, as well as the art of being womanly, whatever that meant . . . unlike Kero, as Rathgar was so prone to remind her whenever she failed to live up to his notion of "womanly."

Selective memory, she told herself bitterly. *He keeps forgetting that he was the one who decided he couldn't do without me.* Wheat-crowned Agnetha was Rathgar's idea of the appropriate sort of deity for a lady to worship—unlike wild, horse-taming Agnira, Kero's favorite. There was a shrine to Agnetha in the Keep chapel, though the other aspects of the LadyTrine were only represented by little bas-reliefs carved into the pedestal of Agnetha's statue. There in the heart of the chapel, Agnetha smiled with honeyed sweetness over her twin babies, her wheat sheaves at her feet, her cloak of fruit-laden vines around her, her distaff dangling from her belt of flowers, sheep gazing up at her adoringly. While on the pedestal, alternating snowflakes and hoofprints were all there was to show of the other two aspects, Agnoma and Agnira. Rathgar approved of Agnetha, occasionally waxing maudlin over his somewhat sketchy devotion when in his cups.

Well, after the feast, the wedding, and the month-long bridal moon, Kero could probably give up the keys of the Keep to Dierna. That would bring an end to the farce of pretending to enjoy being mewed up in the kitchen, still-room or bower day after endlessly boring day. Dierna was pliant enough to satisfy both Rathgar and his son, and she seemed competent when Kero had taken her on a quick tour when the girl first arrived.

Kero shook herself out of her reverie as the servitors appeared with platters piled high with soaked trencher bread. She had them dump the bread into sacks waiting for distribution to the poor. Time for the bowls and eel-pies.

Cook was head-and-shoulders deep into the oven, removing the next subtlety, and Kero overheard one of his assistants giving orders for the pies to be carried out first.

"Hold it right there!" she snapped, freezing the servants where they stood. She stalked to the table, plain brown linen skirts flaring, and countermanded the order, physically taking a pie away from one poor confused lad and shoving a pile of clean bowls into his hands instead. The harried young man didn't care; all he wanted was someone to give him the right thing to carry in, and tell him what he was to do with it.

Kero repeated the instructions she'd given them all for the soup course, as she passed out further piles of bowls. "One bowl for every two guests, put the bowl between them, when you've finished placing the bread, go to the sideboard, get trencher bread, give each guest a trencher, then come back and get a pie."

It made a kind of chant as she repeated herself for each servingman. Outside, Wendar would be directing the men to their tables; no matter that they'd been going to the same places all night. By now they were tired and numb with the noise and the work, and all they were thinking of was when the feast could be over so they could eat and drink themselves into a celebratory stupor.

Dierna was probably beginning to wilt under all this by now. That much Kero didn't envy her. When the older girl had taken her on that round of the Keep duties, she'd been a little shy—and Kero knew very well how sheltered the girls trained by the Sisters tended to be. Not *ignorant,* no; the Sisters made certain their charges were well-educated in the realities of life as well as domestic skills. But perhaps that was the problem; Dierna was like a young squire who has watched swordwork all his young life and only now, at fifteen, was going to pick up a blade. She knew what was *supposed* to happen, but was unprepared for the reality of the situation.

The first of the servitors returned for his pie, and Kero made certain he didn't take it without a towel wrapped about his hands. She wondered, as she passed out towels and pies in a seemingly endless stream, what Rathgar would do or say the first time dinner was inedible or there were no clean shirts for him.

Probably nothing. Or else he'd find a way to blame Kero.

What is wrong with the man? she asked herself in frustration for the thousandth time. *I'm doing the best that I*

*can with what he allows me! It wouldn't be so bad if he
didn't pick faults that no one else cares about. Maybe if
I'd talked him round to doing without me and gone to the
cloister. . . .*

She watched the cook prepare the next subtlety, an
enormous copy of the Keep itself complete with edible
landscaping, and made sure that two men were assigned
to carry *it* out. The mingled odors of meat and fish and
fowl weren't at all appetizing right now; in fact, they
made her stomach churn. When this was all over, the
most she'd want would be bread and cheese, and maybe
a little cider.

Or maybe the problem that made her stomach churn
was the thought of what could have happened if she'd
actually gone to the cloisters. While not mages, the Sisters had a reputation for being able to uncover things
people would rather have been left secret. What if Kero
had gone, and the reputation was more than just kitchen
gossip? What if the Sisters had found her out?

*Father has had plenty to say about Grandmother. "The
old witch" was the most civil thing he's ever called her.
What if he'd found out he had a young witch of his own?*

*He'd have birthed a litter of kittens, that's what he'd
have done. Then disowned me. It's bad enough that I ride
better than Lordan and train my own beasts; it's worse
that I hunt stag and boar with the men. It's worse when
I wear Lordan's castoffs to ride. But if he ever found out
about my apparently being witch-born, I think he'd throw
me out of the Keep.*

The mingled cooking odors still weren't making her in
the least hungry; she helped Cook decorate the next
course with sprigs of watercress and other herbs, chewed
a sprig of mint to cool her mouth and told her upset
stomach to settle itself.

"What if" never changes anything, she reminded herself. *He never did more than play with the idea, and he
didn't want to take the chance that Wendar couldn't handle things. After all, the only thing Wendar has ever done
was keep track of the books and manage the estate.
There's more to managing a Keep than doing the accounts.* She set sprigs of cress with exaggerated care.
*Come to think of it, Wendar may have discouraged Father
in the first place from sending me away. I suppose I can't*

blame him, he has more than enough to do without having to run the Keep, too. That may be why Father kept saying that it wasn't "convenient" for me to go.

Why did Mother have to die, anyway? she thought in sudden anger. *Why should I have been left with all this on my hands?*

For a moment, she was actually angry at Lenore—then guilt for thinking that way made her flush, and she hid her confused blushes by getting a drink from the bucket of clean drinking water in the corner of the kitchen farthest from the ovens.

She stared down into the bucket for a moment, unhappy and disturbed. *Why am I thinking things like that? It's wrong; Mother didn't mean to die like that. It wasn't her fault, and she did the best she could to get me ready when she knew she wasn't going to get better. She couldn't have known Father wouldn't hire anyone to help me.*

And I guess it's just as well I didn't end up with the Sisters, and for more reasons than having witch-blood. They probably wouldn't have approved of me either, hunting and hawking like a boy, out riding all the time. At least at home I've had chances to get away and enjoy myself; at the cloister I'd never have gotten out.

Agnetha's Sheaves—how can anybody stand this without going mad? Kitchen to bower, bower to stillroom, stillroom back to kitchen. Potting, preserving, and drying; then spinning and weaving and sewing. Running after the servants like a tell-tale, making sure everybody does his job. Scrubbing and dusting and laundry; polishing and mending. Cooking and cooking and cooking. Brewing and baking. At least at home I can run outside and take a ride whenever it gets to be too much—

There was a sudden stillness beyond the kitchen door, and something about the silence made Kero raise her head and glance sharply at the open doorway.

Then the screaming began.

For one moment, she assumed that the disturbance was just something they'd all anticipated, but hoped to avoid. This could be an old feud erupting into new violence. Rathgar had, after all, invited many of his neighbors, including men who had long-standing disagreements with each other, though not with Rathgar himself. That was why all weapons were forbidden in the Hall, and not especially welcome within the Keep walls. Except for Rathgar's men, of course. No one would have felt safe guarded by men armed only with flower garlands and headless pikes. Rathgar had anticipated that too much drink might awaken old grievances or create new ones, and rouse tempers to blows.

But after that fleeting thought, Kero somehow knew that this was something far more serious than a simple quarrel between two hot-tempered men, new grievance or old. Rathgar could handle either of those, and the noise was increasing, not abating.

And that same nebulous instinct told her that she'd better not go see what was wrong in person.

She braced herself against the wall with one hand, a hand of cold fear between her shoulder blades, and she realized that it was time to try something she had seldom dared attempt inside the Keep.

She closed her eyes, and opened her mind to the thoughts of those around her.

The walls she had forged about her mind had been wrought painfully over the years, and she didn't drop them lightly, especially with so many people about. At first she had thought she was going mad with grief over her mother's death, but chance reading had shown her otherwise. Her grandmother, the sorceress Kethry, had left several books with Lenore, and after her mother's death, these had been given to Kero along with Lenore's other personal possessions. Kero had never known what had prompted her to pick out that particular book, but she had blessed the choice as goddess-sent. The book had proved to her that the ''voices'' she had been hearing were really the strongest thoughts of those around her. More importantly to a confused young girl, the book had taught her how to block those voices out.

But now she was going to have to remove those comforting barriers, for at least a moment.

The clamor that flooded into her skull wasn't precisely painful, but it was disorienting and *exactly* like being in a tiny room filled with twice the number of screaming, shouting people it was intended to hold.

Steady on—it's just like being in the kitchen—

Her stomach lurched, and she clutched the wall behind

her, as dizzy as if she'd been spun around like one of Lordan's old toy tops.

Pain and fear made those thoughts pouring into her mind incoherent; she got brief glimpses of armed men, strangers in no lord's colors—men who were filthy, ragged, and yet well-armed and armored. She was half-aware of the servants, babbling with terror, streaming through the door opposite her, but most of her mind was caught up in the tangled mental panic outside that door. And now she was "seeing" things, too, and she nearly threw up. The strangers were making a slaughterhouse of the Great Hall, cutting down not only those who resisted, but those who were simply in their way.

Their minds seized on hers and held it. She struggled to free herself from the confusion, wrenching her mind out of the desperate, unconscious clutching of theirs— and suddenly her thoughts brushed against something.

Something horrible.

There were no words for what she felt at that moment, as time stood frozen for her and she knew how a hunted rabbit must view a great, slavering hound. Whatever this was, it was cold, if a thought *could* be cold, cold as the slimy leeches living in the swampy fen below the cattle pastures. There was something sly about it, and filthy— not a physical filth, but a feeling that the mind behind these thoughts would never be contented with pleasures most folk considered normal. Kero couldn't quite decipher them either; what she experienced was similar to what she had "heard" as her ability first appeared—as if she were listening to someone speaking too quietly for the exact words to be made out. There was only a sense of speech, not the meaning.

But worst of all, that brief brush created a change in those not-quite-readable thoughts, as if she had alerted the owner of the thoughts that he—or she—or *it*—was being observed.

The back of her neck crawled, and gooseflesh rose on her arms, as the thoughts took on a new, sharp-edged urgency. Propelled by fear, she managed to tear her mind away, and slammed the doors in the walls of her protections closed.

She opened her eyes, sick and sweating with fear, to discover that far less time had passed than she imagined.

The servants were still clogging the doorway, and the screaming from beyond had only increased.

For an instant, all she wanted to do was to scream and cower with the rest of them—or even faint as some of the kitchen girls had already done, sprawling unnoticed beneath the table. At that moment, something as hard and impassive as the walls around her mind rose up to cut off her emotions. Suddenly she could think, calmly.

The door to the back court—if they come in behind us, we'll be trapped—

Freed from the paralysis of fear, she ran to the back door of the kitchen, slammed it shut, and dropped the iron bar of the night-lock into place across it. The noise behind her was so overwhelming that the sound of the heavy bar dropping into the supports was completely swallowed up in the general chaos.

She whirled, stood on her tiptoes to see over the mob crowding between her and the door, and looked frantically for two people—Wendar, and the cook. Wendar's balding head appeared in a clear spot for a moment next to the table, and she spotted the cook, burly arm upraised and brandishing a poker, beside him. Cook was shouting something, but she couldn't even hear his voice above the others.

Wendar served with Father, and Cook takes no nonsense from anyone—in fact, Cook looks like he's ready to lead a charge back in there!

She dove into the press of bodies and struggled across the kitchen, elbowing and punching her way past hysterical servants who seemed to have no more sense left in them than frightened sheep. As she dragged a last wailing girl out of her way by the back of her rough leather bodice, Kero got Wendar's attention by the simple expedient of grabbing his collar and dragging herself to him. Or more specifically, to the vicinity of his ear.

"We've got to stop them at the door," she screamed, hardly able to hear herself. *"We can hold them there, but if they get in here, they'll kill us all!"*

Most likely Wendar didn't have any better idea of who "they" were than Kero did, but at least he saw the sense of her words immediately. He turned and reached across the table for Cook's shirt; satisfied that he would handle the rest, Kero looked for weapons, snatched up a heavy, round pot lid and the longest meat knife within reach, and ran for the door.

She reached it not a moment too soon.

There was no warning that the invaders had found the half-hidden stair to the kitchen. He was just *there;* a squat, broad shadow in the doorway, sword negligently stuck through his belt, plainly expecting no resistance. He paused for a moment and squinted into the brightly-lit kitchen, then he saw her, and grinned, reaching for her.

Kero had no time to think. Training took over as wit failed.

"This's no dance lesson, girl!" She could hear the armsmaster's bellow in the back of her mind even as she slashed for the man's unprotected eyes. *"This's fightin' o' th' dirtiest—y' hit yer man now an' hit 'im so's 'e knows 'e's friggin'-well been hit!"*

Armsmaster Dent could have been dismissed for teaching Kero *anything* besides archery, and well he knew it. He'd done his best to discourage her when she presented herself beside Lordan for training. It was only when he caught her clumsily trying blows against the pells with a practice blade too long and heavy for her, and realized that Rathgar would assume he'd been training Kero anyway if her father ever found her out there himself, that he made a bargain with her.

In return for a reluctant promise never to touch a longer weapon, he promised to teach her knife-fighting. He hadn't been happy about it, but Kero had made it very clear that it was the only way to keep her out of the armory and the practice ground.

Knife-work was, as Dent put it, the dirtiest, lowest form of combat, and figuring that if she ever really *needed* that training, it would be a case of desperation, he had taught her every trick he'd learned in a lifetime of street scuffling.

By some miracle, knife-work was also the only form of combat suited for the close confines of the kitchen doorway; the only kind of situation where a knife-fighter would be at an advantage against a swordsman. In the back of her mind, Kero thanked whatever deity had inspired that bargain with Dent, and slashed again at the

man's face when he evaded the wicked edge of her blade
with a startled oath.

He reached for his own weapon, hampered by the wall
at his side and the stairs at his back, further hampered
when the quillons caught on his ill-kept armor.

Then she was no longer alone; Cook and Wendar were
beside her, Cook armed with a spit as long as her arm in
one hand and a cleaver in the other, and Wendar (with a
pot over his bald head like an oddly-shaped helm) with
the even longer spit used when they roasted whole pigs
and calves. Cook stabbed at him with the wicked point
of the spit and the man dodged away, moving into Wendar's reach. Wendar brought the heavy, cast-iron rod
down on the man's head, and caved his helm in completely. The brigand fell backward, but another took his
place.

Now there were more men piling down the staircase;
how many, Kero couldn't tell. One of them dragged the
first out of the way, and the man on the stairs pulled him
into darkness.

But the three defenders had the doorway blocked
against all comers, with Kero going low, Wendar, high,
and the Cook holding the middle and protecting them
both with Kero's pot lid. Then one of the young squires
began lobbing ladles of hot turnips over their heads and
into the faces of their opponents, using the ladle like a
catapult. The stairs were already slippery; that made them
worse, and no one fights well with scalding vegetables
being flung in his eyes.

The invaders slashed and stabbed, but with caution.
More of the servants took heart; at least Kero assumed
they did, because suddenly the doorway was abristle with
knives and pokers to either side of her.

At that, the bandits pulled back, retreating up the staircase, slipping and sliding on the stones. It looked to Kero
as if more than one of them was marked and burned or
bleeding.

It was as if she stood outside of herself, a casual ob-
server. Her heart was pounding in her ears, yet she felt
strangely calm. A cluster of three of the raiders stood
just out of turnip-reach halfway down the staircase, staring down at the defenders of the kitchen. It was rather
hard to see them; the press of bodies in the doorway

blocked the light coming from the kitchen, and they themselves blotted out most of the light from above. Kero wished she could see their faces, and shifted uneasily from her right foot to her left.

If they get a log from upstairs and rush us with it, they could break through us, she realized. *Agnira, please, don't let them think of that—*

The men seemed to be arguing among themselves. Kero squinted against the darkness and strained her ears, but could hear nothing but the screaming from the hall beyond. One of them gestured angrily in Kero's direction, but the other two shook their heads, then pulled at his arm.

The argumentative one shook the other man's hand off and started down the staircase. He was big, and very well armored, with a heavy wooden shield. Kero shuddered as she realized that he could rush them behind that shield, and give his comrades the chance to get by the bottleneck of the doorway. It looked as if he had figured that out, too.

But someone behind Wendar threw a carving knife at him. It was a lucky shot—it *thunked* point-first into the man's buckler, buried itself in the wood, and remained there, quivering.

The brigand started, stumbling backward up one step, and swore an unintelligible oath. And he gave in to the urgings of his companions, following them back up the staircase, leaving the kitchen to its defenders.

Now it was Wendar's turn to curse and attempt to follow. Panic seized her throat as she realized what he was trying to do.

Dear Goddess— Kero grabbed his right arm as he charged past her, and hung on, hampering him long enough for Cook to seize his left and prevent him from charging up the staircase after their attackers.

"Stop it!" she shrieked, more than a touch of hysteria in her voice. "*Stop* it, Wendar! You can't possibly do any good up there! You aren't even armed!"

That stopped him, and he stared down at the sooty, greasy spit in his hands, and swore oaths that made her ears burn. But at least he didn't try to charge after the enemy again.

"The table—" Cook said, which was all the direction

they needed. As one they turned back into the kitchen and with the help of the rest of the besieged, hauled the massive table into place across the doorway, turning it on its side, making it into a sturdy barricade that would protect them even if the bandits charged them with a makeshift battering ram.

Then, having done all they *could* do, they waited.

Two

Kero crouched in the lee of the overturned table and tried to keep from thinking about her folk in the hall above, tried to keep her heart from pounding through her chest.

Tried to keep fear at bay, for now that she was no longer fighting, it came back fourfold.

Tried not to cry.

There are trained fighters up there. Nothing you can do will make any difference for them. They can take care of themselves, armed or not.

The servants were watching her; her, Cook, and Wendar. She could read it in their faces, in their wide eyes and trembling hands. If any of the three leaders broke, if any of them showed any signs of the terror Kero was doing her best to keep bottled inside, the rest of the besieged would panic.

She clutched her improvised weapons, her hands somehow remaining steady, but she wished she dared hide her head in her arms, to block out the horrible sounds from above.

She wanted to scream, or weep, or both. Her throat ached; her stomach was in knots. *Why did I ever think those tales of fighting were exciting? Blessed Trine, what's going on up there? Are we winning, or losing?*

How could we be winning? No one up there is armed. . . .

Wendar didn't even twitch. All of his concentration was focused on the staircase—he stared up at the flickering light at the top of the stairs, going alternately white and red with rage. Kero wished she knew what he was listening for.

If this wasn't hell, it was close enough.

* * *

It seemed like an eternity later that the sounds of fighting stopped—there was a moment of terrible silence, then the wailing began.

"That's it," Wendar said, and vaulted over the barricade. This time no one tried to stop him.

Kero couldn't help herself; she followed at his heels. Her skirt caught on the leg of the table as she scrambled over it. She stumbled into the wall, and jerked it loose, tearing a rent as long as her arm in it.

Wendar was already out of sight and she scrambled on hands and knees up the turnip-slimed stairs, pulling herself erect just short of the top, and discovering with dull surprise that she was still holding the knife and pot lid.

She peered out cautiously around the edge of the door frame, and her heart stopped.

Blade and lid dropped from her benumbed hands and clattered down the stairs behind her as she stumbled forward into a scene beyond her worst nightmares.

Someone grabbed her wrist as she staggered past.

Wendar, she realized after a moment. The Seneschal pulled her roughly down beside him, where he knelt at the side of a man so battered and blood-covered she didn't recognize him. Then he moaned and opened his eyes, and she knew—

Dent. Agnira bless!

She'd helped to bind wounds many times before, some of them as bad as any of these, when hunters ran afoul of wolf or boar—her hands knew what to do, and they did it, while her mind spun in little aimless circles until she was dizzy. The blood—there was just so much of it. . . .

Dent died under her hands, but there were others, too many others; she moved from one to the next like a sleepwalker, binding their wounds, sometimes with strips from her ripped skirts, sometimes with whatever else came to hand. Some, like Dent, died as she tried to save them. The others, the lucky ones, often fainted or were already unconscious by the time she found them.

The less fortunate screamed their agony until their throats were so raw they couldn't even whisper.

The hall was a blood-spattered shambles, furniture overturned, food trampled underfoot—and everywhere the women, some huddled in on themselves, were unable to speak, eyes wide and blank with shock; others shrieking, wailing, or sobbing silently beside their dead and wounded.

Of all that host of guests, only a handful remained calm, working white-lipped and grim-faced, as Kero worked, trying to snatch a few more lives back from Lady Death.

One iron-spined woman patted Kero's shoulder absently as she hurried by, eyes already fixed on the armsman laid out on the floor beyond the girl. With a start of surprise, Kero recognized the granite-faced matriarch of the Dunwythie family, a woman who'd never even nodded in Kero's direction before this.

Not that it mattered. Nothing mattered, except to stop the blood, ease the pain, straighten the broken limbs. There wasn't a whole, unwounded man-at-arms in the keep; there wasn't an unwounded *male* except those few menservants who'd fled to the kitchen.

Anyone who had resisted had been killed out of hand. There were young boys and women numbered among the dead and wounded—some of the dead still clutching the makeshift weaponry with which *they* had fought back.

Kero had long since passed beyond mere numbness into a kind of stupor. Her hands, bloodied to the elbow, continued to work without her conscious direction; her legs, aching and weary, carried her stumbling from one body to the next. Nothing broke the spell of insensibility holding her—until the sound of her own name caught her attention. Then she felt someone shaking her and looked up as reality intruded into the void where her mind had gone. Those hands had pulled her reluctantly back to the here and now.

She blinked; two of Dierna's cousins were tugging at her arms, one on either side, weeping, and babbling at her. She couldn't make out what they wanted, they were absolutely incoherent with hysteria. They pulled her toward the dais where the high table had been, sobbing, but before they had dragged her more than a few steps, she heard a young male voice she knew as well as her own raised in shrill curses.

She pulled loose from them and half ran, half staggered, toward the little knot of people clustered about one particular body.

The voice cursed again, then howled, just as she reached them and pulled someone—Cook—away from the figure stretched out on the floor.

It was her brother Lordan, young face twisted with pain, eyes staring without sense in them, ranting and wailing as Wendar bound up a terrible wound in his side.

The Seneschal looked up as Kero dropped to her knees beside him, and then looked back to his work. "It's not a gut-stab," he said, around clenched teeth. "It missed the stomach and the lungs, Kelles only knows how. But whether he'll live—that I can't tell you. Without a Healer—"

He didn't have to finish the sentence. Kero knew very well what his chances were without the help of magic or a Healer's touch. The wound itself probably wouldn't kill him, but blood loss and infection might very well.

There was nothing she could do for him that Wendar hadn't already taken care of. She felt oddly helpless, angry at her own helplessness, wanting to do something and knowing there was nothing productive to be done. She got slowly to her feet to hover just on the edge of the little group, trying to think of anything that might increase Lordan's chances.

I'm of no use here— She hated this—hated being so completely out of control, so afraid that her teeth chattered unless she clamped her jaw tight.

She looked out over the hall and saw that the last of the wounded were being tended to, the dead being carried out, the women too hysterical or paralyzed to do anything being herded over to one side of the hall by a group made up of the old woman who did the Keep's laundry and some of the dairymaids.

Father— she suddenly thought. *Where's Father?* She peered around the group caring for Lordan, looking for Rathgar—and only then saw the battered body laid out on the table, half covered with a pall made up of a table-covering, as if already lying in state.

Oddly enough, seeing him dead wasn't a shock; she wondered if she'd been expecting this from the moment she first looked into the hall. She knew what must have happened. Rathgar would have charged the brigands barehanded and empty-headed the moment they invaded his hall, pure rage overwhelming any thoughts of caution.

She closed her eyes, and tried to summon up a dutiful tear from eyes dry with shock, but all that would come was mere anger, and exasperation. *You were a mercenary, Father,* she thought angrily at the quiet form. *You knew better! You could have ordered the armsmen to play rear-guard and gotten everyone down into the kitchen before they really swarmed the place—but you had to defend your damned Keep personally, didn't you? You didn't think once about anything but that! Did you even think about getting your poor little daughter-in-law out of harm's way?*

She looked around for Dierna, expecting her to be among the hysterical or the half-mad—

—and didn't see her. Not anywhere.

Thinking for a moment that the girl might be hiding behind a chair, or cowering in someone's arms, Kero turned to one of Dierna's two cousins who had caught up with her and were clinging to each other in limp confusion.

"Where is she?" Kero demanded. *If she's hurt, her family will never forgive us.* Part of her calculated their reactions as coolly as a money-changer counted coins. *They'll demand satisfaction—never mind Father died and Lordan may not live out the night, they'll want blood price, and after this disaster, we won't have it.*

The girls stared at her blankly. She grabbed the nearest and shook her savagely. "Your *cousin,* girl! Where is she? Where's Dierna?"

The girl just stared, and stammered. She shook the little fool until her teeth rattled, trying to pry some sense out of her, but got nothing from her or her sister but tears and wailing. Disgusted, she held the girl erect between her two strong hands and contemplated trying to slap a little sense into her.

"She's taken," croaked a pain-hoarsened voice from below and to the right of her elbow.

"What?" Kero let go of the little ninny, who promptly collapsed with her sister into a soggy heap. She looked down at the man who'd spoken; one of the Keep armsmen, lying against the wall on a makeshift pallet of tablecloths and blood-soaked cloaks. Some of the blood

was probably his; he peered up at her from beneath a cap
of bandaging, and his right arm was strapped tightly to
his side.

"She's taken, Lady," he repeated. "I saw. They took
her, and that's when they left."

He coughed; she seized a goblet from the floor and
found a pitcher with a little wine still in it rolling under
the table. She knelt down beside him and helped him
drink; his teeth chattered against the rim of the metal
goblet, and he lay back down with a groan. "I saw it,"
he repeated, closing his eyes. "I been with Lord Rathgar
for ten years now, sworn man. Lady, I don't—this's no
lie. I swear it. There was a mage."

"A—*what?*" For a moment she was confused. What
could a mage have had to do with all this carnage?

The armsman opened his eyes again. "A mage," he
said. "Had to be. One minute, I'm on the wall, hearin'
nothin', seein' nothin'—then there's like a breath of fog,
kinda cold and damp, an' I can't move, not so much as
look around. Then this bunch of riders comes in, nobody
challenges 'em—they get in through the gates, an' I can
see they're scum, but somebody's given 'em good arms—"
The last word was choked off, and he lay for a moment
panting with misery, while Kero clutched the goblet so
hard her knuckles were white.

"Still couldn't move, couldn't yell," he continued,
staring up at nothing. "Couldn't. Then I hear the yellin'
from the hall, an' I *can* move—ran right straight in—right
into the ones waitin' for me." He coughed, and his face
spasmed with pain. "Waitin' around blind corners, like
they *knew* the place, Lady. Got free of 'em, made it as
far as th' hall. That's when I seen 'em take the bride—
Lord Rathgar, he was down, gods save 'em; they got th'
last of her guards, an' they took her. An' that's when the
fightin' stopped; they just packed up and grabbed what
they could an' left." He blinked and focused again on
her. "I tried, Lady. I tried—"

Now she remembered his name; Hewerd. "I know you
did, Hewerd," she said absently. That seemed to satisfy
him. He closed his eyes and retreated into himself.

A mage— That made sense. *Especially when I think how
Father hated mages. Maybe he had an enemy that was a
mage, or became one. He had other enemies, too; maybe*

one of them got together with this mage. They might have been waiting a long time to catch him off-guard, to take revenge when he wasn't expecting it. She shivered, and stood up, staring out over the shambles of the hall, but not seeing it. *That must have been the—thing—the dark thing I touched with my mind. Maybe one of Father's enemies* bought *a mage. That could happen, too. It would have to be someone who knew him well enough to know that he didn't have a house mage of his own. And it would have to be someone who knew about the wedding. . . .*

Agnira's Teeth! She shuddered. *He's destroyed us! There's no one to go after Dierna—there isn't a man fit to ride in the whole Keep! And if we don't at least try— I know her uncle, he'll call blood-feud on us. Kill every last one, take the Keep. . . .*

Dierna's uncle, the powerful Lord Baron Reichert, had used the pretext of familial insult to add to his lands more than once. He wasn't likely to turn down an opportunity like this one—and by the time the King found out about it, the Baron would have ensured that there was no one left at the Keep to argue Lordan's innocence. If they were lucky, they'd escape with their lives. If they weren't—the Baron had no percentage in their survival.

We won't have a chance, she thought bleakly. *Not unless someone goes after her, makes a token try at rescuing her—*

Dierna's sweet, heart-shaped face, and sensitive mouth and eyes rose up like a ghost to confront her. *Dearest gods, the poor baby—*

That last unbidden thought did something unexpected to Kerowyn. She was overwhelmed with dizziness, and reached blindly for the support of the wall. As her hand touched the wall, it faded away, and she was afraid she was about to collapse, to faint like one of Dierna's foolish cousins.

But she didn't collapse; she opened her eyes—but it wasn't the hall she was seeing, it was the road. And, faint shapes in the moonlight, a band of men on horseback.

For a moment she *saw* the girl, bound and gagged, and carried in front of one of the riders, a tall, thin man, in robes rather than armor. Her eyes were wide with shock and fear, her delicate face white and waxen, and she looked closer to eleven than to fourteen.

Anger replaced fear, outrage drowned any other feelings. This was *not* right. The girl was hardly more than a child.

Kero blinked.

The vision—if that was what it was—faded, replaced by another. A plain, simple sword. Then her own hand, taking the sword-hilt as if it belonged to her.

But I can't—

Again, a flicker of Dierna's frightened eyes. *Blessed Trine. Only fourteen, and sheltered all her life. Like a little glass bird, and just as easy to break.*

The visions faded, leaving her staring out at the hall again. The anger retreated for a moment. *I'm the only one left that could follow. If I try to get her back, her uncle won't have an excuse to come after Lordan.* She hugged her arms to her chest and shivered—then the anger returned, stronger this time. *And dear gods—all alone with those bastards—I can't just sit here, playing ninny like those cousins of hers. I can't. It isn't honor, it isn't pride, it isn't any of those things in ballads—it's that I can't sit here knowing what's going to happen to her once they think they're safe, and not try and do something to prevent it.*

Then something else occurred to her, and amid the anger and the fear, there rose a tiny flicker of hope.

And maybe Grandmother will help me.

Suddenly, following after the raiders didn't seem quite so mad a decision.

She turned on her heel and ran for the servants' entrance, but this time instead of going down, she went up, emerging into a corridor that ran the length of the hall itself and led to the family quarters. Her own room was in the first corner tower, where the hallway made a right-angle bend. She snatched a tallow-dip and lit it at the lantern, then ran up the short flight of stairs to the round room above. It was cold by winter and hot by summer, and drafty at all seasons, but it was hers and hers alone—which meant it held things not even Lordan knew about.

She lit her own lamp beside the door and blew out the tallow-dip. As the light rose, she went to the tall, curtained bed, and pulled the mattress off onto the floor.

Instead of the usual network of rope-springs, Kero's bed was one of the old style, a kind of box with a wooden bottom. Only the bottom of *this* bed held a secret. As she had discovered when she was a child, it could be raised on concealed hinges to reveal a second shallow compartment.

It still held a few of her childhood treasures; the dreaming-pillow her Grandmother Kethry had sent, her favorite stuffed toy horse, the two wooden knights Lordan had never played with and never missed when she spirited them out of his nursery and into hers—

But now it held, besides those things, her brother's castoff clothing *and armor;* a set of light chain made for him when he first began training, long since forgotten in the armory. It no longer fit him; he was too broad in the shoulder. But it fit her perfectly. She shed the ruins of her skirts with a sigh of relief, and pulled on breeches, stockings, and sleeved leather tunic. She bound up her hair as best she could; debated cutting it off for a moment, then decided she was going to need it under the helm. The chain mail shirt came next; without a squire, getting into it was a matter of contortion and wriggling, and enough hip-waggling to make a trollop stare. It caught in her hair despite her best efforts; she jerked her head and the caught strands were torn out of her scalp with the weight of the mail.

Finally she settled it into place, jingling noisily, with a final shake of her hips. It covered her from neck to knee, slit before and behind so the wearer could ride. Another leather jerkin went over it, to muffle the inevitable jangling of the rings. She pulled on her riding boots, then turned and headed for the door.

But all she had in the way of weapons were her knives. *I don't know how to use a sword,* she thought, hesitating with one hand on the door handle. *But knives aren't much use against a longer weapon. Maybe I'd better take one anyway.*

So instead of going back the way she'd come, she headed for her brother's rooms and his small, private armory. Hopefully, the raiders wouldn't have gotten that far.

Lordan's rooms were farther down the darkened hall, halfway between her tower and what had been her mother's solar. Kero had never had the leisure to play the lady over a bowerful of maids, nor had she really ever cared for fine sewing even if she'd had the leisure for it, so the solar had been closed up until such time as Lordan took a bride, or Rathgar remarried.

And since the latter had never occurred, Lordan had used the solar as a place to keep his arms and armor so that he wouldn't have to tend it down in the cold, uncomfortable, and gloomy armory. Doubtless their father would have had a fit if he'd known, but Kero hadn't seen any reason to tell him. If Lordan wanted to polish his swords up in the sun-filled solar, why not? Sun had never harmed metal *or* boys so far as Kero had ever heard.

She pushed the door open, and went in; the moon shown full through the solar windows, and the armor on its stand looked uncannily like Lordan for a moment. It gleamed a soft silver where the moonlight struck reflections from the polished metal and those reflections gave it a momentary illusion of movement.

Lordan's swords were hung from the racks where shuttles for the looms had been kept in Lenore's day. Kero knew the one she wanted: one of Lordan's earliest blades, a light shortsword, the closest thing to a knife and hence the one she could probably use the easiest if it came to that.

Lady Agnira, grant it doesn't. . . .

She buckled the belt over her tunic, hesitated a moment more, then resolutely helped herself to a little round helm with a nose-guard hanging on the wall beside it. It might not be much in the way of protection, but it was better than a bare head.

Lordan's rooms next door had a private stair to the stables outside; normally locked, but she and Lordan had made enough illicit moonlight expeditions that she'd long ago learned how to pick the clumsy old lock in the dark.

The door was still locked, but her hands, though they shook a little, still remembered how to tease the lock with the thin blade of her knife. She forced herself to breathe slowly, told herself that this was nothing out of the ordinary, leaned against the door frame, and tried not to think about what she was doing.

It worked; the lock clicked, and the door swung open, hinges creaking.

The stairs gave out on the tack-room, and the shielded light normally kept burning there made her blink, eyes watering. But there were no sounds of restless horses beyond the door, and the tack-room itself was a shambles.

As her eyes adjusted to the light and she picked her way over the saddles and other tack strewn over the floor, she saw why—there were no horses to hear. The stall doors stood wide open; what beasts the brigands hadn't stolen had doubtless been driven off. Witless things that horses were, they were undoubtedly scattered to the four winds, running until they foundered.

So much for sending someone for help, she thought bleakly. *Not even the guests are going to be able to send their own people back, not until some time tomorrow at the earliest.*

Someone had planned this very well indeed.

With one small exception.

Kero hurried to one stall that would have been empty even if one of the guests hadn't brought a high-bred palfrey to install there. Though this was the stall reserved for Kero's riding beast, her Shin-a'in-bred mare spent most of her time in the pastures from the time the last of the winter's snow cleared off until the first of it appeared. Kero generally kept Verenna's tack hung over the side of the stall; it didn't take up much room, since she had never permitted anything other than Shin'a'in tack on the young mare's back. The one thing Rathgar was an expert on was horses, and he'd taught his children himself. Kero tended and trained Verenna with her own hands unless there was an urgent need for her to be otherwise occupied.

The tack was still there; blanket, a saddle with lightweight stirrups that was hardly heavier than the blanket, bitless bridle and reins. She gathered it all up, slipped the hackamore over her arm, and took her back way out of the stables, out into the pasture.

Some of the horses had either jumped the fence or been driven out here—she saw them in the moonlight, dark shapes milling around at the end of the pasture, whinnying their distress. Catching them was going to be impossible until they'd tired themselves out.

Pray Verenna hasn't gotten caught up in their panic, she thought, biting her lip. *If she has—*

Best not to think about it. Kero pursed her lips and whistled shrilly, three times.

And very nearly jumped out of her skin as something warm and soft shoved her in the small of the back.

Gods!

She managed to kill the scream trying to tear its way up out of her throat before she frightened the mare, but she *did* drop all the tack, startling the young horse so that she shied a little and danced away, nervously. Kero, for her part, just stood and shook for a moment. A very long moment, in fact, so long that Verenna got over her startlement and picked her way cautiously back toward her rider before Kero had entirely recovered.

The horse nuzzled her anxiously, and Kero found the steadiness to reach for Verenna and scratch her ears while she regained the last of her own composure. Finally she was able to take the hackamore off her own arm and slip it over Verenna's nose without her hands shaking so much that she'd be unable to get the band over the mare's ears.

Saddling Verenna was a matter of moments. The mare stood on command, quietly, as she'd been taught, while Kero slung the saddle and blanket over her back and fastened the girth. Chest and rump bands were next, as Kero fumbled the buckles a little in the dark, then Kero snugged the girth tight against her barrel. Verenna snorted a little, but was being remarkably well-behaved under the circumstances.

Which is just as well, Kero admitted, as she put her foot in the stirrup and pulled herself up onto Verenna's back. *I'm not sure what I'd do if she decided to get out of hand.*

She rode the mare up to the fence, then leaned over and grabbed the latch on the gate. The pasture gate could be opened from horseback, and Verenna remained quiet, though a little jumpy, throughout the entire maneuver. *At least I don't have the others crowding up around this end, waiting for a chance to bolt.* Verenna was a very light-footed beast, and hardly made more noise than a goat as she pivoted in place so that Kero could pull the gate shut and latch it closed. Kero was counting on that; she'd need every advantage she had against the raiders.

Verenna automatically turned southward as they moved away from the gate at a fast walk; Kero normally rode her along the game trails in the Keep's wild lands, and the shortest way there was along the road south. She shivered under the saddle; horses are creatures of habit, and her world had been turned all round about this evening, first by the invasion of strange men and horses into her pasture, then by Kero's arrival on the heels of the chaos. This business of riding out in the middle of the night had the mare nervous and confused—

And now Kero confused her still further by turning her in an entirely opposite direction to the one she expected. Westward, not southward, and away from the hunting lands and the main village.

She stopped, snorted again, and bucked a little. Kero held her head down, and she fought the reins for a moment more, then settled, shaking her head.

Poor baby, you don't know what we're doing out here in the middle of the night, do you? Kero let her stand for a moment until she stopped shivering, then loosened her reins and gave her a touch of the heel. Obedient, but still snorting a little in protest, the mare headed into the west, up to the least hospitable side of the valley, along a faint track that led to the border of the Keep lands.

Their road stayed a track only so long as it lay within the Keep's borders. From there it turned into a goat path, then into a game trail.

Verenna didn't like it at all; it was bordered by clumps of bushes that swayed and rustled alarmingly, and overhung by trees that made it difficult for either her or her rider to see the path. Any horse bred by the Shin'a'in nomads could pick her way across uneven ground in conditions much worse than this, but that didn't mean she had to like it. Her ears were laid back, and Kero sensed by the tenseness of her muscles that the least little disturbance would make her shy and possibly bolt.

A spooky enough road for a visit to a witch. Kero kept looking sharply at every movement she caught out of the corner of her eye, and starting a little at every sound. She was just as bad as Verenna, when it came down to it. This was the way to her grandmother's home, called "Kethry's Tower." Kero hadn't been up this road very often, but she knew it well enough. As a child, she'd been taken here either pillion behind a groom, or on her own fat pony, and the visits had been at least once a month. Later, though, as Lenore became ill, she'd gone no oftener than twice a year—and since her mother's death, she hadn't gone at all. Not that she hadn't wanted to, but although Rathgar hadn't expressly forbidden it, he'd certainly made his disapproval known. Kero had her hands full running the Keep, and somehow there never seemed to be enough time to visit her grandmother. And Grandmother had never sent any messages urging a visit either, so perhaps *she* hadn't wanted any visitors. . . .

And maybe she still doesn't. But that's a chance I'll have to take.

As Kero remembered it, the place wasn't exactly a tower; it was more like a stone fortress somehow picked up and set into the side of a cliff. Kero scrubbed at her burning eyes with her sleeve, wishing that the Keep had been as impregnable as that Tower—it always looked to her as if it had been grown into the cliffside, or perhaps carved into the living rock, and the only access to it was along a steep, narrow stairway. Witch and sorceress her grandmother might be, but she took no chances on the possibility of having unfriendly visitors.

Verenna stumbled, and Kero steadied her. Now that they were away from the Keep, the normal night sounds surrounded them as if nothing at all had happened back there tonight. Off in the distance an owl hooted, and beyond the clopping of Verenna's hooves, Kero heard tiny leaf-rustlings as nocturnal animals foraged for their dinners.

Mother said that Grandmother had offered to build the Keep into something like the Tower, and Father refused, she remembered suddenly. *Why? He wasn't normally that stupid, to refuse help. Was it just that he didn't want to be any further in Grandmother's debt?*

That could have been. Every thumb's length of property that Rathgar called his own was actually his only through Lenore, and had come as her dowry. And he had resented it, Kero was certain of that; Rathgar was not the kind of man who liked to be in debt to anyone. Stubborn, headstrong, determined to make his own way, to depend on no one and nothing but himself, and to allow nothing to interfere with his plans for his lands and children.

But he loved Mother, she thought, letting Verenna pick her way through the thin underbrush. *I know he loved Mother, and not just her lands. He used to bring her meals and feed her with his own hands when she was too weak to even move. He never said a cruel word to her, ever. He never once even looked at another woman while she was alive, and I don't think he wanted to look at another one after she was gone.*

Verenna's eyes were better in this light than Kero's were; basically all she had to do right now was keep from falling off, and stay alert for stray bandits or wild animals. It was hard to believe that Rathgar was really dead.

Oh, Father. She thought about all the happy times she'd spent in his presence; how he'd taught her to hunt, how proud he'd been of her scholarship. *He could hardly write his own name,* she thought, with a lump in her throat, *yet he was so proud of me and Lordan and Mother. He used to boast about how learned we were to his friends. He used to tell them about how I could keep books better than Wendar, and how Lordan was writing the family history—and then he'd drag Lordan's chronicles out and have me read them out loud to everyone after dinner. And he used to tell us both how we were following in Grandfather Jadrek's footsteps, and how respected Grandfather had been, and how we should be proud to live up to his example.* She could see him even now, sitting on the side of Lenore's bed, with Lordan at his right and herself at his left, and whatever book they happened to be reading on his lap. "Don't be like me," he'd say, solemnly. "Don't pass up your chance to learn. Look at me—too ignorant to do anything but swing a sword—if it hadn't been for your mother, I'd probably be living in a bar somewhere, throwing out drunks by night and mopping the floor by day." And with that, he'd look back over his shoulder, and he'd stretch out his hand and gently touch Lenore's fingertips, and they'd both smile. . . .

What happened? she asked herself, around the tears that choked her throat. *I know he changed after Mother died. Was it because I wasn't able to be like her? He became so critical, that's all I ever saw. There were times when I wondered if he hated me—and times when I won-*

*dered if he even knew I was alive. Maybe if I hadn't been
so completely opposite from Mother, maybe we could
have gotten along better.*

Verenna stopped for a moment, ears pricked forward,
and Kero hastily rubbed her eyes, then peered into the
moon-dappled shadows beneath the trees ahead of them.
She slipped her knife from its sheath as she heard a repetition of the sound that had alerted the horse in the first
place. A rustling noise—as if something very large was
threading its way through the brush.

A crash that sent her heart into her throat—and then it
stood in the moonlight on the path.

A stag.

Verenna shied, the stag saw them, and with a flip of
its tail dove into the brush on the other side of the trail.
Kero's heart started again, and she urged Verenna forward. The mare didn't want to go, and was sweating
when Kero forced her to obey; but once they were past
the spot where the stag had appeared, she calmed down
a bit.

*Maybe it was because he thought I wasn't listening to
him about schooling,* she thought, trying to calm the mare
further with a firm hand on her neck. *I know he thought
I should be spending more time reading and less with the
horses. Dammit, I passed every test the tutor ever set me!
Is it bad that I like to be outside, that I hate being cooped
up inside four walls when I could be out doing things?
What's wrong with that? A book's all right when the
weather's foul and there's nothing else to do, but why sit
and read when the wind is calling your name?*

She'd never been able to figure that out. Lordan,
though—every chance he had, he was at a book or driving the tutor mad with questions. It was as if he got all
of Kero's love of learning as well as his own.

*Books, dear gods, he owns more books than anyone I
know. And if he gets his way, he's going to spend half
Dierna's dower on more books. . . .*

. . . if he's still alive to do it.

Her eyes stung and watered again, and her throat knotted. She rubbed her sleeve across her eyes, and wondered
if he'd live the night.

*If I can just get Grandmother down to the Keep . . . if
she's got the kind of power everyone seems to think she*

*does. Father would have had a cat if he'd known about
the stories I used to pick up in the kitchen. They say she
built the Tower in one night, with magic, just before she
moved out of the Keep and gave it to Mother as her wedding present. They say she has a giant wolf and a demon-
lizard for familiars. They say she can kill you or Heal
you just by looking at you. And if only half of that's true,
she surely will have what I need to save Lordan and get
Dierna back.*

Kero bent over Verenna's neck to keep from getting
hit in the face by a series of low-hanging branches, and
thought about what she'd ask for. Something that shot
lightning, perhaps; a magic wand that called up demons.
Exploding arrows? Maybe the help of that giant wolf?

*With magic even I ought to be able to get Dierna away.
And magic can surely save Lordan . . . unless Grandmother doesn't care what happens to us.*

The thought made her heart freeze, and every succeeding thought seemed worse than the first.

*She never once sent a messenger or anything after
Mother died. Maybe she was angry with Father for taking
Mother away from her. Maybe she really hates the rest
of us. Maybe she thinks we all hate her, and she's gone
all sour and mean. Maybe the magic has gotten to her
brain, and she's gone mad.*

"Lady Kerowyn—" said a voice out of the dark.

Three

"Lady Kerowyn—" said a voice from beneath the shadows of the trees, frightening the breath out of her, closing her throat with an icy hand. There was no warning, no movement beside the road, just a voice coming out of the darkness. It was a voice as harsh as the croaking of crows, and Kerowyn jerked, letting out an involuntary squawk of surprise as she reined in Verenna. The mare jumped and squealed, dancing madly backward, but fortunately didn't bolt.

Her heart felt like a lump of frozen stone, her pulse rang in her ears as she wrestled Verenna to a standstill. Hands trembling on the reins, she peered at the dark shadow-shapes under the trees; there was *something* there, but she couldn't even make out if it was human or not, much less if it was male or female. And that voice certainly didn't tell her anything.

"Who are you?" she replied, hoping her own voice wasn't going to break. "What do you want?"

"I live here," replied the voice, "which is more than I can say for you. What are you doing out here, beyond your father's lands, Lady Kerowyn? Why aren't you safe in your bed, in your father's Keep?"

It sounds like an old woman, Kero decided. *A really nasty old woman. The kind that makes her daughter-in-law's life a misery.* Oddly enough, the mockery in the old woman's voice and words made her feel calmer—and angrier. *"Which is more than I can say for you,"* indeed! "If you really live here, you know that the sorceress Lady Kethryveris is my grandmother," she called back. "I need to see her, and I'd appreciate it if you got out of the way. You're frightening my horse."

"In the middle of the night?" the old woman retorted. "Dressed in men's clothing? Carrying a weapon?" She moved out into the middle of the path, blocking it, but still in enough shadow that Kero couldn't see her as anything other than a cloaked and hooded shape. "What kind of fool's errand are you on, girl?"

Kero tightened all over with anger, inadvertently making Verenna rear and dance. When she got her mare and herself under a little better control, she told the old woman of the raid, in as few words as possible, though she wondered why she was bothering. "I'm going to ask my grandmother for help," she finished. "Now if you'll please get out of my way—"

"Dressed like that?" The woman produced a short bark of a laugh, like a fox. "I think you have something else planned. I think you reckon to follow after these raiders, and try to rescue this girl they took."

"And what if I do?" Kero retorted, raising her chin angrily. "What business is it of yours?"

"You're a fool, girl," the old woman said acidly, then hawked and spat in the dust of the path just in front of Verenna's hooves. "You're a moonstruck fool. That's a job for men, not silly little girls with their heads stuffed full of tales. You're probably acting out of ignorance or out of pride, and either one will get you killed. Go back to your place, girl. Go back to women's work. Go back where you belong."

Every word infuriated Kero even more; she went hot, then cold with ire, and by the time the old woman had finished, she was too angry at first even to speak. Verenna was no help; she reacted both to Kero's anger and to something the mare saw—or thought she saw—under the trees. As Verenna danced and shied, the mare's panic forced her to calm herself down in order to control the horse. She finally brought Verenna to a sweating, eye-rolling standstill a scant length from the old woman.

Whoever she was, the old hag was at least as foolhardy as she accused Kerowyn of being, for she hadn't moved a thumb's length out of the way during the worst of Verenna's antics.

"What I do or plan to do has *nothing* to do with pride," Kero said tightly, through clenched teeth, as Verenna tossed her head and snorted in alarm. "There's no one left down there that's capable of riding out after her. *No one,* old woman. Not one single man able to ride and lift a weapon. All that's down there is a handful of frightened servants and pages, and two old, arthritic men who never learned to ride. If I don't go after Dierna, no one will. If I wait until that so-called "proper" help arrives, she'll be dead, or worse. People who intend to ransom a captive don't ride in and try to slaughter every able-bodied adult in the place. I don't have a choice, old woman.''

She wanted to say more, and couldn't. Fear stilled her voice in her throat. She was right—but—*Everything I said is true—and—everything she said is true. This is going to get me killed, but I've come too far to turn back now. I made my choices back at the Keep.*

"I made my choices, and I'm going to live or die by them," she finished, hoping she sounded brave, but all too aware that she probably sounded like a foolhardy braggart. "And I'm *going* to see my grandmother whether you bar the way or not!"

She touched her heels to Verenna's sides, and the mare bolted forward. The old woman stepped adroitly aside at the last possible moment, and they cantered past her and were out of sight or hearing in a few moments.

Kero reined the mare in as soon as she'd run out some of her nerves; the path was still just as dark and potentially treacherous. *And the last thing I need is for Verenna to break her leg within sight of the Tower. I should be in sight of the Tower by now,* she thought, looking upward through the branches of the trees. *That old woman—in tales she'd either be a demon sent by the mage that took Dierna to turn me back, or a creature of Grandmother's, sent to test me. If she's a demon, the next thing will be a whole swarm of them after me—*

The back of her neck crawled at that thought, and she could not resist the temptation to stop, turn, and look down the path behind her.

Nothing. Just the moving shadows of tree limbs, and an owl winging silently across the road. Even Verenna seemed calmer, no longer fighting the reins, no longer sweating.

So much for the tales, she thought, a little embarrassed by her wild fears. *Sometimes a crazy old woman is just a crazy old woman.*

* * *

The Tower was exactly as Kero remembered it; or at least, the little of it she could see in the darkness was exactly as she remembered. Halfway up the side of the cliff, a single light burned beside the door. There might have been a fainter light coming from a curtained or shuttered window above that, but it was too faint for Kero to be sure it was there.

Verenna whickered inquisitively as she dismounted. The trees and brush had been cut away for several lengths at the bottom of the cliff, leaving a wide expanse of meadow. Not a carefully manicured and tended meadow though; this one was knee-high in grass and wildflowers, and looked very much like a natural clearing.

The moon shone down on this swath of grass unhindered by brush or trees, making it possible for Kero to see quite clearly. There was a hitching post beside the beginning of the staircase; a steep, narrow, open stone stair. Not even a Shin'a'in-bred horse was going to be able to negotiate that; it was barely wide enough for a single human.

And it's a good thing I have a head for heights, she thought soberly, eyeing the stair dubiously. *Oh, well. . . .*

She tethered Verenna to the hitching post, giving her enough lead-rope so that she'd be able to graze a little. *It's too late for wolves, and too early for mountain-cats. I hope.* Once again she looked back down the path, and once again saw and heard nothing out of the ordinary. She turned and started up the staircase, with one hand on the rough stone wall, resolutely looking at the steps and not over the open side. The stone beneath her hand was still warm from the afternoon sun. She forced herself to hurry as much as she dared, taking the relatively shallow steps two at a time; she'd have run, but the footing was too uncertain and the light was deceptive.

By the time she reached the top, she was feeling the strain in her legs. She paused for a moment to square her shoulders and lift her chin, then hefted the cold metal ring set into the door, and knocked. The first blow sounded dull, as if the door was a lot thicker than it looked.

The door began to open before she had a chance to finish the second knock. She released the iron ring hastily, before it could be snatched out of her hand.

A lantern she had not seen bloomed into life beside the door as it opened. The soft yellow light fell on a silver-haired, green-eyed woman who bore a strong resemblance to Kero's mother Lenore. Except for her hair, she showed few signs of age; she was as slim and erect in her soft blue-velvet gown as any girl, and moved gracefully, if slowly. There were a few crow's-feet around her eyes, concentration-lines on her brow, and smile-lines at either corner of her mouth, but otherwise her face was unwrinkled. She was exactly as Kero remembered her—which was eerie. She should have shown *some* signs of increasing age. . . .

"Kerowyn?" The sorceress frowned. "I knew there was something wrong, but—never mind. Come in."

Kero edged cautiously past her grandmother, careful not to touch her, and tried not to stare. There was no telling what she'd take offense at, and Kero had to keep repeating to herself that this strange, ageless woman was her grandmother. *I can't believe she still looks like this. Mother looked older, and not just because she was so sick.* Kethry turned away to close the door, and Kero took the opportunity to glance around while her back was turned.

There was no anteroom; she found herself in some kind of public room that took up the entire bottom floor of the Tower. It was full of comfortable clutter, the kind of things Kero would have expected to find in any woman's rooms. Ordinary things; an embroidery frame by the window, a basket of yarn and knitting beside the fire, cushions piled carelessly everywhere. What furniture there was tended to be worn, overstuffed, and looked as if it saw heavy use. Kero shivered despite the unexpected warmth of the room. The lighting was concentrated near the fire, leaving the rest of the room in shadow, and Kero wasn't certain she wanted to look too deeply into any of those shadows.

Kethry closed the door with a dull *thud,* but did not shoot the bolt home. Kero looked back at her, hoping she hadn't noticed her granddaughter's wandering attention. She turned with a frown on her face, though Kero could not tell if it was because of her, or for some other reason. Kero clasped her hands behind her back, nervously, and waited for her grandmother to speak.

"I felt something—wrong—down in the valley,"
Kethry said vaguely, her brow creased and her eyes looking somewhere past Kero's shoulder. "Something magical. I've been expecting a messenger, since I pledged
Rathgar when he wed Lenore that I would not enter his
domain uninvited—but I didn't expect that messenger to
be you."

She promised Father—dear Agnira! Kero took a deep
breath, and stored that bit of information away for later.
If there was a later. *She looks so odd—blessed Trine, I
hope she hasn't gone senile—* "I'm the only one fit to
ride, Lady Kethryveris," she began.

"Grandmother," Kethry interrupted tartly, her focus
sharpening for a moment. "I *am* your grandmother. It
won't hurt to say so. Sit," she continued, gesturing at a
bench by the door as she took a seat opposite it. "What
happened down there that they sent *you* to bring me
word?"

Kero nodded, a shiver of real fear going up her back,
and gulped. *No, she's not senile. If she still admits she's
my grandmother—wants to admit it—maybe she will help
us—* "Grandmother, nobody sent me. Nobody *could* send
me. I came by myself. It's—it's horrible—" She told the
story a second time, watching as Kethry grew more and
more distant—and more and more collected—with every
word. By the time she was halfway through, her grandmother *looked* like the powerful, remote creature the stories made her out to be. And Kerowyn continued, a sick,
leaden feeling in the pit of her stomach, trying not to
break down in front of this self-possessed, regal woman.

But she began to relive the tale as she told it. Her
stomach churned, and her throat began to close with
harshly suppressed sobs.

*I have to get through this. I have to make her believe
me. I can't do that if I'm crying like a baby.*

She managed to sound relatively calm, or at least she
thought she did, until she got to the part where she'd first
come up from the kitchen. She faltered; stammered a
little—then clenched her teeth and plowed onward.

But she kept seeing the bodies—

And then she came to the part where she saw her own
family fallen victim; first Lordan, then Rathgar.

That was too much; she lost every bit of her composure and fell completely apart.

There was a brief flurry of movement as her grandmother rose—and warm arms clasped and held her.

She found herself sobbing into a blue-velvet covered shoulder, found her grandmother holding her as no one had held her since her mother died. It was something she hadn't known she needed until it happened—

She cried all the tears and fears she'd held in since this nightmare began; cried until her eyes were swollen and sore and her nose felt raw. Kethry didn't say a word, simply held her, stroking her hair from time to time, and it was with a great deal of reluctance that she freed herself from that comforting embrace to finish the story.

She had to do so with her eyes shut tightly against the tears that threatened to come again, her throat thick, and her hands knotted into fists. "Are you going to be all right?" Kethry asked when she had finished.

Kero took a deep breath, opened her eyes, and shrugged. "I'll have to be," she replied. "I told you, I'm the only one left."

Kethry nodded, pushed her down into a chair, and narrowed her eyes—and turned from comforter to something far different.

The sorceress' face lost all animation. She cooled, she became somehow remote.

"The men," she said dispassionately. "Describe them again."

"They didn't look like much," Kero replied, falteringly. "Ratty looking. Like bandit-scum, the kind we'd never hire, except that their armor was awfully good. It wasn't new, but it wasn't dirty enough for them to have had it long."

"No badges, no insignia?"

"Not that I saw," she said, hardly knowing what to think.

"How did it fit them?" her grandmother persisted.

"What?" Now Kero really was perplexed. Her grandmother looked impatient.

"You're no dunce, child, how did it fit them? Well, or badly? Too big, too small, places where it was just held together by jury-rig straps?"

"Uh—" Now that she thought back on it, the armor

for the most part *had* fit badly, gaping places where it was too small on some men, too-large mail shirts spilling over knuckles on others. "Badly, mostly."

"Ah. Are you sure you don't want to go back and see if there's someone that can go after Dierna besides you?" She gave Kero a measuring look. "You look to me as if you've done enough already. I wouldn't say you're up to this, personally."

"No," Kero said as forcefully as she could.

Kethry nodded, and changed the subject. "Did it seem as if anyone was the leader?"

The questioning went on until Kero was ready to scream for the wasted time. And Kethry kept asking her if she was *certain* she didn't want to go back. She answered everything as honestly as she could, but it almost seemed as if her grandmother was now looking for an excuse to dismiss her and her plea out of hand, before she'd even had a chance to voice it. She certainly was just as discouraging and disparaging as the old woman down on the trail had been.

She's not going to listen; she thinks this was all Father's fault and she doesn't care what happens to the rest of us. Kero was shaking now; there was a light in Kethry's eyes that she didn't in the least like. Hard, and cold—uncaring? Perhaps. The sorceress' face was unreadable.

Still, when Kethry seemed to have come to the end of her questions and stood up to pace back and forth with her arms crossed, deep in thought, Kero took a deep breath, and made her carefully rehearsed speech before her grandmother could tell her to take herself off.

I'll never have another chance—

"Grandmother," she said urgently, "I *have* to go after Dierna. If I don't—there won't be anything left of the family by the time her uncle gets done with blood-feud. He *might* leave me alive—but not Lordan."

Kethry blinked, and seemed to shake herself out of an entrancement. "I actually know that, child," she said dryly. "I've had dealings with Baron Reichert before. That man wouldn't be satisfied if he devoured the world. In fact—never mind. I'll tell you later. So what do you want out of me?"

"Help!" Kero cried. "Lordan won't live out the night without a Healer—and I need help, too. A magic weapon,

something that will make it possible for me to get Dierna away from those bandits—''

A lightning-caller, a tame demon—something that can attack them from a distance so I don't have to get too close.

''They aren't bandits, girl,'' Kethry interrupted, her brow creased with a frown. ''At least, that mage isn't. Whoever, whatever he is, he's good, he hid his presence from me right up to the time of the attack—and he wants a virgin girl for something. I would guess he was hired, and the girl is his price for this night's work. I suspect your father made one enemy too many, and that enemy has decided to extract a complete revenge and end him and his line. Or else—'' She gave Kero a sharp glance, and didn't complete her surmise.

There's something she knows that I don't, Kero realized suddenly. *Something she isn't going to tell me.* ''I still need a weapon, Grandmother,'' she persisted. ''And Lordan—''

''Lordan will survive until I get there,'' the sorceress said abruptly, turning so quickly that Kero's heart jumped. ''Trust me on that. And as for your going after those bandits—what makes you think *you* can do anything? You aren't trained in magery *or* weaponry.''

''I have to try,'' Kero said stubbornly. ''I have to. There's no one else, and *you* told me what Dierna's uncle—''

''Why you?'' Kethry repeated.

''Why *not* me?'' Kero stood up, as tall as her shaking knees were permitting, and raised her chin defiantly. ''Why not me—if you'll help, I can do it. You did more with less when you were my age.''

She was all worked up and ready to say a *lot* more, but to her surprise, Kethry nodded. ''There's truth in that, child,'' her grandmother said softly. ''More truth than you know. And now I know who it is I've been waiting for all these years. . . .''

Waiting? For—

''Stay there.'' The sorceress crossed the room to one of the shadow-shrouded corners, and bent over a chest, opening it with a creak of iron hinges.

She turned with a long, slender shape in her hands,

and as she moved into the light again, Kerowyn could
see that it was a sword. Not a very impressive blade; the
hilt was plain leather-wrapped metal, and the sheath was
just as plain.

"Here," Kethry said, holding it out to her. "Let's see
if she'll take to you."

She? Kero reached forward to take the hilt without
thinking, and as she clasped it, Kethry pulled away the
sheath.

For a moment, no more than a breath, writing blazed
up on the blade itself, as fiery and white-hot as if the
sword had just come from the heart of a forge. Kero
gasped, but Kethry only nodded, unsurprised.

"She wants you all right, child. You're the only one
of my daughters or granddaughters she's spoken for. She's
yours now—or you're hers." Kethry slid the sheath back
over the now perfectly ordinary looking blade. "Take
your pick. When she speaks, I don't think anybody de-
nies her."

"What did it say?" Kero asked, aware of—something—
in the back of her mind. A testing—but distracted by
what her grandmother had just said. *Granddaughters?
Daughters? I thought Mother—*

*"Woman's Need calls me, as Woman's Need made me.
Her Need will I answer as my maker bade me."* Kethry
tilted her head sideways to fix Kero with a penetrating
stare. "This is my sword Need, Granddaughter—the
sword I wore for most of my life. Your sword, now; for
well or ill, you're bound to her like you'll never be bound
to another living thing, man *or* woman. But I don't think
you'll rue the bargain."

Kerowyn almost dropped the sword in her surprise.
This was Kethry's famous blade? Even she had heard stories about *this* sword. "B–b–but I don't know how to—"

"You won't have to," Kethry said confidently. "She'll
take care of you. At least in this instance she will—well,
you'll see."

Kero managed to stop gaping and slid the sheath onto
her belt, removing the old blade she'd taken from Lordan's armory. "Grandmother," she said slowly, looking
from the sword to Kethry and back again. "A few moments ago you wanted me to go back home. Now you've

given me *this*—and you're all but throwing me after those raiders. Why?''

Kethry clasped her hands behind her, and stepped back a few paces, looking Kero up and down with a distinctly satisfied expression. ''I was testing you,'' she said calmly. ''What you're about to do is going to change your life forever. Oh, don't look so skeptical; I know what I'm talking about. It will. And the road you're about to take is not for the fainthearted. But you seem to be made of stronger stuff than poor Lenore.'' Kethry nodded, slowly. ''Yes indeed. I think you'll do.''

What happened?
One moment, Kero was standing in the middle of Kethry's Tower, staring at her grandmother. Then there was a moment of dizziness, as if the floor had dropped out from beneath her, and she found herself *here*, at the foot of the stairs.

She blinked, and the moonlit meadow wavered a little in front of her eyes. *Dizzy—blessed Trine—* She staggered two steps forward, her hand outstretched in front of her, stopping herself on Verenna's shoulder. The mare snorted in alarm and jumped, as if *she* hadn't known Kero was there until that moment.

The dizziness vanished. She looked up suddenly, only to see the light in the Tower blink out, leaving it entirely dark.

''Gods.'' She stared up at the Tower, but could make nothing out in the shadows—and something told her that if she climbed all the way back up again, she could pound her fists bloody on that door and never raise a soul. She'd gotten all the answer she was going to get, at least for now.

She looked back down at the sword hanging from her belt. It was *not* the one she'd gotten from the Keep. It *was* the one she remembered her grandmother giving her.

She stroked the mare's neck to calm her. ''I think I've been dismissed, Verenna,'' she said quietly. ''I didn't get the answer I came for—''

But maybe I got a better one, she thought slowly. *And at any rate, it's the only one I'm going to get.*

She clenched her jaw, and mounted before she could turn coward. ''Come on, girl,'' she said to the mare, turning her back down the trail, the way they had come. "We've got a hard ride in front of us."

Tarma shena Tale'sedrin, Kal'enedral warrior of the Shin'a'in Clan of the Hawk, urged her tall gray warsteed a little faster up the backtrail to Kethry's Tower. The mare snorted an objection as she moved from an amble into a running walk; she didn't like taking the back way at night, and she didn't like to be rushed at the end of a journey.

"You're going to like what's coming up even less, old girl," Tarma told the mare, patting her coarse-coated neck. "You only *think* you're getting a warm stable and a rest. I'm afraid we're going to be turning right back around as soon as we find out what my partner's planning."

:So you're going to follow the girl?: asked a rough voice as familiar to her as her own in the back of her mind, a voice carrying overtones of approval. *:Good. I like her; I'd have followed her alone if you'd refused. She has courage.:*

"Oh, that, certainly. Lots of guts, not too many brains, but that's the way of things when you're young," Tarma retorted to the shaggy, calf-sized beast trotting along with its head level with her stirrup.

The *kyree* turned its lupine head up so that his great glowing eyes met hers, and blinked. *:Exactly. Reminds me very much of a certain barbarian Shin'a'in I knew many years ago.:*

"*Barbarian?*" Tarma exclaimed, as her mare's ears swiveled back with surprise. "Who's calling who a barbarian? *You're* the one who eats his meat raw. And fish—blessed Goddess, that's a vile thought."

:Cooking ruins the flavor,: Warrl replied haughtily. *:Some of the most civilized beings in the world eat their fish raw.:*

"Dear Goddess. No wonder they die young. Yes, I'm going after her. I just want to find out what Keth has in mind for both of us." Tarma reminded her mare with a touch of her heels that she was supposed to be trotting. The mare grunted, and grudgingly increased her speed. "Have you picked up anything more from Keth's mage-alerts down on the Keep?"

:No.: Warrl, creature of the magic-riddled Pelagir Hills, had some mage-abilities of his own; how much, he'd never told Tarma *or* her partner. He'd been able to throw off magical attacks in the past that would have killed a man. He'd once managed to feign death, pull Tarma out of a demon-sent trance, and smell the presence of mage-energy. He was also able to speak mind-to-mind with Tarma—which meant, she assumed, that he could do so with anyone he chose.

She'd been quite grateful for those abilities in the past, and never more so than tonight. She'd actually been within a couple of leagues of the Tower, returning from her annual visit to Clan Tale'sedrin, when Warrl had sensed the alarms Kethry had placed on the Keep sounding a danger-signal. They'd pushed their pace, knowing Keth was going to need them—only to have Warrl sense the girl riding hell-for-leather straight for the Tower herself. He knew her, of course; he knew all of Kethry's children and grandchildren, whether or not they knew *him*. He'd played spy for Kethry often enough; Rathgar didn't know of the *kyree's* existence, and what he didn't know about, he couldn't forbid. Warrl's excursions to the Keep were often the only things that kept Kethry from violating her sworn word.

They'd stopped Kerowyn easily enough; even a Shin'a'in-bred horse didn't readily pass something as large and carnivorous as a *kyree*. Tarma had played a part then; testing her while she and Warrl extracted information from the girl's words *and* mind. Tarma had sensed the despair in her voice, the fear she had been trying to cover with bravado.

Poor child, the Shin'a'in thought, wishing she was already guarding the "child's" back. Wishing she'd dared to be sympathetic. *She wasn't ready for this.*

:I'm glad you intercepted her,: the *kyree* said, evidently following her thoughts. *:She still might have tried something like this if she'd been as feather-headed and stuffed full of tales as you accused her of being. If she'd been like her mother—:*

"She isn't, Star-Eyed be thanked." Tarma had very little use for Lenore, living or dead. But then, while Lenore had been alive, the antipathy had been mutual. Contempt on Tarma's side, fear mingled with disdain on

Lenore's. Warrl teased his mind-mate by calling her a barbarian; Lenore had *meant* it. "Lenore wouldn't have done anything other than faint, though. And have hysterics. Girl's well rid of that father, though the boy has promise. We'll get her through this one, then we'll see she finds out about her kin and Clan—then she can make up her mind about what she *really* wants to do with herself."

:Get her through this one first,: the *kyree* interrupted. *She is brave, and resourceful, but—:*

"But, my rump. I did more with less at her age." Tarma said, with more certainty than she felt. *She's what, sixteen, seventeen? No real weapons' training? Dear gods, I was trained all my life, then retrained by the* leshya'e Kal'enedral—

Uncomfortable thoughts. Best to get all the plans straight, then go see that the girl survived this quest of hers. She nudged the mare again, bringing her up to a canter. The mare knew every pebble of the way from this point, and Tarma didn't want to waste any time getting on Kerowyn's backtrail. Warrl barked once, then put on the wild burst of speed of which his kind was capable, and sprinted ahead of her toward the dark, craggy bulk of the cliff housing the Tower.

When Tarma pulled her mare up at cliff-side, Warrl was nowhere in sight, which meant he'd gone on ahead. *:The lady is saddling up,:* came his mental call, thinned by rock and distance. *:We are in the stable.:* Light from a full moon directly overhead showed that the path here curved around the side of what looked to be sheer rock face, heading toward the stair that led to the Tower itself. The rough granite gave lodging-room here only to occasional scrub trees and bushes, and a little moss. There was no sign whatsoever of a stable.

Which was, of course, exactly as Kethry intended.

The mare tossed her head, as Tarma dismounted stiffly, her right hip aching a little from the long ride. *It would have been nice if this mess had managed to happen some time next week,* she reflected wistfully, trying to flex some mobility back into her legs. *Give me a chance to get a hot bath . . . my own bed for a few nights. . . .*

Ah, I'm getting soft in my old age.

As often as she pulled this trick, the mare still balked

when it came to going through the hidden entrance. Tarma pulled off the scarf that had held her hair out of her eyes all day, and blindfolded the mare with it.

And walked into the side of the cliff, leading the docile horse.

This trick wouldn't work for just anyone, of course; only those Keth had keyed into the spell. For anyone else, that granite cliff-face wasn't illusion, it was real, and solid enough to climb. Tarma still hadn't made up her mind about it, and like the mare, she didn't much enjoy passing through it. She kept thinking that one day something was going to go wrong, and she'd get stuck halfway through.

Three steps through absolute darkness, then she and her mare emerged into the tunnel that led to the Tower's stables. The tunnel, the stable, and the ''door'' were the only extravagances Keth permitted herself in the way of magic. The tunnel and stable had been carved from the living rock by magic, and were illuminated by permanent witch-lights. The rock walls of the tunnel were planed and polished until the granite shone like marble, and the yellow globes of witch-lights brightened just ahead of her and dimmed after she had passed. ''Austere, but attractive,'' was what Warrl had called it. It gave Tarma a case of claustrophobia.

Her footsteps and the mare's echoed up and down the tunnel, announcing their arrival. Oddly enough, the Tower—which everyone seemed to think Keth had magicked into place—had already been here when they'd first had their schools at what was now the Keep. Besides the obvious way in, there'd been an escape route down through the cellars. That was what Keth had enlarged into the stables and tunnel, and had concealed with her magic.

The end of the tunnel was considerably brighter than the tunnel itself; Tarma blinked a little when she led the mare out into the stable proper. As Warrl had advised, Kethry was already at work; she'd already saddled her mount and loaded it with packs of medicinal gear. Kethry was no fool; she'd changed into one of her old traveling outfits; knee-length hooded robe and breeches, both of soft, but sturdy beige wool. Now the sorceress had gotten her gray warsteed to kneel so that she could mount the mare's saddle. While Tarma might still be able to mount unaided, these days Keth couldn't, and made no pretenses about the fact.

Poor Keth. She moves so gracefully no one ever guesses how much her bones ache.

:We are not what we were, mind-mate,: Warrl acknowledged ruefully. He had flung himself down beside the cool stone wall where he lay panting after his run. Now that he was in the light, he was even more impressive; not even a wolfhound or the grasscats of the Dhorisha Plains could best him for size. He could—and had—snapped a man's leg in half with those formidable jaws.

"Your timing couldn't have been better, *she'enedra,*" the sorceress said, as her mare heaved herself to her feet. "I saw you were almost home when I checked this morning, then when I sensed the trouble in the valley, I checked on you first, and caught your little conversation with Kerowyn." She checked all the fastenings on the packs as she spoke, making sure nothing was going to come loose. "I'm going to the Keep to see what I can do—"

"Don't worry, I just came down here to tell you I'll be playing guardian to the girl," Tarma interrupted. "You didn't have to ask."

"She isn't as helpless as you might think," Kethry said, knotting her long silver hair up on the back of her head and pinning it there securely. She turned her emerald eyes on her partner, and Tarma for once could not read them.

"So?" She raised an eyebrow.

"I—Need woke for her."

Silence. *Four daughters, a host of granddaughters and fosterlings—not to mention all the students—not one of which woke even a spark from that piece of tin. Dear and most precious gods. For once the damned thing picked a good time to poke its nose in!*

If a sword has a nose.

Tarma took a deep breath, quite well aware that her oathbound sister was waiting for some kind of reaction. "She's neither fighter nor mage. So what's it going to do for her?"

Kethry wheeled her mare and got her head pointed toward the tunnel. "Whatever it has to. Protect her from magic, make her fight like a hellcat. Probably more than that, things I didn't know it could do. All I do know for certain is that with the lives of not one, but *two* young women depending on it, Need is going to stretch to its limits.''

Tarma considered that for a moment. "In that case, I'd better get on my way. And young Lordan isn't getting any better for you standing there.''

When Kethry didn't move, Tarma frowned. "There's something you're not telling me.''

The sorceress grimaced. "I think Rathgar was betrayed. I told Kero that whoever hired the mage and the bandits to pull this raid was probably one of Rathgar's enemies, but I lied to her. I think it was Dierna's uncle. That Reichert bastard.''

Tarma blinked—and swore an oath strong enough to make the witch-lights dim for a moment. "It all makes sense, doesn't it—the fact that the raiders knew about the feast tonight and that almost everyone would be unarmed. That they knew *where* everything was. And that bastard has wanted the Keep since I can't remember when. I didn't like Rathgar, but he deserved better than that.''

" 'That bastard' probably wouldn't be too upset if Dierna's father happened to die and the collateral lands came to him either,'' Kethry pointed out grimly. "Basically, I think you'd better stay alert for other surprises— *and* if you can find anything linking him to this massacre, bring it back.''

Tarma nodded. "I'll keep my nose to the ground.''

Kethry's troubled eyes cleared, and she urged her horse down the tunnel. "That takes a lot of worry off my mind. I'll go do what I can for Lordan.''

"And I'll keep our young swordbearer in one piece.'' Tarma mounted up, much to the displeasure of her horse, and followed her out into the night. "And may the gods ride with all of us.''

Four

The moon was down, but Tarma had no problem following Warrl. Any time she lost him, he'd be sure to set her right with acidic delight. She was far more concerned with her mare's footing in the uncertain light. One false step and the rescue could be ended with a broken foreleg. Shin'a'in-bred horses were damned canny, but accidents could still happen to anyone.

She was glad now she'd left her old mare back with the Clan two years ago, and had taken a younger beast. This was the fourth warsteed to carry the name "Hellsbane," but she was the best so far. Though lazier by nature than the other three, she had keener senses, a superior level of good sense, and an uncanny knack for path-finding.

Warrl was up to his usual high standards; despite a confused trail, he had picked up Kero's track with very little problem. He might be as old as Tarma, but there was nothing wrong with his nose.

I can't imagine how that girl is finding the bandits' trail, though. That had her sorely puzzled. *She's a good enough hunter, but not that good, and not by night—*

:The sword?: Warrl suggested absently. *:Kethry said that we don't know all it can do. We've never seen it in the hands of someone entirely untrained.:*

Tarma snarled a little at the thought of the blade that had caused her and her *she'enedra* so much trouble, and agreed. *I'll tell you, Furface, I've never been entirely happy about that blade. It has too much of a mind of its own. Damn thing came awfully close to getting Keth killed a time or two.*

:The Hawkbrothers call it a "spirit-sword,": Warrl reminded her, as he stopped at a crossroads to cast around for the scent. *:I have often thought it to be more than a*

geas-blade. But your Star-Eyed bound you two, despite Kethry's previous link to it, so I presume it isn't inimical, only—hmm—stubborn?:

Tarma grimaced at the *kyree's* choice of words. *Maybe. Whatever, I'm glad now that the damn thing does have a mind of its own. The only two females in peril for leagues around are Kero and her brother's bride. There're no women in that bandit group, right?*

:I have not scented any,: the *kyree* confirmed, loping off on the fork to the west.

Tarma urged her horse to follow. *Then the goal and the target are clear. There's nothing to confuse the issue. And Kero is going to need all the help she can get.*

:We two are not precisely useless.: The path was leading off into the hills, and presently vanished. Warrl continued to follow with his nose along the bare ground, swiftly and silently.

It was as dark as the inside of a cat with the moon down. Tarma relaxed, rested, trusting to the senses of her mount and Warrl.

:Halt.:

Tarma reacted instantly, and so did her mare. She peered into the darkness ahead of her, and could barely make out a moving blot against the lighter expanse of scrub grass and dirt ahead.

What's up? she thought at him. *She* could not speak mind-to-mind, but *he* could and did read her thoughts. They'd used that little talent of his on more than one scouting foray.

:Interesting. She dismounted here.: Tarma eased herself down out of her saddle, and winced a little when she put weight on her bad leg. She led the mare up to Warrl as quietly as she could to keep from distracting him. He raised his head and sniffed the breeze just as she got there.

:Fascinating. We are somewhere near the bandits' camp. I can scent smoke and many humans, and weary horses. And old blood, and I think, Dierna. Which means the girl Kerowyn somehow knew they were nearby. . . . :

He put nose to ground again. *:The sword, I presume, alerted her. Or possibly is guiding her.*

Or controlling her, Tarma thought sardonically, thinking of times past.

:Perhaps. I think she led her horse off—there—:

Tarma dropped Hellsbane's reins, ground-tethering her, and carefully moved off in the direction Warrl's nose pointed. Within a few feet of the trail, behind a low rise, she found a creekbed with a trickle of water running through it, trees on both sides of it. Where the trees were thickest, she found Kero's mare tethered with enough rein that she could eat and drink.

Satisfied—and pleased that the girl had thought to provide for her horse—she tethered Hellsbane there beside the girl's riding mare, and returned to Warrl.

If it's controlling her, she's at least holding her own. Now what? she asked him.

He moved forward a few feet at a time. *:Ah. Here she dropped to hands and knees. A crawling stalk.:* He raised his head to look at her. *:I would advise the same, based on the strength of the scents.:*

Tarma shook her head in admiration. *Brightest Goddess—the damned blade is finally doing something right. All right, Furface, let's see what you and I can do about cutting around to the other side of the camp.*

Kerowyn halted her horse; she could just barely make out the dirt road ahead, and the fact that this was a crossroads. She stared at the trail and tried to remember what the stories she'd heard had said about her grandmother's geas-blade. There was something about Kethry fighting as if she were a master swordswoman even though she was entirely untrained—which might mean the thing gave her unusual abilities. Could it make one a master tracker, perhaps?

She touched her hand to the hilt, and felt a kind of tingle, as if her hand had a mild case of "pins and needles." There was something there, all right, even if she didn't know what it was.

On the other hand, she wasn't too certain she wanted to find out while she had other options available.

She settled herself carefully in her saddle and opened the protections on her mind. Slowly, this time. The last thing she wanted was to let that slimy thing know she was behind them.

She caught a lot of stray thoughts, full of violence and not very clear or coherent; and when she opened her eyes, she found she was facing westward. Very well, then, west it would be.

Each time she lost the trail, she found it again by cautiously lowering her protections, and "listening." But then the road she followed turned into a path, and the path itself dwindled away to nothing, and it was too dark to try and track the bandits by ordinary means.

Now she *had* no choice. Reluctantly, she eased the blade halfway out of its sheath, and relaxed.

The darkness about her began to lighten, and soon she could see as well as if it was near dawn. For a moment, as she looked around herself in astonishment, she thought she might be having some kind of fit—there were little sparkles of sullen light leading off over the hills. Then she pulled her hand away from the hilt of the sword, and she realized that the little sparkles vanished, as did her ability to see so clearly, the moment her hand left the sword.

So this means, what? She dismounted and put her hand back on the sword. The sullen light reappeared, and as she examined the hard ground, she saw the faint traces of hoofmarks there. This, then, was the direction the bandits had taken.

And the moment she *found* their trail, the light disappeared, although she could still see as well as before.

It's letting me do what I can do. It's—playing tutor, I guess. But the moment I'm in a position where my own abilities can handle things—then it just sort of steps back and makes me take care of myself.

She took the blade in her right hand, the mare's reins in her left, and followed the trail until—something—told her to stop. It just didn't seem right to go on farther.

Maybe it's about time to see what they're up to. She opened her mind, leaning against Verenna's warm, sweaty neck and closing her eyes to do so, and went "looking" for bandits.

She found them all right. An entire encampment of them, with sentries posted all around the little valley they'd taken for their own. Drunk, most of them. Wild, disconnected thoughts. Dierna was there, and still alive—and relatively unharmed. But with her was—

Kero slammed her protections shut, convulsively. *He* was there with her, that cold, slimy, *evil* presence she'd felt before. This time he hadn't sensed her presence, but that was because he was preoccupied. But she had inadvertently come a lot closer to being detected than she really wanted to think about.

She looked around, assessing the possibilities; there was a tiny creek not far from where she was standing, with trees lining both sides. It wasn't much cover, but to all eyes other than hers the night was deep and dark enough to hide just about anything. With the cover provided by the bushes, Verenna would be just about invisible. Now if she could just do something to keep her from making a fuss—

Well, the mare probably hadn't fed terribly well, what with all the confusion for the feast, and then the upset of the raid. If she left Verenna tethered loosely so that she could get at browse and water, that might keep her occupied and quiet.

She led her mare into the copse, right up to the waterside, and tethered her in a tiny clearing right next to the creek. The clearing was surrounded by bushes and trees, and may itself have been part of the creekbed until something changed its path.

Verenna should be safe—and if I don't get back, she'll probably be able to free herself.

She left the little mare tearing up grass hungrily, and proceeded cautiously, afoot at first, then on her hands and knees; opening her mind for brief glimpses of her enemies, until she knew that the farthest sentries were little more than a hill away. She dropped down beneath the bushes, and crawled forward in their shelter.

All this time her sight had been dimming; was the sword taking away her advantage, or losing its power? Or was it that too much profligate use of magic might be somehow visible to the unknown mage? Now her vision was about equivalent to what she'd have under a full moon.

Well, that'll do—she thought just as she heard the careless footsteps of one of the bandit-sentries, and the rattle of the bushes as he pushed through them. She flattened herself under the cover of the brush with her sword still in her hand, face pressed into the gritty dirt, her heart pounding with sudden fear, and waited for him to pass.

He did; making no attempt at quiet. He stalked within

an arm's length of her, armor creaking and jingling, and
never knew she was there.

She didn't start breathing again until he was well out
of hearing distance; didn't get her nose out of the sand
and wipe it on the back of her hand until long after that.

All right, I know where the sentries are, she thought,
her right hand toying nervously with the hilt of the sword
as she peered out from under the branches. *So how do
I avoid them? They seem to be stationed pretty closely
together. Maybe I shouldn't avoid them.*

It was hard to recall the stories—the tales the old mercenaries told when she was supposed to be out of ear-
shot, not the bardic lays. The recollections of old battles,
ambushes, things that would be useful to her now.

*Dent—he told Lordan once, about how he had to get
into an enemy camp. He said the sentries were posted all
around, but they weren't used to working together and
weren't checking in with each other, so they wouldn't
know if one of them had been taken out until his replacement came looking for him. So he got rid of one, and
brought his entire company in through the hole in the
lines. . . .*

Somehow all the fear and grief was behind her now,
now that she was confronting her own life—or death. It
was easier to think; the pain was far away and nothing
was important but the next moment, and the strange excitement that sharpened all her senses.

*If I slip past them, they'll still be at my back, and
dangerous. I could forget that they're there, and one of
them could get me from behind. I can't just slip past
them. I'll have to get rid of one.*

No sooner had she made the decision than she was
crawling forward after the sentry that had just passed her.
She had no real plan, it was just that this particular man
seemed the most careless. She followed him with the
sword still in her hand, able to move with relative silence
through brush that she could see and he could not.

*Maybe if I can come up on him from behind, I can hit
him in the back of the head with the pommel like Dent
showed me—*

She was within a length of him; half a length. He
started to turn—

And suddenly *she* was no longer in control of her body.

As if she was a passenger behind her own eyes, a puppet in the hands of an unseen manipulator, she felt her muscles tense as the man started to peer through the dark toward her. She found herself ducking down and crouching behind the cover of a bush. She hadn't even noticed the bush beside her, much less that it was big enough to hide behind. He even moved a couple of steps in her direction, but couldn't see anything, and she stayed as still as the disembodied puppeteer could hold her. Then, when he turned away, she sprang up, sword-hilt clasped in both hands; and as a wild excitement filled her, drove the blade *through* his body, between his ribs, using all the momentum of her leap. The edges of the blade scraped against his ribs; he arced, and made a kind of strangled gasp, dropping his own blade. She seized him around the neck with her free arm, and shoved the blade completely through him, up to the quillons.

They stayed that way for a moment, then he fell; she braced herself and pulled at the same time, and the blade came free of his falling body. He never even made another sound.

Then, just as suddenly as she had lost control, she regained it. *She* was the one who staggered two trembling steps away from the carcass, mouth open with shock, heart thudding against her ribs. *She* was the one who very nearly turned and ran, ran all the way back to the copse where she'd left Verenna to take her and ride home at a gallop—

Only the knowledge that if she did, they would probably hear her and kill her, kept her from doing just that.

I've killed a man, she thought, legs shaking, sour taste of bile in the back of her throat. Her gorge rose. *I've killed a man, myself—*

Except that she didn't know the blow that had killed him. If it had been her doing, she'd have just hit him from behind with the pommel. Nothing like that was in anything Dent had taught her.

It was the sword. It had to be. Only a magic sword would have been able to manipulate her like a puppet. And Need was, of course, a magic sword, and had been described as giving Kethry the same power it had just apparently given Kero.

I never thought it would happen like that—just take me

*over like that. I thought—I thought it would just sort of
show me how to do things—*

This wasn't what she'd planned at all. She looked at
the blade in her hand and the blood on it with revulsion.
She wanted to drop it right there—

But then, just before she did, another thought occurred
to her.

*I was going to ask Grandmother for a weapon, or a
demon. Would this bandit be any less dead if I'd hit him
with a lightning bolt, or let a demon eat him? What makes
it any better if I kill him with my own hands, or do it
from a distance?*

It wasn't better, of course—

And he hurt and killed my *people. Maybe even somebody I knew.* She steeled herself, steadied her hands, and
forced herself to clean the blade on his tunic. *He could
have chosen an honest living. He's helping keep Dierna
captive. He had a choice, he made it. And I'm making
mine.*

She went back on hands and knees and eased through
the brush toward the camp, making as little sound as
possible. Her hands were getting full of stickers, and her
knees were bruised by rocks—but it was no worse than
some of the injuries she'd picked up berrying or training
Verenna. So far.

So far, thanks to the sword, she'd been lucky.

Thanks to the sword. It still made her skin crawl to
think how it would probably take her over again. She
didn't have a choice, not if she was going to rescue
Dierna, but she didn't *like* it at all. *It just takes over with
no warning. And what else does this thing do that I don't
know about? What if it turns me into some kind of monster?*

But her grandmother trusted it.

There's no reason not to trust it, I guess, she thought,
as a cramp seized her leg. She stopped and eased her leg
out straight, waiting for a moment until it went away.
*But I can't help but wonder how much Grandmother
really knew about it. Maybe it hid things from her, too.*

A cheerful thought.

Just then she reached the edge of a drop-off, with a
screening of brush at the edge. Bright yellow firelight
silhouetting the bushes warned her that the camp was just

beyond them. She wormed her way under the shelter of one of the biggest (and prickliest) of them. It was not an easy job. Tiny twigs caught in her hair and scratched her face; exposed roots caught on her belt and tunic-lacings and held her back.

Finally she reached the edge. The branches of the bushes drooped here, down over the drop-off, making a kind of screen of leaves and twigs between her and the fire. Lifting one branch out of the way, cautiously, she peered down at the camp below, blinking against the sudden light.

Closest to her and about a length below her were a half-dozen men, roaring drunk, playing some kind of game with dice or knucklebones. Two were standing; the rest were sitting or kneeling in a rough circle, watching one of their number cast and cast again. They had tossed their armor aside in a heap right below her, up against the side of the low bluff she hid on. They were filthy, unshaven, and dressed in a motley collection of clothing, some of which had probably been very fine at one time, all of which was now stained, tattered, and so dirty she wouldn't have used it to clean the stable floor.

Beyond them was another collection of similar scum sprawled at fireside, sharing the contents of a wineskin, and squabbling over a heap of loot from the Keep. Then came the fire—badly built, part of it smoking, part roaring—and beyond the fire—

Dierna.

Her bright scarlet dress made a brilliant splash of color that attracted Kero's eyes immediately. She lay half on her side, her pretty face a frozen mask of fear, tumbled at the feet of a tall, thin man in long red robes, the skirt of his robes split fore and aft for riding. He sat on a boulder, sharpening a knife, paying no attention to the antics of his men. Nor, strangely enough, to Dierna, although her legs were exposed to the thigh by the way her dress had torn and fallen open when she'd collapsed (or been flung) at his feet.

He reached down, as Dierna shrank away from him, and grabbed a lock of her long, unbound dark hair. He yanked her back toward him with it tangled cruelly in his fingers—Kero watched her clench her teeth and wince—and cut the lock off with a single stroke of his knife.

Kero bit her lip with sudden speculation. That was *not* what she'd expected him to do.

As she watched, he rose from his impromptu seat, kicking Dierna out of the way impatiently, and took the lock of hair to a flat rock just inside the ring of firelight.

Maybe one of these bastards will go for his back, she thought hopefully. *Having a girl within reach must be driving them mad. If one of them tries something, makes a move for her, that's sure to start a fight. Either the man holding her will react, or one of the others—either way, once a fight starts, it's bound to spread. If that happens, maybe I can get in there and get her out while the fighting's going on.*

But the bandits ignored the robed man; ignored Dierna, which was even odder. Even if this strange man—

Mage. This has to be the mage.

—even if this strange mage had given orders about leaving Dierna alone, scum like this would *not* have been able to ignore her. They'd have been watching her, hoping for the mage's back to be turned, hoping for a chance at her. But she might as well not have been there. They weren't ignoring her—they acted as if they didn't even see her.

Kero turned her startled attention back to the mage. That flat rock—he had some kind of paraphernalia laid out on it, as if it were an altar. He set the lock of hair on a brazier in the middle of the rock, picked up something Kero couldn't make out, and began making passes over the burning hair.

I don't like this. I don't like this at all.

A moment later the hair on the back of her neck was rising, as a circular boundary around the rock began to glow, as if he had piled up a circle of dark red embers. The strange light pulsed at first, then settled down to a steady, sullen glow. There was one small gap in the circle, and the mage put his instrument down as soon as the glow of the boundary settled, and strode through it.

He returned to his boulder, his steps hurried and betraying a certain impatience; he shot out his hand, and pulled Dierna to her feet by her bound wrists. She yelped, a sound that carried above the rest of the noise in the camp—and not one of the bandits looked up.

I like this even less.

The mage dragged the young girl stumbling along behind him, then pushed her through the gap in the boundary. He cleared the flat rock of encumbrances with a single sweep of his free hand, then kicked her feet out from under her and forced her down beside it. He waved his hand again, and the gap in the boundary closed as fire burned from each end of the arc and met in the middle. Then he pulled a knife from the sleeve of his robe, seized Dierna's head by the hair, and before Kero could take a breath, slashed Dierna's cheek from eye to chin.

For one moment, Kero was paralyzed, with herself and the sword warring to take over her body and act. And in that moment of indecision, someone—or some*thing*—else acted.

Outside the circle of firelight, a wild clamor went up. It was a heartbeat later that Kero recognized the sounds for the voices of half a dozen horses screaming with fear. The thunder of hooves was all the warning the bandits got before an entire herd of them, blind with panic, stampeded through the camp. Then the campfire went up in a shower of colored ball-lightning and huge sparks and explosions just as they hammered past, and they panicked further, scattering in all directions.

And as if that wasn't chaos enough, one of the revelers fell into the fire with a bubbling shriek of pain, clutching his throat.

And the bandits panicked as badly as the horses.

That's an arrow! Kero realized, in the heartbeat before her attention was caught again by Dierna and the mage that held her. *There's someone else out there—someone with a grievance and a bow.*

But she had no chance to think about it, because the mage caught her attention again. Something—a cloud of smoke, or blood-colored mist—rose up out of the stone. It was the height of a man, and as broad as two men, and it was lit fitfully from within, like the clouds on a summer night flickering with heat lightning. The mage stepped back, releasing the girl; it gathered itself, coiling and rearing up exactly like a snake about to strike. Then it lunged forward and fastened itself on the blood-dripping cut on Dierna's cheek.

Dierna screamed—high, shrill, the way a rabbit screams when it is about to die.

Kero couldn't move; now *she* was as paralyzed with fear as Dierna. But she didn't need to, for the moment she stopped fighting it, the sword took over.

It flung her out of the bushes, rolling down the bluff in a controlled tumble that somehow brought her up onto her feet just as she reached the bottom. The fire was still exploding, though fitfully; a handful of horses were still trampling anything in their way as they circled wildly through the camp, and there was more than enough confusion for her to get halfway across the campsite before anyone even noticed her.

And even then, the bandits had troubles of their own, for that unknown ally out in the dark was letting fly with arrow after carefully placed arrow, picking off raiders with impressive regularity. There were at least three down on the ground that weren't moving, and two more clutching their sides and screaming. One of the bandits saw her, and charged right at her—

And stopped dead, as Kero raised her own sword against him, without pausing in her headlong charge. Whatever he saw turned his face as pale as milk; he turned, and ran out into the darkness.

That happened twice more as she half ran, half stumbled across the bandit camp, dodging fear-maddened horses and the fires set by the explosions in the campfire. A few unfortunates managed to get in Kero's way. The sword did not grant them a second chance. By now Kero wasn't even trying to fight the sword; she was still wild with fear, but there was a kind of heady exhilaration about this, too; she hardly noticed the men getting in her way except as targets to be dealt with, as impersonal as Dent's set of pells in the armory.

She dodged around the now-blazing campfire, vaulted a body, cut down a fool who tried to bar her way with nothing but a short-bladed knife, taking him out with one of those unstoppable two-handed strokes—and found herself jerking abruptly to a halt at the edge of the glowing circle.

She *couldn't* get across it. There was a real, physical barrier demarcated by that scarlet line. The thin band of crimson might as well have been a wall of iron.

She looked up—and saw the thing still fastened on Dierna's cheek, the light within it growing stronger and more regular, pulsing like a heartbeat. And beyond it the mage smiled thinly at her, and gestured, making a throwing motion.

Yellow-green light in the shape of a dagger left his hands; she tried to duck, but the sword wouldn't release her. So she braced herself instinctively, and cold fear froze her from head to toe.

But nothing happened. The dagger of light vanished as it came within an arm's length of her.

She blinked, trying to comprehend what had just happened. *He threw a magic thing at me. It never touched me. And he expected it to kill me—*

The mage stared in utter disbelief, and backed up a half-dozen steps. That was enough for the sword.

Kero backed up a step under its direction, and it slashed down across the circle of light, as if it were carving a doorway. A portion of the crimson barrier blacked out immediately.

The blade sent Kero leaping across that blacked-out section like a maiden leaping the Solstice fires.

Her jump ended two paces in front of the flat rock, Dierna, and the thing fastened leechlike to Dierna's cheek. Dierna was no longer screaming; she was sprawled across the rock, moaning weakly, as if this creature was stealing all her strength. Her eyes were closed, and she seemed utterly unaware of Kero's presence.

The sword slashed down again, but it was not aimed at the leech-thing. For one horrible moment, Kero thought it was trying to kill *Dierna*—but the hilt twisted in her hands and cut between the girl and the leech-cloud, shaving so close to Dierna's face that the blade flicked away a couple of drops of blood from her wounded cheek.

The mage shouted, something incomprehensible, but angry. The cloud reared back as Dierna came to life and rolled weakly off the rock and out of its way, the strange thing looking more like a leech than ever. Before it could lunge at her and refasten itself to her cheek, Kero had leapt up onto the rock, positioning herself between it and the girl. She slashed at it, cutting nothing, but forcing it to retreat. It glowed an angry sanguine, and seethed at her, the roiling movements within it somehow conveying a cold and deadly rage.

Behind it, the mage chanted furiously, in some language Kero didn't recognize. She somehow knew that the *sword* did, though; for the first time she felt something from it—a strange, slow anger, hot as a forge, and heavy as iron.

Her left hand dropped from the hilt and reached for her dagger at her belt, and threw it.

The mage held up his hand, and the dagger hit his palm—

—and *bounced*, clattering harmlessly to the ground.

Kero *wanted* to run, but the sword wouldn't let her. She could only stand there, an easy target. The mage sneered, and raised his hands. They glowed for a moment, a sickly red, then the glow brightened and a spark arced between them. He brought them together over his head, and pointed—and sent a bolt of red lightning, not at her, but into the leech-cloud.

It writhed, but she somehow had the feeling it was *not* in pain. Then it solidified further—and doubled in size in a heartbeat, looming up over her.

The blade's anger rose to consume her, and she shifted her grip from the hilt to the sword-blade itself. She balanced her sword for a moment that way, as if it was, impossibly, nothing more than a giant throwing knife. It didn't seem to weigh any more than her dagger had at that moment.

Her arm came back, and she threw it, like a spear.

It flashed across the space between herself and the mage, arrow-straight and point-first. And as the mage stared in surprise, it thudded home in his belly, penetrating halfway to the quillons.

He gave a strangled cry, staggered forward two steps, and fell, driving it the rest of the way through his body.

The leech-cloud screamed, somehow inside her mind as well as with a real voice; it seemed to split her skull as completely as any ax-blade.

Kero dropped to her knees and covered her ears, the scream driving all thoughts except the pain of her head from her mind. But she couldn't look away from the thing, her eyes held by the mesmerizing, pulsating lights within it. The light flickered frantically, wildly; the cloud stretched and thinned, reaching upward, and rose to a height of three men—

Then it exploded, vanishing, with a roar that dwarfed the explosions earlier.

Kero blinked dazzled eyes, shaken and numbed, and slowly took her hands away from her ears. There was only silence, the crackling of the fire, and the far-off drum of hoofbeats.

She rose to her feet, shaking so hard she had trouble standing, her knees wobbly. *Dear gods, what happened? I can't have killed that thing, can I?* She waited for what seemed like half the night, but nothing more happened. Finally she pulled herself together, gathered what was left of her wits, and staggered over to Dierna.

The girl lay quietly beside the rock, eyes wide and staring, face as white as cream. She blinked, but that was the only movement she made; for a moment Kero was afraid that she might have gone mad; or worse—not that she would have blamed her.

But when the older girl came into the failing light from the fire, there was sense in her eyes, and she took the hand that Kero offered in both her bound ones, and allowed Kero to pull her into a sitting position.

"K–K–Kerowyn?" the girl stuttered weakly after a long moment of silence. "Is it r–r–r–really you?"

"I think so," Kero replied unsteadily, putting one hand to her temple as she looked vaguely around for something to free the girl's wrists. Although the mage's dagger lay nearby, she somehow couldn't bear to touch it. Instead, she retrieved her own knife and used it to cut through the rawhide of Dierna's bonds.

Once her hands were freed, Dierna clapped her sleeve to her still-bleeding cheek, and began to cry. Kero couldn't tell if she was weeping out of pain, fear, or for her marred cheek.

Probably all three.

She started to look for something to use for a bandage, but when she turned around—

An old woman in a worn leather tunic and armor that fit her as well as the bandits' had fitted poorly appeared out of nowhere between her and the fire.

Kero shrieked, and stumbled back, and turned to run—and shrieked again when she came face-to-face— literally—with the biggest wolf she'd ever seen in her life.

Its eyes glowed at her with reflection from the fire, as she groped frantically after weapons she no longer held.

"*Stop* that, you little idiot," the old woman said in a grating voice from directly behind her. "We're friends. *Obviously.*"

That voice—

She spun around again, just in time to watch the old woman stalk past her toward the body of the mage, the wolf eyeing both of them with every evidence of intelligent interest. The woman surveyed the body for a moment, then leaned over and wrenched her grandmother's sword out of the mage's corpse with a single, efficient jerk. Before Kero could say or do anything, the woman *handed* it to her, hilt first.

She took it, stunned, unable to do anything *but* take it.

"Clean that," the old woman growled, a frown harsh enough to have frosted glass on her beaky face. "Dammit girl, you *know* better than that! Don't *ever* throw your only weapon away! Just because you were lucky once—ah, I'm wasting my time. Take that ninny of a sister-in-law of yours, and get back home."

And with that, the woman turned on her heel and stalked off to the nearest body, wrenching an arrow out of its back. Kero stood staring dumbly as the wolf jumped down off the rock and joined her.

It was only then that Kero noticed that they were the only creatures living or moving in the whole camp. And no few of those bodies were slashed across throat or belly. *Her* work, or that of the sword—in the end, it really didn't matter.

She couldn't help herself; it was all too much. Her guts rebelled, and this time there was nothing to stop them from having their way. She stumbled toward the rock and leaned against it, heaving wretchedly.

She expected Dierna to be having her own set of hysterics, but after the first few heaves, as she dropped her grandmother's sword from her nerveless fingers, the girl helped steady her while she lost dinner, lunch, and breakfast—and then even the memory of food. Finally, when her guts quieted down for lack of anything else to bring up, Dierna wiped her sweaty forehead with a dust-covered velvet sleeve, and helped her to sit down on the erstwhile altar.

She looked around for the sword; it was just out of reach. Dierna followed her gaze, and patted her awkwardly on the shoulder.

"I'll get it," she said, in a voice hoarse with screaming and crying. "You've done everything else tonight. Never mind that horrid old woman."

Horrid old—now I remember where I heard that voice before. The old woman. That was the same voice I heard on the road, the old woman that stopped me on the way to the Tower—

While Dierna picked the sword up with a clumsiness caused mainly by the fact that she was trying not to touch it, and was doing her best to keep it at arm's length away from her, Kero looked around for the old woman.

She was gone. So was the wolf. And all the usable arrows.

"Here," Dierna said, thrusting the sword hilt at Kero. She stared at the girl without taking it; that awful, bone-deep gash was healing right before her eyes, faster than Kero had ever seen anything heal before. By the time she had shaken off her surprise to take the blade out of Dierna's reluctant grasp, the wound had sealed shut and was already fading from a thin pink line to practically nothing, leaving not even a scar.

It Heals? Dearest Agnira, it Heals, too? After turning me into a berserk killer?

And what was that old woman doing here, anyway?

The sound of dancing hoofbeats made her turn, to see one more surprise in a night full of near-miracles.

The enormous wolf had returned. In its mouth were the reins of two horses; Kero's, and one she recognized as coming from the Keep stables. Kero's Verenna was sweating with fear, and trembling so hard that she was plainly too frightened to try and escape, but the other beast was so tired it was paying no attention to its unusual "groom."

The wolf led the horses right up to her, and snorted, which made Verenna grunt and shy. Kero grabbed the ends of the reins dangling from its mouth, and the wolf let go immediately. Verenna jerked her head and tried to bolt, but Kero held her, dropping the sword into the dirt a second time, as the mare rolled her eyes with terror and danced. Finally Kero had to grab her nostrils and pinch them shut, cutting off her air, before she'd calm down.

She glanced around guiltily as she retrieved the sword a second time, but the old woman was still nowhere in sight. She had the feeling that she'd get a *real* tongue-lashing if she didn't clean the blade off after all this. And somehow she didn't want that formidable old harridan to unleash the full force of her scorn.

So how am I going to keep the horses from running off while I clean the damn thing? She looked around for something suitable, and finally wound up improvising hobbles for both horses before tethering them to a bush. She could only hope that would hold; if they bolted, she didn't think the wolf was likely to bring them back a second time.

By now the sword was encrusted with dirt; Kero had to cut a piece from the bottom of her tunic and use what was left in a stray wineskin to get it clean enough to sheath. The fire was dying down by the time she finished, and she sheathed the blade at her belt and looked for Dierna, again expecting her to be collapsed somewhere, as helpless and incoherent as her two cousins.

Instead, she saw the girl sorting through a pile of the loot that was part of one of the bandits' dice winnings, turning things over with a stick, and tossing selected items onto a tattered cloak she had spread out to one side.

"Dierna!" she shouted, and winced when the girl jumped, overbalanced, and fell. She left the horses and walked wearily to give the girl a hand up. "Sorry. But what in the name of the six hells are you *doing?*"

The girl's face took on a stubborn expression. "Looking for my wedding presents," she said.

"You're *what?*" Kero wasn't sure whether to scream, laugh or cry. She'd been kidnapped, her friends and new relations had been slaughtered, she'd very nearly gone down the gullet of some kind of monster. *She lives through all this, and she's looking for a few paltry cups?*

"I'm looking for my wedding presents," the girl repeated. "They're *mine*, they were given to *me*, and I— I'm n–n–not going to let these—b–b–beasts have them!"

Her eyes grew moist, and threatened to spill over, and Kero sensed that she *would* have hysterics if she were prevented from completing her search. "I saw most of them," she sighed. "Some of these bastards were dicing for them. Here, let me help you—by the way, Lordan's all right, or at least he will be by the time we get back. My grandmother, the Sorceress Kethryveris, said so."

"Did she?" the girl replied vaguely, fishing a silver plate out of a pile of trash. "That's good; I'm glad we're going to be able to have the wedding after all. Lordan's a very nice boy."

Kero very nearly choked. *That's* good? *She's happy about the* wedding? *When my father and brother—*

For one moment Kethry had to hold very still, counting slowly, to avoid losing her temper and killing the girl she'd come to rescue.

Stop. Don't kill her. She doesn't realize how she sounds. And don't tell her what you think of her, it isn't going to do any good to shout at the girl. Lordan's the next thing to a stranger, she hasn't known him very long— what, a week or so? And if she didn't marry him, they'd have found another husband for her within a couple of months. Probably not as good-looking or personable, certainly not as young, but equally a stranger—

Dear Goddess, that could have been me.

No wonder she wants her wedding presents more; they're all she really has. The only things she really owns. She doesn't even own herself.

Kero found the last of the set of silver wine cups they were looking for, dented, but still recognizable, and threw it onto the blanket. Dierna looked up then, and the threatened tears did start to fall, as she ran to Kero and threw her arms around her neck. Kerowyn held her awkwardly, as she sobbed into the older girl's shoulder.

"K–Kerowyn, I thought they were going to k–kill me!" Dierna cried. "I thought no one was going to come in time! Y–you were w–w–wonderful—"

She went on in that vein for quite a while. *Poor baby. Poor baby.* Kerowyn just patted her gingerly on the back until the flood subsided, then coaxed her to the side of the spare horse and secured the blanket full of loot to the back of the saddle. The horse was so tired it didn't even object to the noisy bundle.

"Where's the knee-rest?" Dierna asked, trying to find the kind of accoutrements she was used to on a saddle.

"There isn't one," Kero replied, hauling herself up onto Verenna's back. "You're going to have to ride like me."

"Like—but—" Dierna paled, then her lower lip started to quiver. "But—but—I *can't!* It isn't—my dress—it's not *womanly!*"

Kero closed her eyes, and begged Agnira for patience. "Your dress is ruined," she pointed out. "Besides, no one expects to see you *alive*, Dierna. Nobody is going to notice that you're riding astride. Now just slit your dress and let's get out of here before one of those bastards comes back."

And when Dierna hesitated, with the little knife Kero had handed her dangling loosely from her fingers, Kero added, "That leech-thing might not be dead, you know."

The girl squeaked; slit the skirt of her dress so that she could swing her leg over the saddle and get her foot into the stirrup, and mounted with all the haste Kero could have wanted.

Blessed Agnira, spare me from "womanly," if this is what it is, she thought, making the words an unconscious prayer as she took the reins of Dierna's horse to lead it behind her own. *Just—spare me.*

Five

:*So what do you think of the girl now?*: Warrl asked conversationally, as Tarma sorted through the scattered piles of the bandits' belongings.

"I'm pretty impressed," the Shin'a'in admitted, as she squatted on her heels, emptying out a belt-pouch, and separating copper from silver. Not that there was much of the former, and of the latter there was even less, but Tarma was a thrifty soul, and young Lordan was going to need all the help he could get. He was going to have to pay for enough mercenaries to keep his neighbors from getting ideas about annexing his property to theirs. That took ready cash, and silver and copper spent as readily as gold.

"I think I have a fair notion how much of what went on was the damn sword's doing, and how much was the girl's," she continued, pouring the coppers into a large leather pouch that had been a wineskin a few moments ago. "She's got a few brains besides the guts."

:*Unlike a certain barbarian nomad I once knew.*: Warrl chortled; Tarma simply ignored him, and moved on to a pile of looted wedding gifts the girls had overlooked. Of course, it had been *under* one of the men Tarma had shot, which might be why they'd overlooked it. . . .

She shook her head over a blood-soaked silk cloak. *Too bad; that's one wedding present ruined past anyone using it.* She tossed it onto the fire. "I never claimed to have much in the way of brains when I was younger. Now—well, I'd rather do things with a minimum of effort, and that takes planning. That was good work with the horses, Furface."

:*Thank you. And you displayed your customary efficiency with the sentries.*: Warrl nosed something out of the dirt, and batted a shiny little gold pendant toward his mind-mate with his paw. She snatched it up adroitly and dropped it into the appropriate pouch.

"You must be planning something rude; you're complimenting me," she teased him, stripping the body at her feet of everything useful, and tossing various items on the appropriate piles. "I'll tell you though, I had a bad moment back there, when the mage started that blood-rite. I thought that stupid sword would take the girl over and turn her into a nice juicy target before we had a chance to start distracting them."

:You didn't think it knew what we were doing?: Warrl dragged a set of saddlebags over to the fire so that Tarma could rummage through them, then stood beside her, head cocked to one side, watching her work with absent curiosity.

"I've never known what that sword noticed or didn't notice," the Shin'a'in admitted. "I *know* the damn thing's amazing when it wants to be—but I don't think even Keth has ever figured it out, and she's Adept-class. All we know for sure is that it Heals, it gives a mage fighting mastery, and a fighter immunity from magic. And it won't work against a woman."

:And that women in trouble call it the way lures bring in hawks.:

"Too true," Tarma sighed, thinking of all the times exactly that had happened. And all the trouble the sword had gotten them into as a consequence. Not to mention all the *paying* jobs it had cost them. "What did you do with the rest of the nags, anyway?"

:Herded into a blind canyon. They won't be going anywhere. I assumed you'd want them.: Warrl sounded more than usually smug, and with good reason. By the time Tarma finished collecting everything salvageable, there was going to be enough here for at least three pack animals—and the horses themselves would be worth something, ill-used, scrubby beasts though they were. Most of the horses the bandits rode in on hadn't been stolen from the Keep.

:They'll be worth more if Lordan offers them as bonuses to any merc who signs with him than if he sells them,: Warrl pointed out, following her train of thought with his customary ease. *:It isn't often a common merc gets a chance at even a scrubby nag like one of this lot.:*

"Good point; I'll make sure he realizes that." She straightened, and surveyed the remains of the camp. "I think I've gotten everything worth getting. The vultures are welcome to what's left."

:No self-respecting vulture would touch one of these fools.: Warrl sniffed disdainfully. *:Stupidity might be catching.:*

Tarma snorted in agreement as she tied up a bundle of assorted silver plate. "They really weren't terribly bright, were they?"

:Doesn't that strike you as odd?:

Tarma paused with her hands on the last knot. "Now that you mention it," she said slowly, "it does. You might think these fools had never worked together before."

:Hired separately?: Warrl licked his lips. *:Then thrown together—that would account for some of the laxness, the lack of coordination. They did act as if each man was following his own set of orders, and to the nether hells with whatever anyone else was doing. And once back at camp, the only thing they did as a group was to set sentries.:*

"Exactly." Tarma sat back on her heels, and stared at the dying fire without really seeing it. "Now why would someone want to throw a group of scum together that they *know* is going to fall apart the moment the job is over?"

Warrl began pacing back and forth, head swinging from side to side a little. *:One would assume that whoever hired them—wanted them caught?:*

"Good notion. Let's think about this—if everything had gone wrong for these fools, what would have happened to them?" Tarma stood up, and joined Warrl in his pacing.

:If they had not been able to take the girl, Rathgar would have been faulted for not protecting her. And I would guess that in any case the mage was ordered to dispose of Rathgar, no matter what the cost. They certainly had the men to assure that.: Warrl paused in his pacing, and looked up at her. *:Which would leave the estate in the hands of the boy.:*

"Who could be gotten rid of as soon as the bride had produced an heir, or even before." Tarma scratched an

old scar on the back of her hand. "All right—if it had
gone half right, and they'd killed Rathgar, but left a force
of able-bodied men behind to follow, it would have taken
a while to get that force organized. And even if someone
had come pounding after them, they'd have had time to
get rid of the girl, which would give the family an excuse
for blood-feud."

:If you assume the girl is expendable—: Warrl sounded
sour.

Tarma felt just as sour; the Shin'a'in lived and died
for their Clans, and the idea that a man could betray his
own blood for the sake of gain curdled her stomach. Not
that she hadn't encountered this before—but it curdled
her stomach every time. "I think she is, given who's
probably behind the attack in the first place. Keth already
had this one figured. The uncle. Baron Reichert."

:It fits his style:

"Aye, that. He'd put up his own daughter as an expendable, let alone a mere niece." She frowned. "Let's
get the horses. I think that once we're in place, we'd
better make the Keep a lot more secure than Rathgar had
it, or the bride is likely to be a widow before the year's
out. Assuming *she* lives that long."

The sun was approaching zenith by the time Tarma
coaxed the weary, footsore horses through the gates of
walls about the Keep-lands—and by the tingle on her skin
as she passed under the portcullis of the Keep itself,
Kethry had already put a mage-barrier about the place.

The Keep was more than a fortified manor; it was a
small walled town, with a small pasture—or large paddock—within the walls for keeping horses. The quarried
stone walls were "manned" by an odd assortment of
women, old men, and boys, but Tarma nodded with approval as she gave them a surreptitious inspection while
she dismounted and tended to the horse-herd. They were
alert, they were armed with the kind of weapons they
were most familiar with, and they looked determined.
The boys had slings and bows; the old men, spears and
crossbows; the women, knives, scythes, and threshing
flails. By their weathered complexions and sturdy builds,
those women and boys had been gleaned from the farms
around the Keep, and Tarma knew her farmers. Every

mercenary did. They could be frightened off, but if they decided to make a stand, they weren't worth moving against. Farmers like these had taken out plenty of men with those "peasant weapons."

Evidently she was expected; the farmers around the Keep knew her, in any event, from the old days when the Keep had been a school that she'd shared with Keth. Those farmers had long memories, and several recognized her on sight. She even knew one or two, once she got within the walls and close enough to make out faces. One of those was a woman just above the gate, who waved, then turned her attention back to the road, shading her eyes with her hand while she fanned herself with her hat. Leaning on the wall beside her was a wicked, long-bladed scythe, newly-sharpened by the gleam of it, and having seen her at harvest time with that particular instrument, Tarma would not have wanted to rouse her ire.

No one came down to help her, which spoke well for discipline, and that Keth had evidently impressed the seriousness of the situation on them.

I might be old, Tarma thought with a certain dry amusement as she dismounted, *but the day a Shin'a'in needs help with a herd of exhausted horses is the day they're putting her on her pyre.*

Her warmare followed her to the entrance, with the three pack horses trailing along behind. Warrl held the rest of the horses penned in the farthest corner of the court while she pulled packs and tack off her four. When packs and saddle were piled beside the door, she and Hellsbane drove the three tired nags before her, shuffling through the dust, to join the rest. Warrl kept them all in place simply with his presence, and Hellsbane kept them calm, while she opened both stable doors.

She whistled, and through the open door watched Warrl climb lazily to his feet, then bark once, as Hellsbane played herd-mare. That was all the poor beasts needed; they shied away from him, and broke into a tired trot, shambling past her and out into the pasture. She slammed the stable door after them, and walked as wearily as they had back into the stone-paved, sunlit court.

The *kyree* was waiting for her, looking as if he was

feeling every year of his age. *:Are we finished yet?:* Warrl asked hopefully, his tongue lolling out.

"You are," she replied, stretching, and feeling old injuries ache when she moved. "I'd better see what Keth's up to."

:If you don't mind, I'll go get something to eat, and then become flat for a while.: Warrl headed off in the direction of the kitchen-garden. *:I think that under-cook still remembers me.:*

"I wish I could do the same," she sighed to herself. "Oh, well. No rest for the wicked. . . ."

She caught up the pouches of jewelry and money on her way past the pile of packs. *I don't think anyone out here is other than honest, but why take chances?* The Keep door was halfway ajar; she pushed it open entirely, and walked in unannounced.

The outer hall was cool, and very dark to her tired eyes after the brightness of the courtyard. That didn't matter; this place had been her home for years; she knew every stone in the walls and crack in the floors. *As long as Rathgar didn't install any statues in the middle of the path, I ought to be able to find my way to the Great Hall blindfolded,* she thought, *and I'll bet that's where Keth is.*

She was right.

The Great Hall was nearly as bright as the courtyard outside; it was three stories tall, and the top story was one narrow window after another. Not such a security risk as it looked; it was rimmed with a walkway-balcony that could be used as an archers' gallery in times of siege—and the exterior walls were sheer stone. Kethry was in the middle of the Great Hall, supervising half a dozen helpers with her usual brisk efficiency, robes kilted up above her knees, hair tied back under a scarf. She'd set the entire Great Hall up as a kind of infirmary, and she had no lack of patients. Even Tarma was a bit taken aback by the sheer number of wounded; it looked suspiciously as if the raiders' specific orders had been to cause as much havoc and injury as possible in the shortest period of time.

Which may be the case, she reflected soberly, as she threaded her way through the maze of pallets spread out on the stone floor. *The more Rathgar's allies suffered, the better off Reichert would be. They'd be unable to support the boy, and very probably unwilling as well.*

Kethry was kneeling at the side of a man who was conscious and talking to her. She looked up from her current patient at just that moment, and her weary smile told Tarma all she needed to know about the mage's night. Long, exhausting, but with the only reward that counted—the casualties had been light at worst. Tarma nodded, and as Keth continued her current task of changing the dressing on a badly gashed leg, she slowed her steps to time her arrival with the completion of that task.

"Looks like you've spent a night, *she'enedra,*" the Shin'a'in said quietly, as Kethry stood up. "How's the boy?"

"He'll live," she said, tucking a strand of hair under her scarf. "In fact, I think he'll be up and around before too long. I held him stable from a distance as soon as Kero told me what had happened, and I managed to get the one Healing spell What's-her-name taught me to *work* for a change."

Tarma shook her head, and grimaced. "I never could understand it. Adept-class mage, and half the time you can't Heal a cut finger."

"Power has nothing to do with it," Kethry retorted, "and it's damned *frustrating.*"

"Well, if you ask me, I think your success at Healing has as much to do with how desperate you are to make it work as anything," the fighter replied, shifting her weight from one foot to the other and flexing her aching arches. "Every time you've really *needed* it to work, it has. It's only failed you when you were trying it for something trivial."

"Huh. That might just be—well, the boy is fine, and as grateful as anyone could want, bless his heart. The *girl,* on the other hand—" Kethry rolled her eyes expressively. "Dear gods and Powers—you've never heard such weeping and histrionics in your life. Kero came dragging them both in about dawn, and Her Highness was fine until one of her idiot cousins spotted her and set up a caterwauling. Then—you'd have thought that every wound in the place had been to *her* fair, white body.''

"About what I figured," the Shin'a'in said laconically. "Did you truss her up, or what?''

"I sent her up to the bower with the rest of her hysterical relatives," Keth told her, the mage's mouth set in a thin line of distaste. "And I sent Kero to bed, once she'd looked in on her brother. She's made of good stuff, that girl."

"She should be," Tarma replied, pleased that Kero hadn't fallen apart once she'd reached safety. "But it doesn't necessarily follow. Well, I'm for bed. And see that you fall into one sometime soon."

"Soon, hell," the mage snorted. "I'm going now. There's nothing to be done at this point that can't be handled by someone else. There're half a dozen helpers, fresher and just as skilled."

Tarma clutched the tunic above her heart. "Blessed Star-Eyed! You're delegating! I never thought I'd see the day!"

Kethry mimed a blow at her, and the fighter ducked. "Watch yourself, or I'll turn you into a frog."

"Oh, would you?" Tarma said hopefully. "Frogs don't get dragged out of their beds to go rescue stupid wenches in the middle of the night."

Kethry just threw her hands up in disgust, and turned to find one of her "helpers."

The tallow should be ready about now, Kero thought, setting her mortar and pestle aside long enough to check the little pot of fat heating over a water-bath. The still-room was dark, cool, and redolent with the odors of a hundred different herbs, and of all the "womanly" places in the Keep, it was by far Kerowyn's favorite. Dierna was still having vapors every time she set foot outside the bower—now converted from armory back to women's quarters by Dierna's agitated orders—so Grandmother Kethry had entrusted the making of medicines to Kero's hands.

It keeps me busy, she thought, a little ruefully. *And at least it's useful-busy. Not like Dierna's damned embroidery.* Some of the recipes Kethry had dictated from memory, and they were things Kerowyn had never heard of; she was completely fascinated, and retreat to the still-room was not the boring task it usually was.

Retreat to the stillroom was just that, too—retreat. Dierna's relatives, the female ones in particular, were treating her very strangely. Part of the time they acted as if she was some creature as alien and frightening as Tarma's giant wolf. The rest of the time they acted as if she was a source of prime amusement. They spoke to her as little as possible, but she was certain that they made up wild stories about her once they were on the other side of the bower doors.

They certainly don't seem to spend any time doing anything else, she thought sourly, as she carefully removed the pot of melted fat from the heat, and sifted powdered herbs into it. *They're amazingly good at finding other places to be whenever there's real work to be done.*

She beat the herbs into the fat with brisk strokes of the spatula, taking some of her anger at the women out on the pot of salve. She was very tired of the odd, sideways looks she was getting—tired enough that she had continued to wear Lordan's castoffs, rather than "proper, womanly" garb, out of sheer perversity.

I'm cleaning, and lifting, and tending the wounded—when I'm not out drilling the boys in bow or in the still-room, she thought stubbornly. *Breeches are a lot more practical than skirts. Why shouldn't I wear them? Grandmother and that Shin'a'in woman do—*

She had to smile at that. *And they are one and all so frightened of Grandmother and her friend that if either one of them even looks cross, they practically faint.*

The salve smelled wonderful, and that alone was a far cry from the medicines she used to make here. She sighed, and stirred a little slower, feeling melancholy descend on her. Life was not the same; it didn't look as if it would ever be the same again.

It isn't just them, it's everything. It seems as if no one treats me the same anymore. Not the servants, not Wendar, not even Lordan. Why has everything changed? It doesn't make any sense. I haven't changed. Of course, Father—

The thought of Rathgar made her feel guilty. She knew she should be mourning him—*Dierna* certainly was. The girl had ransacked Lenore's wardrobe for mourning clothes, and had them made over to fit herself and her women. She'd carried on at the funeral as through Rathgar had been *her* father instead of Kero's.

She carried on enough for both me and *Lordan,* Kero recalled sardonically. *Maybe it's just that I really never saw that much of him when Mother was alive, and when she was gone, he really never had much to say to me except to criticize. Really, I might just as well have been fostered out, for all that I saw of him. I knew Dent and Wendar better than I knew him!* She sighed again. *I must be a cold bitch if I can't even mourn my own father.*

She heard footsteps on the stone floor outside just then, and the door creaked open. "So here's where you've been hiding yourself," said a harsh voice behind her. "Warrior bless! It's like a cave in here! What are you doing, turning yourself into a bat?"

"It has to be dark," Kero explained without turning, wondering what had brought the formidable old fighter here. "A lot of herbs lose potency in the light."

"I'll take your word for it." The Shin'a'in edged carefully into the narrow confines of the stillroom, and positioned herself out of Kero's way. "My people don't store a great deal, and that little only for a season or two at most. Don't tell me you like it in here."

"Sometimes," Kero told her. "It's better than—" she bit her tongue to keep from finishing that sentence.

"It's better than out there, with the hens and chicks clucking disapproval at you," the Shin'a'in finished for her. "I know what you mean. The only reason they keep their tongues off *me* is because they're pretty sure I'll slice those wagging tongues in half if I find out about it." She chuckled, and Kero turned to look at the old woman in surprise. "We never have been properly introduced. I'm Tarma—Tarma shena Tale'sedrin, to be precise—Shin'a'in from the Hawk Clan. I've been your grandmother's partner for an age, and I'm half of the reason your father disapproved of *her.*"

"You are?" Kero said, fascinated by the hawk-faced woman's outspoken manner. "But—why?"

"Because he was dead certain that she and I were

shieldmates—that's lovers, dear. He was dead *wrong,* but you could never have convinced him of that.'' Tarma hardly moved, but there was suddenly a tiny, thin-bladed knife in one hand. She began cleaning her nails with it. ''The other half of the reason he disapproved of her was because he was afraid of both of us. We didn't know our place, and we could do just about any damned thing a man could do. But that's a cold trail, and not worth following.''

''Are *you* the reason we could get Shin'a'in horses to breed?'' Kero asked, suddenly putting several odd facts together.''

Tarma chuckled. ''Damn, you're quick. Dead in the black, *jel'enedra.* Listen, I'm sorry I was so hard on you, back on the road the other night. I was testing you, sort of.''

''I'd—figured that out,'' Kero replied. The knife caught the light and flashed; it looked sharp enough to wound the wind.

The Shin'a'in nodded, a satisfied little smile at the corners of her mouth. ''Good. I was hoping you might. I want you to know I think you did pretty well out there. About the only time you started to dither was *after* everything was over and done with. You know, you're wasted on all this.''

''All what?'' Kero asked, bewildered by the sudden change in topic.

''All this—'' The Shin'a'in waved her knife vaguely, taking in the four walls of the stillroom and beyond. Kero hid her confusion by turning her attention to the salve, watching her own hands intently. ''This life,'' Tarma continued. ''It's not enough of a challenge for you. You're capable of a lot more than you'll find here. My people say. 'You can put a hawk in a songbird's cage, but it's still a hawk.' Think about it. I have to go beat some of those hired guards into shape, but I'll be around if you need me.''

And with that, she backed out of Kero's sight, and vanished. One moment she was there, the next, gone; leaving only the door to the stillroom swinging to mark her passing.

* * *

"*All* right, you meatheads, let's see a little life in those blows!" Ten men and women—those currently off-duty—placed their blows on the ten sets of pells as if their lives depended on it.

Of course, their lives do *depend on it.*

Tarma roamed up and down the line of hired guards, scowling, but inwardly she was very pleased. These were all reliable, solid fighters, with good references, very much as she and Keth had been early in their careers.

The only difference was that these fighters were well *into* their careers. Ordinarily they had nowhere to go now but down.

Because she'd been able to offer a packhorse apiece with half pay in advance, she'd gotten the cream of the available mercenary crop. None of them were going to be the kind of fighter that legends were made of, but for Lordan's purposes they were far better. Most of them were in their middle years, looking for a post where they could settle down, perhaps even think about a spouse and children. That's why they *weren't* with a mercenary company—going out and fighting every year was a job for the young. . . .

And fools, she thought, *which these gentlemen and ladies are not.* "Put some *back* into it!" she shouted again, feeling a sense of deja vu. How many times had she shouted those same words, in this same courtyard?

Only then, it was into young ears, not seasoned ones. These folks are well aware of the absolute necessity for practice, every day, rain, snow or scorching heat.

Thirty seasoned fighters. That would be enough to give even Baron Reichert second thoughts. And one very special recruit. . . .

As middle-aged as the others, without a single thing to differentiate her from the rest. Even her color and stature—golden skin, and very tall for a woman—were not particularly outstanding among mercenaries. Hired swords came from every corner of the known world, and some places outside it; Beaker had been odder-looking than this woman. She acted no differently than any of the others, not looking for special status, nor making herself conspicuous. Tarma drilled this recruit as remorselessly as the rest, and paid her no more attention, and no less.

Lyla Stormcloud was from the far south and west; past even the Dhorisha Plains. She was half Shin'a'in, with the gold complexion of her father and the black eyes and wandering foot of her mother, a Full Bard who had double the normal wanderlust of that roaming profession. Life with a nomadic Clan had suited her perfectly, and Tale'sedrin, made up as it was of orphans and adoptees, made her welcome there as she might not have been in a "pure" Clan. How they'd gloried in having a Full Bard with them.

A Full Bard with another profession as well, the one she had trained in as a child—the skills and training of which she passed in turn to her daughter.

Assassin.

It's a good thing the Clans didn't know that until long after she'd been accepted on the basis of her Talent and current profession. And it's a damned good thing for her that she admitted it before someone ferreted the information out on his own. But I'm glad it happened, especially now. Try and get an assassin past another assassin. Tarma furrowed her brow in thought, watching Lyla at her sword-work. *Blessings on the Warrior, for sending her mother to Tale'sedrin, and a double blessing that Lyla was willing to pack up and move on my say-so.*

Lordan was in danger as long as Baron Reichert thought him vulnerable. If Tarma and her partner could stay here—well, nothing and no one was going to get past them. Now that Keth was no longer bound by the promises she'd made Rathgar, she could put mage-protections up that would stop any magical attack on her grandson short of an Adept-spell. And if Tarma could possibly have moved in here permanently—

But she couldn't, and knew it. There were other considerations, not the least of which was that she wasn't as young as she used to be. And guarding a target from assassins was a young person's job. That had been when she'd thought of Lyla. After that, it had been a matter of sending a mage-borne message via Keth to the shaman of Tale'sedrin—who just happened to be Kethry's son, Jadrek. And then, when Lyla had agreed to come, some mysterious transaction involving the Tale'edras of the Pelagiris Forest had been negotiated via Jadrek to get her here. *I'm still not sure how she got here as fast as she did. Those Hawkbrothers—they've got to have secrets of magic even Kethry and the other Adepts don't know. Probably only the Clan shamans have any idea what they can do. And they aren't telling, either.*

Even Lyla didn't remember how she'd gotten here; she told Tarma that Jadrek had taken her to the forest edge— and the next thing she knew, she was walking through the open mouth of a cave near the Tower.

Just as well; let them keep their secrets. I don't think I want to know them.

Lordan was now as safe as Tarma knew how to make him. Certainly safer than money could buy. . . .

Lyla was a pleasure to watch; wasting no effort, and certainly almost as good as Tarma in her prime. Better than Tarma was now. Not through fault of training or will, just old bones and stiff, scarred muscles, slower reactions and senses that were no longer as keen—

So the world belongs to the young. At least there're youngsters I'm glad to see have it. Like young Kero.

She hoped she'd said the right things, neither too much, nor too little. Too much, and she might frighten the bird back to its nest. Too little, and she wouldn't realize there was a great big world out here, and a whole sky in which to use her wings.

If I'm any judge, she's got the reactions and the instincts; all she needs is the skill and the strength, and she'll put Lyla in the shade. She has it in her. She has the brains and the guts, too, which means even more—she can be more than even an exceptional merc with those. But if I push, she'll rebel, or she'll be frightened off.

"Good!" she said aloud, and the sweaty fighters lowered their weapons with varying expressions of gratitude. "*All* right, ladies and gentlemen—off to the baths. On the quickstep—march!"

I never thought I'd find myself here, Kero thought for the hundredth time, watching the rest of the wedding guests over the rim of her goblet. She tried not to fidget; tried not to feel as if she was being smothered under all the layers of her holiday dress. *I should be back in the kitchen.*

But she didn't need to be in the kitchen, not anymore. Grandmother Kethry had seen to that. There was a proper housekeeper now—which was just as well, since Dierna was not up to handling the kitchen staff and servers the way Kero had. She was good at knowing what orders to *give* the housekeeper; what servants were best where, which was something Kero had never been able to figure out. She was a marvel at loom and needle, and Lordan was shortly going to find himself in possession of a thriving woolen-cloth trade if Dierna had anything to say about it. She was fair useless in the stillroom, but—

But the housekeeper can do that, too.

This housekeeper was an impoverished gentlewoman, found by Kethry by means of one of her many (and mysterious) contacts. Kero had a vague idea that there was a relative involved in some way.

An uncle? An aunt? Someone connected with some kind of mage school, I think.

There was something about the way she'd been dispossessed, too. Something unjust, that Kethry wouldn't go into when Dierna was around. Could it possibly be something involving Dierna's uncle, the Baron? Well, no matter what the cause, here she was, and grateful for the post. Being neither noble nor servant, she was perfect for the position, which wasn't quite "family," and wasn't exactly "underling."

Perfect, as Kero had not been; she knew that now. Too close to the servants for them to "respect" her properly; that was what Dierna's mother had said.

She'd said a lot more, when she thought Kero couldn't hear. Kero glanced at the lady in question, sitting on the other side of the bride and groom, and lording it over her half of the table. *I'm glad for Lordan's sake she won't be here much longer. I might murder her and disgrace him.*

Thank the gods for grandmother and Tarma, she thought, as Lordan and his bride shared a goblet of wine, and made big eyes at each other. *They were like whirlwinds, magic whirlwinds. They blew in, they created order, and they're about to blow out again before anyone has a chance to resent them. Even Dierna.*

To her credit, through, the bride showed no signs of

resenting Kethry's "interference," despite the plaints of
her own mother. She'd had more than enough on her
hands, even with the aid of the housekeeper. Dierna had
taken over nursing Lordan as soon as Kethry had pro-
nounced him fit for company, and he'd quite fallen in love
with his intended.

They're besotted, she thought resignedly. *I suppose it's
just as well.*

She looked down over the Great Hall, at all the other
guests, like a bed of multicolored flowers in their finery,
and many of them just about as immobile. Fully half of
them couldn't stand, and all of them wore some token of
mourning, but that didn't seem to be putting any kind
of a pall on the celebrations. Wendar saw to it that the
wine kept flowing, and the celebrants were chattering so
loudly that it was impossible to hear the minstrels at the
end of the hall. All enmities seemed to have been forgotten, at least for now.

But she kept catching strange glances cast her way. It
was beginning to make her want to squirm with discomfort, but she kept her seat and her dignity.

I'm a heroine. And I'm an embarrassment.

That just about summed it all up. She looked down
into her wine, and felt the all-too-familiar melancholy
settle over her.

She didn't fit in. She didn't belong. Even her own
brother looked at her as if she had suddenly become a
stranger.

*I rescued Dierna. Which makes me a heroine. Just one
little problem—I'm Lordan's sister.*

She'd already heard some of Lordan's peers teasing
him about his "older brother Kero." It made him uncomfortable, for all that he was deeply, truly grateful,
for all that he'd offered her anything she wanted, right
down to half the lands. And it shamed him. *He* should
have been the one to rescue his bride. Wasn't that the
way it went in the tales? Not his sibling.

Not his *sister.*

She could talk until she was blue in the face about how
it had been Kethry's sword that had done everything.
None of that mattered—because she had gone out on The
Ride in the first place, *without* the help of the sword.

That's what they were calling it now, "The Ride." There were even rumors of a song.

Dierna did not want her in the bower. Not that Kero wanted to *be* in the bower. She most assuredly did not fit in *there*.

But she keeps looking at me as if she thinks I'm—what was it that Tarma said, the other day? She'chorne. Like I'm going to suddenly start courting her. Like I make her skin crawl.

Kero gulped down half the wine in her goblet, and a page immediately reached over her shoulder and poured her more. The rich fruity scent rose to her nostrils, and tempted her not at all.

I wish I dared get drunk.

The hired guards didn't want her in the barracks. It was not that it was "unwomanly" for her to be there by their standards. They had enough women with them already. It was that she didn't fit there because of her status. She was noble, and she was family, and she didn't belong with the hirelings.

And her old friends among the servants kept treating her like some kind of demi-deity.

I don't fit here anymore, she thought, a notion that had begun to make its own little rut through her mind, she'd repeated it so often. *I just don't fit here. If I stay here much longer, I think I may go mad. It feels like I'm being smothered. Tarma was right. You can put a hawk in a birdcage, like a songbird, but it's still a hawk.*

She caught a movement down at the second table, and saw her grandmother and her friend easing out of their seats. It didn't look like a trip to the necessary; it seemed more final. Somehow she knew where they were going. Back to the Tower. *They* weren't needed here anymore, either—so they were making a graceful, unobtrusive exit.

I wish I could do the same—

That was when it hit her.

Why can't *I do the same? Why can't I just go?* She sat up straighter, feeling her cheeks warming with excitement. *I have to return Grandmother's sword anyway—so why don't I follow after them? Maybe they'll be willing to teach me things. Didn't Tarma say they used to have a school?*

The more she thought about it, the better the idea
sounded. And the more intolerable and confining the idea
of remaining here became. Finally she excused herself
from the table—her seatmate didn't even notice—and
slipped out of the Great Hall and into the corridor beyond.

Once there, she hiked her encumbering skirts above
her knees, and ran for her room. There were no servants
in the hall to see her, and although she split one sleeve
of the gown, she no longer cared. Let Dierna give it to
one of her maids.

I certainly won't wear it again.

She slipped out of it as soon as she reached her room,
tossed it in a heap in the corner, and dragged her saddlebags out from under the bed. She rummaged through
chests and wardrobe in a frenzy, discarding most of what
she encountered without a second thought, casting what
she'd decided to keep on the bed.

It was amazing how little she owned that she wanted
to keep. Her armor, Lordan's outgrown castoffs, a few
personal treasures and the jewelry and books Lenore had
left her . . . it all fit into two saddlebags with room to
spare. She started to take a last look around her room—
and realized that it held nothing of her or for her anymore.

So she turned her back on it, and strode out, chain
mail jingling with a cheer she began to feel herself.

Out in the stable, even the grooms were absent, enjoying their own version of the wedding feast. All the better;
that made it possible for her to saddle up Verenna and
ride out without anyone noticing.

The mare came to her whistle and stood quietly while
she saddled and bridled her. She felt Verenna's tense eagerness as she mounted, as if the mare was as ready to
be free of the place as Kero was. She touched her heel
lightly to the mare's flank; Verenna leapt forward. They
trotted across the courtyard, cantered to the gates. She
was at a full gallop as they passed the gates in the outer
wall. Kero laughed as they burst out into the sunshine,
wind whipping her hair, Verenna striding effortlessly under her. Nothing was going to stand in her way now!

But she pulled Verenna up abruptly at the sight of the
two mounted figures waiting for her at the crossroads.

Suddenly sick with dread, she approached them at a walk. *What if they tell me to go back? What if they don't want me? What if—*

"What kept you?" asked Tarma.

Six

This was not precisely what Kerowyn had pictured when she'd asked for teaching.

"Chopping wood I can understand," Kero said slowly, hefting the unfamiliar weight of the ax in her right hand. She eyed her appointed target, an odd setup of two logs braced against the tree, and shifted her hand a bit farther down on the haft. It wasn't a very big ax, and she had the sinking feeling that it was going to take a long time to chop her way through the pile of log sections stacked up at the edge of the clearing. She'd already put a dent in the pile over the past few days, using a larger ax in a conventional manner, but this tool baffled her. It wasn't much heavier than the hand axes some of Rathgar's men had fought with. "I've been cutting wood for you since I got here, and I can see that you still need firewood. But why brace the logs so that I'm cutting at *that* angle?"

Warrl—Tarma's enormous wolf-creature—snorted, flopped himself down in a patch of sun, and laid his ears back in patent disgust. His kind were called *kyree,* so Tarma had told her—and she needed no testimony as to his intelligence; she'd seen that herself with her own eyes. She'd gotten used to his presence over the past weeks, and now she could read his expressions with more ease than she could read Tarma's. It would appear that she was being particularly dense, though for the life of her she couldn't figure out what she was missing.

Tarma chuckled evilly, and leaned against the wood-pile. If Kero had tried that, she'd probably have knocked half the logs down. The pile didn't shift a thumb's length. "But what if you've got it wrong?" the Shin'a'in asked conversationally. "What if we *don't* need you to chop firewood?"

"What?" Kero replied cleverly. She blinked, and did

a fast revision of her assumptions. "You mean you heat that great stone hulk with magic? But I thought you said—"

"That it takes more effort to do something magically than it does to just *do* it, yes," Tarma replied, a maddening little smile on her face. "No, we don't heat it with magic, yes, we use wood, and we still don't need you to chop it. We hire it done. A couple of nice farmer lads with muscles like oxen. So why would I be having you chop wood, and why would I be giving you different sizes of axes to do it with? And now why would I start asking you to work at odd angles?"

Kero blinked again, and the answer came to her in a burst of memory—recollections of Lordan working out against the pells. "Because you want me to strengthen my arms and shoulders," she said immediately. "All over, and not just a particular set of muscles."

"And because while you're doing so, you might as well be useful. Besides, if I make you really chop up wood, you won't hold back. Against the pells you might. Against me, you already do." This time Tarma laughed outright, but Kero couldn't resent it; somehow Kero knew the Shin'a'in wasn't laughing at her expense. It was more as if Tarma was sharing a sardonic little joke. "Out on the plains we were set to working bellows at the forge, toting water for the entire camp, or any one of a hundred other things. Be grateful it's wood-chopping I've got you doing. Ax calluses you're getting now are going to be in about the same places that you'd want sword-calluses."

Kero sighed and took her first, methodical blow. Now that she knew *why* she was engaging in this exercise in frustration, it wasn't quite so frustrating. *And*, she vowed silently, *I'm going to be a lot more careful in placing my hits. I just might impress her.*

She certainly wasn't impressing her grandmother. Kethry had tested her in any number of ways, from placing a candle in front of her and telling her to light it by thinking of fire, to placing various small objects in front of her and asking her to identify which of them were enchanted. She'd evidently failed dismally, since Kethry had given up after three days and told her she'd be better off in the hands of the Shin'a'in.

But she won't take that sword back, Kero thought in

puzzlement, swinging the ax in an underhand arc, repeating the motion over and over, switching from right to left and back again under Tarma's watchful eye. *It's hers, but she won't take it back. I don't understand—it's obviously magical, and no one in her right mind would give something like that away—but she keeps saying that it spoke for me, and it's mine.*

So, marvelous. It spoke for me. Now what am I supposed to do with it?

"Faster," Tarma said. Kero sped up her blows, trying to keep each one falling in exactly the same place; right on top of and within the narrow bite she'd incised on the sides of the logs. Those logs were strapped tightly to either side of what had once been a tree. When it had been alive, it had somehow managed to root itself in the exact middle of this clearing and had taken advantage of the full sun to grow far taller than any of the trees around it. Perhaps that had been a mistake. From the look of the top of the stump, some two men's height above her head, it had been lightning-struck. That top was splintered in a way that didn't look to be the hand of man.

Maybe Grandmother got in a temper one day. . . .

This was not where Tarma schooled her new pupil and practiced her own sword-work; this was just what it seemed, a kind of primitive back court to the Tower, with a large outdoor hearth for cooking whole deer on one side, the pile of firewood ready to be chopped on the other, and in the center, the old, dead tree with iron bands around it. A *big* old, dead tree. Kero could circle what was left of the trunk with her arms—barely.

"That's not too bad," Tarma observed. She pushed herself off the woodpile, and gestured to Kero to stop, then strolled over to the two logs and began examining the cuts closely. Kero wiped sweat from her forehead with her sleeve, and shook her arms to keep them loose.

"That's not too bad at all. And considering what a late start you got—can you finish those in double time?"

She gave Kero the kind of look Dent used to—the kind that said, *be careful what you say, you'll have to live up to it.* Kero licked salty moisture from her upper lip and considered the twin logs. They were chopped a little more than halfway through. The target she'd been creating was just above the iron bands holding them tight to the tree trunk.

So when I get toward the end, they'll probably break the rest of the way under their own weight. She squinted up at the sun; broken light coming down through the thick foliage made it hard to tell exactly where the sun *was*. It was close to noon, though, that was for certain. Her stomach growled, as if to remind her that she had gotten up at dawn, and breakfast had been a long time ago.

The sooner I get these chopped, the sooner I can have something to eat. Some bread and cheese; maybe sausage. Cider. Fruit—and I know she magics that up; pears and grapes and just-ripe apples all served up together are not *natural at any time of year.*

"I think I can," she said, carefully. "I'll try."

Tarma stepped back, and nodded. Kero set to, driving herself with the reminder of how good that lunch was going to taste—

Especially the cider. At double time she was getting winded very quickly; there was a stitch in her side, and she couldn't keep herself from panting, which only parched her mouth and throat. Her eyes blurred with fatigue, and stung from the sweat and damp hair that kept getting in the way. Finally, though, she heard the sound she'd been waiting for; the *crack* of wood, first on one side of the trunk, then on the other. As she got in one last blow, then lowered her arms and backed off from the tree, the two half-logs bent out from the center trunk, then with a second *crack,* broke free and fell to the ground.

Kero rather wanted to fall to the ground herself. She certainly wanted to drop the ax, which now felt as if it weighed as much as the tree trunk. But she didn't; she'd learned *that* lesson early on, when she'd dropped a practice sword at the end of a bout. Tarma had picked it up, and given her a *look* of sheer and pain-filled disgust.

She'd never felt so utterly worthless in her life, but worse was to come.

Tarma had carefully, patiently, and in the tone and simple words one would use with a five-year-old, explained *why* one never treats a weapon that way, even when one is tired, even when the weapon is just pot-metal and fit only to practice with.

Then, as if that wasn't humiliation enough, she put the blade away and made Kero chop wood and haul water for the next three days straight, instead of chopping and hauling in the morning, and practicing in the afternoon.

So she hung onto the little hand-ax until Tarma took it away from her. "All right, youngling," she said in that gravelly voice, as Kero raised a hand at the end of an arm that felt like the wood she'd just been chopping. "Let's get back to the Tower and a hot bath and some food. You've earned it." Then she grinned. "And after lunch, a mild little workout, hmm?"

Kero finished getting her arm up to her forehead, and mopped her brow and the back of her neck with a sleeve that was already sopping wet.

"Lady," she croaked, "Every time you set me a 'mild little workout,' I wind up flat on my back before sundown too tired to move. You're a hard taskmaster."

Tarma only chuckled.

Lunch in the Tower was as "civilized" as even Kero's mother could have wished. The three of them sat around a square wooden table in one of the upper balconies, sun streaming down on them, a fresh breeze drying Kero's hair. Despite the fact that she had braided it tightly, bits of it were escaping from her braids and the breeze tugged at them like a kitten with string. She kept trying to get it back under control, but it persisted in escaping, and finally she just gave up and let it fly. There was no one here to care how "respectable"—or not—she looked.

She felt much the better for her hot bath, though her muscles still ached in unaccustomed places from that little exercise this morning. Furthermore, she knew very well that she was going to hurt even more tonight. But it was a small price to pay for freedom.

Freedom from the bower, from boredom, from pretending I was something I wasn't. That thought led inevitably to another. *So what am I now? What am I supposed to be doing with myself?* And one more—*Why wasn't I like Dierna, content with being someone's lady?*

An uneasy set of thoughts—and uncomfortable thoughts. But problems that, for the moment, she could do nothing about. She forced her attention back to more immediate concerns.

Like lunch.

I don't know where Grandmother gets her provisions, but Wendar would kill to find out. On a platter in the center of the table were cheese, sausage, and bread. Simple fare, certainly not the kind of things one would expect a powerful mage to savor—but they were the best Kero had ever tasted. It wasn't just hunger adding flavor, either; even after one was pleasantly full, the food at Kethry's table tasted extraordinary.

Beside the platter was a second, holding fruit; not only apples, pears and grapes, but cherries as well.

Definitely not natural. Those are fresh apples, pear season is over, grapes are ripe, but cherries won't be for another moon, and apples don't ripen until fall.

But the sun felt wonderful, the apple she'd just cut into quarters was pleasantly tart, and Kero didn't much want to think about anything for a while.

I'm going to enjoy this, however it came about. Father was wrong about Grandmother, and he was probably just as wrong about mages in general.

"Think you're ready for some family history?" Kethry said, casting a long look at her from across the old table, as Kero reached for a piece of sausage. "I think I have a fair number of surprises for you. For one thing, you have some rather—unusual—cousins. Quite a lot of them, in fact."

Kero froze in mid-reach.

The sorceress sat back in her cushioned chair, tucked flyaway hair behind one ear and smiled at her expression. In her russet gown of soft linen she looked nothing at all like a feared and legendary mage. She looked like the matriarch of a noble family.

And I must look like a stranded fish, Kero thought, trying to get her mouth to close.

"Don't look so stricken, child," Tarma said, and reached across the table, picked up the sausage, and dropped it into her hand. "There's no outlawry on the family name. It's just—well, you have a lot more relatives than you know about. Those cousins, for instance."

"I do?" She gathered her scattered wits, and took a deep breath, only then becoming aware that she was still clutching the sausage. She put it down carefully on her plate. "I mean—you said something about *daughters* and

granddaughters earlier, but Mother never said anything—
I didn't know what to think. How many? Did Mother
have a sister or—''

"Your mother had *six* brothers and sisters, youngling,'' Tarma interrupted, grinning from ear to ear at the
dumbstruck look on her pupil's face. She played with
one end of her own iron-gray braid as she spoke. The
tail of hair was as thick as Kero's wrist, and as gray as
the coat of Tarma's mare. ''Your grandmother and I are
Goddess-sworn sisters, and I know I've explained that to
you already.'' When Kero finally nodded, she continued.
''Well, what I didn't tell you was that before I met her,
my Clan was wiped out by the same bandits she'd con-
tracted to stop.''

"It was one of my first jobs as a Journeyman,'' Kethry
put in, after Tarma paused for a moment, staring off at a
long cloud above the trees. ''They had taken over a whole
town and were terrorizing the inhabitants. Tarma followed them there, and I managed to intercept her before
she managed to get herself killed.''

"Huh. You wouldn't have done much better alone,
Greeneyes,'' Tarma replied sardonically, coming back to
the conversation. ''Well. We decided to team up. It
worked, and we actually managed to take out the bandits
and survive the experience. That was when we figured
we'd make pretty good partners.''

"Then things got a little complicated,'' Kethry chuckled, popping a grape into her mouth.

"A *little* complicated?'' Tarma raised both eyebrows,
then shrugged. ''I suppose—in the same way that stealing a warsteed can get the Clans a *little* annoyed. Anyway, the main thing is that we got back to the Plains, she
got adopted into the Shin'a'in, and she vowed to the el-
ders that she'd build a new Clan for me. Eventually she
met and wedded your grandfather Jadrek, and damn if
she didn't just about manage to repopulate Tale'sedrin all
on her own!''

Kethry chuckled, and actually blushed. ''Jadrek had a
little to do with that,'' she pointed out, raising an eloquent finger at her partner.

"Well, true enough, and good blood he put in, too.''
Tarma stretched, tossed the braid back over her shoulders, and clasped both gnarled hands around her knee.

"That's another story. We three raised seven children, all told. When the core group claimed the herds, we added adoptees from other Clans, orphans and younglings who had some problems and wanted a fresh start. Tale'sedrin is a full Clan; smaller than it was before the massacre, but growing. Kind of funny how many young suitors we got drooling around the core and the core-blood—but then, to us, a blond is exotic."

"But—I don't understand—" Kero protested. "If my uncles and aunts are all Shin'a'in, why aren't I? How did I end up here instead of there?"

"Good question," Tarma acknowledged. "The way these things work is that even though Keth vowed her children to the Clan, what she vowed was that they'd have the right to become Clan, not that they *had* to. It's the younglings who decide for themselves where they want to go. We don't make anyone do anything they aren't suited for—the Plains are too harsh and unforgiving for anyone who doesn't love them to survive there. So—when we've got a case like Keth's, vowed younglings of adopted blood, the children spend half their time with the Clans until they're sixteen, then they choose whether they want to become Shin'a'in in full, or go off on their own. Five of those aunts and uncles of yours chose Shin'a'in ways and the Tale'sedrin banner when they came of age to make the choice."

"Mother didn't. And?" Kero asked curiously. *Why would anyone choose to stay here? The Keep may be the most boring backwater in the world.*

"I was getting to that." Tarma gave her one of those *looks*. "Of the two that didn't go with the Clans, one picked up where his mother left off, and took over the White Winds sorcery school she'd founded and set up at the Keep—just moved it off onto property *he'd* swindl—ahem."

She cast a sideways glance at Kethry, who only seemed amused to Kero. "Excuse me. Earned. That's your uncle Jendar. It's not that he didn't like Clan life, it's that he's Adept-potential, and all that mage-talent would be wasted out there. There's another son, and he's mage-gifted as well. That's your uncle Jadrek, only he's a Shin'a'in shaman. But your mother Lenore was last-born, your grandfather died when she was very small and we had some problems with the school that kept us busy. Maybe too busy. She—well—" Tarma coughed, and looked embarrassed. "Let's say she was different. Scared to death of horses, and had fits over the Clan style of living, so we stopped even sending her out to the Plains. Bookish, like Jadrek, but no logic, no discipline, no gift of scholarship. No real interest in anything but ballads and tales and romances. No abilities besides the ones appropriate to a fine lady. No mage-talent."

"In short, she was our disappointment, poor thing," Kethry sighed, and twined a curl of silver hair around her fingers. "She spent all her time at the neighboring family's place, and all she really wanted to be was somebody's bride, the same daydream as all the girls she knew. I scandalized her; Tarma terrified her. Finally, I fostered her with the Lythands until she was sixteen, then brought her back here. She came back a lady—and suited to nothing else."

Kero thought about her mother for a moment, surprised that for the first time in months—years—the thoughts didn't call up an ache of loss. Even when Lenore had been well, she'd been fragile, unsuited to anything that took her outside the Keep walls, even pleasure-riding, and likely to pick up every little illness that she came in contact with. *No wonder she didn't like Tarma or her Clan. Living in a tent for three moons every year must have been a hell for her.*

"So what were you going to do?" she asked carefully. "Mother wasn't the kind of person you could leave on her own. She was better with someone to take care of her."

Kethry smiled slightly, the lines around her eyes deepening. "A gentle way to put it, but accurate. Frankly, I had no ideas beyond getting her married off. I wanted to find a really suitable husband for her, one she could learn to love, but after one experience with suitors, I despaired of finding anyone that would treat her so that she'd survive the marital experience." Her eyes hardened. "That suitor, by the by, was Baron Reichert. Not the Baron then, just a youngster hardly older than Lenore, but already experienced beyond his years. One might even say, jaded."

"One might," Tarma agreed. "I prefer 'spoiled, debauched, and corrupt.' He was never interested in anything other than the lands, and when he saw how delicate your mother was, he damn near danced for joy."

She scowled, and Kero read a great deal in that frown. "Need saw it, too; damn sword nearly made Keth pull it on him and skewer him then and there. First time that stupid thing's been totally right in a long time, and us having to fight it to keep from being made into murderers. But given what's been going on, maybe we should have taken the chance."

Kethry sighed, and leaned forward a little. "Well, we were in a pickle then. I knew Reichert would keep coming back as long as she was unwedded, and Lenore was just silly enough that he might be able to persuade her that he loved her. I was at my wits' end. I even considered manufacturing a quarrel and disinheriting her long enough for Reichert to lose interest. Then your father showed up, escorting a rich young mageling, and looking for work when his escort duties were done. Strong, handsome, in an over-muscled way, full of stories about the strange places he'd been, and amazingly patient in some circumstances. Personally, I thought he was god-sent."

"The fathead," Tarma muttered under her breath. Kero winced a little; not because of what Tarma had said, but because she couldn't bring herself to disagree with it. She'd been here at the Tower for several weeks, now, and with each day her former life seemed a little less real, a little farther distant. She supposed she should be feeling grief for Rathgar, but instead, whenever she tried to summon up the proper emotions, all she could recall were some of the stupid things he'd done, and the unkind words he'd said so often to her.

I'm turning into some kind of inhuman monster, she thought with guilt. *I can't even respect my father's memory.*

"He may have been a fathead, *she'enedra,* but he was exactly what Lenore needed and wanted. A big, strong man to protect and cosset her." Kethry looked up at the blindingly blue sky, and followed a new cloud with her eyes for a moment. "I offered to let him stay on for a bit, and the moment Lenore laid eyes on him I knew she was attracted to him. Give her credit for some sense, at least—Reichert terrified her as much or more than *you* ever did. I was just afraid that he'd notice what he was doing, and manage to convince her he was harmless.''

"Tender little baby chicks know a weasel when they see one," Tarma retorted, scratching the bridge of her beaklike nose with one finger. "That's not sense, that's instinct. Lady Bright, I suppose I should be glad her instincts were working, at least. One year in his custody, and you'd have been out a daughter, *and* lands, *and* probably under siege in this Tower.''

"Probably," Kethry agreed wearily. "Well, to continue the story, that young mage was the last pupil we were going to take; we planned to retire within a few years. So I let Rathgar stick around—and I told Lenore I wanted her to run a little deception on him.''

"*That* part I know about," Kero exclaimed. "If you mean that she pretended to be the housekeeper's daughter instead of yours, so he felt free to court her—" Kethry nodded, and Kero flushed. "When I was little, that seemed so romantic. . . .''

Tarma snorted. "Romantic! Dear Goddess—I supposed she'd think of it that way. We were both afraid that if he knew she was Keth's daughter, he'd never even think about courting her. *We* just wanted her under the protection of somebody who'd take care of her without exploiting her.''

"It all would have worked fine, except for Rathgar himself," Kethry said, shaking her head. "If I'd had any idea how he felt about mages—well, she fell very happily and romantically in love with him, and he was just dazzled by her, and it all looked as if things were going to work out wonderfully. He proposed, she accepted, and I told him who she really was—"

"And the roof fell in." Kero felt entirely confident in making that statement. She knew her father, and had a shrewd guess as to what his reaction to such a revelation would be. Outrage at the deception, further outrage that this *mage* was his beloved's mother. Before long he'd have convinced himself that Kethry had some deep-laid plot against him, and he'd have done his best to pry his poor innocent Lenore out of her mother's "deadly" influence.

"I didn't see it coming," Kethry admitted. "I should have, and I didn't. And at that point, it was too late. My daughter was deep in the throes of romantic love, and Rathgar was her perfect hero. Anything Lenore heard from me on the subject threw her into hysterics. She was certain that I wanted to part them.''

''She thought he made the sun rise and set,'' Tarma said with utter disgust, her hawklike face twisted into an expression of distaste. ''It's a damned good thing he was an honest and unmalicious man, because if he'd beaten her and told her she deserved it, she'd have believed him. How could *any* woman put herself in that kind of position willingly?''

''I suppose I should have expected it,'' Kethry said gloomily. ''I set the whole mess up in the first place. You know what your people say—'Be careful what you ask for, you may get it.' For the first time she had someone around who thought she was wonderful just as she was, helpless and weak, and *wasn't* trying to force her to do something constructive with her life. Of course she thought he hung the moon.''

Tarma threw up her hands. ''I still don't understand it. Keth went ahead with the marriage, because anything was safer than letting Reichert have another chance. Well, that was when Lenore decided Keth and I were old fools and began listening only to Rathgar, and when he saw he had the upper hand, he started making demands. Finally it came down to this: when Lordan was born, he made Keth promise never to set foot on Keep property without an invitation.''

''So that's why—'' Kero's voice trailed off. A great many things started making sense, now.

''I think he was afraid I'd try and take her away from him,'' Kethry said, after a long silence filled only with the sound of the wind in the leaves below them. ''I really do think he didn't care as much about the property as he did about my daughter. On the other hand, I know that he always resented that every bit of his new-won wealth came from me. I think he kept expecting me to try and take over again, to control him through either the wealth, Lenore, or you children.''

Probably. That was the one thing he hated more than anything else, being controlled by someone. Maybe because he got a bellyful of taking orders when he was younger, I don't know. I do know that he'd never have believed Grandmother didn't *have some kind of complicated plot going.*

Tarma got up, stretched, and perched herself on the stone railing of the balcony. "Well, I'm not that generous," she growled. "The man was a common merc; a little better born than most, but not even close to landed. And that was what he wanted all his life—to win lands, and become gentry. That's what most mercs want, once they lose their taste for fighting. Whether it's a farm they dream of, or a place like the Keep, they all want some kind of place they can claim as their own, and that's the long and the short of it."

Kero shifted uneasily on her wooden bench, and put down the last of the sausage, uneaten. She had the vague feeling she ought to be defending Rathgar, but she couldn't. *Both* of them were right. She knew beyond a shadow of any doubt that Rathgar had adored her mother—but she also knew his possessive obsession about his lands.

And she knew that there would be no way that Kethry could ever have convinced him that *she* didn't care about the property so long as her daughter was happy. He simply could not have understood an attitude like that. Kero had heard him holding forth far too many times on the folly of some acquaintance, or some underling, giving up *property* for the sake of a child. And his reasoning, by his own lights, was sound. After all, if one gave up the property now, how could one provide for that same child, or leave it the proper inheritance?

"Destroy a birthright for the sake of the moment?" she'd heard him say, once, when the Lythands had settled a dispute with a neighbor by deeding the disputed land to a common relation. *"Folly and madness! Your children won't thank you for it, when they've grown into sense!"*

And she was sure now that this was the source of his deep-seated bitterness—that he owed everything, not only to his wife's mother, not only to a *woman*, but to a mage. And one who had earned it all honestly, herself.

That must have rankled the most. Mages were not to be trusted; mages could change reality into whatever suited them at the moment. Mages were the source of everything that was wrong with the world. . . .

"That's how and why your folk ended up with a breeding-herd of Shin'a'in horses," Tarma said, startling her out of deep thought. "I don't know if you know how rare it is for us to sell a stud, but we let him have one—an ungelded cull, but still, a stud. He wouldn't listen to Keth about the lands, he didn't have her resources, and he didn't have her capital. He was operating on the edge of disaster, squeaking through season after season, never making a profit. *We* had done fine, but we'd had the Schools. This land is too rocky to be good farm land; the tenants barely managed to make ends meet. Finally I had the Clan bring in a herd of the best culls and sell them to him at a bargain price. *He* figured he'd outbargained the ignorant barbarians. We didn't care; that got him something he could use to maintain the Keep and Lenore without stripping the lands bare or abusing the tenants. Then, when you and your brother were of an age to train your own beasts, I arranged to have a couple of good young mares slipped into the next batch he bought."

She lifted her face to the sun and breeze, and Kero thought she looked very like a weathered, bronze statue. Tough, yet somehow graceful.

"It wasn't all that hard to do," Kethry said wryly. "Really, it wasn't. After all, we were making trips back to the Clan every year to see the rest of my brood. It was more than worth the fuss to get him convinced you two should have them and then convince him it had been all his own idea. It was about my only way of doing anything for you after I pulled back to the Tower and promised to leave you all alone."

"So what do you think of all this?" Tarma asked, finally turning those bright blue eyes back toward Kero. "It isn't often a person gets an entire Clan as relatives, and right out of nowhere, too."

"Am I ever going to get to meet them?" she asked impulsively. "The others, my uncles and aunts and all—"

Tarma laughed. "Oh, I imagine. Eventually. But right now you and I have a previous appointment."

Kero felt a moment of disappointment, then smiled. After all, it wasn't as if everything had to happen all at once. *Look how much has happened in just the past few weeks! I think I can wait a little longer.*

"Then we'd better get to it before we both get stiff,"
she replied, and grinned. "Or before I get a chance to
think about what you're going to do to me at practice!"

The one thing Tarma was an absolute fanatic about was
cleanliness. She insisted Kero take a bath after morning
work and afternoon training, both. There was no short-
age of hot water at the Tower, unlike the Keep—that was
one magical extravagance Kethry was more than willing
to indulge in. Once Kero got over her initial surprise, she
found that she liked the idea of twice-daily baths. Hot
water did a great deal to ease aching muscles, and the
evening bath was a good place to think things over, with
a light dinner and good wine right beside the enormous
tub. Kethry left her granddaughter alone after dinner,
saying when Kero asked her that "everyone needs a little
privacy." Kero was just as glad. She tended to fall asleep
rather quickly after those long soaks, and she doubted
she'd be very good company for anyone.

With unlimited hot water, she found she was following
Tarma's example; drawing one bath to get rid of the dirt
and sweat, then draining it and drawing a second of hot-
ter, clean water to soak in.

The bathing chamber in her room was far nicer than
the corresponding room at the Keep. It was as big as her
sleeping chamber, easily, and the tub could have held two
comfortably. That tub looked as if it had been hollowed
out of a huge granite boulder, then polished to a mirror-
smooth finish. There were convenient flattened places,
just the right size to rest a plate and a cup, at either end
of it. Water, hot and cold, came out of spouts in the wall
above the middle. You simply pulled a little lever, attached to something like a sluice-gate, and the water ran
into the tub. The water itself came from a spring in the
mountain above. Kethry had shown her the cisterns at
the top of the cliff the Tower had been built into—telling
her they were part of the original building.

*The original building. And she doesn't know how old
it is. That's—amazing.* It made Kero wonder who those
builders were—and what they'd been like.

They certainly enjoyed their comforts, she mused idly,
sipping her wine. Set into the wall of the bathing chamber was an enormous window made of tiny, hand-sized,

diamond-shaped panes of glass. Glazing the windows had
been Kethry's addition; the previous occupants had either
seen no need for glazed windows, or had been unable to
produce them. Tonight Kero had noticed a full moon rising, and once she'd drawn her second bath, she blew out
the candles to watch it and the stars. *With all the incredible things those Builders were able to do, I can't imagine
why they wouldn't have been able to make a little glass.
I wonder if they were so powerful that they could actually
keep the winter winds out of the Tower by magic?*

Moonlight filtered through the steam rising from her
bath, and touched the surface of the water, turning it into
a rippling mirror. She had to laugh at her fancies, then,
for the answer was obvious to anyone but a romantic. *Of
course; glass breaks, and Grandmother said herself she
had no idea how long the place stood empty. There are
more than enough crows and robber-rats around here to
steal every last shard. Blessed Agnira, some of Mother's
silliness must have rubbed off on me.*

She laughed aloud, and the water sloshed at the sides
of the tub as she reached for the carafe of wine to pour
herself a second serving. That was when she noticed that
she was nowhere near as sore and stiff as she'd expected
to be.

I must be getting use to this, she thought with surprise.
*By the Trine—I was beginning to think I'd never stop
aching! Funny, though—even when I was so sore I wanted
to die, I still was enjoying myself. . . .*

This afternoon had been the first time Tarma had actually given her a lesson in real swordwork. Admonishing
her to "pretend I'm one of those logs," the Shin'a'in
had run her through some basic moves, then brought her
up to speed on them. Before the afternoon was over, she
had been performing simple strike-guard-strike patterns
against Tarma at full force and full speed—and she
thought her teacher seemed pleased. It had been even
better than yesterday, when Tarma started her on tracking. Once Kero knew what to look for, it had been surprisingly easy to track the movements of a deer, a badger,
and Warrl himself across a stretch of forest floor.

Of course, none of them had been trying to *hide* their
trails. Kero had a notion that if Warrl wanted to hide his

traces, the only way anyone would be able to track him would be by magic.

Most satisfying about today's exercises had been that the skills she'd acquired had been all her own. The sword was hanging on the wall of her room, and Kero wasn't going to take it down until she didn't *need* its uncanny expert assistance—at least where fighting was concerned.

Is that what I want to do? she asked herself suddenly. *Is that what I want to learn?* She pondered the question while the moon climbed higher in the window, and the square of silver light crept off the water and onto the floor, leaving her end of the bathing chamber in darkness. *I suppose it makes sense,* she thought with a certain unease. *After all, it's always been physical things that I've been best at. Riding, hunting, hawking—that knife-fighting I pried out of Dent. The only "proper" thing I was ever any good at was dancing. . . .*

The one thing she'd been able to surprise Tarma with was her expertise with bow. *And then she asked me why I hadn't taken a bow with me when I went after the bandits. When I said that it just never occurred to me, I thought she was going to give up on me then and there.* Kero sighed. *It's so hard to have to think of people as your enemies . . . at least she isn't being as nasty as Dent was to Lordan.*

Dent had been absolutely merciless on his young pupil, never giving him second chances, cursing and sometimes striking him with the flat of a blade, driving him to exhaustion and beyond. And yet once practice was over, he was unfailingly courteous, a kindly man, who'd praise Lordan to his face for what he'd done right, remind him of what he'd done wrong, and then go on to tell Rathgar of Lordan's progress with exactly the same words, praise with the criticism.

He never treated me that way—but why does it feel as if he wasn't doing me any favors by letting me get off lightly? She closed her eyes and sank a little lower into the hot water. *Maybe—because half of what Tarma's teaching me is undoing mistakes I learned to make? Well, at least I can see some progress. I get a little better each day, she shows me something new each day. And she's giving me the same kind of talks afterward that Dent used to give Lordan.*

That felt good; warm and satisfying. There were no "buts" attached to Tarma's compliments. When she said that Kero was doing something well, she meant it, with no qualifications.

I just hope I'm not boring her too much. At least I'm patient. Lordan used to get so mad when he couldn't do something right that he'd storm off the field and go duck his head in the horse trough. And she can't say I'm not determined.

The moon finally rose to a point where there was no light shining in the window at all. The bathing chamber was in complete darkness. And the wine was gone.

I guess it's time for bed, she decided. *Before I fall asleep in the tub.*

She found the plug at the bottom of the bathtub with her toes, took the bit of chain attached to it between her big toe and the rest, and pulled. When Tarma had shown her the drain at the bottom of the tub, she'd been both amazed and amused—the tubs at home had to be bailed by hand, then tilted over on their sides to drain completely. She couldn't imagine why no one had ever thought of something like this before.

She stood up, slowly; a thick towel hung from a rod at the side of the tub; it gleamed softly in the darkness, and she reached for it, then stepped out onto the tiled floor. That was the *only* thing wrong with this chamber; the tile made the floor *cold!*

Cold enough that she dried herself off quickly, and hung the towel back where it belonged. Tarma had given her one of those *looks* when she'd thrown it on the floor, and Kero had managed to deduce that there weren't many servants in the Tower. Thereafter she'd put things away properly.

She pulled on the old shirt she used to sleep in, and walked slowly and silently across the floor to her own room; Tarma wanted her to practice moving quietly whenever possible, so that doing so became habit rather than something she had to think about. Kero had decided on her own that learning to move quietly *in the dark* would be a *very* good idea, so she practiced a little every night.

Once past the doorway, she turned to light the candle she'd left on a shelf by the door. And when she turned back with it in her hand, she thought she'd jumped into a nightmare.

Teeth, that was all she saw at first; huge white fangs, gleaming in the candlelight. And eyes the size of walnuts, shining with an evil, green glow all their own.

Seven

She shrieked, jumped back into the wall behind her, and dropped the candle, all at the same time.

The flame went out immediately, leaving her in the dark. She felt for the wall and edged along it toward the door, hoping to escape into the bathing chamber before whatever it was realized she was moving—and wondering what awful thing had happened that this *thing* had gotten past Tarma and her Grandmother.

:Children,: snorted a voice from—somewhere. It seemed to come from everywhere at once. She froze.

:Child, I am not the Snow Demon. I don't eat babies. I just came here tonight to talk to you.: She didn't move, and the voice took on a tone of exasperation. *:Will you please light that candle again and go sit down?:*

"W–who are you?" she stammered. "*Where* are you?"

:Right here.: Something cold and wet prodded her between her breasts, and she nearly screamed again. *:It's Warrl, you little ninny! You see me every day!:*

"Warrl?" She reached out—cautiously—and encountered a furry head at about chest level. It certainly felt like Warrl.

:And while you're at it, you can scratch my ears.:

It certainly *sounded* the way she'd imagined Warrl would talk. *If* Warrl could talk.

"How are you—" she began. He interrupted her.

:I'm Mindspeaking you,: he said, impatiently. *:It's exactly what you could do if you wanted to, and the other person had the Gift of Mindhearing.:* She felt a brief movement of air and heard the faintest little ticking sound, a sound that might have been the clicking of claws on the floor. *:Do light that candle and come to bed, there's a good child.:*

She went to her knees and groped about on the floor until her left hand encountered the candle. Once lit, she stood up with it in her hand, and discovered that Warrl had resumed the position he'd been in when she first entered the room. Sprawled on her bed, taking up fully half of it.

"Make yourself comfortable," she said sarcastically, more than a little nettled now that her heart had started beating again.

:Thank you, I have,: he replied with equal irony.

She crossed the floor and put the candle into the sconce in the headboard, refusing to look at him the entire time. Only when she had climbed up into bed, and settled herself cross-legged on the blanket, did she finally meet his eyes.

"So if you could talk all this time, why haven't you?" she demanded.

:There wasn't any reason for you to know I could,: he replied calmly. *:Now there is.:*

"And what, pray tell me, is that reason?"

:I want to know why you have been concealing your Gift.:

Her heart stopped again. She couldn't pretend not to understand him; she had the feeling that if she tried to lie mind-to-mind she'd get caught. And she knew very well what he was asking, her mother's books had called this ability to hear thoughts a "Gift."

So she temporized, trying to buy time to think. "I haven't been hiding anything," she countered. It *was* the truth; Kethry hadn't asked her if she could hear thoughts, or given her any tests to see if she could.

Meanwhile, her mind was running in little circles, like a mouse caught in the bottom of a jar. *If Grandmother finds out about this, she'll make me become a mage, and I don't want to become a mage, I want to be like Tarma—*

The *kyree* laid his ears back and winced. *:PLEASE!:* he "shouted" at her, making *her* wince, but bringing that frantic little circle of thoughts to a halt.

He sighed gustily. *:Much better. Thank you. Child, I have no intention of betraying your secret to Kethry, if that is really what you want—but what you just did is precisely the reason why I wanted to speak with you.:*

"What did I do?" she whispered, head still ringing from his "shout."

His ears came back up. *:Every time you feel safe and begin to concentrate on some complicated problem that involves your emotions, you do exactly what you just did. You think "out loud." Very loud, I might add, far louder than you know; I would imagine that one could hear you all the way to the next Keep if one was so minded.:*

"I do?" She shook her head; it didn't seem possible.

:You do,: he insisted. *:Almost as loudly as I just "shouted." And unlike my "shout," which was meant only for your mind, your thoughts are heard by anything receptive. You are fortunate that your grandmother is not Gifted with Mindspeaking, or your secret would be no such thing.:* He flattened his ears, and looked pained; his brow wrinkled in a way that would have been funny under any other circumstances. *:It is very discommoding. And uncomfortable. I won't dispute your right to keeping your abilities to yourself, since they don't involve magecraft, but I must insist that you get training. Quickly. Before you cause an unfortunate incident.:*

Kero bit back her first reply, which was that she *had* gotten training. Obviously what she had learned on her own wasn't good enough.

Not if someone like Warrl can hear me all the way to the Lythands'.

"I can probably take care of it myself," she said cautiously.

He lifted his lip just a trifle, and snapped at the air in annoyance. She shrank back instinctively. His fangs were as long as her thumb, and very sharp. *:Don't you realize I wouldn't be here if that were true? There is no way you can train yourself. And untrained—well, half-trained— you are in terrible danger. You are just very lucky that the mage you killed wasn't strongly MindGifted. If he had been—well, you'd probably be serving his every whim right now. It is ridiculously easy to take over the mind of someone who is Gifted, but untrained; your barriers are weak, and you have no secondary defenses. Right now you are more vulnerable than someone with no Gift at all. And you display that fact to the universe every time you become distressed!:*

But that just led her right back to the same problem;

she didn't *want* Kethry to know about this. And who else
was there that could train her?

She shook her head. "I can't—"

He growled, and sneezed, as if he had smelled something he didn't like. *:Must you be so dense? I'm offering
to train you myself. No one else will ever know, not even
my mind-mate.:*

"You are?" She could hardly believe it. "But why?"

He put his head down on his paws, and sighed. *:Self-
defense, child. Self-defense. I am increasingly weary of
trying to shut you out, and you have at times awakened
me out of my rest. Now, in the interest of peaceful sleeping, shall we work on that so-called shield of yours?
You're going about it all wrong.:*

And I thought I was overworked before, Kero thought
with a little groan, as she opened bleary eyes two weeks
later on a morning that had arrived much too soon. She'd
trained herself to wake as soon as the first light of sunrise
came through her eastern window. It seemed to hit her
closed eyelids candlemarks earlier every morning.

*The worst part of it is, if Tarma knew Warrl was keep-
ing me up half the night, she'd probably let me sleep
later. But if I tell her—no, I can't. I don't know what
she'd think about this, and I know she'd tell Grandmother.*

Kero rubbed her eyes with her knuckles, and sat up
slowly. By the look of the clear, pink-tinged sky, this
was going to be another perfect day—which meant Tarma
would be feeling pretty frisky. Kero was beginning to
look forward to rainy days; even more to days of cold
and damp, with a heavy morning fog. Both conditions
made Tarma's joints ache—she would stay in bed until
late morning, and confine Kero's workouts to sessions in
the practice ring against the pells or other targets. It
wasn't particularly *nice* to be pleased when her teacher
wasn't feeling well—but Kero had found that guilt in this
case was easily outweighed by the pleasure of sleeping
in.

For the past week, she'd been freed from the chopping
and wood-carrying; now she practiced against the pells
and in sword-dances in the morning, had an hour or two
of book-training directly after lunch, and practiced

against Tarma in the afternoon. She no longer wondered what she was going to do with herself—she was going to become a mercenary, like Tarma, and like some of those women Kethry had hired to protect Lordan and the Keep. The only question in her mind now was—what kind of mercenary? The books that Tarma was teaching her from were studies in strategy and tactics—the ways to move and fight with whole armies. At this point, Kero couldn't see why she'd need anything of the sort.

But maybe Tarma had some kind of plan. Kero was perfectly content to learn whatever Tarma wished to teach her, and let the future take care of itself. Tarma was always saying that "no learning, no knowledge is ever wasted." If nothing else, it probably wouldn't be a bad thing for an ordinary fighter to know how whole armies moved, so she could anticipate her orders.

She stretched and arched her back, then wormed her way back down under the warm blankets. *I'll just relax a little longer,* she thought, and reveled in the "silence" in her mind. She hadn't realized just how much she'd been "overhearing" until after Warrl showed her the right way to protect herself; ground, center, and shield. For years there had been a kind of buzzing in back of all her thoughts, as if she was hearing a tourney crowd from several furlongs away. Now it was gone, and the relief was incredible.

She hadn't quite realized how useful this particular ability could be to a fighter, either, until Warrl showed her. He'd proved she could use it to get a tactical advantage in many situations; from doing as she had during the rescue and "reading" the area for enemy minds, to reading her opponent during a combat and countering his moves before he even made them.

But she wasn't entirely happy about using it that way.

She caught herself falling asleep again, and jerked herself back up into wakefulness. She threw back the covers and swung her legs out of bed before she succumbed a second time. A brief trip to the bathing chamber and a splash of cold water solved the problem; the water was cold enough to make her gasp, but she was certainly awake now.

I don't like the idea of reading someone's thoughts without them knowing, she decided, while climbing into her breeches and tunic. *It doesn't seem fair. Maybe if the circumstances were really extraordinary, like going after Dierna alone, it would be all right. I mean, with odds like that, you have to use every advantage you've got. But if I was just one-on-one—no, it's not right.*

She tightened the laces on her tunic, and reached for stockings and boots. *Besides, if I used it a lot, pretty soon I wouldn't be able to hide its existence. Then what? People would hate me, or they'd be afraid of me. It wouldn't be an advantage anymore, it'd be a handicap. No, I don't want that; I've had my fill of being different.*

That led to the same problem that had been troubling her since she came here.

What's wrong with me? she asked herself unhappily, as she laced her boots tight to her legs. *Why is it that I don't want what everyone else does? Every other girl seems to want a husband and a house full of babies. Even Grandmother and Tarma had families, and if Tarma hadn't been Swordsworn, she'd have raised her own children instead of helping with Grandmother's.* She shook her head, her earlier cheer gone. *I don't like children, and if anyone else knew that, they'd think I was some kind of monster. I hate being cooped up inside, and I don't want to have to spend my life taking care of everybody except myself! But all the priests have to say about it is how women should rejoice that they can sacrifice themselves for their families. Blessed Trine, am I the one who's crazy, or is it everybody else?*

But since there was no possible way to answer that question, she jerked the laces of her boots tight with a snarl of frustration, and went out to take out her ill-humor and uncertainty on the pells.

Tarma's private practice ring was indoors rather than outside; a second hollowed-out cave beside the stables, this one with the walls left rough and convoluted. She'd long ago tired of practicing in the cold and wet—and the mere thought of practicing in the snow was enough to make her shiver. Besides, back when she and Keth had held the Keep, she'd gotten used to having an indoor practice ground. This one was much smaller, but she didn't need room for twenty pupils anymore.

Kero was going through her paces; one of the Shin'a'in

sword-dances. And as Tarma watched her, the Sword-sworn's heart sang with pride. Granted it was one of the simplest of the exercises, but Kerowyn performed it so flawlessly that it looked as effortless as breathing.

The girl's a natural, she thought with a kind of astonished pleasure. *Years and years of training younglings, and never a natural in the lot—and now, at the end of my days, I not only get to teach one, but she's an adoptee. My Clan.*

She'd been waiting for Kethry to get up the nerve to ask about the girl for weeks. Keth had been vaguely disappointed that Kerowyn proved out null so far as mage-craft went, though she'd admitted to her partner that the girl seemed more relieved than anything else.

Now, at last, she'd come down to watch Kero work out; and Tarma sensed that she was ready to ask the question.

"Well," Kethry said, as Kerowyn moved into the next exercise in the cycle, this one a little harder than the last. "She looks like she's doing all right. That isn't Need, is it?"

"No, it's a painted wooden practice blade," Tarma told her. "I made it the same size, heft and shape, so she could get used to the weight and balance. Need's up on her wall—*her* decision, and she says the damn thing stays there until she's sure of her own abilities and she knows that what she does is due to her skill, not the sword working through her."

"So?" Keth replied.

"So, what?" Tarma countered, teasingly.

"So *how is she?*" the mage snarled in annoyance. "Is she any good, or not?"

To Tarma's utter amazement, her throat closed, and her eyes filled with tears. She couldn't speak for a moment, and Kethry bit her lip in dismay.

"Oh, no," she whispered. "When she didn't have any mage-talents, I was sure—what are we going to do with her?"

Tarma wiped her eyes on the back of her hand, and coughed to get her voice working again. "Keth, *she'enedra,* you've got it backward. The girl's good. Hellfrost, she's *better* than good. One year, just *one* year of teaching, and Companies are going to stand in line to have her.'' She pulled Kethry into one of the alcoves formed by the irregular walls of the cave, so that Kero wouldn't notice them watching her from the shadows. ''Look at her; look at her move. She's a natural, Keth, the kind of pupil that comes along once in a teacher's lifetime if she's lucky. She's never had anything other than some indifferent training in knife-fighting, but she's taken to the sword as if she was born with one in her hand. She's doing things now that most of my old students couldn't have done after two years of teaching. She could probably earn a living right now, if all somebody wanted was a basic recruit.''

''And in that year?'' Kethry watched her granddaughter rather than Tarma.

''In that year she'll be able to go to the best Companies and they'll take her for officer training. They won't *tell* her that, of course, but she'll be an officer a lot faster than you or I made it. She's not only a natural with a weapon, she's a natural on the field.'' She poked Kethry with her elbow to regain her attention. ''By the way, Warrl said to tell you that you were right; she's a Mind-speaker. He also said to tell you that he's taking care of the training.''

Kethry relaxed. ''Good, and I appreciate his delicate sense of what to promise. You know, I was afraid you were unhappy because she was awful, and you didn't know how to tell me.''

Tarma chuckled. ''Hardly. And hardly unhappy. To get a student like her is amazing enough—but that it turns out to be one of *ours*—well, the only thing that would make me happier would be if Jadrek were here to see her.''

Keth smiled a little. ''He probably knew before we did. And thank Warrl for me; I was afraid she was a Mindspeaker, but since I'm *not*, I had no way to tell. I thought she was shielded, but that could just have been the fact that she was concentrating. She's better off in Warrl's hands—paws—than mine.''

''I think he has his paws full,'' Tarma said, recalling what Warrl had told her this morning. *:As stubborn as ever you were, mind-mate, and as taciturn. She won't tell me anything, I have to pry it out of her. Thank the gods there's only one of her, and I don't have to teach her* *combative mind-magic. She refuses to learn the offensive techniques.:* He had snorted his opinion of her attitude. *:She has all the morals and compunctions as one of those half-crazed Heralds!:*

"In that case, I have a proposition to make you." Kethry took a deep breath before she continued. Tarma restrained a sigh; Keth only did that when she was going to ask something she didn't think her partner would like. "Would you be up to teaching two? Your second pupil will already have had several years of good instruction, so he'll be about at Kero's level, I'd guess."

Tarma considered that for a moment. *I'd like to devote all my attention to her—but she needs some competition.* "Depends," she replied after a moment. "Depends on who the pupil is, and how much free rein I have with him. It *is* easier to teach two, and having someone else around will keep her on her toes. Competition will be damned good for her, especially if she thinks she's having to compete for my attention. But I can't have a brat taking my concentration away from her, and frankly, I won't put up with a brat anymore."

"I got a 'begging' letter from Megrarthon," Kethry replied, watching Kero, and picking absently at a shiny bit of quartz embedded in the rock wall. "It arrived a couple of days ago, but I had to get up the nerve to ask you about Kero first."

"So what's the King of Rethwellan want with us?" Tarma asked, a little surprised. "Was it from 'His Majesty the King, Megrarthon Jadrevalyn' or my old student Jad? And did he mention his overhand?"

"From your old student, and he said the gout in that broken shoulder is just too bad; he's never going to get the overhand swing back. Hopefully, he'll never need it." Kethry sighed; and Tarma knew why. The King's letters had always been very open with both of them, and lately they'd been profoundly unhappy. Rethwellan politics were torturous at the best of times, and he was regretting that his father's sword had ever spoken for *him*. Three state marriages, two of them loveless, had given him a surfeit of sons and daughters, and one of the sons was making life difficult for him. Tarma and Kethry were two of a scant handful of people he could be that open with; Tarma had changed his diapers more than once and had tutored him in the way of the sword, Keth had nursed him through his first love and subsequent broken heart.

Together they had helped put his father on the throne before he was a year old, which made them *very* old friends of the family.

"That middle son of his is being a—"

"*Grek'ka'shen,*" Tarma said in disgust, said carrion eater combining the worst aspects and habits of every scavenger known to the Shin'a'in. It ate things even vultures wouldn't touch, it slept in a bed of rotting detritus from its foraging, and both sexes were known to eat their own young on a whim.

Kethry nodded. "So he's written to you?"

"Not lately, but yes, I got a letter while I was down on the Plains. I just didn't see any reason to depress you with it." Tarma grimaced. "You know, sometimes I wonder if the reason the Rethwellan royal line has so much trouble is because of the wretched things they name their children."

"That's as good a theory as any," Kethry replied, managing not to smile. The names Jad had given his boys were bad enough, but the eight girls' names were worse, all full of historical significance and all as unpronounceable as *kyree* howls. Those awful names were an ongoing joke between the two of them. "Faramentha's as bright and trustworthy a young man as you'd ever hope to see, and Karathanelan is making up for him by causing Jad three times the grief his older brother gave. His latest antic is to torment the youngest boy verbally until the youngster explodes and attacks him. Now the poor lad is getting a reputation for being a hothead and a bully, because Thanel is—"

"A handsome, languid vicious little fop, playing on the fact that he's shorter and lighter than the other boy," Tarma interrupted. "Remember, I've seen him, when I went back up with Faram to deliver him to Jad and see him made heir. That's why I told Jad I wouldn't have him here. At thirteen he'd already made up his mind that since he wasn't the heir, he was going to sleep and charm his way to a crown. He probably will, too. Some little fool of a princess with a senile old father is going to fall for his pretty face, clever wit and graceful manners, and spend the rest of her life pregnant while *he* plays bed games with her ladies, torments her lap dogs, and spends her treasury dry.''

Kethry shook her head. ''From everything Jad says, you're right. I told him it was a mistake to let Irenia raise Thanel instead of fostering him out, and now the mistake is irreversible. Well, the long and the short is that he hopes he can find some place to send Thanel that will keep him out of mischief—but until he does, he needs to get the youngest out of Thanel's reach.''

''Otherwise there's going to be fratricide.'' Tarma nodded. It was a logical solution, and rather elegant. Especially since it would get the hot-headed boy some much-needed discipline and training. ''So he wants us to take the youngest. That'd be Darenthallis, right? Absolute baby of the bunch?''

''Right. He's not mage-talented, so he'll be yours.'' Kethry tilted her head to one side. ''Are you up to this?''

Tarma stretched, feeling every joint creak. ''For Jad's sake—and for the boy's. From what Jad's said, the youngster is a lot like Faram, which means he won't be at all hard to teach. I understand that the boy does have a quick temper, which makes him an easy target for Thanel. I wouldn't see any lad have to put up with that if I can help it. I don't like bullies, and Thanel's the worst kind of bully—a clever one. Although I must say, a lot of this is Jad's own fault. He wouldn't have gotten into this mess if he hadn't been trying to compete with you in the number of offspring he could produce.''

Kethry smiled, the tension draining out of her. ''I was hoping you'd say that. Now, just one other possible problem. My granddaughter is *not* what I would call 'unattractive,' and she's very probably not only a virgin, she has no idea of—''

Tarma grinned evilly; she knew what was coming, and she had no intention of letting Keth slough *this* job off on her. Especially not when she'd agreed to teach a second youngster all by herself. ''Then you'd better tell her, hadn't you? After all, *you're* her grandmother. And you know very well when I start to make the two youngsters work together what's going to happen.''

''But—'' Kethry said, faintly.

Tarma kept right on going. ''I think the experience will be good for both of them, actually. The boy has

probably been playing a poor third to Faram-the-heir and
Thanel-the-beauty. It'll be nice for him to have a young
lady paying attention to *him.*"

"But—" Kethry repeated.

"And you have to admit, *I'm* hardly the one to give
Kero the basics of nature. I'm celibate, remember?"
Tarma was enjoying her partner's discomfort. Keth had
landed her with the job of explaining those basics to every
boy that ever passed through their schools, and since
there were usually twice as many lads as girls passing
through their hands, Tarma found herself with that uncomfortable duty far oftener than Keth. Now the shoe
was on the other foot, and Tarma intended to enjoy the
fact.

"Besides," she finished, "if your own daughter was
such a dunce as to leave her completely ignorant, it's up
to you to rectify the situation."

Kethry's mouth tightened in dismay. "You're right, of
course. And if she's going to join a Company, she's going
to have to know *all* of it."

"Damn right she is," Tarma replied, becoming serious. "From camp-hygiene to post-rape trauma. And
since you worked with the Healers in the Sunhawks,
you're better equipped for that than I am. Those aren't
the kind of problems lads are going to face, and they
aren't the kind of problems I *ever* had to deal with on
my own. But you can take it slowly, I think. Give her the
basics and pregnancy prevention, and take care of the
rest later." She grinned. "Think of it as my fee for
agreeing to take Daren on."

Kethry shook her head. "Still a mercenary."

Tarma chuckled. "That's how you tell a merc is dead;
he just stops collecting paychecks."

Kero knew that there was something in the air; Tarma
had been a little absentminded lately, with that slight
frown she always wore when she was thinking. But once
she'd satisfied herself that *she* wasn't the cause of the
frown, she relaxed. Whatever it was that was bothering
Tarma, it was not under *her* control.

So she kept a weather eye out, but concentrated on the
things that *were* in her power to deal with. She had speculations, but nothing concrete to go on.

Finally all speculations came to an end, when she showed up at the practice ring with her arms full of equipment to find Tarma there already, fully armored (complete with full helm), working out. And Tarma wasn't alone.

There was a young man with her; that was surprise enough. He looked around Kero's age, and she stiffened reflexively as they both stopped what they were doing and turned at the sound of her footstep. He was rather handsome, in a lanky, not-quite-finished sort of way. His long hair was somewhere between brown and blond, his eyes between gray and hazel. He was taller than Tarma, and moved like a young colt that still isn't quite certain where his feet are going to go when he puts them down. His armor was good—*very* good, use on it, but well-maintained and in perfect condition. And there was a surcoat lying crumpled up with some other odds and ends in one of the little alcoves. A surcoat that was as well-made as the armor, and looked as if it was blazoned with some kind of familial device.

All of which added up to one conclusion: he was some kind of nobility. Kero did not like the implications of that.

Tarma waited for Kero to come up to them before speaking. She pushed the face-guard of her helm up, and gave Kero a cool, appraising look. The young man did the same with his helm, then shifted his weight uncomfortably from one foot to the other.

"Kero," Tarma said, in a neutral, even voice, "This is Darenthallis—Daren to us. He'll be training here with you."

Kero's first reaction was of resentment. *Why?* Her second was of jealousy. *We were just fine with the two of us.*

She stepped forward slowly, keeping her expression neutral, but not her thoughts. *They don't need the money—and now Tarma is going to be spending half her time with* him, *which means I won't be learning as much from her. It isn't fair! By the look of him, he could have any teacher he wanted! Why should he steal mine?*

She eyed his armor with envy; up close, it was even better than she'd thought, combination plate and chain mail, the chain mail so fine it looked to have been knitted, with articulated plate that had to have been specifically fitted to him. And he wasn't finished growing yet—which meant that someone, somewhere, didn't care how much it cost to keep fitting him with new armor every time he put on a growth spurt. Then she recognized the name—after all, there weren't that many young men named Darenthallis in the world, and there was only one likely to have armor of that quality.

His Highness, *Prince* Darenthallis, third son of the King.

Which explained how he'd gotten Tarma to agree to teach him, and virtually guaranteed that the Shin'a'in would be spending the lion's share of her time with *him*.

The privilege of rank. Kero's resentment trebled. *I have to earn my way here, and he walks in and takes over.*

But she kept it out of her face and manner; she'd learned to school her expressions long ago. Rathgar took a dim view of resentment and rebellion in his children.

Daren smiled; he looked self-confident and sure of his superiority. Kero's temper smoldered. *Well, we'll just see how superior you are. Especially once we get into the woods. If you've ever had to track anything in your life, my fine young lord, I'd be very much surprised.*

She cleared her throat, and made the first move. "I'm Kerowyn," she said, nodding a little, *not* holding out her hand; she could have freed one to shake his, but she chose not to.

"Daren," he said. "Are you one of Lady Kethryveris' students?"

Ignoring the fact that I'm carrying armor. Assuming I couldn't possibly be anything other than a nice little ladylike mage.

"I'm her granddaughter," she replied acidly. "And I'm Kal'enedral Tarma's student."

Tarma's left eyebrow rose a little, but otherwise her face was completely without expression. "Well, now that you've met," she said quietly, "why don't we get down to business."

Kero's resentment continued to simmer over the next several weeks. Daren wasn't any better than she was, especially not at archery. But he kept acting as if he were, giving her unasked-for advice in a patronizing tone of voice that said *What's a little girl like you doing man's work, anyway?* and made her blood boil.

But she kept her temper, somehow; always turning to Tarma after one of those supercilious little comments, and asking her advice as if she hadn't heard Daren's.

Unfortunately, from time to time this backfired. Tarma would occasionally give her a slow, sardonic smile, and reply, "I think Daren hit it dead in the black." Daren would smirk, and Kero's ears would burn, and she would have to bite her lip to keep from "accidentally" bringing her shield up into that arrogantly squared chin. And then she'd pull her face-guard down and do her damnedest to give him the trouncing of a lifetime.

At night, before Warrl arrived for her evening lesson in mind-magic, she'd lie back in her bath and seethe. *It's not fair*, she'd repeat, like a litany. *He's had the best trainers from the time he was able to walk; I've only had Tarma for a few moons! Why should I have to share her? And what makes him so much better than I am that money and power didn't buy for him?*

But that was the problem, wasn't it; life *wasn't* fair, and power and gold bought whatever they needed to. From people's skills to people's lives. And if anyone happened to be in the way, it was too bad. Money had doubtless bought the near-ruin of her family; power was probably keeping the real perpetrator safe. And now both were conspiring to steal her future—

—if she lay down and let it happen.

I won't, she resolved every night. *I'll make him compete with me for every moment of time. I'll be so much better than he is that Tarma will see she's wasting her time with him and concentrate on me again. I'll do it.*

I have to.

It helped that he was as helpless as a baby in the woods, and when he started, he couldn't even track the most obvious of traces. She would give him advice in the same kind of patronizing tone he used with *her*—and she laughed inside to see how he bristled.

She was planning on doing just that this morning, as she skipped down the stairs to the stable, humming a little tune under her breath. Today was going to be a daylong stalk-and-trap session, a "hound and rabbit game," Tarma called it, and Warrl was going to be the "rabbit."

Daren hadn't yet figured out that Warrl was anything more than a very large, odd-looking dog, and Kero wasn't going to tell him. After all, they were supposed to be using their minds and paying attention to things, and if he hadn't been able to figure out that the *kyree* was something rather different by now, she didn't see any reason to enlighten him.

Besides, it would give her an edge. That edge, combined with her tracking skills, should enable her to beat him to the quarry by whole candlemarks.

The meeting point was the stables; Kero reached them ahead of both Daren and her teacher. A brief look out the window this morning had told her all she needed to know about the weather—today was going to be a typical late-fall day for these parts; cold, wet, and miserable. Even though there were no clouds overhead, Kero had seen them on the horizon, the kind of flat, gray clouds that meant an all-day drizzle. So she'd dressed for it; a waterproof canvas poncho over lambswool shirt, and heavy sweater, sheepskin vest, and wool hose and breeches, and her thickest stockings inside her boots. Daren had dressed for the cold, but not an all-day chill in wet weather; he was wearing mostly leather, which looked very good on him and *would* keep him warm at first, but would do nothing for him once it was soaked. His only concession to possible drizzle was a wool cloak, a bright russet that would stand out in the gray-brown woods like a rose in a cabbage patch. And which was going to get caught on every twig and thorn unless he was very careful. Kero's gray poncho wouldn't; it was belted tight to her body at the waist, and thorns wouldn't catch so easily on the tightly-woven, oiled canvas. Kero hid a smirk with some difficulty.

Tarma glanced at her in a way that Kero couldn't read, but said nothing. Daren just took in the peasant-style clothing, and gave her an amused and superior little smile.

Kero had been toying with the notion of warning him about the oncoming rain, but that smile made up her mind for her. *If he's too stupid to read the weather, and too cocksure to ask advice when he sees someone dressed for weather he didn't expect, he can suffer,* she thought with angry anticipation. *And I can't wait to see him shivering and chafing in that fancy wet leather.*

"I told you yesterday that this was going to be another 'hound and rabbit' game following Warrl," Tarma said, interrupting her thoughts. "I didn't tell you that it would be under different rules."

Kero stiffened, and dropped her thoughts of revenge. She noted that Daren lost his little smile, and fixed his eyes on Tarma as if he was trying to read her mind.

"This is going to be a 'hostile territory' game," the Shin'a'in continued. "Rule one: you're in enemy territory, behind their lines, following a spy. Assume that anything you do or say may give you away to the enemy. Rule two: leave no traces yourselves; assume the enemy may have someone trailing you. Rule three: this is a real scouting mission, which means you are not working alone. Rule four: both of you come back, or you both lose the game."

At "rule three" Kero realized what Tarma was pulling on them. At "rule four," Daren figured it out. The glare of outrage he gave her was only matched by the exasperation she dealt him in return.

She can't—I'm going to be saddled with this overbearing fool all day long? And if I don't keep him from falling on his face, I'm *going to lose the game?* She wanted to tell her teacher exactly what she thought of the idea, and only one thing kept her quiet. The sure and certain knowledge that Tarma was testing her, as she had been tested at the crossroads. Only this time the test was not for courage, but for good sense, and the ability to take orders.

Such considerations did not hamper Daren.

"You can't mean that!" he said angrily. "I've had *years* of training, and you expect me to drag this little tagalong and take care of her—"

"I expect you to take the orders you're given and follow them, young man," Tarma replied evenly, with no display of emotion at all. "I expect you to keep your mouth shut about it. I have my orders from your father. You are to treat me as your commanding officer at all times, and I have your father's full permission to do whatever I like with you. Be grateful this is all I've ordered you to do. How do you ever expect to give orders

that will be obeyed if you never learn how to follow them
yourself?''

Daren stared at her with his mouth hanging open for a
moment, while Kero fumed. *Tagalong, am I? Years of
training, hmm? Then why can't he even follow a rabbit
track a furlong without losing it?*

''I've given you your orders,'' Tarma said, putting one
finger under his chin and shutting his mouth for him.
''Remember the rules.''

She turned on her heel, and went back up the staircase,
leaving the two of them alone in the stable. Daren's
stormy expression did not encourage conversation, so
Kero just shrugged and headed out into the valley.

Daren followed, overtaking her in the tunnel, so that
when they emerged he was in the lead. Kero hung back,
deliberately, so that he would have to wait for her. After
all, under the rules, if he ran off without her, he'd lose.

I'm beginning to see some advantages here, she
thought, as her anger cooled. *Provided I can keep my
own temper.*

The clouds were already moving in; the sky was gray
from horizon to horizon, or at least as much of it as Kero
saw beyond the black interlacing of leafless trees. Daren
waited impatiently for her beside the hidden stable door,
and pointed at Warrl's obvious clawmarks in the dust beside the path.

''He went that way,'' the young man said, and plunged
off into the underbrush, leaving a telltale thread from his
cloak on the very first thornbush he passed.

Kero would have left it, except that *she* remembered
the rules. *Leave no traces.* And since she was being
graded on his moves as well as her own. . . .

She sighed, and picked the russet thread out of the
thorns before she passed on. She was still sucking a stuck
finger when she caught up to him.

''You left this,'' she said sardonically, holding it out
to him before he could accuse her of lagging. He took
the thread from her, his mouth shutting with a snap, and
frowned. Without saying a single word, he turned back
to studying the ground, ignoring her.

She saw that Warrl's tracks vanished here, as his trail
crossed a dry streambed. The obvious answer was something any reasonably smart animal would do—run along

the streambed for a while, then leave it at some point that wouldn't show much disturbance. A bed of dry leaves, for instance.

But Warrl wasn't an animal.

Kero studied the trail, and noticed that the tracks were blurred, the claws dug in a bit too deeply.

He walked backward in his own tracks, the beast! she thought with admiration. *I didn't think he could do that!*

Instead of following downstream (as Daren was moving upstream and obviously expected her to take the other direction), she traced the tracks back, and found where Warrl had leapt out of them and into—yes—a pile of dry leaves off to the side of the trail. There were several old, wet leaves on top of the dry ones, and a few more scattered against the direction of the last winds, showing that the leaves had been disturbed.

She waited beside the telltale traces until Daren came storming back. By that time the expected drizzle had been falling for about a candlemark; and as she had anticipated, his cloak and his leathers were soaked through. He was shivering, and the leather was probably chafing him raw wherever it touched bare skin, and his temper was not improved by his discomfort.

"You were supposed to take downstream!" he shouted. "I had to take both! You lazy little bitch—you're supposed to be *doing* something, not standing around waiting for me—"

"He left the path here," she said, clenching her hands to keep from hitting him. "He walked backward in his own tracks, and then jumped off the trail into that pile of leaves."

Daren looked at her scornfully. "I'm not some green little boy who believes in Pelagir-tales. I'm a prince of Rethwellan, and I've been trained by some of the finest hunters in the world. You—"

She lost her temper, and grabbed the lacings in the front of his leather tunic, then dragged him past the pile of leaves, surprise making him manageable for the necessary few steps. "Does *that* look like a Pelagir-tale, *little boy?*" she hissed, pointing at the very clear pawprint in the mud. "Seems to me you'd better start growing up pretty quickly, so you know what to believe and what not to believe. I've beaten you at this game five times out of six, and you *know* it, so don't you think you'd better stop playing the high and mighty princeling and start paying attention to somebody who *happens* to be better at this than you are?''

He pulled out of her grip, his face growing red. ''Since when does half a year of training give you the right to act like an expert?'' he shouted.

''Since—''

That was all she had a chance to say.

Something very dark, and very large suddenly loomed up out of the bushes just behind her. She never had a chance to see what it was; the next thing she knew, she was flying through the air, and she had barely enough time to curl into a protective ball to hide her head and neck before she impacted with a tree.

After that all she saw was stars, and blackness.

Eight

This was the worst headache she'd ever had—

—and the most uncomfortable bed. It felt like a bush. A leafless, *prickly* bush.

What happened?

Kero tried to move, and bit back a moan as every muscle and joint protested movement. It felt as if the entire left side of her body was a single ache. And her head hurt the same way it had when one of the horses had kicked her and she'd gotten concussed.

"Well?" That was Tarma's voice. "You two certainly made a fine mess out of this assignment."

She opened her eyes, wincing against the light. Tarma stood about twenty paces away; just beyond her was Daren, lying up against another tree, as though he'd impacted and slid down it. Fine mist drooled down onto her face; droplets condensed and ran into her eyes and down the sides of her face to the back of her neck. Her mouth was dry, and she licked some of the moisture from her lips.

Looks like he got some of the same treatment I did, Kero decided, and shivered. Even wet, her wool clothing would keep her warm, but she must have been lying on the cold ground for a while and it had leached most of the heat out of her body.

"You've managed to botch everything I told you to do," Tarma said coldly, arms crossed under her dark brown rain cape. Her harsh features looked even colder and more forbidding than usual. Her ice-blue eyes flicked from one to the other of them. "First you don't even bother to set up a plan, or agree on who is going to do what. Then you, Daren, storm off into the game leaving behind a trail a baby could follow, so that Kero has to spend twice the time she should covering it for you. Then

you, Kero, let Daren waste his time in a fruitless search
when you knew from the moment you saw Warrl's tracks
that he was chasing a wild hare. Then you both start
arguing at the tops of your lungs. An army could have
come up on you and you'd never have known it until it
was too late.''

She glared at both of them, and Kero didn't even try
to move under the dagger of that stare.

''Keth was working with me on this,'' she continued,
pitilessly. ''We decided to make this run dangerous for
you, to teach you that if you fouled up, you'd get hurt;
just like real life. You triggered one of her booby traps
with your arguing. And that's exactly what it caught; two
boobies, two fools who couldn't even follow simple orders to keep their mouths shut. Well, I have a further
little assignment for you: get home. There's just one
catch. Until you cooperate, you won't be able to *find* your
way back.'' She smiled nastily, and turned on her heel,
stalking off into the rain. In the time between one breath
and the next, she was gone, as if the drizzle itself had
decided to step in and hide her.

Kero struggled out of the bush she'd flattened in her
fall. Twigs scratched her, as she slowly pulled herself up
onto her knees, then from her knees, shakily, to her feet.
Her head ached horribly, and she guessed that she was
one long bruise from neck to knee along her left side.
The only good luck she'd had was that she'd fallen into
that bush in the first place. There had been enough dead
leaves and grass between herself and the ground to keep
her out of the mud. Bits of leaves clung all over her,
making her look as if she'd slept in them. She brushed
herself off as best she could, and waited for Daren to join
her.

He used the tree trunk to steady himself as he got to
his feet; he wavered quite a bit getting there, and looked
as if he felt just as shaky as she did. When he saw she
was watching him, he glared at her, and limped off after
Tarma without taking a single backward glance at her.

That little bastard! she thought, indignantly. *Well, two
can play—*

Then she looked around.

She had been in and out of these woods for the past
several months. They weren't *that* far from the back door

to the Tower. It was late autumn, most of the leaves were off the trees, which should have made it easier to see through the woods in spite of the rain.

She didn't recognize *anything* now. She was totally, inexplicably, lost.

And in three breaths, Daren came storming out of the mist, head down, limping along like a wounded and angry bull, and ran right into her.

"Hey!" she yelled, indignantly. He caught her as she started to fall, then shoved her away.

"What are you doing, running into me like that?" he shouted.

"Run—you pig! You ran into me!" she spluttered.

"You weren't anywhere in sight!" he yelled back, turning red again. "You just jumped out of nowhere!"

"I did no such—" but he was gone again, as fast as his bruised legs would take him, this time going in the opposite direction to the one he'd been traveling when he ran into her.

That— she couldn't think of any name that was bad enough to call him. *That swine! That rat! Unreasonable, pigheaded, overbearing, arrogant*— She looked around, angrily, dashing water and wet hair out of her eyes with the back of her hand. That vague shape looming up through the rain, beyond and above the trees—that might be the cliff of the Tower.

I think. . . . It changed from moment to moment, shrinking and growing, and sometimes vanishing entirely behind the trees. *Well, I have to go somewhere. I'll bet I make it back, no matter what Tarma said. And I'll bet he doesn't. All I have to do is head for the Tower and watch for where we were. Or find Tarma's tracks.*

She limped off, keeping her eyes alert for signs of disturbance that marked their travel. She found plenty of little snags of wool, a sure indicator that Daren had been there. And she found traces of his footsteps, and of her own.

But she found nothing identifiable as Warrl's or Tarma's tracks, and though she stopped frequently to reconnoiter, she saw no landmarks that looked familiar, and no sign that the Tower cliff was any nearer. She might as well have been on the other side of the world. She couldn't even tell if she was wandering in circles. The

forest seemed utterly lifeless; the steady dripping of rain
on dead leaves hiding any other sounds when she stopped
and listened. She couldn't even tell where the sun was;
the sky was a uniform gray everywhere. Her head
throbbed, and her stomach knotted with nausea; walking
was torture, but at least it kept her warmer than standing.
When she stopped to try and hear past the falling rain,
she was shivering in moments.

Finally, for lack of anything better to do, she took out
her belt-knife, and began to mark the tree trunks. *At least
this should keep me from going around in circles,* she
thought, slogging her way through heaps of soggy leaves,
shivering with the cold rain that kept trickling down the
back of her neck. *As long as I keep going in a straight
line, I'll come to something I recognize. I have to find
the place eventually. Either I'll run into the cliff, or I'll
run into the path, or I'll find the stream. If I don't do
any of those things, I'll get to the road. I* have to cross
either the stream, the road or the path. There's no other
way off Tower lands.*

Or so she thought. Until she stopped to ease her
bruises, side aching so much she wanted to cry, and
rested a while leaning up against a tree trunk. And when
she felt a little less tired, and started to mark the trunk,
she happened to look at the other side, first.

And saw her own six-armed star chipped carefully into
the bark as Tarma had taught her; the least amount of
damage to the tree that she could manage and still have
the mark visible. It was still so fresh that the wind hadn't
disturbed the fragments of bark still clinging to the tree.

She looked around in a panic, sure she couldn't possibly have touched *that* tree. The place was in no way
familiar. But the mark was indisputably there.

She clung to the rough bark, suddenly faint and dizzy.
*But this isn't possible—I know I'd have seen that huge
pig-shaped rock, or the little cave under it! And the tree
with the hawk's nest in the fork! And there's no way I
could forget that clump of holly, it's the only green thing
I've seen all afternoon!*

Nevertheless, it was her unique marking. In a place
she'd never seen.

She closed her eyes, the dizziness and nausea increasing. She fought them down, telling herself not to panic.

But when she opened her eyes again, fear clutched her heart and made it pound painfully in her temples, for her sight was darkening, too.

Then she realized that it was not her eyesight dimming—the sun was setting, dusk closing in rapidly, and she was nowhere nearer to getting home than she had been from the moment Tarma left them.

Tarma—*she can't mean to leave us out here all night— we're both hurt, and we haven't eaten all day. She'll come and get us. She'll come and get me, surely—none of what happened was* my *fault. I followed the rules.*

For one moment, she let herself believe that. Then, as she thought about how angry her teacher had been beneath that mask of indifference, she knew with a sinking heart that there would be no rescue tonight. *We aren't children. One night in the forest isn't going to kill either of us. We'll just wish we were dead. And even if I followed the rules, I didn't make sure he did. When I saw he wasn't going to measure up, I should have forfeited the game by turning around and going home.*

She heard a thrashing sound behind her, then, the noise of someone forcing his way through undergrowth rather than looking for paths. She knew what it was before she turned. No animal would ever make that much noise, and no animal in the forest limped on two legs.

It's a good thing we're not really in enemy territory— they'd have heard him a long time ago. She moved to the other side of the tree and put her back up against it to watch the dim shape grow more distinct as it neared. Finally it was close enough to make out clearly.

She put her knife away and watched Daren stumble toward her, shivering visibly inside his soggy woolen cloak—no longer a handsome russet, it was mud-stained and snagged in too many places to count. And Daren looked much the worse for wear.

He didn't act as if he saw her. He didn't act as if he saw *anything*.

"Hey," she said wearily, as he started to blunder past her. He stopped dead in his tracks, and blinked as if he was surprised to see her.

Maybe he was. The more Kero thought about it, the more certain she became that her grandmother had a hand in this confusion of what should have been familiar ter-

ritory. Hadn't she read in one of Tarma's books on warfare about a spell that fogged the enemy's mind, and
made him unable to recognize his surroundings?

"K–k–kero?" Daren said, stuttering from the cold.
"Are y–y–you still lost, t–t–too?"

"I guess so," she replied reluctantly. Full dark was
descending, and with it, more rain. Harder and colder,
both. Somebody needed to make a decision here, and it
didn't look as if Daren was up to remembering his own
name.

*We need to get out of this, and we need to find some-
place to hole up for the night, otherwise we're going to
wander around until we drop.* The only place at all close
was that enormous rock she'd noticed earlier; the size of
the Keep stables, and right now that little hollow place
under it was the closest thing they were going to get to
real shelter.

"Look," she said, grabbing him by the elbow and
pointing at the stone outcropping. "There's just enough
room under that rock that we can both squeeze in out of
the rain. Right now even if I knew where I was, I
wouldn't be able to find my way back. In a candlemark
you won't be able to find your hand at the end of your
arm."

For a moment, it looked as though Daren was going
to protest—he frowned and started to pull away from her.
But evidently he was at the end of his resources; he gave
in as she tugged at him, and they both stumbled through
the downpour to the shelter of the overhang.

It was a lot drier in the little cave than she had thought,
and the cave itself was larger than she had estimated. As
she crawled on hands and knees into the hollow, feeling
her way with her left, dry sand gritted under her probing.
Dry, relatively clean sand; there didn't seem to be anything in here but a pile of dry leaves blown into the back.
No snakes, for instance—and mercifully few rocks. There
was enough room for both of them to get completely out
of the weather if they squeezed in tightly enough, and
the leaves cushioned them from the worst rough edges of
the rock wall. Without being asked, Daren pulled off his
soggy cloak and draped it over both of them. Shamed a
little, she squeezed some of the water out of her outer

sweater and handed it to him—wet wool stretched, and he managed to get it on over his tunic.

Her prediction of coming darkness proved true; within moments after they took shelter, it was impossible to see anything out beyond the mouth of the cave. For that matter, it was impossible to see anything *in* the cave.

"At least we don't have to worry about bears or wolves or anything," Daren said after a long silence. Both of them had finally stopped shivering, even though Kero doubted that either of them was really warm. She thought, with a longing so sharp that it hurt, of hot tea and her hot bath, and a fire in the fireplace in her room. *This isn't fair. I wouldn't be out here if it wasn't for him playing the fool. I wouldn't be bruised and battered if he'd had any sense.*

Still, being surly wasn't going to accomplish anything. And if he decided she was insulting him and left in a huff, she'd freeze. Together their bodies were keeping the little hollow of their shelter tolerable. By herself she'd shiver herself to pieces. "You think we're safe because nothing with any sense would be out in this rain?" Kero asked. "You're probably right. Unless there's any truth in the stories about water-demons—and I doubt either of us would be of much interest to a water-demon."

"Not even water-demons are going to stumble around in this," Daren replied, his voice dull and dispirited. "Dear gods, I hurt. Even my hair hurts."

"I know what you mean," Kero told him, glumly. "The colder I get, the stiffer my bruises get." She hesitated a moment, then said, "You know, we could have handled this better."

"You mean *you*—" He stopped himself. "I guess you're right. We. I just—I never thought you were serious about all of this. And I didn't think there was any way you could keep up with me. You're a *girl.*"

"So? Half of the mercs Grandmother hired for the Keep are *girls,*" Kero retorted curtly. "Half of the mercs that put your father on his throne were *girls.* His sister, the Captain of the Sunhawks, was a *girl.* I'd have thought it would have occurred to you by now that being a girl doesn't mean your mind is dead, or that you can't handle anything more dangerous than a needle."

"You're going to become a *mercenary?*" His voice spiraled up and broke on the high note. "But—why?"

"Because I have to keep myself fed and clothed somehow, your highness," she said sourly. "Nobody's going to give me anything. My father was a common merc himself before he married my mother, and Grandmother's the only family I've got besides my brother. I'm not going to live out my life on her charity or as the old maiden aunt if I can help it. I've seen too many old maiden aunts, taking care of every chore the wife finds inconvenient. And I really don't have any interest in selling anything other than my sword."

She thought by his coughing fit, followed by an embarrassed silence, that she'd made him blush.

Finally he cleared his throat, and asked, "Just exactly what are you? You speak like a noble, but you dress like a peasant half the time—a *male* peasant, at that."

"That's because dressing like a peasant is a lot smarter than you think in conditions like this 'hound and hare' game," she pointed out, shifting a little to ease an ache in her hip. "The grays and browns blend right into the forest. And you can't fight in skirts and tight bodices. Or hunt, or ride, or do much of anything besides look attractive. You'd discover, if you ever bothered to look closer, that a lot of the peasants working in the fields that you think are men and boys are actually women."

"They are?" Evidently this had never occurred to him.

"How in hell are you supposed to swing a scythe with a skirt in the way?" she asked him. "You'd have your skirt in ribbons! As for us, we were supposed to be thinking 'enemy territory,' right? So I was dressed like a peasant, hard to see, and if anyone did see me, they might not think I was anything dangerous. And I was warm, might I add; peasants know how to dress for bad weather. And there you are in a bright red cloak, in the middle of a dead forest. I suspect we'd have been tagged for that alone."

"Oh." He sounded gratifyingly chagrined.

"So you just found out for yourself how well those hunting leathers of yours keep you warm in the rain," she persisted. "You didn't pay any attention to the weather this morning, you didn't ask Tarma about it either, did you? I've never once heard you ask what the weather was going to be like when we were going to be out all day. It's been unseasonably good since you arrived, if you want to know the truth.''

"You could have told me," he replied sullenly.

"Why?" Her own repressed anger was warming her better than all her shivering. "You come in here and take my teacher's time away from me, you treat me like I'm too stupid to know that you're insulting me with your superior attitude, you act like you expect me to be excited about the so-called 'privilege' of training with you. Why should I tell you *anything?* Why should I share my edge with *you?* You haven't done a thing to deserve it.''

He stiffened as she spoke, and she waited for the outburst she knew would followed her words.

It never came.

"Why is it that you're here, Kerowyn?" he asked slowly. "All I know is that you're Lady Kethry's granddaughter. I thought—I guess I thought you were just playing at this business of learning from Tarma, but you're talking about really going out and selling your sword—"

"I'm not talking about it, I'm going to *do* it," she told him firmly. Her stomach growled, reminding her that it had been a long time since she'd last eaten. "I don't have much choice in the matter, not unless I want to live on my brother's good will until he decides to find an appropriate husband for me. If anyone would take me at this point; there's no telling. I've certainly scandalized all of Dierna's family. And of course that assumes I'd sit right down and marry whoever he found for me, like a good little girl, which I don't think I'm minded to do.''

And if some of the hints about the Baron that Grandmother's dropped are true, I suspect he'd have an interest in keeping me from producing any competition for the Keep. Kethry had never actually accused the Baron of anything, but Kero was perfectly capable of putting facts together for herself, including a few that Kethry didn't know about. The Baron had been quite interested in the proposed marriage, and had sent a very handsome set of silver as a gift—yet had sent no representative to the wedding. Which argued for the fact that he might well have known that something was going to happen.

And he was in an excellent position to plan for it to happen. She was very glad that Tarma had hired all those

guards, those very competent guards. Doubtless Kethry
was keeping a magical eye on the place as well, since the
promises she'd made to Rathgar were void with his death.

"I don't know why your brother would have any trouble finding a husband—" Daren began.

Something about the way he said that crystallized the
problem that had been going around in her head for
weeks. She interrupted him. "What if I don't *want* him to
'find me a husband'? What if I'm perfectly happy without
a husband? Why should everyone think I'm supposed to
be overjoyed about getting wrapped up in ribbons and
handed off to some man I've never even met? I'm not so
sure I'd want to be handed off like a prize mare to anyone
I *have* met!"

"But I thought that was what every girl wanted," he
said, with what sounded like honest bewilderment. "My
sisters all do, or at least, that's all they talk about."

"Not Tarma," she reminded him. "Not Grandmother.
Not your Aunt Idra. And not me. Does every *man* drool
at the idea of going out and hacking people to bits?"

"Well," he admitted, "No. My cousin—"

"Well, nothing," she interrupted again. "Every man
doesn't want the same thing. Then why should every
woman want the same thing? We're not cookies, you
know, all cut out of identical dough and baked to an
identical brown and sprinkled with sugar so you men can
devour us whenever you please." She was rather proud
of that simile, and preened a little in the dark—but the
talk of cookies made her hunger all the worse.

"No," he replied. "Some of you are crabapples."

For once her mind was working fast enough. "At least
crabapples don't get devoured," she snapped. *Though I'd
eat crabapples right now, if I could find them.* She'd have
turned her back on him, if she could have, but there
wasn't room in their shelter.

"It's not any easier on a man, you know," he said
after a sullen silence broken only by the steady pattering
of rain on dead, soggy leaves. "We get presented with
some girl our parents have picked out for us, we have no
idea what she's like, and we're expected to make her fall
deliriously in love with us so that she goes to the altar
smiling instead of crying. And then we're supposed to
live up to whatever plans our fathers have for us, whether

or not we actually fit what they have in mind. I'm just lucky. Faram's the best brother in the world, and I don't *want* the crown—he thinks I'd make a good Lord Martial, and I've always been pretty good at strategy, so I'm not going to have to do anything I hate. And since I'm the youngest, nobody's going to be expecting me to pick out a bride until I want one. Poor Faram's got to choose before Midsummer, and the gods help him if there isn't at least a sign of an heir by Winter Solstice.''

All this came out in a rush, as if he'd been holding it in for much too long. Kero realized as she listened to him that she felt oddly sorry for him.

Maybe too much power and position is as bad as too little.

''So what are they forcing *you* into?'' she asked quietly. ''There must be something.''

He sighed, and winced halfway through as the sigh moved ribs that probably hurt. ''I like the idea of planning things, and I like fighting *practice,*'' he said. ''It's like a dance, only better, because in court dances you spend an awful lot of time not moving much. But—I've never—actually killed anyone—''

''I have,'' she said without thinking. ''It's not like in the ballads. It's pretty awful.''

She felt him wince again. ''That's what I was afraid of,'' he confessed. ''I'm afraid that—I won't be able to—'' He swallowed audibly, then seemed to realize what she'd said. ''You've *killed* someone?'' he said, his voice rising again,

''Well, the sword did—''

''You're *that* Kerowyn?'' he squeaked. She couldn't tell from his voice if he was pleased or appalled.

''I'm *what* Kerowyn?'' she asked. ''I didn't know there were more of me.''

''The one the song's about, the one that rescued the bride for—'' he faltered. ''—for her brother—with her grandmother's magic sword.''

''I guess I must be,'' she said wearily, ''since there can't be too many Kerowyns with magic swords around. The sword did most of it. It was more like *it* was the fighter, and I was the weapon.''

''If I'd known you were that Kerowyn,'' he began. ''I wouldn't have—''

"You see?" she said through a clenched jaw. "Why should it have made any difference in the way you treated me? Deciding that someone's serious just because they've had a bloody *song* written about them is a pretty poor way to make judgment calls, if you ask me. Grandmother and Tarma had plenty of songs written about *them,* and most of them were wrong."

"It's just—just that when I heard the song—I wished I could meet you," he whispered. "I thought, that's a girl that I could talk to, she doesn't have any stupid ideas about honor, she just knows what's right. And then she goes and does something about it."

"Well, you're talking to me now," she replied sourly, hunching herself up against the bed of leaves, wishing she could find a position that hurt a little less.

"I guess I am." Another long silence. "So what was it really like?"

"If I hadn't been sweating every drop of water out of me, I'd have wet myself," she told him bluntly. "I've never been so scared in all my life."

Somehow it was easy to tell him everything, including things she hadn't told her grandmother, the anger she'd felt at Rathgar for being so stupid as to die and leave them all without protection, the same anger at Lordan for being unable to take up the rescue himself. She didn't cry, this time; she wasn't even particularly saddened by the losses anymore. It might all have happened to some-one else, a long time ago, and not to her at all.

He told her about his father, his brothers; quite a bit about Faram, not so much about Thanel. She guessed, though, from what little he did say that Thanel was a troublemaker, a coward, and a sneak. The worst possible combination. Fortunately, their father seemed well aware of that; Kero just hoped he'd considered the possibility that Thanel might well try to arrange for an "accident" to befall his older brother. Daren didn't say anything about that, and Kero decided that it wasn't her business to bring it up.

They dozed off sometime during the night; for Kero it was an uneasy sleep, she woke every time he moved, and every time one of her bruises twinged. And it was hard to sleep when her stomach kept gnawing at her backbone. When the sky began to lighten, she just stayed awake. The moment it was bright enough to see, she nudged him; he must have been as awake as she was, because he pulled the cloak off them without a single word, and they both crawled out of their shelter.

The rock they'd hidden under was no longer pig-shaped; it was a very familiar castle-shaped outcropping that Kero had seen a hundred times. They were no more than a few furlongs from the Tower.

Daren blinked stupidly at the rock; undoubtedly he recognized it, too, but he didn't say anything. So far as Kero was concerned, this only confirmed her suspicion of last night, that Kethry had cast some kind of glamour over the area that wouldn't lift until they cooperated.

Well, they were cooperating now.

She caught Daren's eye; he nodded. They got them-selves as straightened up as possible, then dragged them-selves back to the Tower, figurative tails between their legs. Kero wasn't sure what Daren was thinking—and saw no reason to try and find out—but she had to admit that they'd pretty much brought this whole mess on them-selves.

And she had a shrewd guess as to what was going to be awaiting them.

She was right. Daren preceded her; he stopped for a moment behind the outcropping that hid the entrance, said something too low for Kero to hear, then went on in. She followed, with the relative warmth of the stable closing around her like a cozy blanket. Tarma stood im-passively just inside the stable door, leaning against the rock wall as if she had been there all night and was pre-pared to go on waiting.

She looked them both up and down, face unreadable.

"There's food in your rooms," she said. "Get a hot bath and feed yourselves, then get your rumps back down here. I'll be waiting in the practice ring."

After the bath and the food, Kero felt a little closer to human. Today wasn't going to be pleasant, but as she climbed stiffly into warm—dry!—clothing, she had to ad-mit that she'd spent worse.

And I know damn well that if we don't exercise those bruised muscles, we're going to stiffen up. Then tomor-row will be twice as hard.

She closed the door of her room behind her, and ran into Daren on the staircase down. Daren was bewildered, she could read it in his face—and resentful; she could read *that* in the way he carried his shoulders, stiff and hunched.

"What's the matter?" she asked.

He looked over his shoulder at her, as if he halfway expected her to ridicule him. "If I was home," he said hesitantly, "after something like last night, I'd have been, well, fussed over. They'd have sent servants up with my favorite food, gotten someone to massage me, probably sent me to bed—"

He stopped, and she realized her expression had probably betrayed some of her disgust. She made herself think about what he was saying, and realized that he wasn't to blame for the way other people had treated a prince of the blood.

"Look," she said, trying to sound as reasonable as possible. "Do you think that's what would happen in battle conditions? You're going to be in worse shape than *that* at the end of each day if there's ever a war fought."

He obviously took the effort to think about what she had just said, in his turn, and stopped on the staircase. "I guess you're right," he replied. "There wouldn't even be any hot baths, much less all the rest. We'd probably be sleeping in half-armor, and eating whatever the bugs and rats left us."

"Exactly. If this had been a foray during a war, we'd have been lucky to get the food and dry clothes." She looked at him in the dim light, and shrugged.

"I guess—I guess if I'm supposed to be learning how to command armies, maybe I'd better start getting used to a couple of hardships now and again."

There was the sound of sardonic applause from below them, as the light from the landing was blotted out. Tarma stood for a moment on the first step, still clapping slowly, then took the stairs up toward them at a very leisurely pace.

"It's about time you finally figured out why you're here, young man," she said, one corner of her mouth turned up in something that was not quite a smile. "Now, I have a bit of news for you both. Your day is only beginning."

The exercises she set them were harder than anything she'd given them before, and any resentment or residual anger Kero had felt was lost in the general exhaustion. Daren was in worse shape than she was, since his bruises were deeper and more extensive.

By the time she crawled—literally—up the stairs to her room, she was quite ready to fall into her bed and sleep for a week.

But her day wasn't over yet.

She was as tired as she'd ever been in her life, including when the entire Keep, staff and family, had gone out to get the tenants' harvest in to save it from a storm. Given a choice, she'd have gone straight to bed, stopping just long enough to eat something and drink enough wine so that she didn't ache quite so much.

But she knew she didn't have a choice; another hot bath would do more good for her bruises and stiff muscles than all the sleep in the world, and unless she wanted to wake up aching a lot more than when she'd gone to sleep, she was going to have to take the time for another bath.

She'd just eased herself down into that bath when she had a visitor. Not two-legged this time, but four.

She didn't even realize he was there; when he wanted to he could move as silently as a shadow. She was lying back in the tub with her eyes closed when he MindSpoke her, startling her so that she jumped.

:Might one ask what, exactly, you thought you were doing out there yesterday? Besides playing the fool, of course.:

"Me?" she spluttered. "I was the one playing by the rules! He—"

:By the letter, perhaps. Not the spirit.: The *kyree* sat like a great gray wolf just out of range of any stray splashes. *:You knew very well that I'm not simply some kind of well-trained performing animal. Why didn't you tell Daren that?:*

"Do you think for a moment he would have believed me?" she asked angrily. "Up until last night he didn't think *I* had a mind, so why should he credit you with one?"

:It was your job to convince him,: Warrl said coldly.

*:That is what teamwork is about. If you have knowledge
your fellow does not, you are obliged to enlighten him.:*

"Why?" she retorted. "It would have wasted time. I
knew what you were, that was enough."

*:Why? Because withholding information could get both
of you killed. What if something incapacitated you? What
if I, as the enemy, used the fact that you withheld that
information to split the two of you up? That was exactly
what happened, didn't it? You let him follow a wild hare
and sat down and waited. If I had been a real enemy, I
would have disposed of him, then come up behind you
and disposed of you. But you were too busy feeling superior to worry about that, weren't you?:*

"Me? I—" The accusation was as unfair as anything
else that had happened in the last day. She was trapped
between anger and tears, and the tears themselves were
half caused by anger.

He continued to sit, and stare, an immovable icon of
conscience. *:You finally get in a position where you have
the upper hand, and you misuse your opportunity. You
could have found a way to convince him that you knew
what you were talking about, and you could have done
it in such a way that he would have felt surprised and
grateful. After that, he would have been much more at-
tentive to any suggestions you made. Instead you jeop-
ardized him, yourself, and the mission, all out of pique.:*

"No, I couldn't! I—" She was completely unable to
continue; she tried, and choked up.

*:When you become a mercenary, whether you work
alone or with a Company, you will often be forced to
cooperate with those you dislike. You will find yourself
working for those who hold you and your skills in contempt. If you continue on in your present pattern, you
will, if you are lucky, succeed only in getting yourself
killed. If not—you may bring down hundreds with you.:*

Warrl's eyes glowed, blue as ice and hard as the finest
steel. *:I advise you to think about this,:* he said, after a
long pause during which she wasn't even able to think
coherently. He waited again, but when she didn't reply,
he simply rose to his feet. So smoothly did he move that
not a hair was disturbed; he could easily have been a
statue brought to life by magic. He pierced her with those

eyes once more, and padded out as silently as he had arrived.

She pulled the plug on the bath, too upset and tense now to relax. The water flowed out smoothly, with scarcely a gurgle as she climbed out. She seized the waiting square of cloth and jerked it from the hook beside the tub, then toweled herself dry, rubbing hard, as if to rub those unkind, untrue accusations out of her mind.

Unkind, untrue, and *unfair.* She stalked out of the bathing chamber and flung herself down on her bed, seething. *I'm not the one that went pelting up the trail, leaving tracks and traces a child could read! I'm not the one that decided he knew what was happening without bothering to consult his partner! I'm not the one that decided to divide the party—he wanted me to go downstream while he went up!*

She turned over onto her back and stared at the ceiling. The more she thought about Warrl's little lecture, the angrier she became.

What gives him the right to sit in judgment over me anyway? What gives an overgrown wolf the right to dictate what I should and shouldn't have done? How could he possibly understand? He isn't even human!

She was still simmering when exhaustion finally caught up with her and flung her into sleep.

Daren appeared the next morning at the common room; breakfast was a self-serve affair she sometimes shared with Tarma and her grandmother. Daren sported sunken cheeks and enormous dark circles under his eyes. Since she didn't have a mirror, Kerowyn couldn't have said if she looked the same, but she was very much afraid that she did. It had not been a restful night, to say the least.

"Well, you look like hell," Kero greeted him over the buffet table, handing him a piece of hot bread.

"Thank you," he replied. "If you're curious, it's mutual. Where in hell does she get all this food? I haven't seen a single servant since I got here."

"Magic, I suppose," Kero replied. "Although . . . you know, not that much of it has to be *cooked.* Just the bread and the oat porridge. Everything else could be set beside the bread ovens to warm. I've never seen the kitchen; it could be just on the other side of that wall. I

have no idea how they'd vent ovens this deep in the cliff—
that would be magic, but I've seen stranger things in this
place.''

''Like the bathing chambers?''

''Hmm.'' She eyed the table; the ham and bread would
reappear at dinner, the fruit and cheese at lunch, the
hard-boiled eggs would keep for quite a while, and the
oat porridge would be gone at this meal. All four of them
liked a good big bowl of it, laden with sugar and swim-
ming in cream.

''One cook and two helpers could take care of all this
and more, and still have time for the helpers to double
at light cleaning and laundry,'' she said. ''We all clean
our own rooms, that means the only places a servant
would have to clean would be the common rooms.''

Daren blinked at her in surprise. She dished out her
own bowl of porridge, loading it down with maple sugar
and sweet raisins, leaving just enough for him. ''How do
you know all that?'' he asked.

''All what? Household nonsense?'' Tarma and her
grandmother had evidently just finished; they were dis-
appearing together through one of the doors that was always kept locked. Kero knew what was on the other side
of that one, though—her grandmother's magic workroom. She'd visited it once, and had no desire to do so
again.

Daren completed his selection and followed her to one
of two small tables beside the hearth. ''I thought you said
you weren't interested in marriage and a family.''

''I'm not. I took care of the Keep for five years after
Mother died, and for most of two years before that.'' She
made a face, and cut a careful bite out of her ham slice.
''I hated it. But I learned it anyway. Why do you look
like you spent the night tossing?''

''Because I did,'' he replied. ''Rotten dreams.''

She put her knife and fork down. ''You, too?''

He nodded, then stopped in mid-chew to stare at her.
Finally he swallowed, and asked, ''Were you in the middle of some kind of battle? In a scout group? And you
went off looking for something in a party of about six?''

She nodded. ''And you were there, and we had an
argument about something?''

''Yes. And then?'' He leaned forward.

"Then—you wouldn't listen to me, or I wouldn't listen to you; I can't remember which. But the party split, and we both missed something really important, because when we got back, we'd lost half the scouts, and we discovered that the enemy had cut around behind us—"

"And everyone on our side was dead." He sagged back in his chair, his eyes closed. "Oh, gods. I thought it was just a dream—"

"It was just a dream," a new voice entered the conversation. Kethry's. Daren jumped, then tried to leap to his feet.

"Sit," Kethry ordered him; she was in russet today, the color Daren's cloak used to be, but as if to underline what Kero had told him earlier, she was not wearing a gown, she was in breeches and a long tunic. "If it had been a prophetic dream, certain warnings would have been triggered, and I would have known."

"If it wasn't prophetic," Kero asked hesitantly, "What was it?"

Kethry smiled, as if she had expected exactly that question. "A warning," she said. "This place—seems to trigger things like that. It's happened perhaps a dozen times since we moved here. It's not showing any possible future so far as I've been able to tell—it's showing you the general outcome of a negative behavior pattern."

"So what we saw isn't going to happen to us?" Daren asked hopefully.

"No, not likely," Kethry repeated. "and you won't dream it again unless you continue the pattern."

"But if we do, we get the same dream over and over?" At Kethry's nod, Daren grimaced. "Pretty effective way of getting someone to break the pattern."

"Evidently the builders of this Tower thought so." Kethry patted him on the shoulder in a very motherly fashion, turned and vanished back through the heavy wooden door leading to her workroom.

Daren sighed, and turned back to Kero. "Will it help to say that I've been a blockhead and I apologize?"

She considered him with her head tilted to one side for a moment. "Will it help to tell you I've been just as pigheaded as you?"

He smiled. "It's a start."

"Good," she replied. "Let's build on that." Then she

laughed, feeling a burden lifting from her mind. ''Besides, I'd do a lot more than just apologize to avoid another two days like the past two!''

But Warrl was destined to have the last word, although he was nowhere in sight.

:It's about time,: said a sardonic voice in her mind. *Humans!:*

If Daren wondered why she was choking on her porridge, trying not to laugh, he was too polite to ask.

Nine

Kero studied the sand-table, the terrain laid out in miniature, the tokens that stood for civilians, stock, fighting men and women. *Bloodless warfare,* she thought to herself. *All the fighting reduced to numbers. Is that how generals see us?*

Had it been a year since that quarrel with Daren? It must have been, since it was winter again. Tarma had gradually begun teaching them other things; strategy and supply, tactics and organization. Every daylight hour was spent in some kind of study; from their weapons' practices to reading the fragmentary accounts of the wars of the ancients. Even their ''leisure'' hours usually had something to do with their studies.

''All right,'' Tarma said, leaning over the sand-table. She indicated the tokens that represented the enemy forces, tokens she had just put in place. ''There're the opposing forces. What have you got, Daren?''

He studied his tokens, cupped in the palm of his hand, and placed them carefully in the sand. ''Five companies of foot, one of horse, one of specialists. In country like that, the horse is useless.'' He placed a token with a painted horse's head on it behind the ''lines.'' ''I need another company of foot and two of specialists if I'm going to hold you off. Mountain fighters, irregulars, if I can get them.''

''Which means you hire. Kero, what have you got for him to hire?'' Tarma leaned over the table, resting her weight on her hands, and watched Kerowyn through narrowed eyes.

She represented the Mercenary Guild and the freeswords. ''According to the list you gave me, he can get what he wants, but he's going to have to make some choices.'' She studied the roster, and wondered what he was going to pick—and what his resources would bear. She didn't know what he had to draw on; Tarma did, but while she was playing the enemy, she would pretend she didn't know.

He studied his handful of papers again. "So, what are my options?" he asked her.

"First, there's a full bonded Company of foot, they're at-hire, and their base is within three days' march of your position; you'll have to send a messenger across the Border, though, so I hope your relations are good with King Warrl over there." She grinned at the *kyree*, who was playing all the neutrals in this little game.

:I'll think about it,: Warrl replied genially. *:Depends on what nice present he sends me.:*

Kero grinned; she knew Daren couldn't hear the *kyree*, which made Warrl's comments all the more amusing. Daren consulted his list again. "I can afford to send him a bribe of some fine beef-stud stock under pretense of a trade mission. That's in my private holdings and won't make me raise taxes."

Warrl laid his ears back and looked hurt. *:Bribes? How crude. I don't know . . . well, I suppose I must, crude or not.:* He stood on his hindlegs, put his forepaws on the edge of the table, and nudged the little flag that signified "clear passage."

"Thanks, your majesty." Daren studied his sheaf of papers with a frown on his face. "All right, I can pay for the foot Company with surplus in the treasury. So what about these irregular fighters?"

"That's where you get the choice," she told him. "You can either hire two more bonded Companies, you can hire one bonded Company and one free-lance, or you hire the free-lance Company and set up recruiting posts and hire enough free-lancers to put another temporary Company together. The bonded Company will work with the free-lance Company, but not with a put-together force. There's more than enough of the individual free-lancers in your area. Free-lancers would be cheaper, about half the cost of Companies the same size." She looked up at him. "That's the first time I recall Tarma giving us that option. She's always had bonded Companies in the game, no free-lancers."

"Quite true," Tarma replied, nodding. "You've gotten used to those options. Time to spice up the game with a little more reality. By the time you need them, Daren, bonded Companies will usually have been hired by someone else.''

Daren pursed his lips. "Hmm. The treasury is getting mighty lean . . . Tarma, what's the difference between free-lancers and a bonded Company?''

"Free-lancers are just that: individual hire-swords. Some of them may have bought into a Company, some may be totally on their own. They're cheaper because they haven't posted bond with the Mercenary Guild.'' She stood up, and Kero noticed her flinching a little.

Her joints must be hurting again. I keep forgetting how old she is. We're going to have to start working out against each other more, now that the weather's turned cold. Save our teacher for the things only she can teach us.

:Thank you,: Warrl said softly into her mind.

"Kero, did you say some of those free-lancers were a Company, or am I dealing entirely with individuals?'' Daren asked. "I don't want to hire individuals; it would take too much time to get them coordinated and I'd have to detail one of my own officers to command them. According to these notes, I don't have that kind of time, and I don't think I have an officer to spare. And besides, I know I remember you saying that the bonded Company won't work with something just thrown together.''

Kero looked at the list again. "One Company, the rest on their own.''

Daren winced. "Well, I'll be hiring one bonded Company, anyway. Now, what's the difference between a free-lance Company and a bonded Company?''

Tarma licked her lips. "It's easier to tell you what free-lancers aren't. A bonded Company has posted a pretty hefty bond with the Mercenary Guild, on top of the individual dues each hire-sword's paid into the Guild. What *that* means is that they have to follow the Guild Mercenary Code. If they violate that code, the Guild pays the injured party damages, then takes it out of the bond. *Then* they take it out of the offending party's hide, and they are not gentle, let me tell you! And if *you* violate your contract, the Guild will fine *you,* and you won't be able to hire bonded fighters for at least a year. Maybe more, depending on the severity of the offense.''

"What's this 'Code,' anyway?'' Kero asked. "You've never mentioned that before. You've talked about the Guild code of conduct for individuals, but not a Company code.''

"It's pretty simple. Whatever is in the terms of the contract is followed by both parties, to the letter. Bonded Companies do not pillage in the countryside of their employer, and pillage only in enemy territory with permission of the employer. That takes care of cutting your own throat in a civil war.'' Tarma looked at both of them. "Can you figure out why?''

Kero was marginally quicker. "Easy; if you keep everybody on *your* side from looting, the locals are going to come over to you, and that's going to make big problems for the opposition if they aren't doing the same.''

"Good. And really, what's the point of wrecking your own tax base? All right; if a bonded Company or one of its members surrenders, they are permitted to leave the battlefield unmolested and report to a neutral point. They'll get ransomed by the Guild; that's why the individual members pay their dues every year. You know about the individual Code, so I won't go into that.'' Tarma leaned against the sand-table. "They won't switch sides in mid-contract, they won't follow a mutiny against their employer, they won't fight a suicide-cause, but they'll do their damnedest to get their employer out of a bad situation in one piece. Because of the twin Codes, bonded Companies are more reliable and trustworthy than unbonded. That's why they're expensive.''

Daren examined the table again. "I've got a bad situation here. I think maybe I'd better take out a loan, or go find a buyer for some Crown properties and go the distance for two bonded Companies.''

"What would you do if I set up the situation like this?'' Tarma moved two of her counters away and placed them farther along the Border.

Daren studied the table again. "Hire one bonded and one free-lance, and see if I couldn't negotiate with my neutral neighbor to take a stand. Those two Companies are threatening his territory, too.''

"Good. What about this?" She pulled the counters off the table entirely.

"The bonded foot and the free-lance guerrillas. Then I'd arrange things this way—" He set up his counters against hers, accepting the two mercenary counters from Kerowyn. "—and I'd put the free-lancers right *here*. They're not going to pillage my countryside because that's all rocky hillside; once I move the sheepherders out, there's nothing there to pillage, which means every profitable move for them to make will be against the enemy and not against me." He moved around the table, and looked at the situation from Tarma's angle. "What's more, they can't mutiny, they're on the end of the supply line and all I have to do is cut them off. I think they're relatively safe to trust there."

Tarma studied his setup, and smiled, slowly. "Excellent. Let's play this and see how it runs. Kero? The first move is yours."

Kero had the most interesting time of it; according to Tarma's profile sheets, the free-lance guerrillas were a newly-formed Company, and fairly unreliable, but the bonded foot were an old, established Company with a nice subgroup of scouts that made up for the deficiencies of the free-lancers. And Daren had set up a situation in which the very worst that could happen would be the free-lancers deserting; with a howling wilderness between them and civilization, they were, Kero judged, less inclined to do that. They played the game out over the course of two hours, and in the end, Daren's side won. During that time he'd even found the bribe that would bring Warrl in on his side, so the victory cost him less than he'd feared.

"Good, all the way around," Tarma applauded. "I'm proud of you both. Daren, did you see why Kero's Companies did what they did?"

"Pretty much, though I was kind of surprised at the versatility of the foot." He smiled over at Kero, who returned it, feeling warmed by it.

"That's one thing you'll often find in a good bonded Company; they've trained together with many weapons, and they have their own support groups." Tarma yawned. "Even the best Companies have gotten shafted now and again; the Guild imposes fines, but that's *after* the damage has been done. That's why they like to have everything they need under their *own* control.''

''Well, those two extra hedge-wizards may have saved the day.'' Daren yawned, too, and Kero fought to keep herself from echoing it. It had been a long day, but a good one. This victory against Tarma on the sand-table had been the dessert to the meal; they didn't often win against her.

''I'm off to bed, children,'' the Shin'a'in said, blowing out the extra lanterns, leaving only the four set onto the corners of the table for light. ''Savor your victory; I'll get you tomorrow.''

''No doubt,'' Kero laughed. ''So far you've beaten us five games out of seven.''

''Keeps you on your toes,'' the Shin'a'in retorted on her way out the door. Warrl grinned at them, and padded after her.

Kero collected the tokens, while Daren smoothed out the sand in the table. ''Good game,'' he said, handing her a token that had gotten half-buried in the sand. ''You know, it's a lot more fun being your friend than your enemy.''

''In the game, or in general?'' she teased.

''Both.'' He put his arm around her shoulders and hugged her. She returned the hug—but there was a different feeling about the way he held onto her tonight, keeping her close a breath or two longer than he usually did, sliding his hands down her arms before letting her go.

''Tired?'' he asked, something in his voice telling her than he hoped she'd say ''no.''

''Not really.'' She put the flags and tokens away in a drawer under the table, and looked up at him expectantly. She wasn't tired, either—not with him looking at her the way he was. ''Feel like talking a while?'' she asked hopefully, her muscles tensing a little with anticipation. Was she reading more into his words than was really there?

''If you don't mind.'' It wasn't her imagination, there was an odd light in his eyes, an appreciative glint she'd been seeing quite a bit, lately. ''Your room or mine?''

''Yours,'' she said. ''It's cleaner.'' She laughed, but the way he kept watching her was sending an oddly exciting chill up her spine. She stretched, and came close to giggling at the way his eyes widened. She blew out the rest of the lanterns, and headed for the door.

"Only marginally," he replied—but instead of letting her precede him, he caught her hand in his as she walked past him.

She stopped for a moment, then gave his hand a squeeze. He returned it, and caressed her palm with his thumb as she tugged at his hand and got him moving out the door. She shielded her mind with studious care; right now she couldn't afford any leakage. . . .

She knew what was going on; she'd begun to hope he found her attractive several moons ago, and it was a distinct thrill to see him responding, though she truly wasn't trying to flirt. Even if she hadn't figured it out, Tarma had taken care to let her know a couple of days ago. *"You're young, attractive, and here,"* she'd said bluntly. *"He's young, attractive, and not very sure of himself— though I doubt he's a virgin. You're a friend, so you aren't threatening. If you want to go to bed with him, go right ahead. But make sure you're protected."*

She'd been relieved—but disappointed. *"Is that all it is? Just—availability?"*

Tarma had shaken her head. *"Child, even if it was love everlasting—which we both know it isn't—he's a prince of the blood, and you're going to be a common mercenary. He can't afford to marry you, and you shouldn't be content with anything less. Your potential is enormous, or that damned sword of Keth's wouldn't have spoken for you. You have no right to fritter your life away as Prince Daren's mistress. You have things to do—so enjoy yourself now, but know that when it's over, you're going to go out and do them."*

But with Daren's hand holding hers possessively, and then Daren's arm around her shoulders as they climbed the stairs together, it was difficult to keep Tarma's advice in mind.

There was another side to it all as well—a kind of relief. *I'm all right, I'm not she'chorne or anything. I'm not so different from the other girls after all. Daren wants me, and I want him. . . .*

That was not such a bad feeling, being wanted. He liked her as a friend, and wanted her as a woman—a good combination, if she could keep it from getting serious. She'd followed part of Tarma's advice; she was protected. *That* much Lenore had taught her; the moon-flower powder all the time to control moon-days as well as preventing pregnancy, or child-bane afterward—though moon-flower was better for you, easier on the body.

They reached the top of the stairs, and Kero was glad that there weren't any servants; there was no chance that they'd be interrupted or gawked at knowingly. She had the feeling anything like that would put Daren off entirely. She felt overheated; flushed and excited, and with odd little feelings in the pit of her stomach and groin.

Daren had to let go of her to get his door open, and that seemed to make him shy again; he followed her inside without touching her and made a great fuss of clearing off a chair for her to sit in.

He carefully avoided looking at the bed, and she followed his example, pummeling her brain for some way to make him feel comfortable again. If it had been warmer, she would have suggested they go out on his balcony—his room had one, hers didn't. But it was freezing out there, literally; the ice on the ponds would be thick enough to skate safely on, come morning. Cold hands and feet were not conducive to romance, and the temperature out on the balcony was likely to chill the hottest lust.

Her throat tightened, and she flushed for no reason. Suddenly she was afraid, though of what, she couldn't have said. To cover the fact, she ignored the chair and sprawled out on the sheepskin rug in front of the hearth, half reclinging against a cushion.

Talk. Say anything.

"If you could be anything in the world," she said, staring at the flames, as he sat down hesitantly beside her, "What would it be? Anything at all—anything you wanted, king, minstrel, beggar, whatever."

He thought about it; she took a sidelong glance at him, and saw that his face was set in a frown of concentration. "You know, I think I'd be a merchant. I'd get to travel anywhere, see everything I ever wanted to. I'd be a rich merchant, though," he added hastily. "So I could travel comfortably."

She chuckled. "Like one of Tarma's proverbs: 'What

good is seeing the wonders of the world when you're too saddle sore to enjoy them?' ''

He laughed, and relaxed a little, letting his hand rest oh-so-casually on hers. ''What about you?''

''Being a rich merchant would be nice,'' she agreed. ''But I'd rather be the kind of person that travels just because she wants to. Not tied to a caravan or a trading schedule.''

''Ah,'' he said, nodding wisely. ''A spoiled dabbler.''

''A *what?*'' she said, sitting up straight, pulling her hand away.

''A dilettante,'' he teased. ''A brat. A—''

He didn't have any chance to go on, because she hit him with a pillow.

That attack engendered a wrestling match which he, heavier and stronger, was bound to win—unless she resorted to tactics which would have ended any further plans for the evening. But it was a great deal of fun while it lasted—the more so because she discovered his one weakness, and turned the contest into something much more even.

He was ticklish.

Very ticklish, especially down both sides and on the bottoms of his feet.

She managed to get his shoes off while tickling his sides. Protecting one meant that the other weak point was vulnerable, and the moment he curled up into a ball, she grabbed his feet and ran her nails along the soles. When he thrashed helplessly and got his feet away from her, his sides were exposed. Before long, she'd turned the tables on him.

She tickled him unmercifully, until they were both laughing so hard their sides ached. Finally neither one of them could breathe, and they tumbled together on the rug, completely unable to move.

''You—'' he panted, ''—cheat.''

''No such—thing,'' she replied, trying to brush her hair out of her eyes with one hand while she held onto his bare foot with the other. ''Just—obeying—my teacher.''

''Exploiting the enemy's weakness?'' He was getting his breath back faster than she was, and he managed to

eel around so that her head was in his lap. "But Kero—
I'm not your enemy."

"Aren't you?" she began, when he stopped all further
conversation with a kiss.

It was in no way a chaste or innocent kiss. It picked
up where the last of their tentative explorations had left
off, and carried them to the logical conclusion. Kero let
go of his foot, and groped for the laces of his tunic. His
hands slid under her shirt and cupped her breasts with a
gentleness that vaguely surprised her, stroking them with
his callused thumbs.

The tunic-lacings foiled her hands, which seemed to
have lost all dexterity. She broke off the kiss, and cursed
the things; he laughed, and got out of the tunic without
bothering to unlace it, tossing it off somewhere into the
dark. The loose shirt, a copy of her own, was easy enough
to slide her hands under—which she did, holding him
closer to her, feeling her blood heat at the play of muscles under his skin.

"Beast," she said, and went back to the kiss. He sank
slowly to the floor, taking her with him, his hands moving against her skin under her shirt. She pushed his shirt
up out of the way, the better to touch him. He rolled over
to one side to give her hands more room to roam.

This time he broke free with a yelp as his bare back
came into contact with the stone floor. "I *hate* cold
floors," he said ruefully, as she giggled at his woebegone
expression. Then he scrambled to his feet, and pointed
off into the dark. She couldn't see his face from that
angle, and she couldn't see past the light cast by the fire,
so she jumped to *her* feet—

Only to find herself scooped up, and launched across
the room, to land in his bed. A moment later, he was
beside her.

"Oh, my," she said, "Where do you suppose *this*
came from?"

He didn't even bother to answer, and in a moment, she
didn't really want him to.

Shirts and breeches were everywhere, being tossed out
of bed or shoved to one side. Somehow she managed to
get out of her clothing without tearing anything; he wasn't
so lucky. He couldn't get the wrist-lacings on his shirt to
untie, and with a muttered oath, he snapped them.

His hands and mouth were everywhere; well, so were hers. Every touch seemed to send a tingle all over her, seemed to make her want more.

They explored each other, a little awkwardly sometimes; she hit him in the nose with her elbow, once, and he knocked her head against the footboard. Kero hardly felt it when she collided with the carved wood, every inch of skin felt afire, and she was propelled by such urgent need that she could have pursued him over the side of a cliff and never noticed.

It hurt, when he took her—or she took him, whichever; she wanted him as much as he wanted her. But it didn't hurt that much, and he was as gentle as his own need would let him be. And she began to feel something else, something she yearned after as shamelessly as a bitch in heat. Just out of reach. . . .

It was all over too soon, though, and she was left feeling as if something had been left undone; unsatisfied and still *hungry* somehow.

Sated, he just rolled happily over into the tumbled blankets, and went right to sleep.

She could have killed him.

Twice.

She curled up on her side, stared into the dark, and listened to him breathe. And wondered, *What did I do wrong?*

Later, she figured out she hadn't done anything wrong. Practice, as with anything else, made both of them more proficient, better able to please each other. Eventually the outcome equaled the anticipation, and neither went to sleep unsatisfied.

She finally understood what all the fuss was about—and the obsession. She understood—but she felt herself somehow apart from it; her desire was satisfied, but whatever it was that awakened real passion in others had not touched her.

And nothing ever quite made up for the letdown of that first night.

And he never understood, or even noticed.

Winter became spring, then seemed to run straight into autumn without pausing for summer. There were never enough hours in the day for everything. Kero often wondered what possessed her, to have consented to this.

She often wondered if she were doing the right thing. She had no doubt that a conventional life would be far, far easier.

And I wouldn't have to rise with the sun unless I really wanted to.

The wooden practice blades were nowhere in sight, which was a little odd. Kero exchanged puzzled glances with Daren, then looked away before the glance could develop into anything more intimate.

I don't know how much longer I can keep this as "just friends," she thought, staring at the sandy floor of the practice ring. *Grandmother was worried about me getting my heart broken, but it seems as though it's going to be the other way around. I really like Daren—but—*

But. Blessed Agnira, I'm a cold-hearted bitch. I ought to be on my knees with thanks that he's in love with me, or thinks he is. Instead, all I can think of is "how can I pry him loose?"

On the other hand, Tarma was right. There is no way I would ever be allowed to marry him—

Not that I'd want to.

Tarma's entrance broke into her ruminations, and she looked up gratefully at her teacher. *All this thinking is making my head hurt.* Daren, who had been reaching for her arm, stiffened, and pulled away a little, and Kero breathed a sigh of relief.

Tarma's eyes flicked toward Daren, though she gave no other sign that she'd noticed him moving. "I think you're ready now for something a little more serious," the Shin'a'in said gravely. "It's about time you both got used to handling the weapons you're going to fight with. Not that you're going to practice all the time with them," she added, holding up a long hand to forestall any questions, "But you're going to be working out at least a candlemark every day with them. I can approximate the weight and balance of your real weapons with your practice swords, but I can't duplicate it—and your bodies will know the difference."

She handed Daren a long-sword, two-edged, but with a point as well. The blade was magnificent, and the jewel in the hilt, a ruby so dark as to be nearly black, was worth Kero and all of her family combined.

For her part, she took up Need with a certain amount of trepidation. Although she felt a kind of tingle when she first set hand to hilt, the sword showed no other signs of life.

Which suited her very well. Over the course of that single night, she'd had her fill of being the tool instead of the wielder.

"Tarma," she said, hesitantly. "Is this a good idea? I mean, I thought I was supposed to be learning swordsmanship, but if I'm going to use Need—"

Tarma chuckled. "Don't worry about it. First off, you'll be bouting aginst me, not Daren, and she won't let you harm a woman. Secondly, she works in peculiar ways. Now that you've established your talents as a swordswoman, she'll never help you fight again. Ah, but magic now, that's where she'll protect you. So far as I know, there isn't a magicker in the world can harm you while you hold her."

"So *that's* how it works," she murmured without thinking.

"Exactly. That's why she did both for you when you went after Lordan's bride; you were neither fish nor fowl yet." Tarma grinned. "Now, since she's no more than a very good blade in your hands—defend yourself, girl!"

Blessed Agnira, it's been a long day. Kero hung her sword in its rack, pulled her armor off and draped it over its stand, and stretched. *Tarma was right about having to get used to Need's weight and balance. There's a distinct difference between her and that practice blade.* She stretched again, reaching for the ceiling, feeling shoulders pop. *That hot bath is going to feel so—*

She started for the bathing chamber—and realized she was still holding her sword.

That's odd. She frowned. *I could have sworn I hung her up.*

She turned back toward the wall rack, and tried to place the sword in its cradle. Tried.

She couldn't make her hands let go.

"Oh, no you don't," she muttered. "You've done that to me once. No more."

She put the sword in the rack, and concentrated on freeing her left hand, one finger at a time.

Let. Go. Of. Me. She stared at her hand as if it didn't belong to her, concentrating until she had a headache, a sharp pain right between her eyebrows.

One by one, she loosened her fingers; one by one she pried them off the scabbard. As she released the last of them, she felt something in the back of her mind stretch, and snap.

She pulled her right hand away, quickly, before the sword could take control of her again.

"I'll thank you to keep your notions to yourself," she told it frostily, ignoring the incongruity of talking to an inanimate object. Then she turned, and walked deliberately back to the bathing chamber. She "heard" something, as she "heard" thoughts, faint and at the very edge of her abilities to sense it. It sounded like someone grumbling in her sleep . . . disturbed, but not awakened.

She ignored it and drew her bath.

Whatever it was, it went away while she was undressing, and by the time she slid into the hot water she wondered if she'd only imagined it.

But as she lay back, relaxing, she began to feel a kind of pull on her mind, as if something had hold of her and was trying to tug her in a particular direciton.

Since the direction was her bedroom, she had no doubt who that "someone" was.

She ignored it, and it grew more persistent; then painful, like a headache in the back of her skull. *Stop that,* she thought sharply, sitting up in the bath. The pain eased off, but the tugging was still there. She sat back and thought for a few moments, then she put up her very best shields, the shields even Warrl had not been able to break through.

The tugging stopped. She waited for several moments, but whatever the sword was doing did not seem to be able to penetrate the shielding.

You ruled my grandmother, sword. You're not going to rule me. She closed her eyes, leaned back again, and let the bath relax all her muscles for her.

Finally the water cooled, and she felt relaxed enough to sleep. She opened her eyes and stared at the wall, thinking. *I can't keep shields like this up forever. If I'm lucky, I won't have to. If I'm not, though, this is going to be an interesting little power struggle.*

She lowered her shields, slowly, waiting for the sword to resume its insistent nagging. *You may be older, with all manner of magic behind you,* she thought at it, *but I'll bet I'm a lot more stubborn than you are.*

Nothing.

It's a good thing Daren was too tired after practice to be interested in bed games tonight.

She waited for a moment, then left the shields down and climbed out of her bath. *This is too easy. It's not going to let me off this easily.* She dried herself, and went back into her room to lie down on the bed. *If I were Need, what would I do? A straight-on attempt didn't work . . . anytime she starts on me again, I can bring my shields up and block her out. So the next logical move would be to try something subtle.*

It occurred to her, as she pulled the covers up a bit tighter around her ears, that it was possible she had inadvertently weakened the sword's hold on her by *not* using it during the first few moons she'd owned it.

Those books of Grandmother's—they had something about soul-bonding in them. I think I still have them, in fact. She sighed. The bed was so warm—and the room was already getting chilly. And she was so awfully tired. . . .

Still—I need the information more than I need the sleep. She gritted her teeth and flung back the covers resolutely, flinching as she swung her legs over and put her feet on the cold floor. At least the Tower was heated a lot better than the Keep. There, this deeply into winter, she could put a mug of water down beside her bed, and it would be frozen all the way to the bottom by morning.

She wrapped herself up in a robe, groped for the candle on the table beside the bed, and took it to the fireplace. She scraped away enough of the ash to expose a coal and lit her candle at it.

The books were right where she thought she'd left them; pushed into the corner of the bookcase next to her desk, ignored in favor of the volumes on the history of warfare and strategy and tactics that Tarma had given her to read. She'd been working her way through them with the interest and enthusiasm she hadn't been able to muster for the books of poetry and history her tutors had assigned her.

I think it was the red one, she decided, studying them as she tried to recall which one held the information she wanted. *But—oh, never mind. There're only three of them.* If there was one thing that studying under Tarma had taught her, it was never to discard a book. You never knew when something in it—even in so innocuous a volume as a book of poetry—could prove useful.

She pulled them out and scurried back to bed with them, putting the candle-holder beside the bed, and pulling the blankets up over her legs.

She began leafing through the first book, looking for the section on enchanted objects and soul-bonding. It *was* where she remembered it, and she read it carefully this time, paying special attention to anything that might apply to Need.

Finally she closed the book, put all three of them on the table, and blew out the candle. She turned over onto her side and watched the embers glowing in the hearth, while she thought about what she had read.

It seemed that, by her determination to learn swordwork on her own, she had inadvertently weakened the blade's hold on her. According to several sources quoted in that book, the first few moons were the critical ones in a soul-bonding. Close physical proximity was required after the inital contact, as well as frequent use of the object in question.

So by hanging her on the wall, and not touching her, I kept her from getting the hold on me that she had on my grandmother. And probably everyone else that had her over the past however-many years.

So the soul-bond had been set in, but lightly. Had Kero been a magic-user, this could have been an unfortunate situation. It might even have been a disaster, depending on how much the magic-user in question was likely to depend on the sword's ability to take over and provide fighting expertise. It was probably just as well that Kethry had been deeply soul-bonded to the thing, given some of the stories Kero had heard from her, and from Tarma.

But to protect Kero from *magic*, it simply needed to be in physical proxmity to her. Which meant it probably didn't need to be bonded to her at all—

Except that it wants to know just who it's fighting for. And it probably needs to have some kind of bond to make sure it can protect the bearer at all levels. But it's got a light bond, so to protect me, now, it's got everything it has to have.

It probably wasn't going to like that, though. Given what Kethry told her about the way the sword had behaved in the past. . . .

I'll bet it's going to fight me, trying to get what it wants. I'm not going to give in. Now, I wonder—should I give this thing up?

If I can. . . .

Kethry had never said anything about the sword deciding to switch owners before the present owner was ready to lose it.

It could happen. All it would have to do would be to decide that it doesn't want to protect me right at the moment some sorcerer has me targeted. Well, that was true enough—except that would also be violating the blade's own purpose.

Given that it's refused to work against some fairly nasty characters simply because they were female, I don't think it's likely to drop me in the middle of danger.

That still didn't answer the question of whether or not *she* wanted to be rid of the thing.

I don't think so. It's too valuable. And—I don't mind paying for that value with a little altruistic work now and again. Truth to tell, it's something I'd probably do on my own anyway. The sword is just going to tell me when it needs to be done, and who needs help.

It was getting harder and harder to keep her eyes open, especially since there didn't seem to be a good reason to stay awake any longer.

But as she drifted away into sleep, she couldn't help but wonder just how much of a fight the sword was going to give her. And who was going to come out the victor.

The next four weeks were a constant reminder that a potent Shin'a'in curse was, "May your life be interesting."

The moment she fell asleep at night, she dreamed. Vivid, colorful dreams of women in peril, in which she rode up, and put their peril to rout. Dreams of a life on the move, in which all innkeepers were friendly, all companions amusing, all weather perfect—in short, a life right out of the ballads.

Finally, on Warrl's advice, she took the sword down off the wall, and unsheathed it. With it held in both her hands, she thought directly at it, unshielded.

I'm not thirteen, and you're not going to gull me with hero-tales, she told it firmly. *Save them for minstrels and little children.*

Was it her imagination, or did she hear a sigh of disappointment as she hung the blade back up on the wall?

In any event, the dreams ended, only to be replaced by darkly realistic ones. Night after night, she was witness to all the evil that could be inflicted on women by men. Abuse and misuse, emotional and physical; rape, murder, torture. Evil working in subtler fashion; marriages that proved to be no more than legalized slavery, and the careful manipulation of a bright and sensitive mind until its owner truly believed with all her heart in her own worthlessness. Betrayal, not once, but many times over. All the hurts that could be inflicted when one person loved someone who in turn loved no one but himself.

This was hardly restful.

And during the day, any time she was not completely shielded, the sword manipulated her emotional state, making her restless, inflaming her with the desire to be out and on the move.

But she wasn't ready, and she knew it. Even if the blade didn't.

Every day meant fighting the same battle—or rather, mental wrestling match—over and over; the sword saying "Go," and Kero replying "No."

And to add the proper final touch, Daren was all-too-obviously becoming more and more infatuated with her. And infatuation was *all* that it was, Kero was pretty certain of that. She had a long talk with her grandmother about the differences between love and lesser emotions, and to her mind, Daren did not evidence anything other than a blind groping after someone he thought was the answer to all his emotional needs.

Or as Tarma put it, much more bluntly, "He's barely weaned, and you're a mature doe. In you, he gets both mate *and* mama. I hate to put it that way, child, but emotionally you're years ahead of him. . . . Young Daren isn't in love with you, little hawk, he's in love with love.''

Kero hadn't said anything, but she'd privately felt Tarma had wrapped the entire situation up in one neat package. Daren would make someone a very good husband—when he grew up. She was fairly certain that when he did so, it would happen all at once—but he'd have to be forced into the situation.

Meanwhile, he wasn't going to. Not with someone like her around.

He was making some hints that had her rather disturbed, hints she hadn't confided to anyone.

Hints that he would be willing be actually *marry* her, if that was the only way he could keep her. As if he thought she could be kept! That was keeping her awake at night as much as the dreams were.

Then, one night, he did more than hint. He told her that he would talk to his father about ennobling her if she'd just come with him to the Court. And there was only one reason for him to make that offer that she knew of. He was serious about her.

And she didn't love him. She liked him well enough, but her answer to the question ''Could you live without him?'' was most decidedly ''yes.'' If he left tomorrow and she never saw him again, she would miss him, but she'd go right back to her sword-practice without a second thought, and her sleep would hardly be plagued by dreams and longing.

She got up early the next morning, after a particularly bad night, to pace the cold floor and try to get herself sorted out.

It was at least a candlemark till dawn, but she just couldn't lie there in bed anymore. She lit the candle and got dressed in the chill pre-morning air, and began walking the length of her room, pacing it out as carefully as if she was measuring it.

I like Daren, she thought, rubbing her arms to warm them. *He's clever, he's intelligent, he's flexible—he's not bad in bed, either. He wouldn't ever hurt me deliberately.*

But the sword had filled her few sleeping hours with some fairly horrific scenes. And if she married Daren, there was no way she could do anything about problems like the ones the sword was showing her.

The prince's wife just can't go riding off whenever the mood takes her. In fact, I doubt very much that the prince's wife would be able to enjoy half the freedom Kerowyn does.

That's really what it came down to: privilege, or freedom? The relief of being "like every other girl," or the excitement of being like no one else, of setting her *own* standards? Power and wealth, or the ability to, now and again, right a wrong?

If she married Daren, she would never again be able to totally be herself.

If she didn't, she'd spend the rest of her life keeping her head above water, and wondering if the next sword thrust, the next arrow, was Death's messenger.

Security, or liberty?

It was enough to give anyone a headache, and she had an incredible one, when, in the pearly-gray moment of pre-dawn, someone tapped lightly on her door.

She nearly tripped over her own feet in her haste to answer it; she was expecting Tarma, but it was Daren.

He was white and shaking, and from the tear streaks on his face and his reddened eyes, he'd been crying. He tried to compose himself, his upper lip still quivering as he tried to breathe more calmly.

Kero stood, frozen, with her hand still on the door latch. She couldn't even begin to imagine why Daren would look this way; surely he hadn't been upsetting himself that much over *her*, had he? But his next words told her everything she needed to know.

"Kero—" he said, hoarsely, as tears began to trickle down his face once again. "Kero, it's—my father's dead."

Ten

For one long moment, she couldn't seem to do anything but stand there stupidly, staring at him. Then his shoulders began to shake with silent sobs, and she reacted automatically, pulling him inside, taking him over to the bed and getting him to sit down on the side of it.

"What happened?" she asked, bewildered. Last *she'd* heard, the King was in excellent health, and Prince Thanel had been safely married off to the Queen of Valdemar. *Dear heavens, that was over a year ago. Closer to two. Daren expected to be called home then, but it didn't happen, and that was when he started making hints about getting me ennobled. Have we been here that long?*

She tallied up the seasons in her mind, and realized with a bit of shock that she had been Tarma's pupil for over three years. She glanced reflexively at the mirror built into the wardrobe, and the Kerowyn that looked back at her, hard, lean, eyes wide with surprise, was nothing like the ill-trained girl that had arrived here.

Never mind that. Right now I have to get some sense out of Daren. She held Daren against her shoulder and let him cry himself out; that was the best thing she could do for him right now. As the pink light of dawn filled the room, he got a little better control over himself, and groped after a handkerchief. As usual, he'd forgotten one. She'd never been quite so conscious before of the fact that he was younger than she by at least a year. At this moment he felt more like her brother than her lover.

"Th–thanel," he stammered at last. "It was all Thanel. He's dead. A week or so ago. He tried to murder his wife."

He what? But his wife— "He tried to assassinate the *Queen of Valdemar?*" she exclaimed. "Dearest gods— but what does that have to do with your father?"

"When they told Father, he—I don't know, something happened. Maybe his heart g–g–gave out on him. There's a branch of Kethry's mage-school not far from the capital; they sent word there and one of the mages sent word to Kethry and she w–w–woke me." He choked up again, and couldn't get anything more past his tears. She patted his back absently, one part of her intent on comforting him as best she could, but the rest of her mind putting together all the possible ramifications.

Valdemar isn't particularly warlike, and they just finished that mess with the Tedrel Companies. Tedrel "Companies," indeed. Trust Karse to find an entire nation of low-life scum, and hire them on as free-lancers . . . then complain when Valdemar routs them and they turn back on Karse to loot their way home. Serves them right—

She gave herself a mental shake and got back on the right trail. *But that was just before Daren came. Valdemar took some pretty severe losses, and they can't possibly have recovered enough to declare war.*

Right. So—Thanel tries to take out his wife, I assume so that he can take the throne. He must have failed. I need to know who caught him and what they did with him. The King gets the news, and promptly collapses, then dies, which puts Thanel's brother on the throne . . . no love lost there, which means he could possibly placate Valdemar.

Damn. I need to know how Thanel tried, and whether or not he had any help, either from here, or from inside Valdemar itself.

She tried to calm Daren down a little, but he was incoherent; she hadn't realized he cared that much for his father. So she just held him close, rocking him back and forth a little; it felt like the right thing to do, and it seemed to soothe him as well. He didn't utter a sound after she stopped asking him questions, and that made her heart ache all the more for him. Those silent sobs bespoke more emotional pain than she had ever felt in her life. . . .

Finally he stopped trembling; the storm of voiceless weeping that shook him went the way of all storms. She continued to hold him until she felt a little resistance, as if he wanted to pull away from her. Then she let him go, and he slowly raised his head from her shoulder.

Sun streamed in Kero's window; ironically, it was going to be a beautiful day, but all prospect of enjoying it had just flown with the migrating birds. Daren winced away from the light, his eyes dark-circled, swollen and red, his face still white as the snow outside. "I think you should get some rest," Kero said quietly. "I know you don't think you'll be able to sleep, but you should at least go lie down for a while."

He bristled a little, which she took as a good sign. At least he wasn't going to fall over helplessly and let her take charge of his life.

"Really, if you don't at least go put a cold cloth on your eyes, you aren't going to be able to see out of them," she insisted. Finally, he nodded, and stood up.

"You'll come get me if you hear anything, won't you?" He seemed to be taking it for granted that she would be with her grandmother and Tarma.

That was as good an idea as any. "I will," she promised, and got up to lead him out the door.

They parted company at his door, and she raced down the hall to the stairs, then took the stairway down as fast as she could without killing herself.

The common room was empty, but there was light coming from under the door leading to Kethry's "working rooms." Kero hesitated a moment, torn by the need to find out more information, and her reluctance to pass that doorway. Finally curiosity won out, and she tried the latch.

The door swung open at a touch, and Kero pushed it aside. At the far end of the room, Kethry was seated at a small, marble-topped table, bent over a large black bowl, and Tarma sat beside her, face utterly impassive. There was a light source inside the bowl itself; Kethry's face was illuminated softly from below, her unbound silver hair forming a soft cloud about her head. Kero coughed delicately; Kethry ignored her, but Tarma looked up and motioned to her to join them.

She picked her way gingerly across the cluttered room. She was never entirely sure how much of the clutter was of magical use, and how much was simply junk, relegated here to be stored. That huge, draped mirror, for

instance—or the suit of armor that couldn't *possibly* have
fit anything human, or even alive, since the helm was
welded to the shoulders and the face-plate welded shut
besides.

Mostly she tried not to look at much of anything. There
were some stuffed animals—she thought they were animals—on shelves along the walls; shapes that didn't bear
too close an inspection if one wanted pleasant dreams.

As she neared the two women, she saw that there was
movement down in the bottom of that bowl; the light
eddied and changed, casting odd little shadows across
Kethry's face. When she finally reached them, she saw
with a start of astonishment that there was a tiny man
looking up at Kethry from the bowl, gesturing from time
to time, and making the light change. Behind the man
was a kind of glowing rose-colored mist, and the light
appeared to be coming from that soft and lambent haze.

"It's only an image," Tarma said softly, as Kero found
a stool and placed it beside her. "It's Keth's son, your
uncle Jendar."

"—so, according to the Herald, the prince had been
part of this conspiracy for some time. One of the other
Heralds, their Weaponsmaster, somehow got wind of the
assassination attempt, and when Selenay rode out for her
exercise, he took a group of young warriors with him
and followed her at a discreet distance. So when the con-
spirators ambushed her, they got something of a surprise—first of all, none of them expected Selenay to be
much of a fighter, second, they didn't expect the rescue
party. Thanel was fatally injured during the fight. He
died a couple of candlemarks later."

"That's just as well," Kethry replied, her posture relaxing just a bit. "Is there any sign that Thanel might
have gotten any help from Rethwellan?"

"None that anyone there has come up with, and no
one at Court seems very inclined to look for it here."
The bearded figure cocked his head to one side, a gesture
that made him look very like his mother. "Mother, do
you want me to look into it?"

"No, not really," she replied. "I'd just as soon leave
that to Valdemar. At this point it isn't a threat to Rethwellan or the royal family, and I hope you'll forgive me
for being insular, but that's really all I care about."

Jendar shook his head. "If you insist. I will have to admit that I'd just as soon not deal too closely with the Heralds. They're well-intentioned, and really good people on the whole, but they're too intense for my taste. Too much like you when that sword wanted you to do something."

"And the one time I was in Valdemar was enough for me," she replied. "I'm glad I was just barely across the border. Have you ever been there?"

He shivered. "Once, like you, just barely across the border. I kept feeling eyes on the back of my neck, but when I'd try to find out what was watching me, I could never find anything. I got the feeling that whatever it was, it was very unfriendly, and I had no intention of staying around to find out what it was and why it felt that way."

"It gets worse if you work any magic," she replied soberly. "Quite a bit worse. By the way, this is your niece, Kero."

The tiny man peered up at Kero out of the depths of the bowl. "Looks like she takes after the Shin'a'in side," he said, with what Kero assumed was a smile of approval. "Kero, if you are ever in Great Harsey, look us up. The school is just above the town, on the only hill within miles. We're not hard to find, there're only about forty of us here, but the town itself doesn't number above two hundred."

She swallowed, with some difficulty. "Uh—thank you. I—uh—I'll be sure to do that."

The man laughed merrily, and Kero saw then that he had his mother's emerald-green eyes. "Just like every other fighter I've ever met—show her magic, and she curls up and wilts."

"Yes, and what do you do when someone has a sword point at your throat?" Kethry retorted with a hint of tired good humor.

"I do my best to make sure I'm never *in* that particular situation, Mother dear," he replied. "So far that strategy has worked quite well. Kero, child, if magic bothers you, I suggest you try Valdemar. They seem to have some kind of prohibition against it up there. In fact," he continued thoughtfully, "I seem to have one demon of a time even mentioning magic to them. Don't know why. It might be interesting to see what happens to Mother's nag of a sword north of the border.''

"That's an experiment I'd rather not see tried," Kethry told him. "Is that all you have for us?''

"That's all for now," Jendar said, dropping back into a serious mode. "I'll contact you the usual way if anything more comes up. I know they'll want the young man here as soon as possible; get him on the road tomorrow, if you can. You might tell him, if he seems interested, that his brother is definitely assigning him to the retinue of the Lord Martial with a view to making him Lord Martial in a few years. I'd guess three years at the most; the poor old war-horse is on his last legs, and losing Jad has done something to him. He was looking particularly tottery this morning. Tarma, I hope the young man is up to the challenge.''

"He's up to it," she said firmly. "I wouldn't turn him loose if he wasn't. Remember, I held him back when Thanel went north because he wasn't ready.''

"Good enough, I'll let the word leak into the Council. Take care, Mother.'' The man bowed once, and the light in the bowl winked out.

Kethry raised her head, slowly, as if it felt very heavy. "Thank the Windlady I'm an Adept," she said feelingly. "The Pool of Imaging took it out of me when I was *young*. I hate to think what I'd be feeling like these days.''

What—oh, right. Adepts can pull on energy outside themselves to work magic, Kero remembered. Learning the capabilities of the various levels of mages was something both Kethry and Tarma had insisted she and Daren learn. *"Knowing what your enemy's mages can and can't do may help you win a fight with a minimum of shed blood,"* Tarma had stressed. *"Daren, that blood should be as precious to you as your own, if only because each fighter lost is a subject lost—Kero, you're talking about the fighters to whom you are obligated in every way, and they in turn are your livelihood, so a fighter lost may well represent next year's income lost. Sounds cold, I know, but you have to keep all of that in mind.''*

"What was that?'' Kero asked carefully.

"It's a spell only Masters and Adepts can use,'' Kethry said, pulling her hair off her forehead and confining it with a comb. She looked terribly tired, and her eyes were as red as Daren's had been. "It's basically a peacetime communication spell—it's draining, it's as obvious as setting off fireworks, and it leaves both parties open to attack. But the advantages far outweigh the disadvantages to my way of thinking."

"You can talk to the other person as easily as if you were face-to-face," Kero said wonderingly. "I had no idea that was possible."

"Like a great many spells, it's one we tend to keep quiet about," Kethry told her with a wry twist to her lips. "There are a fair number of war-leaders out there who wouldn't care how dangerous the spell was to the caster, if that was the kind of communication they could get."

"I can see that—was that really my uncle?"

"In the flesh—so to speak—and kicking," Tarma said. "He's the one that took over your mother's White Winds school and moved it up near the capital. He's got a fair number of friends on the Rethwellan Grand Council, so as soon as anything happens, he knows about it. Useful sort of relative."

"I just wish he was a little less interested in politics, and more in the school," Kethry said a bit sharply. "One of these days he's going to back the wrong man."

"Maybe," Tarma replied evenly. "Maybe not. He has unholy luck, your son. And he's twice as clever as you and me put together. Besides, you know as well as I do that to keep the school neutral the head has to play politics with the best of them. The only reason you survived down there was because you were protected by the crown, and if that wasn't playing politics, what is?"

"I yield," Kethry sighed. "You're right, as usual. It's just that I hate politics."

"Hate them all you want, so long as you play them right," Tarma replied. "All right, little hawk," she continued, turning to Kero, "Now you know as much as we do. Need anything else?"

Tarma hadn't said anything, nor had Kethry, but Kero sensed that they wanted to be alone. She had no idea how well they had known the King, but he *had* been Tarma's pupil, and they had known his father very well. All things considered, it was probably time for a delicate withdrawal.

"I don't think so," she said. "Thank you."

"How's the lad?" Tarma asked as she turned to leave.

"He's probably fallen asleep by now," she said, recalling that she'd left him sprawled over his bed in a state
of exhausted numbness. "I think he'll do a little better
knowing Faram wants him. From what he's said, he's a
lot closer to his brother than he was to his father."

"Not surprising," Tarma said cryptically. "Well, I'll
let him know the news when he wakes up."

That was a definite dismissal, and Kero left as quickly
as she could without actually hurrying. It was with a
certain relief that she closed the door on Kethry's workroom. She walked slowly toward the fireplace, feeling at
something of a loss for what to do next. She was the only
person in the Tower—except, perhaps, for the seldom-
seen servants—who was left entirely untouched by the
King's death. Untouched, though not unaffected, for this
affected Daren—

She went up to her room, pulled a chair up to her
window, and sat gazing out her window at the snow-
covered meadow below the Tower, not really thinking,
just letting her mind roam. She sat there the rest of the
morning and on into the afternoon, before thoughts crystallized out of her musings. Uncomfortable thoughts.

The King was calling in his brother, and Daren would
be leaving in the morning, which left her the only student
at the Tower. There wasn't much more that Tarma could
teach her now that she wouldn't learn just as quickly
through experience. There were things she needed to
learn now that only experience and making her own mistakes would teach her.

In short, it was time for *her* to leave as well.

Leaving. Going out on my own. The thought was
frightening. Paralyzing.

At that moment, someone tapped on her door, shaking
her out of her trance. "Yes?" she said still partially
caught in her web of thoughts, and the visitor opened the
door slowly and cautiously.

"Kero?" Daren said softly, shaking her the rest of the
way out of her inertia.

"Come in." She turned away from the window,
searching his face, though she really didn't know what
she was looking for. "Are you—"

"I'm all right," he said, walking toward her, slowly. As his face came into the light, she saw that he looked a great deal calmer. In fact, he looked as if he had come to terms with the news, and with his own feelings. "I really am. They told me that Faram wants me home."

As he said that, his face changed, and there was hope and a bit of excitement beneath the mourning.

"That—I was kind of afraid Faram had forgotten me," he said shyly. "It would be awfully easy to. And—and I thought, he's had one brother turn on him, he might not trust me anymore either. I wouldn't blame him, you know, and neither would anyone else. I'd be tempted, if I were in his place, and I knew he was safely tucked out of the way with two of my father's old friends keeping an eye on him. I thought that might even be the reason Father sent me out here in the first place, to get me out of the way, with someone he trusted making sure I didn't turn traitor on him. I thought maybe that was why he didn't send for me when Thanel went off to Valdemar."

Kero nodded, slowly. That was sound reasoning; in fact, in his place, she'd probably have suspected the same thing.

"But Faram wants me. More than that, he wants me to apprentice to the Lord Martial." There was suppressed excitement in his voice, and a light in his eyes. "It's just about everything I ever dreamed of, Kero—"

"And you deserve it," she interrupted him, with as much emphasis as she could muster. "You've worked for it; you've earned it. Tarma herself would be the first to tell you that."

"And now you can come with me," he continued, as if he hadn't heard her. "There's nothing stopping me from having you with me. Faram studied under Tarma, he knows Kethry, we won't even have to go through that nonsense of getting you ennobled so we can be married—"

Married? "Whoa!" she said sharply. "Who said anything about getting married?"

That brought him to a sudden halt. His eyes widened in surprise at her vehemence. "I thought that was what you wanted!" he said, in innocent surprise. "I want you with me, Kero—there isn't anyone else I'd rather be married to—"

"Do you want me enough to have me apprenticed alongside you?" she asked pointedly.

He stared at her in shock, as if he could not believe what she was saying. "You know that wouldn't be possible!" he exclaimed. "You're a girl! Women can't do things like that!"

"I'm your equal in blade and on horseback," she replied with rising heat. "I'm your better with a bow and with tactics. Why shouldn't I work at your side?"

"Because you're a *girl!*" he spluttered. "You can't possibly—it just isn't *done*—no one would permit it!"

"Well, what would I be able to do?" she asked. "Sit on the Council? Act as military advisor?"

"Of course not!" He was shocked—despite all their talking, all the things they had done together—by the very idea. *Not so enlightened as we appeared to be, hmm?*

"Well, will I be able to keep in training?" She waited for him to answer, and didn't much care for his long silence. "All right, what *will* I be able to do?"

"Ride some, and hunt—genteel hunting, with hawk and a light bow," he said, obviously without thinking. "Nothing like the kind of hunting we have been doing here. No boar, no deer, good gods, that would send half the Court into apoplexy! You can't offend them."

"In other words, I wouldn't be able to do a single damned thing that I've been trained and working at for the past three years," she pointed out bitterly. "I can't offend them—by 'them' I assume you mean the men—by competing with them. You want me to give up everything I've worked for all this time, and even my recreations."

"You could advise me in private," he said hastily. "I *need* that, Kero, just like I need you! And we could practice together."

"In private, so no one would know your lady wife can beat the breeches off you two times out of three," she said acidly, deliberately telling the truth in the most hurtful way possible."

"Of course, in private!" he replied angrily. "You can't do things like that where people can find out about them! After all, you won't be a common mercenary! Do you think I want anyone to know—"

"That I'm your equal, and their superior. How good I am." She stood up. "In short, you want a combination

of toy soldier and expensive whore; your delicate lady in
public and whatever else you want out of me in private,
with no opinions or thoughts of my own—except in private. Thank you, no. I told you that night we first talked
that I wasn't prepared to sell anything other than my
sword. That hasn't changed, Daren. And it isn't likely
to.''

She rose to her feet and stalked toward the door, so
angry that she no longer trusted her temper with him and
only wanted to be away from him so she wouldn't say or
do anything worse than she already had. She grabbed her
cloak as she passed the door, and he made no move to
stop her.

She was walking so fast, and was so blind with suppressed fury, that she didn't realize until she was down
in the dimly lit stables and on her way out the tunnel to
the rear entrance that she had also snatched up Need on
her way out.

She paused. For one moment that startled and alarmed
her. Was the sword controlling her—had she so lost her
temper that she'd lost her protections against its meddling? Then common sense reasserted itself. *Just good
reactions,* she decided. *Finally I've gotten to the point
where, when I head out of my room, I snag a weapon
without thinking about it.* She flung the cloak over her
shoulders, fastened the clasp at her throat, and belted the
sword beneath it. *Doesn't it just figure,* she thought angrily, as she strode out into the chill late-afternoon sunlight, *that when I finally get to the point that I'm reacting
like a professional fighter, Daren pulls* this *on me? Offering me anything I want—as long as I don't do anything
that embarrasses him. Like act like a human being capable of thinking for herself.*

Another thought occurred to her, as she pictured the
kind of pampered pet Daren seemed to want her to become. *Dierna would have given her soul for an opportunity like this. . . .*

Suddenly she stopped dead in her tracks, just outside
the hidden entrance to the stables, the wind molding her
cloak tight to her body. *So what's wrong with me? Why
don't I want this easy life on a platter?*

She shivered, and pulled the cloak closer about her as
another whip of breeze nipped at her. *Why am I going*

*out to fight for a living? Why do I want to? What kind of
fool am I, anyway?*

She resumed her walk, but at a much slower pace. She
paced the hard-packed path through the forest with her
head down, eyes fixed on the frozen snow, but not really
seeing it. *If he's offering this to me, it pretty much ne-
gates what I first told him, that I'm going to be a mercenary because no one is going to keep me fed and clothed
. . . he's offering that. I don't have to do this. So why do
I still want to?*

She raised her head, and looked around, half hoping
for some kind of omen or answer. There were no answers
coming from the silent forest, only the mocking echoes
of crows in the distance and the steady creaking of snow
underfoot. There were no answers written against the sky
by the bare, black branches, and no revelations from the
clouds, either. She walked onward, following the familiar path to the river out of habit, her nose and feet growing numb and chill.

Well, she decided finally, *I suppose one reason is that
I'm good at fighting. It would be a damned shame to let
that talent go to waste. It would be stupidity to let someone else do the job who isn't as good at it as I am. . . .*

The wind died to nothing, and her cloak weighed down
her shoulders as if embodying all of her troubles. That
thought led obliquely to another. *I'm good at fighting. Of
course, it would be nice if there wasn't any fighting, if
bandits would stop raiding, and people would stop making war on each other, and everyone could live in peace.
But that isn't going to happen in my lifetime—probably
not for a long, long time. So it makes sense for people
who are good at fighting to go out and do it—because if
they're good at it, that means the fewest number of other
people die.*

That was essentially what Tarma had said to both of
them, a hundred times over; that her job and Daren's was
to learn everything they could about advance planning,
to protect those serving with and under them, to keep
their casualties to an absolute minimum.

*But there are going to be people like bandits, like the
Karsites, who don't care how many people die. People
with no conscience, no honor. I know that a lot of folk*

think mercs don't have either—but if that's true, then why the Codes?

It was all beginning to come together, to make a vague sort of sense. She stopped again, and squinted her eyes against the westering sun. *There's always going to be fighting. I can't see the world turning suddenly peaceful in my lifetime. People of honor have to be a part of that, because if they aren't, the only ones fighting will be the ones who don't care, who have no honor, and no concern for how many others die. Right. That's why I'm doing this. In a funny kind of way, it's to protect the Diernas and Lordans, the people who would be the victims. Even if I'm getting paid to do it, it's still protecting them.*

Because if all the fighting is done by people with no conscience, there won't be any safety anywhere for the people who only want peace.

That was the answer she was looking for. She felt tension leaving her, as she turned her back on the setting sun, and headed home with her shadow reaching out before her, black against the blue-tinged snow.

I'm good now, but I have to become very good. Special. So special that I can pick my Company and my Captain, pick someone with a Company so good he can choose when he won't take a job, because it's for the wrong side and the wrong causes. Just like Grandmother and Tarma did.

And that was why she wouldn't give in to Daren, and to what he was offering. The love he was offering came with restrictions, restrictions on what made her unique. If he truly loved what she was, rather than what he thought he saw, he would never have placed those restrictions on her.

And last of all, I don't love him, she thought soberly. *I like him, but that's not enough.*

If she took him up on his offer of marriage, she would be offering him considerably less than true coin. She didn't love him, she didn't think she could ever learn to love him. In time, she might even come to hate him for the lie he was making her live.

What if one day he outgrew this infatuation, and found someone he really *did* love? That would be a tragedy as horrible as anything in any of the romantic ballads. Worse, really; there they'd be, living double lies, and trapped in the agreements they'd made when neither of them was thinking particularly clearly.

What if *she* found someone?

But that notion made her grin, sardonically. *Right. Me in love. About as likely as having my horse decide to talk to me. I may not be* she'chorne, *but I don't think there's been a man born that could be my partner, and I won't settle for anything less than that.*

No, liking Daren was entirely the wrong reason to go through with this charade of his. It would be just as false as putting on a dress and pretending to be something she wasn't for the sake of appearances.

And it was ironic that the things that made her so different—and that he now deplored—were the things that had attracted him to her in the first place.

If he wants a woman to be different, why does he want her to be the same as every other woman? she asked herself, as she stood just inside the stable door, waiting for her eyes to adjust to the dimness inside. *Men. Why can't they ever learn to think logically?*

Daren found himself caught between anger and bewilderment. First Kero stormed off and left him standing in the middle of her room, torn between frustration and feeling foolish. He couldn't understand what was wrong with her; why couldn't she see that she was going to have to adjust herself to what people expected of her? The world wasn't going to change just because she was different! He'd offered her something any woman in her right mind—and certainly every single woman at Court—would have pledged her soul to have, and she stormed off because he'd told her the truth of the matter, and how she would have to change.

He waited for her to come to her senses and return, to apologize and take his hands and say she never wanted to fight like that again—

But she didn't come back, and she didn't come looking for him after he returned to his own room. Tarma showed up, toward sunset; she looked older, somehow, and he guessed that her father's death had hit her pretty hard.

"Well," she said. "It's official. Faram wants you up there yesterday, so you'd better get yourself packed up. You'll need to be on the road tomorrow."

"Will I need an escort?" he asked, a little doubtfully. He didn't really *want* one, and a retinue would slow him down.

Tarma shook her head. "I don't think so. You can take care of yourself quite well, youngling, and if you have any enemies out there, they won't be looking for one man and his beasts, they'll be looking for a damned parade."

He sighed. "Well, I guess this is the end of my stay here. I've—not precisely *liked* it, but—Tarma, I appreciate all you've done for me. I can't really say how much, because I won't know exactly how much you've taught me for years yet."

She smiled a little. "Then you're wiser than I thought, if you've figured that out. Wise enough to know that you'll be better off packing up now so you can leave straight away in the morning."

"Does Kero know I'm leaving tomorrow?" he managed to get out. Tarma looked at him oddly for a moment, then nodded.

"I told her," the Shin'a'in said, her expression utterly deadpan. "She didn't say anything. Did you two have a fight?"

He started to tell her what had happened between them, then stopped himself; why, he didn't really know, unless it was just that he didn't want anyone else to now about this particular quarrel. "Not really," he said. "It's just I haven't seen her all afternoon. . . ." He let his words trail off so that Tarma could read whatever she wanted to in them.

She nodded. "Good-byes are a bitch," she said shortly. "Never got used to them, myself. Travel well and lightly, *jel'enedre*. I'll miss you."

She gave him a quick, hard hug, and there was a suspicion of tears in her eyes. Then she left him alone in his suddenly empty room. Left him to pack the little he had that he wanted or needed to take with him. Not the clothes, certainly, except what he needed to travel with— Faram would have him outfitted the moment he passed the city gates in the finest of silk and wool, velvet and leathers. Not the books; they were Tarma's. The weapons and armor, some notes and letters. A couple of books of his own. His life here had left him very little in the way of keepsakes. . . .

And where was Kero? Why didn't she come to him?

She didn't appear at his door any time that evening; he finished packing and tried to read a book, but couldn't concentrate on the words. Finally he took a long hot bath, and drank a good half-bottle of wine to relax. He thought about his father; he and Kero had that in common as well, after the first shock, he was having a hard time feeling the way, perhaps, he should. He hardly knew the King—he'd spent more time away from Court than in it, mostly because of Thanel. Faram had been more of a father than Jad. The King had been the King, and word of his death was enough to shock any dutiful subject into tears. If it had been Faram, now—

He finished the bottle, tried once more to read, then gave up and climbed into bed. He more than halfway expected Kero to drift in through his door after he blew out the candle.

She has to come, he thought. *She has to. She loves me, I know she does. And our lovemaking has always been good—once I get her in bed, I can make her see sense, I know I can.*

But no; though he waited until he couldn't keep his eyes open anymore, despite tension that had his stomach in knots and his shoulders as tight as braided steel, she didn't come.

By morning, he'd finally begun to believe that she wouldn't. That he'd said the unforgivable.

He hadn't expected her, but as he was saddling up his old palfrey, Tarma came down the stairs to the stable to see him off.

He'd never had more than cursory contact with Lady Kethry, and he wasn't surprised when she didn't appear at her partner's side, but he was unexpectedly touched to see Tarma again.

"Couldn't let you go without a parting gift, lad," she said. "You'll need it, too. Take Roan."

"Take *Roan?*" He could hardly believe it. The gelding he'd been using was a fine saddle-bred of her Clan's breeding; he was astonished and touched, and very nearly disgraced himself by breaking into tears again.

"Dear gods, we've got Ironheart and Hellsbane, plus a couple of mules. He'll be eating his head off in the stable if you don't take him." She led the gelding out of his stall and tethered him beside the palfrey. "Look at him, he'd be perfectly happy to do just that. I'd say it's your duty to save the overstuffed beggar from his own stomach."

"In that case," he said, "I guess I have no choice."

"Never try to cross a Shin'a'in, boy," she told him gravely. "We always get our way."

"So I've learned." He dared to reach for her bony shoulders and hug her; she returned it, and they both came perilously close to damp eyes.

"Now get out of here before I have to feed *you* again," she said, pushing him away, gently. "Star-Eyed bless, but the amount of provisions we've had to put in to keep you fed! You and that gelding make a matched set!"

It was a feeble joke, but it saved him, and he was able to take his leave of her dry-eyed, saddle up Roan, and ride off down the path to the road.

Then, as he stared back at the Tower, his eyes burned and stung after all.

She didn't come.

She hadn't even come to say good-bye.

He turned his back on the place resolutely. She'd made her choice; he had to get on with his life. Only his eyes kept burning, and not all the blinking in the world would clear them. He was rubbing them with the back of his hand, when like the ending to a ballad, he heard hoofbeats behind him—hoofbeats he recognized; the staccato rapping of Kero's little mare's feet on the hard-packed snow. He'd know that limping gait anywhere, any time; Verenna had favored her right foreleg ever since an accident in his second year here, and he knew her pace the way he knew the beat of his own heart.

He turned his gelding to greet her, his heart filled to bursting. *She came to her senses! She's coming with me! I won her over—*

Then as she came into view, he felt a shock, and stared, his eyes going so wide he thought they were going to fall out of his head.

It was Kero, all right. With her face made up like one of the Court flowers, her hair in an elaborate arrangement that must have taken hours to do. In a dress. A fancy, velvet dress, a parody of hunting-gear. It was years, decades out of date, and she must have gotten it out of her grandmother's closet.

She looked like a fool. It wasn't just the dress, it wasn't even *mostly* the dress, old and outdated as it was. It was that she was *simpering* at him, her eyes all wide and dewy, her lips parted artfully, her expression a careful mask of eager, honeyed anticipation.

"Oh, *Daren*," she gushed, as she rode within hearing distance. "How could you ever have thought I'd stay behind? After all you've offered me, after all we've meant to each other, how could you have ever doubted me?"

She rode up beside him and laid a hand on his elbow, a delicate, and patently artificial gesture. "I thought over what you'd said, and I realized how *wise* you are, Daren. The world isn't going to change, so I might as well *adapt* to it! After all, it isn't every day a *prince* of the *blood* offers to make *me* his *consort!*"

She giggled—not her usual hearty laugh, or even her warm, friendly, sensuous chuckle, but a stupid little giggle. Her mare sidled a little, and she let it, instead of controlling it.

That's when it dawned in him. She was acting exactly the way those little ninnies at Court had been acting—vacuous, artfully helpless, empty-headed, greedy—

Sickening. He pulled away from her, an automatic, unthinking reaction.

Abruptly, her manner changed. The artificial little fool vanished as completely as if she had never existed. Kero looked at him soberly, the absurd riding habit, painted cheeks and ridiculous hair all striking him as entirely unfunny. Verenna tried to sidle again, and this time Kero controlled her immediately.

"I just gave you everything you said you wanted me to be, yesterday. That's exactly the way you asked me to behave."

"In public!" he protested. "Not when we're together!"

"Oh, no?" She tilted her head to one side. "Really? And how private *is* a prince of the blood? When can you be absolutely sure that our little secrets won't be uncovered? When can you guarantee that we won't be interrupted or watched from a distance?"

He was taken rather aback—and vivid recollections

came pouring back, of private assignations that had become public gossip within a week, of secrets that had been out as soon as uttered, of all the times he'd sought privacy only to find watchers everywhere. Roan stamped impatiently, reflecting his rider's unease.

"Even if you can get away from your courtiers," she persisted, her brows creased as she leaned forward earnestly in her saddle, "even if you can escape the gossips, how do you keep things secret from the servants? They're everywhere, and they learn everything—and what they learn, sooner or later, the entire Court knows."

She sat back in her saddle, and watched his face, her eyes following his. "Besides, what you live, you start to become. The longer I act like a pretty fool, the more likely I am to turn into one. Is that *really* what you want from me?"

"No!" he exclaimed, startling Roan into a snort. "No, what I love about you is how strong you are, how clever you are, how much you're like a friend—the way I can talk to you like another man—"

He stopped himself, appalled, but it was too late. She was nodding.

"But *this* is what you asked me to become," she replied, taking in dress, hair, and all with a single gesture. "Daren, dearheart, you don't *really* want me as a lover, you want me as a *friend*, a companion. But I can't be a companion in your world—I can only be something like this."

He tried to say something to refute her, but nothing would come out.

"Daren, you have a companion and partner waiting for you—someone who needs your help and support and the fact that you love him, and needs it more than I ever will," she said softly, but emphatically. "Your brother is and will be more to you than I ever can. Or ever should. And once we'd both gotten to the Court, you'd have found that out. I could never be more than a burden to you then, and it would frankly be only a matter of time until my temper made me an embarrassment as well."

"I—you—" he sputtered a while, then shook his head, as his gelding champed at the bit, impatient to be off. "I—I guess you're right," he said, crestfallen. "I can't think of any reason why you should be wrong, anyway."

He looked down at his saddle pommel for a moment, then defiantly met her eyes. "But dammit, I don't have to like it!"

"No, you don't," she agreed. "But that doesn't change anything."

She stared right back into his eyes, and in the end, he was the one who had to drop his gaze.

"Daren," she said, after a moment of heavy silence, broken by the stamping of horses, creak of leather, and jingle of harness, "Wait a couple of years. Wait until I've found my place. Then I can be your eccentric friend, that crazy female fighter. Princes are *expected* to have one or two really odd friends." She chuckled then, and he looked up and reluctantly smiled.

"I suppose," he ventured. "You might even do my reputation some good."

"Oh, definitely." The smile she wore turned into a wicked grin. "Just think how people will react when they know I'm your lover. 'Prince Daren, tamer of wild merc women!' I can see it now, they'll stand in awe of your manhood!"

He blushed—all the more because he knew damned well it was true. "Kero—" he protested.

"Are we friends again?" she said abruptly.

He blinked, his eyes once more filling with tears, and this time he did not try to pretend they weren't there. "Yes," he said. "Although why you'd want a fool like me for a friend—"

"Oh, I have to have *someone* I can borrow money from," she said lightly—then reached across the intervening space between them and hugged him, hard.

And when she pulled away, there were tears in *her* eyes as well.

"Just you take care of yourself, you unmannered lout," she whispered hoarsely. "I want you around to lend me that money."

"Mercenary," he replied, just as hoarsely.

She nodded, and backed her horse away slowly.

"Exactly so, my friend. Exactly so." She halted the mare just out of reach, and waved at him. "And you have places to go, and people waiting for you, Prince Daren."

He turned his horse and urged it into a brisk walk, looking back over his shoulder as he did so. He halfway expected to see her making her way toward the Tower, but she was still sitting on her horse beside the path. When she saw him looking, she waved once—more a salute than a wave.

The departing salute he gave her was exactly that. Then he set his eyes on the trail ahead. And never once looked back.

Kero waited until Daren was out of sight, then turned her horse's head toward the Tower.

I'm not sure what was more surprising—him developing good sense, or me developing a silver tongue. She hadn't quite known what she was going to say, only the general shape of it. She certainly had not expected the kind of eloquent speech she'd managed to make.

One thing that was not at all surprising; she was already missing Daren—but she wasn't as miserable as her worst fears had suggested. Which meant, to her way of thinking, that she was *not* in love with the man. Deep in the lonely hours of the night she'd had quasi-nightmares about successfully sending him away, then discovering she really *couldn't* live without him.

She sighed, and Verenna's ears flicked back at the sound. "Well," she told the mare, "I guess now it's my turn to figure out exactly what I'm going to do with *my* life."

And Need chose that moment to strike.

Kero had a half-heartbeat of warning, a flash of *something stirring*, like some old woman grumbling in her sleep, just before the blade began exerting its full potential for pressure. She managed to keep it from taking her over entirely, but she could not keep it from disabling her.

It did its best to overwhelm her with a desire to run away from all this, to be out running *free;* a desire so urgent that had she not already fought one set of pitched battles with the sword, she'd have probably spurred Verenna after Daren, overtaken, and passed him. Now she knew these spurious impulses for what they were, and she met them with a will tempered like steel, and a stubborn pride that refused to give in to a piece of metal, however enchanted. She had just enough time to toss Verenna's reins over her neck, ground-tying her, before the sword took over enough of her body that making Verenna bolt for the road was a possibility.

Then she sat, rigid and trembling, every muscle in her body warring with her will. It wasn't even going to be possible to get back to the Tower and get help from Kethry—assuming Kethry, having spent years under the blade's peculiar bondage, even *could* help. *Damn you,* she thought at the blade, as her body chilled; and Verenna shuddered, unable to understand what was wrong with her rider, but sensing something she didn't at all like. *Damn you, I know who and what I am, and what I want and even why I want it—and if a man I like isn't going to be able to pressure me into changing that, no chunk of metal is going to be able to either!*

Muscle by muscle, she won control of her body back. She closed her eyes, the better to be able to concentrate, and fought the thing, oblivious to everything around her.

Finally, candlemarks later, or so it seemed—though the sun hadn't moved enough for one candlemark, much less the eight or nine it *should* have taken for the fight—she sat stiffly in her saddle, the master of her own body again. She waited warily for the sword to try again, as her breath and Verenna's steamed in the cold—and she sensed that the sword *would* try again, unless she could devise some way of ending the struggle here and now.

She stripped off one glove and placed her half-frozen hand on the hilt. *Listen to me, you,* she thought at the blade, and sensed a kind of stillness, as if it was listening, however reluctantly. *Listen to me, and believe me. If you don't stop this nonsense and leave me alone, and let me make my own decisions, I'll drop you down the nearest well. I mean it. Having a blade that will protect me from magickers may be convenient, but damn if I'm going to lose control of my life in return!*

She sensed a dull, sudden heat, like far-off anger.

Look, you know what I've been thinking! I agree with your purpose, dammit! I'm even perfectly willing to go along with this agenda of helping women in trouble! But I am, by all that's holy, going to do so on my terms. And you're going to have one hell of a time helping women from the bottom of a well if you don't go along with this.

The anger vanished, replaced by surprise—and then, silence. She waited a moment longer, but the sword might as well have been a plain old steel blade at that point. Not that it felt lifeless—but she had a shrewd notion she'd made her point.

"Silence means assent," she said out loud, and put her glove back on. Then, bending over and retrieving the reins, much to Verenna's relief, she sent the mare back toward the Tower.

But the last thing she expected was to be met at the stable by Tarma.

The Shin'a'in took Verenna's reins from her once she'd dismounted, and led the mare toward her stall, all without saying a word. Kero waited, wondering what was coming next. A reproach for not taking Daren up on his offer? That hardly seemed likely. But Tarma's silence portended *something*.

Tarma tethered Verenna to the stall, but instead of unsaddling her at once, put a restraining hand over Kero's.

"I'd have said this within the next couple of months," she began, "But sending Daren back is just letting me say it sooner. You're ready, little hawk. Think you're up to losing the jesses?"

Kero blinked. "To go where?" she asked, after a moment of thought. "Knowing you, you have a plan for me."

Tarma nodded, her ice-blue eyes warming a little. "Experience is going to be a better teacher than I am, from here on," she said, "And I've been looking around for a place for you for the past couple of moons. As it happens, the son of a good friend of mine just took over a bonded Company. They're called the Skybolts; they're scout-skirmishers, like my old Company, the Sunhawks. Lerryn Twoblades is the Captain's name; he's got a reputation for honesty, fair dealing, and as much honor as anyone ever gives a merc credit for. He'll have you, and gladly, if you want to go straight to a Company."

"And if I don't?" Kero asked, curious to know just what her options were.

Tarma shrugged. "You could go out on your own, and I have some referrals for the Jewel Merchants Guild caravans, but your skills would be better used in a Company like the Skybolts. You could go home, if you really want. You could go after Daren, you're even dressed for *that*," she said wryly. "But it's time for you to go—before you stop wanting to."

Silence hung thick in the stable; even the horses sensed something was afoot, and weren't making their usual noise. Finally, Kero nodded. "I thought this would happen in the spring, but I'm ready—or as ready as I'll ever be. And I'll go to the Skybolts; I'd have to be a fool to turn down an offer like that."

Tarma relaxed, and smiled. "I try not to train fools," she replied. "And—Kero, you're of the Clan—I want you to take Hellsbane."

"What?" Kero asked, incredulously. "I can't do that!"

"Why not?" Tarma retorted. "You've been training with her all damned year; you're better with her than I am. Leave Keth your Verenna—a saddle horse isn't going to do you much good as a merc, anyway, you'll spend far too long getting her battle-trained. I'll still have Ironheart, Keth is never going to need a battlemare again, and to tell you the truth, she's always been a shade uneasy about riding them. She'll be just as happy with Verenna, and your girl will be a lot happier with us."

Warrl appeared like a shadow behind the Shin'a'in. :*She's right, you know. Hellsbane is warrior-trained, like you. It would be a shame for* her *potential to be wasted.*:

Kero shook her head, part in disbelief, part in amusement. "I can see I've been outvoted."

Tarma's hoarse voice roughened still further with emotion. "You're kin of my Clan. You're the closest thing I'll have to a daughter. You're my only true protégée. And you're the best damned warrior I've ever trained. I want you equipped with the very best." Then she smiled, and her voice and eyes lightened again. "Besides, after you see the rest of the gear Keth and I got you, Hellsbane is going to seem like an afterthought!"

Kero found it very hard to speak, or even swallow. "I don't know what to say—" she began.

Tarma pulled the saddle off Verenna, and led the relieved mare back into her stall. "You can start with 'thank you,' and we'll take it from there. Think you'd be ready to take the road by the end of the week?"

"I—" Kero faltered. "I—"

"If you are," Tarma continued, "Keth can start the

messages out to Twoblades, and we can start fitting your fancy new armor to you so you don't disgrace us when you get there.''

''I can be ready,'' she managed. ''As ready to leave as I'm likely to be. I wish—I wish I didn't have to leave. Or that I could take you with me. . . .''

Tarma snorted. ''Not likely. I *did* my share on the lines. Chick can't go back in the shell, and a young hawk can't unfledge. Time for you to try your wings.''

Time for me to see what it's like out there on my own. Time, maybe, to really live—

''And maybe fly,'' she said, thinking aloud.

''Oh, you'll fly, little hawk,'' Tarma answered. ''You'll fly.''

BOOK TWO

Two Edged Blade

Eleven

"Great Jaesel," Shallan said, her bright blue eyes widening in awe at the sight of what blocked the well-pounded trail, "What in hell is *that?*"

She must have unconsciously tightened her legs, because her high-strung gelding bucked, then bounced a little sideways, blundering into Hellsbane.

Trouble— Kero exerted immediate pressure on the reins, so the mare only laid her ears back, rather than reacting with the swift snap of teeth she would ordinarily have indulged in.

Shallan swore, made a fist and thumped her restive mount between *his* ears, and the fractious beast subsided. Once again the scouting party turned their collective attention toward the untidy sprawl of humanity across their path. "Sprawl" was definitely the operative term, Kero decided. There was a tangle of about twenty or thirty men, some standing, most in variations of "fallen," all interlaced with ten-foot (thankfully) headless pikes.

"Didn't the sergeant from Bornam's Bastards say something about recruiting from the area last night?" asked a male voice from right behind Kero. *Gies,* she identified automatically; of the twins, he had the deeper voice. "I think so," replied his identically-swarthy brother, Tre, and she knew she'd picked the right name for the right twin. "The sergeant wasn't real optimistic."

"I'd say he had reason not to be," Shallan replied, shaking her ice-blonde head in disgust. "And from the look of this, we'd better detour before they get themselves sorted out and stand up." A few more of the men got themselves untangled from the rest and stood aside. Their sergeant wasn't shouting—mostly because, from the

crimson color of his face, Kero reckoned that he was
holding off a fit of apoplexy by will alone.

"Aye to that," Kero said. She was nominally the head
of this group, but only during the actual scouting foray,
and they weren't in the field at the moment. "Let's take
the back way."

The four scouts turned their horses' heads and went
back the way they'd come in, following the pounded-dirt
track between hacked-off patches of scrubby brush. Behind them the sergeant finally regained his voice, and
began using it.

The four Companies Menmellith's Council had hired
for "bandit eradication" had bivouacked in a canyon, but
not a blind one; there were at least four ways into the
area that Kero knew of, and she had no doubt the twins
knew a couple more. The "back way," which was the
other, nominally traveled, route in, took them over some
rough ground, but their horses could handle it; they were
all Shin'a'in-bred.

A few furlongs along the scrub-lined dirt trail (which
steady commerce over the past few days had pounded
into the soil), the human track was bisected by a game
trail that led off through the weather-beaten bushes and
tired, stunted oaks. That "back way" was good for a
goat or a mountain-deer, but not terribly attractive to
humans afoot or humans with horses, which made it unlikely that they'd run into any more delays getting back
to camp.

In fact, the back way was so quiet there was still wild-
life living along it. Birds flew out of the trees as they
passed, and a covey of quail watched from beneath the
shelter of a thorn-bush. "Gods," Shallan said, thumping
her horse again as he shied at a rabbit bolting across their
path. "Gods. Green recruits. Thanks be to Saint Keshal
that Lerryn won't put green 'uns in the field."

"Could be worse," Tre observed. "Could be levied
troops from Menmellith and Rethwellan out here."

Shallan groaned, but Kero shook her head. "Menmellith, maybe, but not Rethwellan. Rethwellan won't even
officially be our hire. Officially, they've 'loaned' the
Council the cash to pay for us. Got that from a letter."
She didn't say from whom. Everyone in the Skybolts
knew about her friendship with Daren—and knew equally

well that she wouldn't trade on it. But she could, and would, pass along any information he happened to drop, whether by accident or design.

"Oh?" Shallan and the other two looked studiously indifferent, which told Kero they hadn't heard this particular tidbit of gossip. "Why's that?"

"Simple enough. *We* all know that Karse is funding these 'bandits'—assuming they aren't already part of the Karsite army. But outside of these Borders?" Kero shrugged. "Anyway, that's why it's us, and why Rethwellan's out of it. We're not official units of any army. Whatever we do, it can't cause a diplomatic incident. *And* if we happen to get carried away, and it turns out that the subsequent bodies *were* part of the Karsite army, well, Karse has violated the Code so many times that the Guild not only wouldn't fine the offenders, they *might* even be rewarded. Unofficially, of course."

"Of course," Tre agreed brightly. Kero looked back over her shoulder. The identical smiles on both twins' faces could only be described as "bloodthirsty."

Or maybe it was just greed. It wasn't too often that a bonded Company had free rein to loot, but that's exactly what the Menmellith Council—their putative employers—had given them. Not that Kero blamed them. Probably half of what was in the possession of the "bandits" had belonged to folk hereabouts first. If anybody got it, the locals would rather it was friends than enemies.

Rethwellan had granted Menmellith client-state status and semi-autonomy shortly after Daren had been born. *Supposedly* this was a kind of thanks-offering for the birth of a third son; in actuality, now that she'd seen the state with her own eyes, Kero suspected that the King had seized on the first available excuse to liberate his land from a considerable drain on the royal coffers. Menmellith was mostly mountain, hellishly hard to travel in, constantly raided by Karsite "bandits," and probably impossible to govern or tax effectively. *Now* it was governed by its own fractious, taciturn folk, served as a buffer between Karse and the lusher lands of Rethwellan, and the King need only hire the occasional merc Company to clean things out now and again, instead of being forced to keep a detachment of the army there on permanent duty.

"We're fairly useless at the moment, you know," Shallan said, as her horse picked its way daintily across a dry streambed that formed part of the trail. "They're just sending the scouting parties out to make sure everything's still where it's supposed to be."

"I know," Kero sighed. If there was one thing she'd learned with the Skybolts, it was that warfare consisted mostly of waiting. "I'm not even supposed to report to anyone unless we *do* see something odd. I suppose it wouldn't be so damned bad if we could see something going on, but the bastards are *not* coming out of that canyon."

"Can't say as I blame them," Gies said laconically. " 'F I'd got m'self trapped in a blind canyon, wouldn't be comin' out either. They c'n hold us off long as the food'n'water last, an' we just might get bored an' go away."

Shallan laughed; not a sound of amusement, it was a particularly ugly laugh. "Between them, the Wolflings and the Bastards are likely to make things real uncomfortable for them in there. Then when they pop out, *we'll* be waiting. And so will the Earthshakers."

Kero preferred not to think too much about that. It was going to cost the two Companies of foot quite a bit in blood to shake the "bandits" out of their lair. By contrast, the Company of heavy cavalry and the Skybolts' skirmishers had it easy, if dull.

But when the "bandits" did emerge, they'd be like any desperate and cornered creatures, and Shallan was likely to get a bellyful of fighting.

But it wouldn't profit anyone to say that out loud, so Kero held her peace, and kept her eyes on the uncertain trail. The last thing she needed to do would be to lame Hellsbane.

"Stand," Kero told Hellsbane. The gray stamped restlessly once more, but then obeyed with no other sign of rebellion. Kero tapped her right foreleg, and the warsteed lifted the massive hoof and set it in Kero's waiting hands.

She pulled the hoofpick out of her belt, and began cleaning the packed muck out of it with studious care. There was a lot of gravel around here, and Kero did not intend to find herself with a lamed horse because of a moment's carelessness. Shallan had already lost the use of her remount that way.

"I could really get to hate Menmellith," she told Hellsbane conversationally. The gray flicked her ears back with every evidence of intelligent interest. "I can see why Jad let them hare off and become a client-state. There's nothing here but sheep, rocks, and bone-headed shepherds. Certainly nothing worth keeping. Why Karse keeps trying to invade them, I'll never know." She thought for a moment, then added, "Unless it's just one more example of how crazy the Karsites are."

She finished with the right forehoof, and moved back to the hind. "*Stand,*" she repeated, with a little more force this time, as some noise from the next camp over made Hellsbane roll her eyes and fidget. She straightened long enough to see what all the fuss was.

A small forest of poles was marching straight for the picket lines, and horses up and down the line were starting to stamp and look nervous.

Blessed Agnira—pikemen again? That's Joffrey's Wolflings! What fool sent pikemen to drill next to picketed horses? Don't they know how much battle-trained horses hate pikes? They're going to have the whole line spooked in a minute! She was just about to head them off, by intercepting them and launching into a powerful flood of abuse, when someone beat her to it.

" '*Alt,* damn yer 'ides! I said *right* march, not bleedin' left!''

The line came to an abrupt and picture-perfect halt. The Wolfling's pike-sergeant strode around the back of the (now stationary) formation, face red as a sunset, veins bulging out on his forehead. "Jecrena's bleedin' *arse,*" he bellowed, "ye'd think ye was a lot o' plowboys, not perfeshnal *so*jers!" From there his tirade went into extreme sexual and scatological detail as to the habits and probable ancestry of his charges. Kero leaned against Hellsbane's rump, listening in astonished admiration. His language was colorful, original, and quite entertaining. She'd been with the Skybolts for quite a few years now, and had never quite heard anything like it.

I should be taking notes, she thought, watching the sergeant get his men turned back in the right direction.

The horses were definitely calming down, now that the pikes were going the *other* way. *You never hear anything like that around our camp.*

But that was at least in part because horseback skirmishers didn't drill the way pike and line swordsmen did. No sergeants, for one thing.

Kero went back to Hellsbane's hooves, glad to have thought of *something* to do. *"There's a lot of waiting involved in warfare,"* Tarma had said many times over. Kero had never quite believed her at the time.

She did now.

Well, it could be worse, she consoled herself. *We could have Rethwellan regulars with us. Then every merc in the Companies would be getting the long-nosed look when he dared poke his head out of camp. What in hell is it that makes every conscript farmboy who can't tell his brain from his backside and wouldn't know what three quarters of the Code meant think he's morally superior to a merc?*

She sighed; the question wasn't worth losing sleep over. Every merc ever born was a misfit; that's why most of them wound up as mercs in the first place. *Lady knows I'm no exception*, she thought glumly. *Last time I went home, Dierna acted like I was going to eat the baby, and Lordan carried on as if he thought I was planning on stealing the boys, the horses, the sheep, or all three.* Each time she visited, she was more of a stranger, and after the last time, she'd just about made up her mind never to go back again.

My only real friends are here, anyway, she reflected, picking at a bit of gravel lodged in Hellsbane's left hind hoof. The warsteed switched her bound-up tail restlessly, but didn't object. Kero had remarked once that Hellsbane's behavior was a lot more like a dog's than a horse's, and Tarma had only smiled and replied cryptically, "Why do you think we won't let them breed to anything but their own kind?" After that, Kero had taken extra care when spring came around and Hellsbane went into season.

Then she discovered that such care was entirely unneeded. The warsteed was perfectly capable of fending off unwanted advances, and she evidently hadn't yet found the stallion that measured up to her own high standards.

Hooves clean, Kero loitered on the lines, replaiting the gray's tail, and watching the Wolflings drill. Those long pikes were a lot harder to manage than anyone but a fighter could imagine. All in all, it made her grateful to be with the Skybolts.

Twoblades' Company actually began as what Idra's Sunhawks came to be; an entirely mounted force of specialists. In every one of the campaigns Kero had served in up until now they'd been constantly busy; their greatest asset was that they were *versatile* as well as highly mobile. Every one of the Skybolts could double as a scout, and when they weren't on the battlefield, they could ride messenger detail. Not this time, or at least, not now.

There were constant scouting forays, of course, just to make sure that the enemy hadn't found a way out of the trap, but that was the only thing like work going on for the Skybolts. That unwonted leisure was beginning to have an effect on the Company. *Which is why I'm out here, and not in camp.* In general, there were only three pursuits available to a merc when forced into idleness: gambling, drinking, and sex. Kero was too shrewd to be lured into the first, too cautious for the second, and as for the third—

I'm an odd fish in a pond full of odd fish, she thought, a little sadly. *Between the sword and this so-called Gift of mine. . . .*

The Gift was the main reason she didn't drink; when she did, her carefully-wrought shields came down, and the guard came off her tongue. Only *once* had she let that happen; she'd frightened a tavern full of hard-bitten soldiers into sobriety with the things she'd said about them. Only some fancy verbal footwork the next day enabled her to convince them that they'd misheard most of it, and luck had given her the rest. So she didn't drink at all now; at least, not to get drunk and not in company, which set her apart from most of the rest of the Company.

She was terrified of what would happen if they ever *did* find out the truth. *Mercs have too many secrets to appreciate anyone, even someone they trust, to be rummaging around in their minds. Every one of us was driven into this life by something, and most of us don't want anyone else to know what that is. Even me. If anyone*

*ever found out about this "Gift" of mine, I don't know
what I'd do.*

The sword now—that set her apart in another way. She
was Kethry's granddaughter—that was no secret—and by
now everyone seemed to have heard the song of "Kerowyn's Ride." It would have been impossible to hide the
fact that she still had the blade; she wore it all the time,
and wouldn't take it off (so common gossip had it) if she
went to bed with someone. Well, that wasn't quite true—
but she'd learned that being too far away from it could
be torture.

There'd been a really bad rainy season a couple of years
ago; they'd had to cross a flood-swollen river, and Kero's
packhorse had gone under. That was before she'd taken
to wearing the blade all the time; she'd thought for the
crossing that it was safer strapped to the packs. She'd
just barely made it onto the riverbank when the pain of
the overstrained soul-bond started. The Company Healer
had thought it some sort of curse, until she'd gasped out
an explanation of just *what* it was she'd lost—between
spasms of blinding agony that left her helpless even to
speak. The entire Company had gone out into the storm
to look for the damned thing and bring it back.

They'd found it, before sunset—but that put her in a
position of debt she was determined to repay. After a lot
of careful thought and consultation with the Company
hedge-wizard she'd found a way; she'd coaxed the blade
(with much emphasis on how many females were in the
Skybolts) into extending its anti-magic protection to in-
clude a fair amount of ground in her immediate vicinity.
Actually, *her* protections covered more area than the
Company mages could, which made her rather popular
when the mage-bolts began to fly.

Thinking about that, she patted the hilt of the sword
the way she patted Hellsbane's neck. *Now that I've got
you cooperating, my lady, you're even more useful than
you were to Kethry. I've heard more than one Skybolt say
he'd sooner trust your abilities than that hedge-wizard of
ours.*

For a moment, at the back of her mind, she seemed to
hear a kind of sleepy murmur of pleasure; but it was too
faint for her to be certain. She'd never yet figured out
how much—or how little—intelligence the sword had. Or

how much it understood or even heard of what she said to it. These occasional little whispers, like the vague mutterings of a sleep-talker, were the closest she ever got to communication.

Many of the Skybolts were a little fearful of the blade, as well as respectful of it and its powers. So that set her apart as well.

Then there was the problem of sex. . . .

Not within the Company. There's too much potential for trouble, and I have to live with these people.

There *were* pairings within the Company, and some of them worked very well. But some of them didn't, and when that happened, it spilled over onto everyone else. *And in the middle of a campaign that could get people killed.*

Tarma had warned her about that, too, and she'd been right. *"You don't sleep around in the Company,"* she'd said. *"They're your family, and you don't bed your brothers. Or sisters,"* she'd added as an afterthought.

Wise advice. But it made Kero very much a loner—and in a case like this, bivouacked leagues away from civilization, it also didn't leave her very much to do.

All my jewelry-carving equipment is back at the winter quarters; I never thought I'd need it now. I suppose I could go find the Healer and get her to teach me how to knit those ankle-braces, she thought, combing her fingers through Hellsbane's coat. *Or I could roach the mare's mane. Or I could poultice the stone-bruise on Shallan's remount. Or I could find some flat river pebbles and draw up another set of hound-and-stag stones for someone. Come to think of it, Shallan wanted a set.*

As if the thought had summoned her, Shallan strolled up to the picket line, currycombs in hand, hoof-pick in her belt, short, white-blonde hair gleaming like a cap of silver-gilt in the sun.

"What's the word?" Kero asked her. "Anything new on the grapevine?"

"Word is that we're supposed to take prisoners," she replied, tossing one of the currycombs to Kero. "Word is there's some pretty good circumstantial evidence that these whoresons really *are* Karsite regulars, but nothing direct. Lerryn wants to prove it, and the rest of the Captains are in agreement."

"So we take prisoners?" Kero asked. "Which means afterward, we make somebody talk."

"Contract says they're bandits," Shallan pointed out with bloodthirsty glee. "*Karse* says they're bandits. Bandits don't fall under the Code. Which means when we've got 'em, we make 'em talk. However."

"And if it turns out they're Karsite regulars?" Kero persisted.

Shallan shrugged fluidly, the leather of her tight black tunic moving with her shoulders. "Five years ago, 'bandits' murdered just about every man in Feldar's Teeth *after* they'd surrendered. Three years ago a half-dozen men from the Doomslayers—actually prisoners of war, and waiting for Guild ransom—were tortured by Karsite priests. And what was ransomed later was a clutch of completely mindless husks. Two years ago, more of these 'bandits' overran the Hooters' winter quarters and killed the civilians—while the Hooters themselves were out putting down a rebellion in Ruvan, and weren't even *near* Karse." Shallan's voice betrayed the tense anger her face and posture wouldn't reveal. "Each time, the Guild levied a *big* fine. Each time Karse just *paid* it. No denial, not even a comment—they just *paid* it."

Kero frowned, dusting her hands off on her mud-brown leather breeches. "That's odd."

"Odd? Great gods, it's a slap in our face! It's like they're saying we're so lowly, such vermin, that they *want* everyone to know what they did." She dropped her voice, so that Kero had to lean closer to hear. "Look, Kero, I know I'm a year younger than you are, but I've been in the business since I was fourteen. My mama was a Sunhawk. I've seen a hell of a lot, most of it not real pretty by civilian standards, and most of it doesn't bother me any more. This is my *job*, you understand? And I don't get worked up about things that go on in it—but I'll tell you right now, for what I've seen the Karsites do to my friends and *their* friends, well, I'd kill 'em for free and dance on the graves after."

Kero knew Shallan was tough, for all that Shallan was a head shorter than she was, and looked frail enough for a wind to blow away. That fragility was entirely false; Shallan was as tough as the black leather she wore, and as impervious to damage, and in all the time she'd been with the Skybolts, Kero had never seen Shallan frightened.

But she was frightened now, afraid of the Karsites, and all her brave words about "killing them for free and dancing on the graves" couldn't hide that.

For a heartbeat or two, Kero felt trapped by the blue intensity of Shallan's eyes. Then she broke free of that hypnotic gaze, aided by Hellsbane's restive stamping. Shallan could do that, now and again; but only when she felt so strongly about something that it was worth living or dying to her.

"I don't know about taking prisoners," she said quietly, turning away and going back to work on the gray's dusty hide. "The more I hear about the Karsites, the less I want to do with them. Almost seems like if you acted like they do, you'd be in danger of becoming like them. But if Lerryn wants prisoners—well, that's an order, isn't it?"

"Aye, that," Shallan agreed. Kero did not like the tone of her voice.

Dear gods, she sounds like she'd be perfectly happy to volunteer for the crew who're going to be "persuading" these prisoners to talk—assuming we catch any. And now that I think about it, she's not the only one to sound that way about these so-called bandits, or the Karsites in general.

She felt a little sick. For all that they were the enemy, for all the atrocities *they* had meted out, she couldn't picture herself handing the same treatment back to them. Kill them, yes, but cleanly. She couldn't agree with Shallan's attitude. *They're so damned vindictive about this, all of them. But maybe I'm the one who's out of line, here. Shallan's lover lost a sister in some fight or other— there're others in the Skybolts that lost friends and family along through here, over the past five years or so. Maybe it's me. Maybe I just don't feel that angry at them because I just can't seem to get really attached to anyone, not even my own blood-kin.*

She leaned into the strokes of the currycomb, and thought back to the incidents that had started her on this whole career, trying to recapture exactly how she felt when she saw her brother wounded, her father dead.

Just—responsibility. That's all I really felt that I can

remember. That someone had to take care of the mess, and I was the only one possible. Dear gods, what's wrong with me? Why am I so cold?

Maybe it's just that I've never really had anyone get close enough that I could honestly say I loved him, except Mother.

But that didn't seem natural either. Other people seemed to be falling in and out of love all the time, but for her, nothing ever seemed to get involved but her body, and sometimes, her mind.

The first lover is supposed to be such a big thing—but with Daren there didn't really seem to be more at stake than friendship and—well—the desires of the moment.

She cast a glance over at Shallan when she thought the other woman wouldn't notice. Her companion could—and did—wax passionate about causes and people at the drop of a gauntlet. This got her into trouble more often than not, but Shallan had no intention of changing, maintaining that it was better to live life hard and completely.

Kero was just the opposite; after those flare-ups with Daren she had never again actually fought with anyone. She saved her anger and her energy for the battlefield; off the field, she thought everything through, planned for every possible contingency, then went coldly and self-reliantly straight for her goal.

Sometimes I go after what I want with such single-mindedness that I frighten myself, she thought, watching Shallan grooming her horse as if by brushing out every speck of dirt she could wipe the Karsites from the face of the earth. *I'd hate to see what the others think of me.*

Uncomfortable thoughts, and not likely to improve her disposition. She was glad to have them interrupted by a shout from the direction of camp.

She looked up over Hellsbane's shoulder, as Tre waved, his dull scarlet shirt identifying him even at a distance. He'd never yet worn the thing out on scout, but he inevitably changed back into it as soon as they hit camp. "Kero! Shal! Back to camp on the double! Meeting!"

She waved back to show that they'd heard, and tossed the currycomb to Shallan. The younger woman caught it deftly, and the two of them ducked under the picket line and trotted toward the mess tent.

"I wonder what it's about?" Shallan said, trotting

along with an ease that reminded Kero of Warrl's lazy lope. Her eyes glinted with an eagerness that Kero thought held just a hint of battle madness. "Maybe they've decided to put on a push so we can get this over with!"

At that point, they reached the edge of the growing crowd, so Kero was saved from having to make a reply. Most of the Skybolts had already gathered at the mess tent when they arrived. They worked their way around to the side; as leader of a scout party, Kero had just enough rank to get in fairly close to their Captain.

Lerryn Twoblades did not look like much of a fighter. He wore the same scuffed leathers as any of his Company; his only concession to rank was a round pin of carved silver Kero had made him, showing two crossed swords bisected by a lightning bolt. Thin and not particularly tall, and just now at rest, he wasn't very imposing, either. But when he rose to speak, it was immediately apparent that he was whipcord and steel over bone, and moved with a lazy grace that spoke volumes to anyone who had studied hand-to-hand combat. Those limpid brown eyes missed nothing; those foppish curls covered a skull with frightening intelligence inside it. There wasn't one single horse in the entire camp he couldn't handle, up to and including Hellsbane, which had surprised the hell out of both Kero *and* her horse. And all he had to do was say three words, and it was no secret why the Skybolts were fanatically devoted to their Captain.

He scanned the crowd slowly to let the muttering die away. Only when he had relative silence did *he* speak, in a calm, but carrying voice. "We've voted, and we've decided to make a push," he said. "Otherwise we let these whoresons force us to piss away our troops against them, while there may be groups out there we *haven't* bottled up taking pieces out of the Border."

There was the start of a cheer—when he raised his hand for silence. He got it, too—something that never failed to impress Kero.

"The Skybolts won't be fighting," he said firmly, "and I'm not taking any volunteers to go on temp to the other Companies. And *that's* an order."

Agnira—there're going to be some objections to that,

and for sure— And there were; a storm of them. People began shouting and waving their hands to get his attention, for all the world like a crowd of unruly children. Lerryn simply let the hotheads have their say, then held up his hand again.

"It's not *our* kind of fight," he told them, his eyes moving from face to face so that in the end, every one of them would have been willing to swear that the Captain talked to him, directly. "We aren't trained, any of us, in the kind of line fighting there's going to be. Most of us are runty little bastards," he continued, with a rueful grin that included himself with them. "We couldn't take on a big man in a shoulder-to-shoulder situation, not when we've built careers and training on speed and agility. We couldn't use our short-swords or horse-bows, and those little round target shields would be damned useless against maces and axes. We can't do any damn good with unfamiliar weapons, afoot, against heavy infantry. And if you all really think about that, and are honest, you'll agree with me."

There was more muttering, and some vehement head-shaking, but not much. Lerryn's words made sense even to the most belligerent among them.

The Captain spread his hands in a gesture that said wordlessly, *Look, I don't like this any more than you do, but we all know the facts when we see them.* "We've done our job," he said. "No one can fault us—we're the ones who tracked them, and we're the ones who harried them and trapped them here in the first place. It's time for the others to do *their* job, and now we have to get out of the way so they can do it without interference. Hmm?" He tilted his head slightly to one side; there was more muttering—Shallan, predictably, was one of the mutterers—but it quickly died away.

"Don't think we're getting off easy," he said, "I'm deploying half of you as outriders to make sure nobody gets away. If there's a breakout, you'll be fighting—and you outriders are as important as the front liners. More. That's the place where we'll have a good shot at taking prisoners. We don't want anyone to escape to take word back to—wherever."

Tactfully not saying what everyone is thinking. Kero's lip twitched. *We can say it, but because he's Captain, he can't. Not till it's proved. That "wherever" is Karse, and if they get back with word of this, the Karsites may send a bigger force before we're ready for it.*

Lerryn looked them all over once again, the breeze blowing his long hair back from his face. "The rest of you, get the camp packed up and ready to move on the instant. Pack up your friends, if they're out on patrol. Once the siege is broken, we'll be moving as fast as we can, back to a secured zone."

Again, not saying what he can't—but he expects there to be prisoners, and I'll bet my next bonus he's been told we'll have custody of them. We're the fastest, and if we can get the prisoners to a secure lockup, we can have them singing like woodlarks before the Karsites even know we have them. I'd bet on Abevell for that secure lockup. Town's practically carved into the side of the mountain.

Lerryn waited for any further comment, but the Skybolts knew their leader, and that his decisions were final. Later, when they were all behind friendly walls, they'd find out *why* those decisions had been made. Until then, they were willing to take it on faith that there were reasons.

"Dismissed," he said, and singled out a dozen scout-leaders with a pointed finger before they all dispersed. Those chosen followed him back to his tent. The rest milled restlessly for a moment, then drifted back toward the camp in twos and threes to begin the breakdown.

Kero was not among the select, but she hadn't expected she'd be; after all, her group had already *been* out this morning, and Lerryn wasn't the kind of Captain to impose double duty on someone without a compelling reason. She was relieved, both that the Skybolts were not going to be involved in the fight, and that she wasn't going to be part of the harriers.

It's too much, she decided, making noncommittal answers to Shallan as they walked through the orderly rows of tents to their own. *Running people down on horseback, like I was hunting rabbits—hellfires, I don't even hunt rabbits on horseback! I'm just glad I don't have to be part of that. I think maybe the Captain figured that out, too. He gave me that kind of look. I don't think he likes it either.*

Shallan's tent was the closest, and the blonde dove into

it with another moan of complaint. "—and just my luck, Relli's with Hagen, which means *she'll* be in on it and I'll have to pack her stuff up!"

Sure enough, the tent was empty, and Shallan threw herself at her lover's belongings with grim determination. Kero took herself off before she could be coerced into helping. Relli was something of a clotheshorse, and Kero did not want to take responsibility for the least little crease that "ruined" a tunic.

Her own tent was the same size as Shallan's but seemed larger, since she had it to herself. Technically these were four-man tents, but only if you stacked everyone together like logs, and no one had more than a single backpack of possessions. Two fit fine; one was perfect, so far as Kero was concerned. Lerryn didn't care about sleeping arrangements so long as everyone was under canvas and *someone* took responsibility for the tent itself. If they took on anyone without his own shelter and they ran out of Company tents, Kero might be ordered to share, but until then, she had her privacy.

She was glad of it, as she packed her belongings down with practiced ease, and began rolling her bedding. The trapped bandits were going to be massacred. She knew how completely logical that was. And she didn't like it. If she'd had a tentmate, she'd have had to talk about it, and she didn't want to. *The sooner I can shake the dust of this place from Hellsbane's hooves, the better I'm—*

Suddenly she heard something on the edge of the camp. Confused shouting, too far away to make out words, but there was no mistaking the tone. There was something wrong, desperately wrong.

For only the second time since she'd joined the Sky-bolts, she dropped her mental shields and searched for a coherent picture among the jangle of thoughts—looking for the person who *knew* what was going on.

Lerryn.

She found him, on the picket line, directing incoming scouts who were galloping up to the line in panic, while the Company hedge-wizard sent up the emergency "come in" signal beside him.

The thoughts in his mind were clear and organized, as cool and unpanicked as her own would be if she were in his place. Though what she read there would have sent anyone else into the kind of panic the rest of the camps were showing.

For all the guesses had been right—these were no "bandits" the Companies had pinned, these were Karsite regulars. But somehow, some way, they had gotten word of their position across the Border, and Karse had sent out a real army to close in behind and catch the Companies in a pincer maneuver. The odds, depending on who Lerryn talked to, were either two or three to one, in the Karsite favor.

Kero pulled out of Lerryn's mind as invisibly as she had insinuated herself in, glad now that she had not given in to temptation and had brought only what Hellsbane could comfortably carry. The tent would have to be abandoned, of course. There was no percentage in standing and fighting, and there was only one way of dealing with this trap before they were all caught in it.

Run.

Each Captain cared only for his own at this point— which was the biggest weakness of a force comprised of mercs. Kero could not help but pity the heavy infantry, the Wolflings—they had no one to cover for them and harry their pursuers. She had no idea how *they* would get away.

On the other hand, she thought, with a twinge of guilt at her selfishness, *I don't want to be the one covering their rear, either.*

She flung herself out of her tent with all of those things of her worldly goods that she needed to survive on her back and in her two hands; no more, with the addition of a ration pack for herself and her horse, than Hellsbane could carry and still run. Everything else she left without a second thought.

Not everyone was so pragmatic; she and Shallan had to physically tear Relli away from her wardrobe and drag her toward the picket lines. The Wolflings, in the next camp over, were already on their way out, pouring over the "back way," as fast as their feet could march. The Skybolts of all the Companies were the likeliest to survive intact; with each of them mounted on light, agile horses, and with so much broken ground available to hide them. That is, the *Company* would survive; as always, the survival of an individual was problematical.

Shallan and Relli were nearly the last to arrive; Relli took one look at Lerryn's grim expression, and shut her mouth on the last of her laments. Without another word, the trio accepted their ration sacks from the quartermaster, tied their packs behind their saddles, and mounted up.

Lerryn waited until the last straggler joined them, before mounting his own beast—a rawboned roan a full hand taller than anyone else's beast—that was renowned for being able to lose any rider but Lerryn within ten heartbeats of mounting.

"We're in trouble, people," he said without preamble. "The Karsites have the main road blocked, the back way is full of foot troops, and the other four tracks in have watchers on them. We stayed till last to give the foot a head start and let our own scouts get in. Now it looks like we're stuck. Suggestions?"

"East, for Karse," Gies said. "They won't be expecting that. And we found a game trail over the top of the cliff at the northeast end of the valley. We never bothered using it, 'cause it's a bitch to get up."

"We'll take it," Lerryn said instantly. "Gies."

The scout took the lead, the rest fell in behind him in a loose formation, as the last of the Wolflings vanished over the game trails. Kero wished luck on their departing backs.

They were all going to need it.

Twelve

There had been watchers on that game trail; not as many as on the other ways out, but enough. Gies thought he had all of them tagged, and Lerryn sent Skybolts out to take care of them—but either Gies had missed one, or someone slipped up. One of the watchers had gotten away from their counter-ambush.

No one knew until they'd gotten out of the valley and were headed toward one of the roads that would bring them back to safety. That was when they discovered that the Karsites had mounted skirmishers, too. With more bows, and faster horses, and—most telling of all—more men.

The escape had turned into a rout; fighting, then running, then fighting again. Somehow they all managed to stay together; desperation gave them speed and cunning they didn't know they had. They managed to leave their attackers behind in confusion, giving them just enough lead to get reorganized.

They headed north at top speed, taking advantage of a stream to break their trail, at least temporarily. At sunset, Lerryn had split the force, taking half of them with him, leaving half with his second in command. Shallan and Relli had gone off with the Captain; Kero had stayed with Icolan Ar Perdin, the second, a dour little man who had survived more routs than Kero cared to think about. The half with Lerryn had ridden south; Icolan took his group northward again, and a little east.

They hoped to confuse their pursuers enough to give both halves time to get to safety. But bad luck followed Icolan's troops, for the Karsites made up their minds quickly on discovering the split trail, and chose their half as the ones to follow.

Bad luck, or a curse, Kero thought, as she guided

Hellsbane afoot through the darkness, stumbling now and again over a root or a rock. Some of the others were already muttering things to that effect, for it seemed uncanny, the way the Karsites had been able to find them after the split. No matter what they did, how carefully they covered their trail, if they stopped to rest even for a moment, a scout sent along the backtrail would return with the unwelcome news that they were still being followed.

She held her mare's rein loosely; Hellsbane's ears and nose were infinitely superior to hers, and Hellsbane had twice been able to detect followers before Kero had.

Unless I unshielded, and looked for them with my thoughts. No—I'm afraid to. What if they've got someone stronger than me with them?

Warrl had warned her about the dangers of meeting someone unfriendly, with a far more powerful Gift. Such a one could take Kero over, hearing with her ears, seeing with her eyes.

For everyone's sakes, I can't take the chance, she decided. *As long as I don't crack my shields, I'm safe. If I do—I could be risking more than myself. I could betray the entire group.*

That was something she would not chance, however tempting it was to use that ability of hers to check on their pursuers.

Hellsbane's natural sensitivities of ear and nose were why *they* were tailmost, ready to call an alert in case the Karsites found them yet again.

It might have been a curse following them; it might also have been the workings of Sunlord Vkandis, the Karsite god. Kero was pretty certain that she had seen priestly sorts among those "bandits" but hadn't had any hard evidence although she'd reported her suspicion. Lerryn had just shrugged; he'd never had any dealings with a deity or demi-deity, friendly or otherwise, and so was inclined to doubt the power of clerics. But Kero had a feeling that it had been the priests of the Sunlord that had gotten word back to Karse of the siege, and not by physical messengers, either. As Kero had every reason to know, there were other means of communication besides physical messengers.

They were practically on the Karsite Border, and Kero

had heard from Tarma the kind of proprietary interest a deity could have for Her people—and the ways in which She could, if She chose, intervene—down on the Dhorisha Plains. If the Sunlord chose to enlighten His priests as to the location of their avowed enemies—well, it certainly wouldn't be unheard of.

Or there was another, more arcane, explanation. The religion of the Sunlord forbade the use of magic. But the ability to work magic was both an inborn Gift as well as the result of study. So where did all the mages born in Karse go?

Kero had *her* suspicions, and had ever since she found out about the prohibition. The mages born with the Gift went into the priesthood, of course; the priests of the Sunlord could easily say their magics were god-granted miracles, and no one would be any the wiser.

That could be the other reason for being pursued; they could have a mage on their trail—and since the hedge-wizard Tarres had gone with Lerryn's half of the Skybolts, it didn't take much guessing to figure which half would be followed. The half without the mage attached would be much easier for another mage to track, especially since Tarres was undoubtedly working his earth-magics to hide the mercs from mage-sight. Kero had tried to communicate with her sword to get the damned thing to cover their trail magically, but it had been as unresponsive as an ordinary piece of steel.

The trail ahead opened up into a clearing; suddenly there were stars overhead instead of interlacing tree branches. Kero picked out the sounds of many horses and a few whispers, and deduced that Icolan had decided to halt them.

"What's up?" she whispered, as soon as she came within range of the closest shadow-shape.

"Conference," the shape whispered back, one hand on its horse's nose to keep it silent. Not a halt for rest, then. That was a disappointment, but hardly a surprise. Kero turned Hellsbane around and pointed *her* head along the backtrail, making use of the mare's superior senses to keep watch for the rest of the party. "Guard," she said into the gray's ear, and slipped the rein over her arm, leaving Hellsbane relatively free. While the mare guarded the trail with ears and nose, Kero slipped her water bottle off the front of the saddle and took a long-wished-for drink. Her stomach was too knotted with fear and tension to even think about eating, but some of the others had taken advantage of the brief rest to snatch a mouthful or feed a handful of grain to a horse.

Finally the word went around the circle; ''There's a fork in the game trail. We're splitting again.''

Kero sighed; it was a logical move, but not one she relished. And it meant they'd be moving on into the night. She patted Hellsbane's neck comfortingly; the mare wasn't going to like this either.

They split twice more during the grueling, half-blind trek through the darkness, and when dawn trickled pale pink light over the hilltops and through the thick trees, there were no more than twenty riders left in Kero's group. She didn't know any of them terribly well, except for the leader, the head of all the scout-groups, a colorless woman known only as Lyr.

She mounted with the rest at Lyr's signal, and they formed a group around her. ''I know you're all tired,'' the scout-leader said in a flat voice, ''But we still have at least one party on our tail. I'm going to try something; back there in the dark they may have lost track of who was following what, and if you're with me on this, I want to head straight across the Border into Karse itself.''

The hard-bitten man in worn leathers on Kero's right coughed as if he was holding back an exclamation or objection. Lyr turned her expressionless eyes on him for a moment.

''I know what you're thinking, Tobe,'' she said, with no sign of rancor. ''You're thinking I'm crazy. Can't say I blame you. Here's my thought: if we head straight across the Border, open like, and stop trying to hide the backtrail, they *may* think they've gotten confused in the dark and they're following one of their own groups. Border won't be patrolled that thickly here; they save the heavy patrols for farther in.''

''They do?'' said a stocky girl that had just joined before the beginning of this campaign, a brown-haired, brown-eyed, brown-skinned girl with ''farmer'' all over her. But she had to be good, or she wouldn't be a Skybolt. ''Why?''

"Bandits," Lyr said succinctly. "Real ones. Karsites let 'em stay here, both to confuse the issue when their regulars come across raiding, and to discourage their own people from trying to cross over into someplace else. So there's a kind of buffer zone along here that the Karsite patrols don't bother with."

The girl nodded, her lips tightening a little. "Which means that's something we'll have to look out for, too."

Lyr shrugged. "It's them, or the real Karsites behind us. Bandits would only kill us if we lost."

"A good point," the girl replied bleakly, and from her tone, Kero guessed that this was yet another Skybolt who had personal experience of the Karsites.

"Sounds like a good plan to me," Kero said quietly when Lyr looked to her, and she saw several others nodding, including the brown girl.

"Then let's go for it." Lyr turned her horse around, and sent the beast trotting east, toward the Border. During the night, they had gone from dry, scrub-covered hills to lusher lands, thickly covered with the kind of trees Kero felt justified in calling a "tree." The hills were taller, too, and although they were also rockier and more precipitous, the soil seemed richer here. If this was the kind of territory Karse was trying to claim, Kero could understand their reasoning, although she obviously couldn't agree with it. Within a few furlongs, the game trail came out above a *real* trail, one with the signs of shod hoofprints on it. Instead of avoiding the trail, as they had been, Lyr led them right down onto it, and they rode along single file as if they belonged here. Kero, who was riding tail again, had to keep reminding herself *not* to turn and look behind. It felt as if there were eyes and arrows trained on her back the moment they broke out of cover, even though she *knew* their followers couldn't possibly have gotten within line-of-sight yet.

Only the presence of birds and an occasional rabbit or squirrel along the trail gave her any feeling of real comfort. If there had been someone ahead of them, there wouldn't *be* any birds to startle up as they were doing. If there was someone following them off the trail, the birds would be similarly disturbed—and the only birds on the wing Kero saw were those who were going about normal business, not those whose straight-line flights showed them to be frightened into taking wing.

She saw Lyr watching the birds, too, and coming to the same conclusions, for the scout leader's shoulders relaxed marginally.

Gradually, as the morning lengthened, and the sun rose above the trees, she lost that feeling of having watchers behind her. Lyr stopped the group from time to time—but she didn't send one of the others back to look for pursuers as Kero had expected she would; she went herself. The first two times she returned with the faintest of frowns, but the third, just before noon, she returned with just as faint a smile.

She let them all stop when their path intersected with a clear, cold river, which horses and riders were equally grateful for. She didn't say anything, but everyone knew; they were no longer being followed, and it was safe to rest for a little, eat, and rest and water the horses.

Watering the horses came first for all of them. At the beginning of their flight, quite a few of the Skybolts had remounts with them—very few horses had the stamina of Hellsbane, and most scouts had two or even three extras. Now those remounts were gone, lost in the fighting, and after a steady night of riding, the beasts were weary. Not lathered, but worn, without any reserves. When Lyr finished watering her horse, unsaddled and quietly tethered it and spread some grain for it to eat, the rest of the group sighed with relief and followed her example. Their horses were their life—and it had worried all of them to have to treat them this way.

"Who wasn't out yesterday?" Lyr asked, and got four hands in reply. "All right," she said. "You four are first guard. Wake four more about mid-afternoon—who're my volunteers?" Kero was about to raise her hand, but someone else beat her to it. So instead, she tethered Hellsbane, munched a handful of dried fruit, and laid herself down on what looked like bracken with her bed-roll for a pillow, pausing only long enough to loosen the straps of her armor a little. She was asleep as soon as she'd wriggled into a marginally comfortable position.

It seemed as if she'd just closed her eyes, but when she woke to a hand shaking her right shoulder—right was for "safe" waking, left for when you wanted someone to wake up quickly and quietly because of a bad situation—she sat up and rubbed her eyes without a grumble. Her waker was Tobe, and he smiled sympathetically as she blinked at him. However short a time it had seemed, the sun *was* a lot farther west than it had been when she'd dropped off to sleep, and there was no doubt she'd gotten the full amount of rest promised.

Satisfied that she was awake, Tobe moved on to the next fallen body. Kero levered herself up out of the bracken, wincing a little at bruises and rubbed places, and glad she was still too young to suffer from joint-ache from sleeping on the ground. *And gods be thanked for keeping me in one piece through all this—may you continue to do so!* She walked stiffly to streamside, up current of where the horses were, and knelt down on a wide, flat stone on the bank. Tobe joined her as she gathered a double-handful of cold water and splashed it over her face. It felt wonderful, especially on her gritty eyes.

"Fill your water skin," he advised. "Lyr says we're right off our maps, and she has no idea when we'll hit water next."

Kero nodded, and splashed her face again, wishing she dared bathe. Going dirty could be dangerous as well as unpleasant; if the enemy used dogs or pigs as guards, or if their horses were trained (as was Hellsbane) to go alert at an unfamiliar scent, you were a fool not to bathe as often as you could.

But there was no hope for it; there was no time. She compromised by taking just long enough to strip off her armor and change the tunic and shirt underneath; Lyr and several of the others were already doing the same, so it was safe to assume she wouldn't take Kero's head off for causing an unnecessary delay. Dirty shirt and tunic were rolled as small as possible and went into the bottom of the pack.

Food and drink came next; Hellsbane got her full ration of grain first, plus Kero pulled a good armful of grass for her, then Kero dug out a handful of dried meat and another of dried fruit. She resaddled Hellsbane while both of them were eating, promising the mare a good grooming as soon as possible. A kettle was making the rounds; when she accepted it from the brown girl, it proved to be half full of some kind of herb tea. Kero raised an eyebrow at her, but the girl shrugged; so Kero dipped the tin cup in it and drank it down.

It was *feka*-tea; double-strength and unsweetened, it was bitter as death and a powerful stimulant. Some of the scouts used it on long patrols; Lyr must have found someone with a supply—assuming she didn't have any herself—and made up a sun-brew while they all slept. A black kettle left in the sun to steep made tea as strong as anything boiled, and Lyr was too canny to risk a fire. They'd probably all need this tea before the night was over; too little sleep had killed plenty of times, as someone nodded out and fell behind the rest on a trek like this one.

When the kettle finished its round, Lyr took it from the last to drink and beckoned them all close to her; they stood shoulder to shoulder in a huddle, like children before a game. "We're in Karse now, in the buffer zone," she said quietly. "There'll be no fires while we're here, nothing to bring us to the attention of anyone—a Karsite patrol wouldn't have a fire either; they make cold camps always unless they're in a siege. We're going a little farther east, riding this trail until just after sunset. Then we'll be turning north, through the night, then west as soon as we hit anything that looks like a road. Once we start going west, we'll be traveling entirely by night. The Karsites do that, sometimes, and it'll be harder for someone to tell that we aren't a patrol of theirs if we meet 'em after dark. *If* that happens, is there anybody who speaks Karsite better than me?"

The brown girl spoke up. "Me mum's Karsite," she offered.

"Can you give me a bit of a speech about going west to harass the heathen, with all the Sunlord crap attached?"

The girl spouted off a bit of liquid gabble; difficult to believe that a people as intransigent and violent as the Karsites had such a beautiful language. Kero didn't understand it, but Lyr evidently did; she nodded in satisfaction. "Better than me by a good furlong; right, if we run into a patrol, *you're* the leader. Think you can reckon what to tell 'em without me coachin' you?"

"Aye," the girl asserted sturdily, blushing a bit.

"Mum useta tell us what them officers was like—bit like the Rethwellan reg'lars, only stuffed full of that religious dung and stricter about orders and rules. So long as I keep insisten' it's orders we're followin', and praise Vkandis often enough, should be all right. The half of 'em can't read nor write, so havin' verbal orders isn't going to make 'em think twice.''

Lyr looked satisfied, and patted the girl on the shoulder. "Right, then, let's mount up and make some time.''

They turned to their horses—and that was when Hellsbane flung up her head and screamed a warning.

Kero didn't even stop to think; she just threw herself across the clearing and into the saddle. She didn't quite make it before the horse lunged; she only got halfway over, clinging with both hands and gritting her teeth as the mare threw herself sideways to avoid a swung ax. The ground had sprouted armed men, it seemed—Hellsbane's scream had been the only warning before the attack. Lyr *must* have left someone as a guard, but just as surely, those guards were dead now.

Hellsbane pivoted. Kero managed to use the mare's momentum to swing herself properly up into the saddle; she pulled Need then, and looked for a target. Battle fever took over; she was wide awake and alert, feeling as fresh as if she'd risen from a feather bed with a full night's sleep behind her. There was someone else operating behind her eyes now, someone who took a fierce enjoyment in dealing death and evading it. Later, she'd be tired and a little sick—but not now. Not now, when her heart raced and the blood sang in her ears, and everything seemed sharper and clearer than it ever was outside of a fight. . . .

She had plenty of targets to choose from. As motley as these attackers were, they had to be *real* bandits, but they outnumbered the Skybolts, and they knew how to fight. In general, a mounted fighter has the advantage over an unmounted man, but these bandits knew how to negate that advantage.

In fact, even as she looked for a target, she spotted a snaggle-toothed, bearded man swinging for Kero with a hooked pike designed to catch in her armor and unhorse her.

Assuming Hellsbane let him. . . .

The mare saw him as soon as Kero did; she reared a little in place, to warn her rider, then reared to her *full* height, flailing out with both hooves and crow-hopping forward on her hind legs as she did so. He was *not* expecting that, and froze, mouth open, staring at the horse. Those powerful hooves caught and splintered the pike, then came down squarely on the head of the wielder.

He collapsed, going down without a sound. Hellsbane dropped down on his body, just to make sure of him; then spun on her hindquarters to take out the ax-wielder she'd evaded earlier with her formidable teeth, while Kero took care of a sword-bearer who had come up on the opposite side. The fool shouldn't have been flinging a sword around his head; Kero took off the swordsman's hand, while Hellsbane snapped inches away from the axman's face. The axman tried to get out of her way, stumbled backward and fell, and she surged forward to trample him.

A large shadow—hoofbeats—Kero sensed someone coming up from behind, but Hellsbane was already ahead of her; the mare lashed out with her hindfeet and caught another horse squarely in the jaw. Kero clung to the saddle while the mare pivoted again, quick as a snake, bringing her into striking position as the injured horse started to stumble. Hellsbane lashed out with forehooves this time, and caught the horse in the neck and shoulder. The other horse started to fall. The rider was flailing both arms for balance, and wide open; Kero's slash opened his stomach, leather armor and all. Hellsbane scrambled over their bodies, pivoted again, and Kero found herself facing a pair of swordsmen.

This time she signaled Hellsbane to charge them; they weren't quite ready, and she figured they'd scatter if they saw the mare coming for them. They did; Kero cut at one as she passed, though she didn't think she'd done him any real damage.

That gave her a bit of breathing space, and now that she had a chance to look up, she saw that she was alone, and no longer in the clearing. The others were just barely within sight, far downstream. Somehow she'd gotten separated from them—and it seemed as if the bandits thought *she* was a far better prospect and were concentrating their efforts on her.

Maybe it's Hellsbane, she thought, parrying yet an-other sword-stroke, just now noticing that her arm was getting tired and heavy. *She's a tempting target, even if they don't know what she is. Dear gods, what am I think-ing? I've got to get back to the rest!*

She urged the mare in the direction of the others, but once again they were cut off, and Kero had a confusing impression of being forced, step by step, toward the bank of the river.

The river! If I can get to it, I'll at least have one di-rection they can't come at me from!

She gave Hellsbane the signal; the mare needed no further urging. She gathered herself and surged toward the beckoning water, while the bandits tried to intercept them. She wouldn't have any of it; though they prevented her from making that bank, she got within a few feet, running two of the bandits right off the bank in the pro-cess. She screamed, and rushed again, heading farther downstream, away from the vanishing Skybolts, but once more toward the riverbank.

Kero blinked as they burst through the brush and came out on a low bluff above the water. This didn't seem to be the same river they'd camped beside; it was much wider and deeper, the opposite side farther than Kero would care to swim, seeing how rapid the current was. But this higher bluff made a good place to make a stand—

Hellsbane had other ideas. She had no intention of stopping on the top of the bluff. She plowed through the last of the bushes, kept charging straight on, and plunged over the edge, headfirst into the cold water.

"Well," Kero said to her horse, as she was wringing out her shirt, "At least we lost them."

Hellsbane munched soaked grain and dry grass, stol-idly ignoring the results of Kero's none-too-gentle min-istrations. The mare had quite a few wounds after the encounter; cuts and slashes, and a few scrapes. None of her injuries were too deep, but Kero had stitched them anyway. Hellsbane was amazingly good about being doc-tored; she didn't even object too strenuously to having minor wounds stitched up.

As for herself, she'd come out of it pretty much un-scathed—other than being half-drowned. Soaked, but unwounded. Bruised and battered by the rocks in the river, tired to death and cold. She hadn't lost any equipment this time, which was no small blessing, but she was completely lost.

She had no idea of where she could be, either. She had a vague idea of where they had gone in, at least in relation to a mental map she'd been constructing, but once off that map, she might as well have been on the other side of the world. The river's powerful current had swept them downstream, to the south, the opposite direction she'd last seen the rest of the troop heading. Hellsbane had hit the water right where it swirled away from the bank in an irresistible flow, and once out of the grip of it, she could *not* get the mare turned to take the western bank that she'd jumped from. There was no help for it; the mare was convinced that the western bank held nothing but enemies and would not swim back to it. Kero had given up, and let her make for the opposite shore. By the time Hellsbane had made the eastern bank, they'd been carried at least a league downstream.

Now the western sky was a bloody red above the trees; night would be falling soon, and she was out in the middle of Karsite territory, completely alone, with every possession she still owned soaked through and through. Even if she'd had a map, it wouldn't have survived.

There were a few notable exceptions to the destruction; her bow had been wrapped in oiled cloth, which had fortunately survived the plunge. It was all right, as were her little medical pack and her fire kit. But everything else was a wet mess. Unfortunately, that included the rations.

The journey-bread was inedible; the rest, jerked meat and dried fruit, and Hellsbane's grain, was in a sad state. The little that was left would last a couple of days before going bad; after that, she and Hellsbane would have to live off the land.

"I could look on the bright side," she said to the mare. "At least we have water. And I got that bath."

But I'm cold now, with no chance to warm up. The best I can do is wring my clothes as dry as I can, stuff myself on what food hasn't been ruined, and walk Hellsbane north. If I'm lucky, my clothes will dry on me without sending me into a chill.

Then she thought better of that idea. *There's only me, and no road. Maybe not. Maybe I'd just better see if I can't rig up a shelter and try for a trail or a path in the morning.*

Tarma had taught her how to rig a shelter in about any territory; in a forest, it wasn't too difficult a task. A little work with her ax and she had enough supple willow and pine branches to weave into a lean-to. As the last sliver of the sun vanished on the horizon, she fabricated a woven mat that should cut the wind, and shed most of the rain if she happened to be *completely* out of luck. With the last of the light she gathered dry leaves and layered first leaves, then all her clothing, then another layer of leaves beneath it. The water-soaked jerky was even less appetizing than it was when dry, but she wolfed it down anyway. It was still food, and if she didn't eat it, she'd have to throw it away.

She hung Hellsbane's saddle blanket under a bush, and turned the saddle upside down to dry.

That was all she could do at this point, except to tell Hellsbane, "Guard." The mare went on the alert, and Kero crawled into her bit of shelter, already shivering. She was sure she'd never get warm, and equally certain she'd never sleep.

She was wrong on both points.

"North or south?" she asked Hellsbane. The mare flicked her ears forward but made no commentary.

Her clothing was dry, her bedroll still soggy. Hellsbane's blanket was dry, though, so after she saddled the mare and strapped the packs on her, she opened up the bedding and draped it over Hellsbane's rump, like a pathetic attempt at barding. The mare craned her head around for a look, and snorted in disgust.

There was a vague tugging sensation that Kero recognized as coming from Need. *West,* it urged. She took one look at the river, even wider here than where she'd gone in, and told it to hold its tongue. Or whatever it used for one.

She mounted, settling herself over bedding and all, hoping they wouldn't encounter anything unfriendly. If they had to make a run for it, they'd lose the bedroll.

"South, I guess," she said out loud. "I haven't a

chance of catching up with the others, and they won't wait for me. We *were* going north and east, so if I go south and can get back across this river, I should be in the right area to make for the Border again.''

Nothing answered her, not even a bird. She could hear birds elsewhere, off in the forest, but her movements had frightened them into silence here.

It made her feel like a creature of ill-omen, a harbinger of death. Something even the birds avoided—

Until she caught sight of a bold green-crested jay swooping down out of the trees to steal a bit of the ruined, discarded journey-bread.

Then she laughed, shakily, and cast off her feelings of impending disaster. *Hellfires,* she thought, as the mare picked her way between the trees, *I've already had my quota of disasters. I should be about due for some good luck.*

But the imp of the perverse wasn't finished with her yet—or else, perhaps, there truly was a curse in operation. She found a path—a well-worn path leading from the river—and followed it just out of sight, afoot, leaving Hellsbane tethered in a safe place hidden by the underbrush. It was just as well that she hid the horse—because the path led to a village, one with formidable walls, and the village was placed across the only real road south.

She discovered, by watching the place for half the morning, that it was a very active village—the headquarters, so it seemed, for the local Karsite patrols. The riders coming in and going out were not in uniform, but they rode with military discipline and precision, and Kero twice saw priestly robes among them.

She cursed to herself, but crawled back to where she had left Hellsbane and retraced her steps to her cold camp, where she destroyed every sign that a scout had been there. There was no hiding the fact that someone had been here, but she did her best to make it look as if the camp might have been the work of children.

I only hope that Karsite younglings run off to play soldier in the woods the way we did, she thought grimly, as she sent Hellsbane picking her way through the forest, trying to keep her on things that wouldn't show hoofprints—stone, pine needles, and the like. She'd muffled the mare's hooves in leather bags, which should confuse things a little, but Hellsbane hated the "boots" and Kero wouldn't be able to keep them on her for very long.

The river turned west, but the terrain forming its bank worsened and they had to leave it and move farther east. By mid-afternoon they hit another trail. This one also had the tracks of horse hooves on it, but they were broad hooves, unshod, and hopefully marked only the passage of farm animals.

Late afternoon brought increasing signs of habitation, and once again Kero tethered the mare deep in the brush and went on alone, afoot.

The territory away from the river was turning drier; there were woods down in the valleys, but the hills themselves supported mostly grass and bushes. She climbed a tree when she picked up sounds of humans at work, and realized, as she surveyed this newest village from the shelter of its highest boughs, that this change of vegetation was going to make traveling even more difficult. It would be hard to stay hidden, and impossible to disguise the mare as anything but what she was.

This village was much smaller than the first, and did not appear to be harboring any of the Karsite forces other than a single priest. He herded every soul in the village into the center of town as the sun went down, leading them in a long—and evidently boring—religious service. Kero snickered a little, watching some of the worshipers nodding off in the middle of the priest's main speech.

When the last edge of the scarlet sun finally sank below the horizon, he let them go. They lost no time in seeking their own little cottages.

Kero watched them until full dark, then went back for Hellsbane, satisfied that no one would be stirring out of doors except to visit the privy. As darkness covered the cottages, her sharp ears had caught the sounds of bars being dropped over doorways all across the village. These people feared the dark and what it held—therefore darkness was her friend.

Therefore I won't be getting any sleep tonight, she added with a sigh, as she took Hellsbane's reins in her hand and moved cautiously toward the sleeping village, walking on the side of the road and ready to pull the mare into cover at the first sign of life other than herself. *I wonder how they get the troops to travel at night if the common folk are so afraid of the dark?*

Then, again, maybe the troops are what they're afraid of.

The village itself was not the kind of untidy sprawl of houses she was used to; this place was a compact huddle of thirty or forty single-storied cottages, mostly alike, ranged on three sides of the village square. The fourth side was taken up by four larger homes, and what Kero presumed to be the temple, and the entire village was surrounded by an area that had been cleared entirely of brush and trees, leaving nothing but grass. The arrangement made it possible for her to skirt the edge of the village without leaving the shelter of the trees, and still see anything moving among the houses.

The place was uncanny, that much was certain. Once again she had the feeling that there were eyes out there, but this time she *also* had the feeling those eyes were somehow missing her. There was definitely something in that village; something that held the inhabitants silent and hidden in their houses, something that scanned the night for anything that didn't belong there. *Like me,* she thought, glad she'd put Hellsbane's "boots" back on, and equally glad that the mare was too well-trained to give her away with a whicker to the farm beasts. *It's looking for something like me, only it can't find me. Maybe—maybe Need's finally doing something. Damned if I'm going to drop shields to find out!*

It seemed to take half the night to creep past the village; and once past, she didn't relax her vigilance in the least. She stayed in the shadow of the trees for furlongs, then she mounted the mare and rode out on the road to the east, and she didn't leave that cover, not even when the village was long past.

That vigilance paid off shortly before dawn, when she thought she heard hoofbeats ahead of her. The sound faded after only an instant, but she found a gap in the brush and dismounted to lead the mare into its concealment. There she waited.

And waited.

She began to feel like a fool, but not even that would send her out onto the road again before she knew without a shadow of a doubt that there was no one else on it.

Then—she felt that *searching* again, and froze. Once again it passed over her, but she felt as helpless as a mouse stuck in an open field, knowing there's a hawk overhead ready to stoop the moment it moves.

The feeling passed, but before she could take Hellsbane out onto the road, she heard hoofbeats, the same as before, but much nearer—practically on top of her position. *Some quirk of the hills echoed them up in time to warn me,* she realized numbly. *Blessed Agnira! If I hadn't heard them—*

It was a long time before she could convince herself to move.

East and north, a little west, then north again; never any closer to her goal, never any idea of where she really was. She was in sheep country now—there were fewer priests, which was a blessing, but shepherds are lonely and inquisitive folk, the kind she wanted to avoid at all costs.

Twice she dropped all caution and used her Gift to help her raid farms for food. Each time she felt that searching "eye" pass over her some time later, as if she had inadvertently set off some kind of alarm by her use of Thoughtsensing. After the second time, she resolved to tighten her belt further. Nothing was worth feeling that *presence* out there, looking for her.

Hellsbane was a hardy soul, and could live quite happily on grass alone since she wasn't seeing heavy activity. In fact, fully half the time Kero walked and led her instead of riding, especially at night.

She slept by day, whenever she could find cover enough to hide the mare. She dreamed almost every night; vague, odd dreams involving Need, Need and an old woman, and a very young girl barely into her teens. They weren't very coherent dreams, and they involved things that seemed to be right out of the wildest of legends, so far in the past that they bordered on incomprehensible.

It was after the first of those dreams that she encountered the first *priestess*—as opposed to priest—of Vkandis.

She had slept most of the day, knowing that there was another village to pass that night, and at sundown had worked her way down toward that village to keep watch until everyone was safely tucked up for the night. Right on schedule, a cowled and robed figure appeared from the rock-walled temple and assembled the villagers. She wondered idly if this village's sunset service was going to be as dull as the other ones she'd overseen when the figure threw back its cowl to reveal a head of wild, scarlet curls and an unmistakably feminine face.

Shock held her in place; further shock kept her frozen for a moment, as the priestess raised her head and stared directly at the place where she lay concealed.

Only the sun saved her; there was a service to conduct, and Kero was under the impression that if there was an earthquake, battle-charge or erupting volcano in progress at sunset, the followers of Vkandis would *still* conduct their devotions to the last ray of light.

Halfway into the service, Kero managed to shake off her paralysis, and crawl back to where she'd left Hellsbane tethered. This time she did *not* wait until sunset; she mounted Hellsbane and rode farther eastward, giving the village a wide berth, and pulling every trick Tarma had ever taught her to confuse and conceal her trail.

Thereafter, following every one of those dreams, she'd encounter a female devotee of Vkandis. And every single one of them seemed able to detect either her, or the sword.

It was unnerving, not the least because she hadn't known—nor had anyone else to her knowledge—that there *were* women placed so highly in Vkandis' priesthood. Up until this time everyone *she'd* ever talked to had spoken of the cult as being exclusively male, and certainly the little anyone outside of Karse knew of it painted the credo as being thoroughly misogynistic.

Certainly the Karsites had very little use for women in general, and positively despised fighting women like the ones in the ranks of the Skybolts, reserving particularly gruesome treatment for them when caught.

And yet—the order of Vkandis was a *militant* order. Every one of the women Kero had seen had worn a sword. The order of Vkandis deplored the use of magic—yet she had felt magic searching for her, and these women seemed perfectly willing to employ something like enough to magic as to make no difference.

It appeared that whatever the outside world knew of

Karse and the state religion, there were things going on within it that were not to be discovered until one penetrated into the country itself. What those things meant, Kero had no idea, except that *she* had better keep her head down and her behind well-hidden, or she wasn't going to be telling anyone of her discoveries. Except, perhaps, an inquisitor.

I think I've been in hiding forever, she thought dispiritedly, from her concealment among the rocks above the road. Sundown would be soon, and then she could get on her way.

For all the good it does me.

Hoofbeats signaled a Karsite patrol; she'd learned that the military were the only groups that traveled mounted. She watched yet another of those woman-priests riding by her, this one evidently in too much of a hurry to do more than raise her head in startlement as she passed Kero's hiding place in the rocks above the road. And once again, she wondered what the presence of high-ranking women in the priesthood meant.

Maybe all that it means is that they haven't much use for women except inside boundaries. Like it's fine for women to do anything *for the glory of the Sunlord, but outside the priesthood they'd better not even think of doing anything besides stay at home and breed more worshipers for the Sunlord. . . .*

Not for the first time, she wondered if she ought to abandon Need. She'd had half a dozen very narrow escapes so far, and she had the feeling that the only reason she hadn't been caught was the blade's belated realization that just because these were women, they were *not* friendly toward Need's current bearer.

But if she did abandon it, the thing would only end up in the hands of some poor, ignorant child, who would very probably be dead the first time one of the *male* priests took advantage of his power and position to abuse one of his flock. Kero had long ago realized the same thing could have happened to *her* if Tarma hadn't been playing guardian that night. The blade had no sense of proportion, and seemed to have a varying regard for the safety and health of its bearer.

Or worse, the thing could end up in the hands of one

of these priestesses, and Kero couldn't even guess what would happen then.

Anything, she reflected, brooding down on the now empty road. *I think Need is a whole lot older than even Grandmother guessed. That probably accounts for a lot of the things it does. Anything that old has a set of priorities and plans that are a whole lot different from those of us who're likely to die if someone puts a hole in us.*

In fact, the more she thought about it, the easier it was to imagine some of the things it was likely to do.

Take over one of those priestesses and lead a religious crusade, for one thing. The Karsites tend to go in for that sort of amusement in a big way. Seems to me that was how the Sunlord ended up as the state religion in the first place. At least I think I remember one of those history books saying something like that; and that's when the Karsites really got strange.

She snorted to herself. *Figures. Make someone a devout, fanatical anything, and his brain turns to mulch. Well, I sure's fire don't want to be the cause of another crusade among the Karsites.*

And there was no indication the sword would even let her go in the first place. If she tried to abandon it, she might end up in agony.

Dusk was falling, and it was time to be on her way. Over the past few days, the sparsely-forested hills had been giving way to pine groves, with mountains looming up in the distance. Kero had the feeling she was very near the Karse-Valdemar border; she was certainly far enough north.

She'd never expected to get up here in her lifetime.

I wish to hell I wasn't here now.

She put her head down on her arms, and allowed herself a painful lump in her throat. *I want* home, *I want out of here!* she wailed inside her mind. *I want to see the winter quarters, and Shallan, and Tre—I want cooked food and a real bed—I want a bath—I want to sleep without having to wake every few breaths because I think I hear something—*

She was tired right down to the bone, and her nerves were like red-hot wire. She started out of sleep lately at the least little sound, but she knew if she didn't keep herself at this kind of a pitch, she'd lie down one night and wake only with the point of a Karsite sword in her throat.

But worse than the rest was despair, the feeling that she'd never get back, never see familiar faces again, never see home, or what passed for it. And the loneliness. She'd thought she was cold, unfeeling—now she knew differently. She might not need people as desperately as Shallan did, but she needed them all the same.

Usually she could shake the mood after letting it have her for a few moments, but not tonight. Tonight despair followed her down off of the hill to the little valley and the brook she'd left Hellsbane tied beside. It rode as her companion, unseen, but profoundly felt, as she followed behind the Karsite patrol—behind *always* being the safest place to be, with the Karsites. It covered her with a gloom as thick as the dusk—and it was almost the death of her.

It was only when Hellsbane snorted and balked, and the sword threw a jab of agony into her head, that she pulled up and realized that there were voices ahead of her. She rode Hellsbane off into the forest, and dismounted, leading the horse quietly under the pines and up onto a tiny game trail above the floor of the valley and the road running through it. The crushed pine needles gave off a sharp scent that made her pause for a moment. That scent could disguise the mare's and make it possible for them to work around the patrol ahead of them without alerting the Karsites' horses.

She took handfuls of needles stripped from the bough, crushed them between her palm and her armor, and rubbed the resulting mass over Hellsbane's coat. The mare sneezed once and gave Kero a rather astonished look, but didn't really seem to object.

That accomplished, she spotted a good place to overlook the road; tethered the mare, and wriggled her way down to it on her stomach.

A rock outcropping offered little in the way of concealment, but the dusk itself provided that. She got into place just in time to see the patrol that had passed her earlier, returning with a prisoner.

A very obvious prisoner; a man, tied to the saddle of a much-abused mule. A man dressed entirely in white.

Thirteen

Something about the white uniform tugged at a half-buried memory in the back of her weary mind. *Something to do with a priesthood? No, that can't be it. . . .*

She was still trying to make the connection, when she saw something else moving below her; something moving so silently that if it hadn't been for the color—or lack of it—she'd never have spotted it. And if it hadn't been for the man, she wouldn't have thought—''horse''—she'd have thought—''ghost.''

Or fog. That was what it resembled; a bit of fog slipping through the trees.

But put white-clad man together with white horse, and even a tired, numb-brained merc knew what *that* meant. This prisoner was one of the Heralds, out of Valdemar.

And the Karsites appreciated the Heralds even less than they appreciated female fighters.

That horse is no horse at all, at least not according to Tarma, she thought, keeping her eyes glued to the vague white shape as it flitted from one bit of cover to another. *She said it was—leshy'a, I think. A spirit. Huh. Looks pretty solid for a spirit. Doesn't look particularly magical, either.*

The Karsite troop had stopped in the middle of the road, and were conferring quietly, with anxious looks cast up at the mountainside above them, and back behind them, where they had been. The—what was it?—*Companion,* she remembered now—the Companion froze where it was. The man seemed oblivious to it all, slumped in his saddle—but Kero had the oddest feeling that he wasn't as badly hurt or as unaware as he seemed.

But it's going to take a lot more than wits and a magic horse to get you out of this one, my friend, she told him

silently. *An army would be nice. Or at least one friend
free and able to convince the Karsites he* is *an army.*
   Or she—
   Instantly she berated herself for thinking like a fool.
This man had no claim on her or her sympathy. Valdemar
hired no mercs, and probably never would. She had no
loyalty to his land and no personal feeling for him . . .
except that the Karsites were not going to be gentle with
him. And there but for Need and the blessings of the
gods, rode she. . . .
   Damn it, you're almost out of here! You aren't *an army,
you aren't even in good fighting shape right now, and he
isn't a female, so Need won't give a fat damn about him.*
   The priestess gave a peremptory order, cutting off all
further discussion. The rest of the party dismounted and
began leading their horses off into a little blind canyon,
probably to make camp, while she took charge of the
prisoner. She rode up beside him, pulled his head up by
the hair, and slapped his face, so hard it rocked him in
his saddle—he would have fallen but for the grip she had
on his hair. The slap echoed among the rocks as she let
go, and he slumped forward over the pommel. Even as
far away as Kero was, there was no mistaking the priestess' smile of cruel anticipation.
   Kero made up her mind then and there. *Fine. He's a
Herald. There's probably going to be a reward if I rescue
him, and even if there isn't, he can get me out of here
through Valdemar. I'm getting him away from that bitch.*
   Part of her yammered at the back of her mind, telling
her that she was *insane* for doing this, for even thinking
about rescuing the stranger. After all, *she* wasn't in the
clear yet, she was all alone, and the idea of rescuing
someone *else* was sheerest suicide.
   She ignored that part of herself, and wriggled backward, keeping herself right down on the rock and ignoring scrapes, until she was out of sight of the road. But
though she ignored good sense, she did not ignore caution—there was no telling if the Karsites had deployed a
scout to check the woods. She kept as low and as quiet
as a hunted rabbit, slipping from one bit of cover to the
next, working her way toward Hellsbane by a circuitous,
spiraling route.
   The woods seemed empty of everything but birds—of

course, another scout, a good one, might not have disturbed them any more than Kero did. Still, there was no one out here that *she* could spot, which probably meant that the Karsites felt secure enough not to bother with perimeter checks. Which meant they also might not bother with perimeter *guards*. If so, her task took on the aura of the "possible."

When she reached her horse, she tied up Hellsbane's stirrups, fastening them to the saddle, before muffling the mare's hooves in her "boots." Hellsbane pricked up her ears at that; she knew very well what it meant, though it wasn't something Kero did often. She was to guard Kero's back, following her like a dog, until Kero needed her. Tarma had drilled both of them remorselessly in this maneuver; it wasn't something every warsteed could learn to do, but Hellsbane was both obedient and inquisitive, and those were marker traits for a mare that *could* learn the trick. Hellsbane had learned her lessons well.

The priestess and her charge had already moved on, but it wasn't at all hard to guess where they had gone— even Lordan could have figured it out. The troop had trampled down vegetation on both sides of that little path leading off the main road. Kero waited, watched and listened long enough for her nerves to start screaming. She crossed the road in a rush, like a startled deer, then went up the side of the hill, planning to follow their trail from above. Hellsbane followed, making no more noise than she did.

She found them at the end of the path, bivouacked in a little blind canyon, thick with trees. And by now the sun was setting somewhere beyond the trees; it was slowly growing darker. That was bad enough—it was going to be damned difficult to get him loose in a setup like that, and harder still to get him *out*—but worse was that there were more of them now than she'd seen in the original group. Where they came from, or whether they were already here when the priestess and her charge arrived, she had no idea.

It didn't much matter. The odds had just jumped from five to one to about twenty to one.

Hellfires, she thought, watching some of the "new" ones tie their prisoner "securely." The Karsite idea of "secure" was enough to make her joints ache in sympathy; ankles tied to wide-set stakes, arms bound behind his back over a thick tree limb, wrists secured to ankles so that his only possible posture was kneeling, and no position could be comfortable, even if he was as boneless as Tre.

That was no way to treat anyone you intended to keep for very long. Which argued that they *didn't* intend to keep him for very long.

I can still walk away from this, she told herself, settling her chin on her hands, the smell of old leaves thick in her nostrils. *I'm not involved yet. They haven't seen me, and not even his horse knows I'm there—and he isn't a woman, so Need won't give me any trouble about leaving him. . . .*

But the more she saw, the less palatable the idea of leaving him in their hands became. Whatever else he was, this Herald was a fellow human being, and a pretty decent one if all the things Tarma and Kethry had said about his kind were true. From the look of things, the priestess was about to try a little interrogation, and Kero knew what that meant. She'd seen the results of one of those sessions, and was not minded to leave even a stranger to face it.

Besides, if these bastards were stopping this close to the Border to question him, there must be an urgent reason to do so. Which meant that the reward for his release would be a good one, and the information he held in his head must be valuable to someone. And if she *could* get him loose, he must know the quickest way out of Karse and across that Border into Valdemar, where she'd be safe, if not welcome.

And from there she could get home. . . .

That clinched it, the thought of "home" set up a longing so strong it overwhelmed any other consideration.

There has to be a way, she thought darkly. *There has to be.* She watched through narrowed eyes as the woman rolled up the arms of her robes and picked up one of the irons she'd placed in the fire, examining it critically, then replacing it. *Huh. So far, that priestess hasn't even looked up once. So either she can't sense me, or Need—or whichever of us these women are somehow detecting—or else she's too busy. Either way, if I'm very careful, I might be able to do a little reading of their thoughts. Maybe I'll overhear something that'll help.*

She unshielded carefully, a little bit at a time, and sent a delicate wisp of thought drifting down among them, the barest possible disturbance of the currents down there—

And suddenly her little finger of thought was seized and held in a desperate mental grip.

Blessed Agnira! Panic gave her strength she didn't know she had. She snatched her mind away, and lay facedown in the leaves, heart pounding wildly with fear. Her first, panicked thought was that it was the priestess; her second, that it was some other mage down below there. But there was no sign of disturbance in the camp, and no one shouted a warning or pointed in the direction of her hiding place. She throttled down her panic, and extended her probe a second time, "looking" for the presence that had seized her.

It snatched for her again, a little less wildly, but no less desperate.

:Who are you?: she thought, forming her statement clearly, as Warrl had taught her.

:Eldan. Who are you? I thought I was the only one out here!:

:Kerowyn—:

:You have to help me get loose,: he demanded, interrupting her, his mental voice voice shaking, but firm beneath the fear. *:I've got to get back to report!:*

:Fine,: she told him. *:What's it worth to you? Or should I say, to Valdemar?:*

That stopped him. *:What?:* He seemed baffled rather than shocked. He literally did not understand what she meant; that was crystal clear from his thoughts.

:What is it worth to you to be freed? How much,: she repeated patiently. *:Money, my friend. What's the reward for getting you loose? I'm not in this for my health. There're easier ways of making a living.:*

:I—: he faltered, *:I—I thought you were a Herald—:*

Silence then, as he began to take in the fact that she plainly was something else.

:Obviously not, friend. To clarify things for you, I'm a professional soldier. A mercenary. Now do you want me

to get you free, or not?: She couldn't resist a little barb. *:Those irons are going to be very hot in a moment.:*

She waited for him to respond, and it didn't take long. He named a figure. She blinked in surprise; it was more than she would have considered asking, and she would have expected to be bargained down. *Either he's more important than I thought, or he has an inflated opinion of his own worth. Either way, I'm holding him to it.*

:Bond on it?: she asked.

He gave his bond, seeming a little miffed that she'd asked. *:My Companion will help you on this, too,:* he added.

Well, that only bore out everything Tarma had told her about the spirit-horses. *:All right—:* she said, and noted that he seemed a little surprised that she took that last so calmly. *:Here's what we'll do. . . .:*

The Karsites had counted on the fact that they were in a blind canyon to protect them from attack on three of the four sides, and probably were assuming that since the canyon was thickly wooded, that would make fighting difficult for an opponent. But while the slope Kero was hidden on was indeed steep, it was not too steep for a Shin'a'in warsteed. And she had *trained* in the woods.

They charged ''silently,'' without a cry, Kero knowing that the Karsites would not recognize the crashing of her horse through the underbrush for an attack until it was too late. She had her bow out, and neither her aim nor her arrows had suffered from lack of practice. The enemy fighters silhouetted themselves most considerately against the fire; she picked off four of the Karsite guards, two of them with heart-shots and two through the throat, while still on the way in.

Already battle fever had her, and her world narrowed to *target; response.* There was no room for anything else.

Meanwhile, commotion at the mouth of the canyon signaled the Companion's charge. Kero had felt a little guilty about putting the unarmed horse there, but the Companion was *not* going to be able to cut Eldan free, and she was.

Hellsbane skidded to a halt beside the kneeling Herald, and Kero swung her leg over the saddle-bow and vaulted off her back, letting off another arrow and getting a fifth score as she did so.

Weeks spent behind the Karsite lines had given her a rough command of their language; she heard the shouts, and realized that from the plurals being used that they had mistaken the gray warsteed for a white Companion, and herself for another Herald—it would have been funny, if she'd had any time to think about it.

She slashed at the Herald's bonds, while the Companion charged down and trampled two more Karsites in his way, and Hellsbane reared on her haunches and bashed out the brains of a third. The ropes to his ankles and wrists were easy enough to handle, but just as she was getting ready to saw at the thongs binding Eldan's arms to the log, two more of the Karsites rushed her. She tossed a knife at the Herald's feet while parrying the first Karsite's rather clumsy attack. *He* was easily dispatched, but his friend arrived, and another with him—

Hellsbane got there first, half-reared and got the first from behind, and the Companion fought his way to the Herald's side. Now at least she didn't need to worry about having to guard him while he cut himself free.

She thought she'd been hit a couple of times, but the wounds didn't hurt. Since they weren't slowing her down, she ignored them as usual. The horses were doing the job of four or five fighters, charging and trampling every sign of organization and scattering people before them like frightened quail—and Kero began to think this was going to work—

Then she wheeled to face an opponent she sensed coming up behind her—

And her sword froze her in mid-slash.

The new opponent was the warrior-priestess. A woman. And Need would not permit her to carry out her attack.

LetmegoyoustupidBITCHofahunkoftin! she screamed mentally at the blade, seeing her death in the smiling eyes of the priestess, in the cruel quirk of her lips, in the slow, preparatory swing of the priestess' mace—

Then a tree limb swung down out of the gathering darkness, and with a resounding *crack,* broke in half over the woman's head.

The priestess dropped the mace, and fell to the ground like a stone.

Need let Kero go, muttering into the back of her mind in sleepy confusion, then subsiding into silence. "Thanks," she told the Herald, with all the sincerity she could manage.

"Anytime," he replied, grinning.

But there were still far too many Karsites in this camp, and the stunned disbelief that took them when their leader went down wasn't going to last much longer.

Kero made a running jump for Hellsbane's saddle, vaulting spraddle-legged over the mare's rump and landing squarely in place. The Herald followed her example a half breath behind.

And she couldn't help it—she indulged in a blood-curdling Shin'a'in war-cry as they thundered out the canyon mouth, running over two more Karsites who weren't quick enough to get out of the way.

Let 'em figure that *out.*

"Have we gone far enough, do you think?" she asked Eldan wearily, about a candlemark before dawn.

"I certainly hope so," he replied, his voice as dull and lifeless as hers. "And I doubt very much they're going to follow our trail. Where in Havens did you learn all that? That trail-muddling stuff, I mean."

"It's my job," she reminded him, and looked up at the sky, critically. There were still stars in the west, but the east was noticeably lighter above the thick pines. It was time to find somewhere to hide for a while.

"We need a cave, or a ledge overhanging some bushes, or something," she continued. "We're going to need to hide for at least two days, maybe three, maybe more, so it's going to have to stand up to some scrutiny. I want a cave, I really do."

He looked bewildered, and not particularly happy. "Two days? Three? But—"

She cut him short. "I know what you're thinking. Trust me on this one. I'm hurt, you're hurt, and the Karsites are going to expect us to make straight for the Border. We need time to recover, and we need time for our trail to age. If we hole up back here, and stay here, we'll get

in behind them. They won't look for us to come from
that direction."

Herald Eldan was hardly more than a dark shape
against the lighter sky, and she realized that she really
didn't know what he looked like. He shook his head dubiously, then shrugged. "All right, you obviously know
what you're doing. You did get me out of there." He
gestured grandly. "Lead on, my lady."

Ordinarily, that would have caused her to snap *I'm nobody's* lady, *much less yours*, but something about Eldan—an unconscious graciousness, a feeling that he'd
treat a scullery maid and a princess with the same courtesy, made her smile and take the lead, afoot, with Hellsbane trailing obediently behind like an enormous dog.

She knew what she was looking for, when she'd started
searching here among the cliffs off the road, following
the barest of game trails, and she had the feeling she'd
find it in these uneven limestone slopes. A cave. Somewhere they could could hide and rest and not have to
worry about searchers. Above all, though, their hiding
place had to be big enough for the horses, too—maybe
Eldan's Companion could make himself into a drift of
fog and escape notice, but Hellsbane was all too solid.

She tried several places that looked promising, but
none of them were near big enough. She began watching
the sky with one anxious eye; the rising sun had begun
to dye the eastern horizon a delicate pink, and once the
Karsites had completed their morning devotions, the hunt
would be well and truly up. There was one advantage; a
small one. Bats would be returning to their lairs for the
day, and bats meant caves.

There was a ledge—and she thought she saw a dark
form flit under it.

She fumbled her way up to it, tired limbs no longer
responding, reactions gone all to hell. Predictably, she
tripped, completely lost her balance and grabbed for a
bush.

She missed it entirely. She fell down the slope with a
strangled cry, rolling over and over, landing in a tangle
of bushes—

And falling through the clutching, spiky branches, into
blackness with a not-so-strangled shriek. She got a face

full of gravel, and rolled farther, finally hitting her head, and seeing stars for a moment.

She lay on her back in the darkness, her ears ringing, wondering what she was doing there.

"Kerowyn?"

She blinked, trying to remember where she was, and who that voice could belong to.

"Kerowyn?" The voice certainly sounded familiar.

She sat up, and her head screamed a protest—but it all came back. Eldan, the rescue—*Right*.

"I'm in here!" she cried, hearing her voice echo back at her from deeper in the darkness with an elation not even her aching head could spoil.

"Are you all right?" She looked in the direction of the voice, and saw a lighter patch in the dark. That must be the entrance, screened off by bushes so thick *she* hadn't even guessed it was there.

"Pretty much," she replied, getting carefully to her feet, and sitting right back down again, prudently, when her head began to spin. "Can you bring the horses in here? Right now my knees are a little shaky."

"I think so." There were sounds of someone thrashing his way through bushes, leaving, then returning. "It looks big enough. Hang on, I'm going to make a light."

She winced at the sudden flare of light, and looked away, toward the rear of the cave. Interestingly, she couldn't see an end to the darkness. When she looked back again, Eldan had a candle in one hand, and was leading Hellsbane in, the horse whickering her protest at being taken through scratchy bushes, but obeying him readily enough.

Which was a miracle.

"She should be breaking your arm, you know," she said conversationally, as Eldan coaxed the mare down the slippery gravel slope to the bottom of the cave. "She's trained not to obey anyone but me, or someone I've designated that she's worked with in my presence. She should be trying to kill you, or at least hurt you."

"One of my Gifts is animal Mindspeech," he said, just as casually. Then he dropped the reins, grinned at her thunderstruck expression, and scrambled back up the slope, leaving the candle stuck onto a rock.

"Oh," she said weakly to the mare. "Animal Mind-speech. Of course. I should have known. . . ."

"Doesn't this hurt?" Eldan asked, peeling blood-soaked and dried cloth away from a slash on her leg. The wound wasn't deep, but it was very messy; she was bleeding like the proverbial butchered pig.

And now that they were safe, it definitely did hurt. Quite a bit, as a matter of fact.

"Yes," she replied, from behind gritted teeth. "It hurts."

"Then why don't you yell a little—it might do you some good."

"It isn't going to do any good to howl, much as I'd like to," she pointed out. "And there might be someone out there to hear me."

He sighed, and repeated what he'd just told her earlier. "One of my Gifts *is* animal Mindspeech, my lady. If there *was* anyone out there, the wild things would know it, and I'd know it. The only creatures that are going to hear you are some deer and a couple of squirrels."

"Call it force of habit, then," she replied, clenching her fists while he continued to clean the wound as he talked.

She'd already done the same service for him, finding mostly bruises, and a couple of nasty-looking cuts and burns where the priestess had tried a little preliminary "work" on him. He proved to be quite a handsome fellow; lean and muscular, a little taller than she was, with warm brown eyes and hair of sable-brown, but with two surprising white streaks in it, one at each temple. He had high cheekbones, a stubborn chin, and a generous mouth that looked as if he smiled a great deal.

"I don't think this needs to be stitched," he said, finally, "Just bandaged really well."

"That's a relief." She allowed herself to smile. "Thanks for taking care of everything. I'm sorry I had to find this place with my head."

Eldan had spent a couple of candlemarks pulling up armloads of grass and bringing it into the cave for the horses, then hunting up food for the humans. That was when he'd assured her that his Gift of understanding animal thoughts would keep him safe. Somehow she hadn't been too surprised that he'd brought back roots, edible fungus, and fish. Obviously if there was going to be any red meat or fowl brought in, she would have to be the hunter. And that would have to wait until tomorrow, since she'd managed to give herself a concussion when she fell.

But the ceiling of the cave was high enough that a fire gave them no problems, and the hot fish, wrapped in a blanket of clay and stuffed with the mushrooms, together with the roots roasted in hot ashes, tasted like the finest feast she'd ever had.

"How in the Havens did you ever become a mercenary?" Eldan asked, wrapping a bandage around her leg, and securing it.

"Sort of fell into it, I suppose," she replied. "I expect this is going to sound altogether horrible to you, but I happen to be good at fighting. And I didn't want the kinds of things considered acceptable for young ladies."

"Like husbands and children?" To her mild amazement, Eldan nodded. "My sister felt the same way. It's just that I can't imagine anyone with the Gift of Mind-speech being comfortable with *killing* people."

"I don't use it, much. The Gift, I mean. Wouldn't miss it if it got taken from me." She felt a little chill; Eldan was the only person besides Warrl to know about this so-called Gift, and the idea frightened her as nothing else in the past five years could. "Don't—let anyone know, all right?"

"There's no reason why I should," he assured her, and somehow she believed him. "But I must admit, I don't understand why you'd want to keep it secret if you don't use it that much."

"I live with mercenaries," she pointed out to him. "People who value their privacy, and who generally have secrets."

"Ah." He nodded. "Where, among the Heralds, such Gifts are commonplace, and we understand that one doesn't go rummaging about in someone else's mind as if it were a kind of old-clothes bin. There's a certain protocol we follow, and even the ordinary, unGifted people understand that in Valdemar."

For a moment she tried to imagine a place where that would be true, a land where she wouldn't be avoided for such an ability, or considered dangerous. She shook her head; places like that were only in tales.

"Well, we're different," he admitted. "Let me look at that slash along your ribs, hmm?"

She pulled off her tunic and pulled up her shirt without thinking twice about it; she'd have done the same with Tre or Gies, or Shallan. But when Eldan cleaned the long, shallow cut with his gentle hands, she found her cheeks warming, and she discovered to her chagrin that she found his touch very arousing.

That's not surprising, she rationalized. *We both came very close to death back there. The body does that, gets excited easily, after being in danger—I've seen Shallan vanish into the nearest bushes with Relli, both of them covered in gore. Coming close to death seems to make life that much more important. Hellfires, I've felt that way plenty of times, I just never did anything about it because there wasn't anyone around that I wanted to wake up with.*

He's somebody I wouldn't mind waking up with.

She caught the way her thoughts were tending, and sternly reprimanded herself. *But that's no reason to start with him.*

:You know, my lady,: whispered a little caress of a thought across the surface of her mind, *:just because you've always been afraid of something, that's no reason to continue to fear it.:*

For a moment she was confused, then angry with him for eavesdropping on her thoughts, until she realized he was talking about Mindspeech, not sex. But the touch of his mind on hers was as sensuous as the touch of his hands just under her breasts; the only other Mindspeaker she'd ever shared thoughts with was Warrl, and he was not only unhuman, "he" was a neuter. She had never felt anything quite so intimate as Eldan's thought mingling with hers . . . there were overtones that speech alone couldn't convey. A sense that he found her as attractive as she found him; an intimation that his body was reacting to the near-brush with death in the same way. . . .

We're going to have to stay in here until the hunt dies down, she thought absently, more than half her attention being taken up with the feel of his warm hands soothing her aching ribs, and the silken touch of his thoughts against her mind. *It's going to happen sooner or later— we're both young, and we're both interested. There's no earthly reason why we shouldn't. If we don't, things are only going to get very strained in here.*

She caught his hands just as he finished bandaging her ribs, and slowly, and quite deliberately, drew him toward her.

He was surprised—oh, not entirely, just surprised that she was so forward, she suspected. There was just a sudden flash of something like shock, and only for a moment. She deliberately kept her mind open to his touch, and after a brief hesitation, his thoughts joined hers as their lips met, and he joined her on her bedroll.

She prepared to kiss him, parting her lips, only to find he'd done the same. She chuckled a little at his evident enthusiasm; he slid his hands under her shirt, over the breasts he had been trying very hard *not* to touch a moment before. She undid the fastenings of his breeches and helped him to get rid of them, while he rid her of shirt and underdrawers.

Tired and battered as they were, they moved slowly with each other, taking their cues from the things picked out of each other's minds. Making love mind-to-mind like this was the most incredibly intimate and sensuous experience Kero had ever experienced; and it was evident that Eldan was no stranger to it. In fact, given the evidence of her senses, she'd have to account him as very experienced in a number of areas, with a formidable level of expertise.

Quite a difference from Daren.

At some point, the candle burned out, leaving only the fire for illumination; she hardly noticed. She saw him just as clearly with hands and mind as she did with her eyes.

One more thing that was different from Daren: incredible patience. It had been a very long time since her last lover; Eldan was understanding, and gentle—and made certain she was fully satisfied, sated, in fact, before taking his own pleasure, pleasure in which she joined, thrilled by the overwhelming urgency she felt rushing into her from his mind. He arched his back and cried out, then slowed, breathing ragged and spent, and came to rest atop her. They lay together entwined, and gradually Kero realized he was falling asleep and fighting it. She soothed the back of his neck with a delicate brush of fingertips, and he sighed at the wordless exchange and gave up the fight. He withdrew from her, gently and slowly, still aware of all the sensations of each others' bodies. When she was certain he wasn't going to wake, she carefully disengaged herself, found another dry piece of wood, and threw it on the fire, giving her a little more light to see by. She reached out and caught a corner of his bedroll, shook it out, and draped the blankets over both of them.

As she settled in beside him, she noticed the Companion stare at him and sigh, before turning toward the entrance of the cave in a "guard" stance. That was the last thing she saw as she fell asleep.

When she woke, Eldan was already awake and about; in fact, that was what had awakened her. Wisely, he did not attempt to move quietly—anything that sounded like "stealth" would have sent her lunging to her feet with a weapon in hand. She woke just enough to identify where she was, and who was with her—then enjoyed the unwonted luxury of taking her time about coming to full consciousness. There was no hurry; she certainly wasn't going anywhere. . . .

Especially not today. Today she was one long ache, from the soles of her feet to the top of her head. Just bruises and muscle aches, of course; the cuts would be half-healed scars by now. Or, more accurately, half-Healed scars. She suspected that the wounds she had taken had been a *great* deal worse when she'd gotten them—but one of Need's attributes was that she Healed the bearer of just about anything short of a death-wound. She'd surreptitiously made certain that the sword was under her bedroll, well padded to avoid making a lump, before she'd undressed to have Eldan tend to her injuries. She didn't have to be in physical contact with it for it to Heal her; it just had to be nearby, but under her bedroll was where she liked to put it when she had hurts that needed to be dealt with. She *certainly* would never have slept with a concussion without Need's Healing.

She wondered what Eldan would make of her rapid recovery.

I hope he'll just think a little self-Healing is one of my abilities. I'd rather not have him asking too many questions about Need. Grandmother said there was something odd about Heralds and magic, and I'd rather not find out what it is.

Eldan had set about organizing the cave into a place where they could stay comfortably for several days. Just now he was heaping bracken into a depression and covering it with a layer of grass, and after a moment, she figured out why. It was to be a bed, of course; much more comfortable than a couple of bedrolls on the cold stone floor. She watched him, blinking sleepily, as he laid her saddle and his own upside down to dry, and spread both horse blankets out to air.

"A nest, little hawk? You're far more ambitious than I am," she said with a yawn.

He looked up, and grinned. "Here," he said, tossing her clothing. "It's clean. I washed it all while you were asleep."

She shrugged off the covers and ran a hand through her hair, grimacing at the feel of it. "I almost hate to get into clean clothing when I'm as dirty as I am."

"That's easily remedied, too," he told her. "This is a limestone cave, and that means water. There's a tiny trickle at the back of the cave. Enough to keep all of us supplied, and clean up a little, too."

One of the things she'd stolen on her forays after food had been a bar of rough brown soap; harsh with lye, but it would get her clean. It had been in her packs; Eldan had evidently found it when he'd rummaged around looking for the medical supplies (such as they were). He handed the soap to her, with a scrap of cloth that had once been part of her shirt. *He* didn't have much, besides his bedroll and some clothing.

"Come keep me company," she said, heading to the back of the cave and the promised water. Sure enough, there was a little stream running across the back of it, in one side and out the other, with a rounded pool worn by its motion. Cold, too. She winced as she stuck her hand in it, but cold was better at this point than dirty.

"So how did you manage to find such attractive company?'' she asked, as she scrubbed ruthlessly at dirt that seemed part of her, harsh soap, cold water, and all.

"Well, I was all tied up at the time—"

"I meant the *Karsites,* loon," she said, splashing water at him. He ducked, and grinned.

"Be careful, or you'll put out the candle," he warned. "And I don't have many. We really ought to make do with firelight. So, you want to know how I happened to be keeping company with Karsites? I'll tell you what, you answer a question, and I'll answer one. Fair enough?"

"Well—" she said cautiously.

"I'd like to know where you got such good training in your Gift if you never told anyone about it," he interrupted eagerly. "Your control is absolutely amazing!"

"I told one other—person," she admitted, reluctantly, "Actually, he came to me, because I was—uh—making it hard for him to sleep at night." She ducked her head in the cold water, more than the chill of her bath making her shiver. Years of concealing her abilities had made a habit of secrecy that was just too much a part of her to break with any comfort. The silence between them lengthened. "Look," she said, awkwardly, her hair full of soap. "I'd rather not talk about it. It—it just doesn't seem right. I really don't use it that much, and I'd rather forget I had it."

He sighed, but didn't insist. "I guess it's my turn, hmm? Well, it's stupid enough. Or rather, I was stupid enough. I was just across the Border, in a little village. Not spying, precisely, just picking up commonplace information, gossip, news, that kind of thing."

She turned to stare at him. "Wearing *that?* Blessed Agnira, what kind of an idiot are you?"

"Not *that* much of an idiot!" he snapped, then said, "Sorry. I wasn't that stupid, no, I was wearing ordinary enough clothing, and I'd walked in; I'd left Ratha out in the woods, outside the village walls. I thought my disguise was perfect, and I thought my contacts were trustworthy, but obviously, something went wrong. I *think* someone betrayed me, but I'll probably never know for sure. Anyway, when they first hauled me outside the walls, there were only a couple of the guards and no

priestess; Ratha tried to get me loose, and they got one
of my saddlebags even though they couldn't catch him."

"And when they found the uniform, they couldn't resist dressing you in it." She rinsed out her hair, and
dried herself with the rag he handed her. With a smile
of amusement, she recognized the rest of her ruined shirt.
"I can see their reasoning. Makes it all the more evident
to the priestess that they really *had* caught a Herald."

He nodded, and she pulled the clean clothing on, dripping hair and all. "So, that's it. Short and unadorned."

*Except for the reason you were over here. Just gath-
ering "information," hmm? With the ability to read
thoughts? Not bloody likely. You were posted to that village to eavesdrop on everything you could, and you're
more of a fool than I think you are if you haven't realized
I'd figure that out. So you Heralds aren't quite as noble—
or as stupid—as you claim. There's such a thing as morality, but there's such a thing as expediency, too. I just
hope you save your expediency for your enemies.*

But she didn't say anything, just strolled over the uneven surface of the cave floor to their fire.

"So how did *you* end up here?" he asked, handing her
a roasted tuber and her water skin. "The closest fighting
I know of is on the Menmellith border, and you're leagues
away from there."

"Sheer bad luck," she told him. "The worst run of
luck I could have had except for one thing—nobody's
managed to kill me yet, that I know of."

He smiled at that, and she described the rout, the flight,
the dive into the river, and her continued flight deeper
and deeper into enemy lands.

"—so I ended up here," she finished. "Like I said,
sheer bad luck."

"Not for me," he pointed out.

She snorted. "Well, if your chosen deity brought me
all this way to save your hide, it's going to cost you double. I may not be able to collect from a god, but I can
certainly collect from you!"

He laughed. "If any outside forces had any part in
bringing you up here, it wasn't at my request," he protested. "I mean, not that I wasn't praying for rescue, but
they *caught* me only yesterday, and you've been on the
run for—what? Weeks?"

"At least," she said glumly. "Seems like months. Sometimes I think I'm never going to make it back home alive."

"You will," he replied, softly.

She just shrugged. "So, are you going to introduce me to your friend? It hardly seems polite to keep acting like he's no brighter than Hellsbane."

Eldan brightened. "You mean, you—"

"My weaponsmaster told me about Companions," she said, cutting him off. "They're—s—s—"

And suddenly, she was tongue-tied. She literally could *not* say the word, "spirit."

"Special," she got out, sweating with the effort. "Absolutely the intellectual equals of you and me. Right?"

"Exactly." He beamed. "Ratha, this is Kerowyn. Kerowyn, Companion Ratha."

"Zha'hai'allav'a, Ratha," she said politely, as the Companion left his self-appointed watch post at the entrance and paced gracefully toward her. "That's Shin'a'in, the greeting of my adopted Clan," she told both Ratha and his Herald. "It means, 'wind beneath your wings.' My Clan's the Tale'sedrin, the Children of the Hawk."

She didn't know *why* the Shin'a'in greeting seemed appropriate; it just fit. Ratha nodded to her with grave courtesy; Eldan's eyes widened.

"Shin'a'in?" he exclaimed, and turned to look at Hellsbane, dozing over her heap of fresh-pulled grass. "Then— surely that's not—"

"She's a warsteed, all right," Kero said with pride. "And probably the only one you'll ever see off the Plains. Her name's Hellsbane. Smart as a cat, obedient as a dog, and death on four hooves if I ask it of her."

"That much I saw." He got up and walked over to the mare, who woke when he moved, and watched him cautiously.

"Hellsbane," Kero called, catching the mare's attention. *"Kathal, dester'edre."*

Hellsbane relaxed, and permitted herself to be examined minutely. Eldan looked her over with all the care of a born horseman. Finally he left her to return to her doze and seated himself back by the fire. "Amazing," he said in wonder. "Ugliest horse I've ever seen, but under that hide—if I were going to build a riding beast for warfare, starting from the bone out, that's exactly what I'd build.''

"My weaponsmaster claims that's what the Clans *did* do,'' Kero said. "The gods alone know how they did it, or even if they did it, but that's what she claims.''

"Amazing,'' he repeated, shaking his head. Then he raised it. "So, tell me about this weaponsmaster of yours. And how in the Havens did you manage to get adopted into a Clan?''

She smiled. "It's a long story. Are you comfortable?''

They were both a lot wearier than either of them thought. He told her to start at the beginning and she took him at his word. She told him about the ''ride''—and to her embarrassment, discovered that the song had made it as far as Valdemar. Once past the decision to leave home and beg some kind of instructions from her grandmother, she caught him yawning.

"I'm not—oh—that boring, am I?'' she asked, finding the yawns contagious.

"No,'' he said, "It's just that I can't keep my eyes open.''

"Well, I don't think any Karsites are going to creep up on us in the dark,'' she admitted, "And it's well after sundown. I never once noticed anyone moving around after dark except army patrols. And even *they* wouldn't go off the roads.'' She did not mention the strange and frightening instances when she'd felt as if she was being hunted; she had no proof, and anyway, nothing had ever come of it.

She got up and went to the tangled heap of blankets, intending to throw them over that invitingly thick bed of bracken he'd made. Eldan joined her in the task, still yawning.

"They seem to think that demons travel by night,'' he said, shaking out his blanket. "It seems that people vanish out of their houses by night—whole families, sometimes—and are never seen again. And not surprisingly, the ones that vanish are the ones that are the least devout, or have asked uncomfortable questions, or have shown some other signs of rebellion.''

She thought about the army patrols she'd seen moving about at night, and was perfectly capable of putting the two together. "Hmm. Demons on horseback, do you suppose? In uniform, perhaps?"

"A good guess," he acknowledged.

"Makes me very grateful I wasn't born in Karse."

Eldan spread the last of the blankets over the improvised bed, and tilted his head to one side. "Not all the 'vanished' end up dead, my lady," he said. "Some of them end up in the priesthood."

"Not a chance!" she exclaimed.

"I hadn't finished. They retain their skills—but they've forgotten everything about their old life. *Everything;* it happened to someone I was watching as a possible contact. She had a Gift of Mindspeech, one that was just developing. When I next saw her, she didn't recognize anyone she had known before. Her mind was a complete blank—and her devotion to the Sunlord was total." He nodded as she felt the blood drain from her face.

"You mean—everybody with these 'Gifts' winds up in the priesthood—and someone in the priesthood strips their minds?" The idea was horrible, more horrifying than rape and torture, somehow. Rape and torture still left you with your own mind, your own thoughts.

"Someone in the priesthood wipes their minds *clean.* Everything that made them what they are is gone. I've been able to trigger old memories in someone suffering from forgetfulness after a head injury—" (She filed that away for future reference.) "—but I have *never* been able to do so in one of the priestesses." He sighed. "Some would say that they are still better off that way than dead, but I don't know."

She shivered uncontrollably. "I'd rather be dead."

He put his arms around her to still the shudders. "Now I've told you something that's sure to make you have nightmares," he said apologetically. "I am sorry. I didn't mean to—"

She snuggled closer in a lightning change of mood, heat in her groin kindled by the warmth of his arms around her, and the feel of his strong body against hers. "You can do something to make me forget," she pointed out, and nibbled delicately on his earlobe.

"So I can," he laughed.

And proceeded to do just that.

* * *

Today there *were* hunters out there, though none were near the cave, and neither of them wanted to risk going out. Quite a few hunters were prowling the hills, in fact— and at least a half-dozen priests. The escaped Herald and his rescuer, it seemed, were very much sought after.

Ratha was the one who warned Eldan about the priests, fortunately before the Herald tried any Thoughtsensing. With that in mind, he pinpointed the enemy and identified the priests through the eyes of the animals about them. He would have liked very much to touch the minds of their horses, so that he could overhear what they were saying to each other, but both of them felt that particular idea was far too risky.

"Maybe if you're ever in a trap you can't break out of," she said. "In fact, I'll tell you what I'd have done if I'd been in your shoes with your Gift back when they had you. I'd have waited until they were sure I was helpless, and then I'd have spooked their horses. Run a couple of them through the fire to scatter it, and they wouldn't have been able to see you getting away. Then I would have hidden real close to the camp until I saw a good chance to get the hell out of there. Like I told you, they don't expect a prisoner to stick around."

Eldan looked at her with considerable respect. "There are times I wish I could convince you to come back with me, and this is one of them. I'd *love* to put you in charge of a class at the Collegium."

She shuddered. "Thank you, no. I'd rather face a siege."

There were other, more disturbing, searchers. Twice, Kero "felt" those searching "eyes" she'd sensed before—this time they were angry, and she could feel the heat of their rage preceding and following them. The first time, she was watching at the entrance to the cave and didn't get a chance to see if Eldan felt them, too. But the second time was just after dark, when they were both lounging beside the barest coal of a fire, not wanting to risk a light being seen, and she instinctively flattened herself against the stone floor of the cave, blood turning to ice-water in her veins.

She looked over at a whisper of sound, and saw that Eldan had done the same thing.

"What *is* that?" she hissed, as if speaking aloud would bring the thing back.

"You felt it, too?" He also seemed impelled to whisper his words. "I don't know what it is. It isn't any kind of Thoughtsensing I've ever run up against before. It doesn't seem exactly like Thoughtsensing. It's like—" he groped for a description "—like there's actually some *thing* moving half in our world, and half in another, and the reason we can feel it is because it happens to be leaking its thoughts. Like it isn't shielded."

She considered that for a moment. "And demons walk at night," she said.

He stared at her. "Demons are only in stories!" he exclaimed indignantly, as if he thought she was trying to make a fool out of him. Then he faltered, as she continued to watch him soberly. "Aren't they?"

"Not in my grandmother's experience," she said, sitting up slowly, "Though I can't vouch for having seen one myself. But consider how *some* of the people who vanish at night do so out of their own houses, with no one else in the family aware that they're gone until the next day."

He contemplated that for a moment, as he pushed himself off the floor, and she watched his face harden. "If that's got even the barest possibility of being true, then it's all the more important that I get back to report." He did not, at that moment, look like a man she wanted to cross.

"I'm doing the best that I can," she pointed out without losing her temper. "After all, I have quite a bit riding on getting you back, myself!"

He stared at her for a moment, as if he wasn't certain just what she was. She watched curiosity slowly replacing anger in his expression. Finally he asked, "If I hadn't agreed to your price back there, would you have left me in their hands?"

It would serve you right if I said "yes," she thought, but honesty compelled her to answer otherwise. "If I could have gotten you loose, without getting myself killed, I would have," she said. "But instead of taking you to Valdemar, I'd have convinced you it was safer to go through Menmellith. And once across the border and with my Company, I'd have turned you over to the Mercenary Guild as a war prize. *They* would have ransomed you back to Valdemar. I'd have lost ten percent on the deal, but I still would have gotten paid.''

He stared at her, shocked and offended. ''I don't believe you!'' he spluttered. ''I can't believe anyone could be so—so—''

''Mercenary?'' she suggested mildly.

That shut him up, And after a few moments, his anger died, and was replaced by a sense of the humor of the situation. ''All right, I was out of line. You have a right to make a living—''

''Thanks for your permission,'' she replied sarcastically. *I'm really getting just a little tired of his attitude. . . .*

He threw up his hands. ''I give up! I can't say anything right, can I? I'm sorry, I *don't* understand you, and I don't think I ever will. I fight for a cause and a country—''

''And I fight for a living.'' She shrugged. ''I'm just as much a whore as any other men or women that make a living with their bodies, and I don't pretend I'm not.''

And maybe that's the real difference between us. Mercs are the same as whores, people who devote themselves to causes are like one half of a lifebonded couple. We do exactly the same things, just I do it for money, and you do it for love. Which may be another form of payment, so—maybe he still should do something about that attitude. She shrugged, feeling somehow just a little hurt and oddly lonely. It appeared that being able to read people's minds didn't necessarily make for less misunderstandings.

Which is as good a reason as any to keep from using it so much I come to depend on it, she decided. *If it can't keep two people who like each other from making mistakes about each other, it isn't going to keep me from making mistakes about other things.*

''So,'' she said, when they knew there probably weren't going to be any repetitions of their visitation, and both of them had gotten a chance to cool down a little, ''I don't know about you, but I am not going to be able to get to sleep for a while. Not after having *that* cruise by overhead.''

Eldan sighed, and looked up from the repairs he was trying to make to his clothing, using a thorn for a needle and raveled threads from a seam. "I'm glad I'm not the only one feeling that way. I was afraid you might think I was being awfully cowardly, like a youngling afraid of the dark."

"If stuff like *that* is out in the dark, I'd be afraid of it too!" She relaxed a little. *He isn't going to be difficult. Thank the gods.* "I don't know if being awake is going to make any difference to *that,* but I'd rather meet it awake than asleep. So let's talk. You know everything that's important about me—"

He started to protest, then saw the little grin on her face, grinned back and shrugged.

"All I know about you is that at some point in your life you decided to make a big fat target out of yourself." She fixed him with a mock-stern glare. "So talk."

Eldan put down his sewing, and moved over to her side of the fire, stretching himself out on their combined bedroll.

Also a good sign.

"To start with, I didn't 'decide' to become a Herald; no one does. I was Chosen."

The way he said the word made it pretty clear that he was talking about something other than having some senior Herald come up and pick him out as an apprentice. To Kero it had the sound of a priestly Vocation.

"Before that, I was just an ordinary enough youngling, one of the middle lot of about a dozen children. We had a holding, big enough that my father could call himself 'lord,' if he chose, but he made all of us learn what hard work was like. When we were under twelve, we all had chores, and over twelve we all took our turn in the fields with our tenants. One day I was out weeding the whiteroot patch, when I heard an animal behind me. I figured one of our colts or calves had gotten out—again—and I turned around to shoo him back to the pasture. Only it wasn't a calf, it was Ratha." Eldan sighed, and closed his eyes. As the firelight flickered over his peaceful expression, Kero guessed that memory must be one of the best of his life.

Silence for a moment. "So what's Ratha got to do with it?" she asked, when he didn't say anything more.

"What's—oh. Sorry. The Companions Choose us. You can't just march up to Haven and announce you want to be a Herald, and your father can't buy you an apprenticeship. Only the Companions make the decision on who will or will not be a Herald." Ratha whickered agreement, and Kero glanced over to see him nodding his head.

Well, if they're like the leshya'e Kal'enedral, *that makes sense. A spirit would be able to see into someone's heart, to know if he's the kind of person likely to forget how to balance morality and expediency.* Ratha looked straight at her for a moment, and his blue eyes picked up the firelight in a most uncanny manner. And he nodded again. She blinked, more than a little taken aback.

"When they're ready to go out after their Chosen, Companions will show up at the stable and basically demand to be saddled up. It's kind of funny, especially to see the reaction of new stablehands." He chuckled. "I was there one day when six of them descended on the stable, each one making it very clear he wanted to be taken care of *right now*, thank you. I had someone call in some of the trainees before the poor stableboy lost his mind. Anyway, I knew what Ratha's standing in the middle of the vegetable patch meant, though to tell you the truth, I'd always fancied myself in a Guard uniform, not Herald's Whites. I think my parents were rather relieved, all things considered; one less youngling to have to provide for. And we weren't that far from Haven, they knew I'd be back for visits, probably even several times a week. Mama made a fuss about 'her baby' growing up, of course, but it's always seemed to be more as if she did it because she thought she should."

Both of them grinned at that. "Couple of my mates have had send-offs like that," Kero offered. "And no doubt in anybody's mind that they weren't just as cared-for as anyone else in the family, just when the tribe's that big, *somebody* has to go eventually."

"And it's a relief when it's on their own. Aye." Eldan nodded vigorously. "Other than that, things were no different for me than for any other youngling at Collegium. Average in my classes, only thing out of the ordinary was the animal Mindspeech. Had a turn for disguise. Got to know this little bit named Selenay pretty well, gave me a bit of a shock when I found out she was the Heir, though!''

Knows the Queen by given name, hmm? The thought was a little chilling; it pointed up the differences between them. To cover it, she teased, ''If I'd known that, your price would have been higher.''

He opened his eyes to see if she was joking, and smiled when he saw that she was. ''That's it,'' he concluded. ''That's all there is to know about me. No famous Rides, no bad scrapes until this one. Nothing out of the ordinary.''

Kero snorted. ''As if Heralds could ever be ordinary. Right. Tell me another one.''

''I collect rocks,'' he offered.

''Great pastime for someone who spends his life on horseback.''

''I didn't say it was *easy,*'' he protested, laughingly.

Kero laughed with him. ''I should confess, then. I make jewelry. Actually, I carve gemstones. Now *that* is a portable hobby.''

''I used to write bad poetry.''

She glared at him.

''I stopped.''

She made a great show of cleaning her knife and examining the blade. ''Wise man. If you'd told me you still did, I'd have been forced to kill and eat you. And the world would have been safer. There's nothing more dangerous than a bad poet, unless it's a bad minstrel.''

She said that with such a solemn face that he began laughing. ''I think I can see your point,'' he chortled, ''I think in your position I'd start using my extra pay to put bounties on Bards!''

''I've thought about it,'' she said wryly. ''And not entirely in jest. Traditional Bardic immunity *can* lead to some misusing their power, and Bards have no one making sure they behave themselves the way the Healers and you Heralds do.''

''Only the Guild,'' he acknowledged, soberly. ''They're pretty careful in Valdemar, but outside? I don't know. I'll bet Karse is using theirs.''

''They're using their Healers,'' Kero pointed out. ''No Healing done outside a temple of the Sunlord. When they're in the mood, they even go hunt down their poor little herbmen and wisewomen. The only reason they don't go after midwives is because the priests can't be bothered with something that is only important to females.''

Eldan's expression sobered considerably. ''I didn't know that. There wasn't anyone like that in the villages I'd been watching. Makes you wonder. About what else they're using, I mean.''

''That it does,'' said Kero, who had a shrewd notion of what they were using. Dark magics? It was likely. And no one to stop them. You might as easily stand in the path of a whirlwind.

And all that was pitted against the two of them.

The night seemed darker, outside their cave, after that. and when they made love, it was as much to cling to each other for comfort as anything else.

The hunt stayed in their area for longer than Kero had expected, which led her to believe that the priestesses *were* getting some kind of indication of where they were. During that time, she got to know Eldan very well; possibly better than he knew. A mercenary learns quickly how to analyze those he will be fighting against or beside—and everything Kero learned led her to trust Eldan more.

Despite having used his powers to spy on the Karsites, he was truly sincere in his refusal to abuse them. He hadn't been so much prying into peoples' minds as simply catching stray thoughts, usually when people were speaking among themselves. As Kero had herself learned, there was a ''pre-echo'' of what they were about to say, a moment before the words emerged, and to someone with her Gift, those thoughts could be as loud as a shout.

To Kero's mind, that was no more immoral than setting spies in taverns, and establishing listening holes wherever possible.

As her concussion healed, they split the chores between them—the only exceptions being hunting. Eldan would happily eat what she killed, but he couldn't bear to kill it himself. That was fine with Kero; he knew what plants and other growing things were edible, and she didn't. So she hunted and he gathered, in the intervals between Karsite patrols, a situation she found rather amusing.

Two days after the hunt moved on, they left their hiding place. The hunters had made no effort at concealing their tracks, which pleased Kero no end. That meant that the Karsites were convinced their quarry was somewhere ahead of them, and they wouldn't be looking for them in the rear.

They traveled by night, despite the demons, or whatever they were. Kero had the feeling that Need was both attracting the things and hiding herself and the Herald from them. Kero did her best to recall every little tidbit she'd ever read or heard about such things.

Some information didn't seem to apply, like Tarma's story about Thalkarsh. Whatever was being used to find them didn't seem terribly bright, which argued for it being something less than a true demon.

Maybe a magical construct, but more likely an Abyssal Plane Elemental. Just about any Master-level mage could command one of those, and they *weren't* too bright. They were attracted by places where the magical energy in something or someone made a disturbance in the normal flows of such energy—but once they were in the area, they would not be able to find the source of the disturbance if it was strong enough to hide itself well. Just as it was easy to see a particularly tall tree from a distance, but next to impossible to find it once you were *in* the forest.

That was how she explained it to Eldan, anyway, but something forced her to couch it in vague terms that could apply to the mental Gifts as well as the magical. Although she couldn't explain away the part about it being magic-made itself, she found herself telling him glibly that the thing might be a creature out of the Pelagirs, invisible and intangible, but nevertheless there. Where *that* explanation came from, she had no idea, but she sensed that he accepted it a little better than he would have taken anything that smacked of "true" magic.

They found a hiding place by the light of dawn—an overgrown hollow, covered completely with leafy vines so that she wouldn't have guessed it was there if she hadn't been paying close attention to the topography of the land. The vines themselves were supported by bushes on either side of the hollow, but nothing actually grew down *in* the hollow itself. It wasn't as secure as a cave, and it certainly wouldn't form much of a shelter if it rained, but it was big enough for all four of them, and offered excellent concealment.

It was then, as they made love in sun-dappled shade, that Kero realized there was something out of the ordinary in her relationship with this man. She felt much closer to him than she had ever felt to anyone, except perhaps Tarma and Warrl, and found herself thinking in terms of things *he* might want as much as things *she* wanted.

It was such a different feeling that finally she was forced to admit she was falling in love with the man. Not just lust (though there was certainly enough of that in the relationship), but love.

Shallan would have laughed her head off. She always claimed that one day the "Ice Maiden" would thaw—and when she fell, she'd go hard.

Looks like she was right, Kero thought with a feeling very like pain, curling up against his back, with her head cradled just behind the nape of his neck and one hand resting on his hip. *Damn her eyes, anyway. I wonder how much money she had riding on it?*

It certainly hadn't been hard to fall for him. He was kind, personable, clean, very easy on the eyes; a "gentleman" in every sense of the word. He treated her like a competent human being, neither deferring to her in a way that made it seem as if he was patronizing her, nor failing to say something when he disagreed with her. He did *not* treat her like a freak for being a fighting woman the way most civilians did.

In fact, he treated her like one of the Skybolts would have, if she'd taken one as a lover. He treated her like a partner, an equal. In all things.

She moved a little bit closer; it was cold down in the hollow, but she wanted spiritual comfort as well as physical. Right now she was feeling very lost. . . .

He knows my best-kept secret. He's shared his thoughts with me.

Was that enough to make up for the differences between them?

Was anything?

* * *

Eldan crouched in the shelter of the branches of a tree beside Kerowyn, and fretted. *I have to get back. Selenay needs to know all this, and she needed to know it a month ago. Every moment wasted here could cost us.*

But the Karsite patrols on the road below didn't seem in any mood to indulge his needs. Even though the sun was setting, painting the western sky in pink and gold, the riders on the blue-shadowed road running between the hills below them showed no signs of heading back to their barracks. Kerowyn glanced over at him, and her lips thinned a little.

"You're not making them get out of the way any faster by fuming," she whispered. "And you're tying your stomach up in knots. Relax. They'll leave when they leave."

She just doesn't understand, he thought, unhappily, as the riders disappeared around a bend, heading north. *How am I ever going to get it through to her? She doesn't care when she gets home—hellfires, she hasn't even got a home—*

"Look, I need to get back to the 'Bolts just as badly as you need to get home," she continued, interrupting his train of thought. "We could still try cutting back toward Menmellith—"

If we go to Menmellith, it'll take three times as long to get back. Dammit, why can't she understand? He knew if he said anything, he'd sound angry, so he just shook his head vehemently, and tried to put on at least the outward appearance of calm. She looked away, her expression brooding, the last rays of the sun streaking through the boughs of the tree, and striping her hair with gold. He wondered what she was thinking.

She wants to avoid Valdemar. I want to bring her into Valdemar with me. If she can just see what it's like, she'll understand, I know she will.

Somewhere north above the road, Ratha was scouting, uncannily invisible among the trees. He settled his mind, closed his eyes, and reached out for the dear, familiar presence.

:Hola, hayburner!:

:Yes, oh, hairless ape?: Ratha had seen an animal trainer with an ape at one of the fairs, and the beast had

sported a pair of twin streaks in its hair that were nearly identical to Eldan's. The Companion hadn't let him forget it since.

:Never let up, do you?:

:I'm trying to lighten your mood, Chosen,: the Companion replied. *:You are going to fret yourself right off that branch if you don't calm yourself.:*

:Is that second patrol showing any sign of moving?: he asked anxiously, ignoring the advice.

He felt Ratha sigh. *:Relax, will you? They've settled in, but they haven't set up a permanent camp. I think they plan on moving before nightfall. In any case we can get by them above the road; I found a goat track.:*

Eldan stifled a groan. The last time Ratha had found an alternative route, they'd been all night covering a scant league of ground. *:How—ah—''challenging'' a goat track?:*

There was a hint of amusement in Ratha's mind-voice. *:Challenging enough. It'll be good for you.:*

Eldan Sent an image of his still-livid bruises. *:That's what you said about the last one you found.:*

:I have four legs instead of two, no hands, and I weigh a great deal more than you do. If I can make it over, you can.: Ratha sounded a little condescending, and more than a little impatient. *:All the fuming in the world isn't going to get us to Valdemar any faster. We'll get there when we get there.:*

:You sound like Kero,: Eldan replied, opening his eyes a little and taking a sidelong glance at the mercenary. She had been watching him, and he saw her swallow and look away. She knew he was Mindspeaking Ratha, and as always, it bothered her. *I wish she'd get over that, too.*

:She's had many lessons in patience. You could profit by her example.: Ratha hesitated for a moment, and Eldan had the feeling the Companion would have said more, but was uncertain if he should.

On the road below them, the Karsites finally reappeared, going back the way they had come. That just left the patrol Ratha was watching. As the last of the sun dropped below the horizon, the wind picked up, and gusted a chill down Eldan's neck. He felt a little more of a chill at Ratha's next words.

:You are very—fond of this woman,: Ratha said, finally.

:I think I'm in love with her,: Eldan told his Companion, cautiously, relieved to have it out in the open between them at last, but not certain he liked the phrasing or the tone of Ratha's statement.

:I—think you are, too,: Ratha replied, obviously troubled. *:I am glad for you, and yet I wish you were not.:*

Eldan had never hidden anything from his Companion, and he didn't intend to start now. *:Why?:* he asked, bluntly, determined not to let things rest with that. *:What's wrong with her? I know you like her.:*

:The patrol is moving off now,: Ratha replied brightly.

:Thank you. And you're changing the subject.: Eldan wasn't about to let Ratha get off that easily. *:I won't be able to move out of this tree for at least half a candlemark. I'm not going anywhere. Just what, exactly, is wrong with Kero?:*

Ratha sounded reluctant to answer. *:She doesn't understand you—us. She can't understand how we can be loyal to people we've never seen, be willing to stand between them and harm, and for no gain. She does not understand loyalty to a cause. And yet—:*

:What, yet?:

:There is something about her that is very noble. She abides by her own code. And she has been very good for you. You are more—alive, since being with her.:

:I feel more alive.: Eldan pondered Ratha's statements; caught Kero watching him with an odd little smile on her face, and felt his heart clench. This strange, frighteningly competent woman was not like anyone else he'd ever encountered. She was—like a perfect Masterwork sword; she could have given any of the famous beauties at Court tough competition, with her long, blonde hair, her finely chiseled features, her pale aquamarine eyes—

Competition? No. She'd never take second place to anyone. She's not only beautiful, she's polished. There's nothing about her that hasn't been honed and perfected until it's the best it can be. Beside her, any other woman looks like a pretty doll; no fire, no spirit. Except maybe the Heralds—but—

His relationships with other Heralds had never gone beyond friendship and a little intimate company. And *he* almost always had to initiate the latter.

Kero initiated lovemaking as often as he did; pouncing

on him, giving him soft little love-bites and growling like a large playful cat—languidly rubbing his shoulders or scratching his back, then turning the exercise into more intimate caresses. He shivered a little, a smile playing around the corners of his mouth. She was a truly remarkable, exciting, bedmate—

But she was more than that. She treated him outside of bed like an absolutely equal partner, taking on her share of the chores without a quibble, substituting things he couldn't do—like hunting—without an argument.

And she had entered his thoughts the way no one else, man or woman, ever had. He wanted to show her his home, to see her excitement, her reactions. He wanted to share everything with her.

He wanted, most of all, to make her understand. Because he wanted to hear her say she was willing to be his partner from now on. . . . *:I want to get her into Valdemar. I know once I get her there, she'll understand, she'll see what it's like for us, and she'll understand everything.:*

:If she ever could, *she—:* The Companion cut the thought off, and Eldan wondered what it was he almost said.

:She what?:

:It doesn't matter. Not now. Just an idle speculation. I agree, we should get her into Valdemar if we can. I think it would make all the difference.: He felt Ratha's reticence, and didn't press. Whatever it was, if it was important enough, Ratha would tell him in his own time.

:You are clear, now,: the Companion concluded. *:I will check ahead.:*

Eldan double-checked the road through the eyes of every bird and beast he could touch, and confirmed Ratha's statement. He opened his eyes again, and touched Kero on the elbow, carefully.

"We can go," he said quietly. "We've both checked."

"Good," she replied, a hint of relief in her voice. "I was beginning to wonder if I was going to spend the night in this tree."

She caught the branch she was sitting on and swung down to the one below. Eldan followed her, marveling at her agility, and her ability to move so well in the twilight gloom.

"Oh, I can think of worse places to spend the night than in a tree," he replied lightly, as he lowered himself down onto the ground beside her.

"So can I, and I've probably been in most of them. Can we take to the road?" She dusted her hands off on her breeches, and unwound Hellsbane's reins from the snag she'd tethered the mare to.

"So far. Ratha's going on ahead. He says he's found a goat-track we can use if more of those patrols show up."

She turned a sober face toward him. "I hope he's finding cover for us in case more of those—things—show up. I don't want to meet one of them out in the open with nowhere to hide."

"No more do I." He shuddered at the thought of it, and marveled at her courage, who'd encountered the creatures—whatever they were—alone, without panicking.

She's incredible, he thought for the hundredth time, as he followed directly in Hellsbane's tracks. *I have to get her back to Valdemar. I have to. She'll never want to leave. . . .*

Fourteen

They're thinking at each other again, Kero observed, trying not to cringe. With Eldan sitting and the Companion lying beneath a roof of living pine boughs, the Herald gazed deeply into Ratha's eyes, both of them oblivious to everything around them. The ground was invisible under a litter of pine needles that must date back ten or twenty years. They'd left Kero on guard while the two of them conferred. If Kero hadn't known the sky was clear, she'd have sworn there was a storm coming; it was that dark under this tree.

She looked away after a few moments, and decided that halfway up this same pine tree would be just about the best lookout point. She should be able to see quite a distance up the main valley from there. And she wouldn't have to watch Eldan and his Companion.

As usual, they'd traveled by night, stopping just before dawn to find a place to hole up in during the day. For the past night they'd been paralleling the main road down the center of a series of linked valleys. The closer they got to the Valdemar border, the less populated the countryside became—but the terrain was a lot rougher, and the alternatives to the main roads fewer. Their hiding place this time had been a little pocket-valley off the main vale. And it wasn't a place where Kero would have stopped if she'd had any choice. There was a shepherd's town—not a village, but a town, rating a main square, a marketplace, and the largest temple of the Sunlord Kero had seen yet—at the head of the valley. This had been the best they could do, and it hadn't been a terribly secure place to stay. A good-sized stand of tall pines with branches that drooped down to the ground ensured that there was no grass here; there was no water either, no one would stumble across them bringing his sheep to pasture. The pines themselves provided cover; one sheltered Hellsbane, one protected Ratha, and one kept the two of them hidden beneath the tentlike boughs.

But it was still open, and too close to that town to make any of them feel comfortable. Kero knew she slept lightly, and she was fairly certain the same could be said of Eldan and Ratha. After they woke, Eldan seemed preoccupied, and finally asked Kero to stand watch while he and his Companion talked.

Kero had a shrewd notion that strategy was not going to be the subject—that *she* was. She had gotten the impression more than once that Ratha liked her, but didn't entirely approve of her. Certainly the Companion wasn't likely to approve of her as a long-term liaison for his Herald.

He thinks a lot like his Herald, she reflected, climbing through the scratchy pine boughs carefully, to avoid making the tree shake. They couldn't afford any carelessness; there had been too many near-escapes in the past few days. The hunters were getting thicker, and more, not less, persistent.

Somehow, in the next couple of days, they had to make a try at the Border. Which meant that parting from him was only days away. She settled herself on a sturdy limb, and blinked her burning, blurring eyes back into focus. *Blessed Agnira, what am I going to do?* Standing watch didn't occupy a great deal of her attention, which meant she had more than enough left over to worry. *I'm in love with this man. He's in love with me. Should be a happy ending in there somewhere, if this was only a ballad. . . .*

She bit her lip to keep from crying. *The whole relationship is impossible, that's all there is to it. It's all the same problems that I had with Daren, only worse, because I* do *love him. I want to be with him more than I've ever wanted any other person in my life.*

But that was the key: any other *person*. Her independence had been dearly bought, and she wasn't about to give it up now.

If she went with him, giving up her position in the Skybolts, what would she do in Valdemar? The regular army might not take her, and if they did, she would undoubtedly find herself on the wrong end of rules and regulations every time she turned around. With her record, she could ask for concessions from a Company that she could never get from a regular army force. Her peculiar talents did not fit into the parameters of a regular army. She wasn't a foot or line soldier, she wasn't heavy or even light infantry, and she was in no way going to fit into heavy or light cavalry. She was a scout—well, that was a job for the foot soldier. She was a skirmisher—that was under the aegis of either light infantry (bow) or light cavalry (sword). She knew more about tactics than most of the regulation officers she'd met, and that would certainly earn her no points. Lerryn encouraged the input of his junior officers, but that simply wasn't so, outside of mercenary Companies.

That assumed they'd even take her in the first place; many regular armed forces wouldn't accept former mercs because they tended to have an adverse effect on discipline.

Which would leave me living on his charity. Not a chance. I won't ever put myself in that position again. Despite the lump in her throat and the ache in her chest at the thought of parting from Eldan, the resolution remained. *Never. I have my own life, and I'm going to lead it.*

He just didn't understand what could lead someone to fight for a living, and it didn't look as though he ever would. She'd tried to point out that if a relatively ethical person didn't do the fighting, that would leave it to unethical people—he'd stared at her as if she was speaking Shin'a'in. For her part, she could not understand his fanatical devotion to an abstract: a *country.* What on earth was there about a piece of property that made it worth dying for? Never mind that territorial disputes were what paid for a merc's talents, more often than not—she still didn't understand it. In a way, she was as alien to him as one of those Karsite priestesses. She disturbed him more than they did, because he *knew* they were alien—she was the woman he loved, and seemed completely rational to him—until she would say something that completely eluded him, or *he* would say something that made no sense to her.

There were other differences, too; serious ones. Like his attitude toward Mindspeech. The way he shared his

thoughts so freely with Ratha made her skin crawl and
her shoulders tighten defensively. *No one should be able
to get inside your mind that closely.*

It makes you vulnerable, she thought, with a shiver of
real fear. *What happens when you open yourself that
much to anyone? Gods and demons, the power that gives
them over you . . . even if they never use that power, it's
a point of weakness that someone else can exploit. And
will. There's never yet been a breached wall that someone doesn't use to invade.*

Then there was that fanatical devotion to duty of his.
He'd make it back to Valdemar if it killed him, just to
get information back there personally. *It isn't sane,* she
thought grimly. *It just is not sane. There are a dozen
ways he could get that news back, and if he took all of
them, that would virtually guarantee it* would *get there.
Maybe not as quickly, but it would get there. But it has
to be by his own personal hands. . . .*

He frightened her; as much as she loved him, she
feared him, and feared *for* him. She was torn between
that love and that fear, and when you added in her reluctance to place herself in a position where she would be
dependent on him, there was only one conclusion she
could come to.

*It's impossible. Oh, gods, it's impossible. And I still
love him. . . .*

She clutched the trunk of the tree in anguish, bark
digging into her palm, the pain keeping tears out of her
eyes. She fought to keep control, finally attaining it just
as Eldan himself appeared under the tree, waving at her
to come down.

She took a couple of deep breaths to make sure the
lump wasn't going to return, and to steady her nerves.
Then she waved back, grinning down at him, as if nothing was wrong.

The faint frown left his brow and he grinned in return.

We've more important things to worry about, she told
herself as she slipped down the tree as carefully as she
had climbed it. *Right up at the top is staying alive to
reach the Border in the first place.*

A rock was digging a hole in Kero's stomach, but just
now she didn't want to move to dislodge it. ''Where are

they all coming from?'' Eldan whispered, as they watched yet another of the Sunlord's priestesses pause just below the entrance to their current hiding place. She pulled back the cowl of her robe, and stared up at the face of the cliff above her. It looked blank from that angle; the ledge they were lying on obscured the entrance, and Kero had seen it only because she had been up in a sturdy oak spying out the land when she'd spotted it. And it couldn't be reached from the floor of the valley; they'd had to backtrack and come up over the ridge to get down to it.

Hopefully that meant no one would look for it. Except the priestess, like all the others, seemed to have sensed *something*.

From up here, they couldn't make out her features; they could just barely distinguish her face from her blonde hair. The scarlet robe she wore was a sure sign of high rank, though—the only rank above scarlet wore gold, and there were *never* women in gold robes. Against the green meadow below them, she looked like some kind of exotic flower.

''I have no idea where they're all coming from,'' Kero whispered back. That was at least half a lie; at this point she was fairly sure they were tracking Need somehow. It would make sense, since neither she nor Eldan ever used unshielded Mindspeech. Since magic was forbidden, it followed that the priesthood had some way of detecting its use. And Need was created with magic; even when she wasn't actually doing something, she must be ''visible'' to someone capable of detecting magic. And no doubt she could hide herself, but she had to know she was endangering her bearer, and her bearer wouldn't know *that* until a priestess actually was in sight.

Kero held her breath, waiting. Surely *this* time the camouflage would break; they'd be spotted. This red-robe was the highest ranking priestess they'd seen yet; all the rest had been white-, blue-, or black-rank. Surely this time would mark the end.

The woman pulled her hood back up over her head, and rode off across the meadow.

Kero let out the breath she'd been holding.

Eldan put his arm across her shoulders and hugged her

wordlessly. She snuggled into his shoulder for a moment, content just to enjoy it, and his warm presence.

But her mind wouldn't stop operating.

That's the third priestess today. We see two and three search parties every day. It's getting harder and harder to find a place to hide by dawn.

Some of that was to be expected; they were right on the Border now, and there were regular Border patrols all the time. Eldan had mentioned that, and mentioned, too, how he'd avoided them in the past. But he had not mentioned ever seeing the clergy out on these hunts before, an omission Kero found interesting.

But although he was trying to pretend that this kind of activity was entirely normal, it was fairly obvious that he was worried. Quite worried.

Which meant that a good number of these patrols were new, and probably called out to find them.

He knew the priestesses were able to pick up something about them, but he didn't know what, and so far Kero had been able to keep Need's abilities from him. So far he hadn't asked any awkward questions, and so far he didn't seem to have made the connection that only the female clergy were detecting whatever it was. It helped that he seemed utterly incurious at moments when she'd have expected a barrage of questions. That *was* odd, but no odder than the fact that she was literally unable to talk about anything involving real magic to him. Absolutely, physically, unable. She'd tried, and in the end, couldn't get the words out of her mouth.

She suspected Need had a hand in both those conditions, though she had no idea what it was doing, or why. But she was getting used to that.

She didn't *like* it, but she was getting used to it.

And it was doubtless the fact that Need was attuned to women's problems that was the reason for the priestesses detecting her, and not the priests.

That maddeningly logical part of her kept right on reasoning as she tried to enjoy the moment with his arm around her. *We've had three narrow escapes,* it said, scoldingly. *Each one got narrower than the one before it. There's no doubt about it: Need is bringing in the priestesses. We're never going to make it across the Border together.*

He'd given his word to send her his ransom, and she had every reason to believe his word was good. She had no logical reason why she should stay with him. In fact, if she wanted to ensure his survival, she *should* leave him. With the target traveling westward, this little section of the Border should be empty long enough for him to get across.

She inched back into the cave, grating along the sandstone, with a hollow feeling in the bottom of her stomach. She'd known all along she was going to have to face this moment, but that didn't make it any easier now that it was here.

She stood up and dusted herself off once inside. It would be stolen rations tonight, Karsite rations. One of those narrow escapes had been just this morning, and had ended in the death of the scout who'd discovered them making their way across the ridge. His body was in a tiny hollow just below the trail, stuffed into a cavelet barely big enough to conceal him. His horse had been run off in a state of sheer animal panic, thanks to Eldan. His rations now resided in their saddlebags. Eldan had been a little squeamish about robbing the dead, but she'd just taken everything useful without a comment, and after a moment, he'd done the same.

Eldan joined her back in the tiny cave. There was just barely enough room for them and the horses, though she could never bring herself to think of Ratha as a "horse." She never looked at him without a feeling of surprise that there was a "horse" standing there, and not another human.

Eldan handed her a strip of dried meat. She accepted it, and pulled her water skin out of the pile of her belongings.

"So," he said, around a mouthful of the tough, tasteless stuff, "It looks like tomorrow isn't going to be a good day to try a crossing."

She swallowed her own mouthful. It had the consistency of old shoes, and was about as appetizing. She found herself longing for the Skybolts' trail-rations, something she'd never have anticipated doing. At least those had been edible.

"We probably ought to hole up here for a while," she offered, feeling her heart sink and tears threaten at the

lie. "Probably they'll give up when they don't find anything, and leave this area clear for us to make a try."

Eldan nodded. "That sounds right. And we've got
supplies enough. All we need is water, and one of us can
go down after it about midnight."

"I'll do that tonight," she replied. "I'm better at
night-moves than you are."

He smiled in the way that made her blood heat. "I'll
agree to that," he said huskily. "And we've got all day
to wait. What do you say to doing something to make the
time pass a little faster?"

"Yes," she said simply, and reached for him even as
he reached for her, desperation making her want him all
the more. For this would be the last time, the very last
time. . . .

She shielded her thoughts and exercised every wile she
had to exhaust him, both out of a desire for him that
made her ache all over, and out of the need to make him
sleep so deeply that little would wake him—and certainly
not her departure.

Then she dozed in his arms, wanting to weep, and far
too tired to do so.

Finally the sun set, and she woke out of a restless half-
sleep full of uneasy dreams, fragments of things that
made no sense.

She extracted herself from his embrace without making him stir, packed up her things, and waited while the
sky darkened and the rising moon illuminated the
meadow below. Tears kept blurring her vision as they
trickled unheeded down her cheeks. She wasn't even going to get to say "good-bye."

She'd left a note for him, on top of the remaining rations, advising him to stay where he was for as long as
they held out, then make his crossing attempt. She told
him that she loved him more than she could ever tell
him—and dearest gods, those words had been hard to
write—and she told him that she could not go with him.
"We're too different," she'd said. "And we're too smart
not to know that. So—I took the coward's way out of
this. I admit it; I'm running away. Besides, I hate saying
good-bye. And don't you forget you owe me; I have to
replace my gear somehow!"

She didn't look back at him, where he was curled up

against the back wall of the cave; that would only make it harder to leave. Instead, she saddled Hellsbane and strapped on the packs, then led her toward the mouth of the cave, knowing that the familiar sound of hooves on rock would never wake him.

But Ratha was suddenly *there,* between her and the entrance, blocking her way.

Before she could react to that, a strange voice echoed in the back of her mind. *:Where are you going?:* it said sternly, *:And why are you leaving in stealth?:*

She gulped, too startled by this sudden manifestation of Ratha's powers to do anything more than stare. But the Companion did not move, and finally she was forced to answer him.

Mindspeech was *not* what she would have chosen if she'd been offered a choice, but if she spoke aloud, she might wake Eldan, and then she'd never be able to leave him. . . . So although it made her stomach roil to answer the Companion that way, she ordered her thoughts and ''spoke'' as clearly as Warrl had taught her.

:I have to go,: she told Ratha. *:I'm putting Eldan in danger while I'm with him.:*

:He was in danger when you found him,: the Companion pointed out with remorseless logic. *:What difference does your leaving make?:*

She took a deep breath, and rubbed her arms to get rid of the chill this conversation was giving her. *:It's the sword,:* she said finally. *:It's magic, and I'm fairly sure that's what has brought the hunt down on us. More than that, it is magic that only works for a woman, which may be why the priestesses are involved. And it's very powerful, I really don't know how powerful.:*

The Companion's blue eyes held her without a struggle. *:So,:* Ratha said finally. *:Your sword must be attracting these women. I agree that may be why no priests have hit on the trail. Why not abandon it?:*

:And leave it for them to find?: she flared. *:Do you want something like that in the hands of your enemies? It may not let me go, but if it does, be sure it will have a new bearer before the sun dawns. My bet would be on a priestess finding it, which might be good for your land or bad. I don't think any of us dare take a chance on which it would be.:*

:True.: Ratha seemed to look on her with a little more favor. *:And by taking this sword of yours away, the hunters all follow you, and you leave the Border here open to our crossing. You sacrifice your safety for ours, becoming a target leading away from us.:*

:I think so,: she said with a sigh. *:I hope so. I'm going to double back to Menmellith, which would have been our logical move if we'd been blocked here. That should make sense to them, and since they've been following the sword and not an actual trail, they'll follow me and ignore you.:*

The Companion nodded. *:You are very wise—and braver than I thought. Thank you.:*

He moved out of the way, and she led Hellsbane past him, onto the narrow ledge and the path that led up to it, still refusing to look back.

:Good luck,: she heard behind her as she emerged into the moon-flooded night. *:May the gods of your choice work on your behalf, Kerowyn. You are deserving of such favor. And may we all one day meet again.:*

That started the tears going again; she blinked her eyes clear enough to see the path, but no more. She had to move slowly, because she was feeling her way, and she was profoundly grateful that Hellsbane was surefooted and *could* see the path. She couldn't stop crying until she'd reached the ridge above the cave. There, she took several deep breaths, and forced herself to stare up at the stars until she got herself under control.

It's over, and I've finished it myself. Ratha and his own sense of duty will keep him from following. It never had a chance of working between us anyway, and at least I've ended it while we were still in love.

She closed her eyes, and rubbed them with the back of her hand, until the last trace of tears and grit was gone. Then she set Hellsbane's nose westward, and descended the ridge, heading for Menmellith. Soon the hunters would be following, and she needed a head start.

I've done brighter things in my life than this, she thought, cowering in the shadow of a huge boulder and wishing that she wasn't quite so exposed on the top of this ridge. But this was the only place she had been able to find that had any cover at all, and she *had* to see down her backtrail. Without Eldan, and his ability to look through the eyes of the animals about him, she was finding herself more than a bit handicapped.

The hunters had found her in the middle of the night, as she crossed from the heavy oak-and-pine forests into pine-and-scrub. She'd felt those unseen "eyes" on her just about at midnight, and this time they hadn't gone away until she had crossed and recrossed a stream, hoping the old saw about "magic can't cross running water" was true. By the time dawn bloomed behind her, the human hunters were hot on her trail, and not that far away, either. The best she could figure was that the "whatever-it-was" had alerted its masters, and they, in turn, had alerted the searchers directly in her path.

Dawn saw her doggedly guiding the mare over low mountains (or very tall hills) that were more dangerous than the territory she'd left behind, because the shalelike rock they were made of was brittle and prone to crumbling without warning. She didn't dare stop when she actually *saw* a search party top a ridge several hills behind her, and caught the flash of scarlet that signaled the presence of the red-robe among them. So there was to be no rest for her today; instead, she set Hellsbane at a grueling pace across some of the grimmest country she'd ever seen. This area was worse than the near-virgin forest, because she kept coming on evidence that people *had* lived here at one time. Secondary growth was always harder to force a path through than an old forest; tangly things seemed to thrive on areas that had been cleared for croplands, or where people had lived. This growth was all second- and third-stage; pine trees and heavy bushes, thorny vines and scrubby grass. All things that seemed to seize Hellsbane's legs and snag in Kero's clothing.

She had left Hellsbane drinking and got up on another ridge to look back about noon, and as she peered around her boulder, she saw the trackers still behind her, spotting them as they rode briefly in the open before taking to cover. This time they weren't several ridges away; they were only one.

She swore pungently, every heartache and regret she'd been nursing since leaving Eldan forgotten. She had something more important to worry about than heartbreak. Survival.

Hellfires. They're good. Better than I thought. And they were gaining on her with every moment she dallied.

She slid down the back of the ridge and slung herself up on the mare's back, sending her out under the cover of more pine trees. And the only thing she could be grateful for was that the day was overcast and Hellsbane was spared the heat of the sun.

They're going to catch up, she thought grimly. *They know this area, and I don't; that's what let them get so close in the first place. I'm in trouble. And I don't know if I'm going to get out of it this time.*

She wanted to ''look'' back at her pursuers, tempted to use her Gift for the first time in a long time—

And stopped herself just in time.

That isn't me, she realized, urging Hellsbane into greater speed as they scrambled down a gravel-covered slope. *Something out there* wants *me to use my Gift, probably so they can find me. Or catch and hold me until they come.*

She fought down panic; Hellsbane was a good creature, and bright beyond any ordinary horse, but if *she* panicked, so would Hellsbane, and the warsteed might bolt. If Hellsbane took it into her head to flee, Kero wasn't sure she'd be able to stop her until she'd run her panic out.

And that could end in her broken neck, or the mare's, or both.

Kero kept Hellsbane in the cover of the trees, even though this meant more effort than riding in the open. She looked automatically behind her as they topped the next hill, and saw not one, but two parties of pursuers; both coming down off the slope she'd just left, and both parties so confident of catching her now that they weren't even trying to hide. They couldn't see her, but they could see her trail; she wasn't wasting any time trying to hide it.

They were perhaps a candlemark's ride from her, if she stopped right now. The temptation to leave cover and make a run for it was very great. If she let Hellsbane run, she might be able to lose them as darkness fell.

Assuming that *their* horses weren't fresh.

Hellsbane had been going since last night, and she couldn't do much of a run at this point.

They could. And would.

Kero sent the mare across a section of open trail when they dropped out of sight, hoping to get across it before they got back into viewing range. This was one of the worst pieces of trail she'd hit yet; barely wide enough for a horse, bisecting a steep slope, with a precipitous drop down onto rocks on one side and an equally precipitous shale cliff on the other.

No place to go if you slipped, and nowhere to hide if you were being followed.

She breathed a sigh of relief as they got into heavier cover before the hunters came into view. She hadn't wanted to rush the mare, but her back had felt awfully naked out there.

Thunder growled overhead; Kero looked up, pulling Hellsbane up for a moment under the cover of a grove of scrub trees just tall enough to hide them. She hadn't been paying any attention to the weather, but obviously a storm had been gathering while she fled westward, because the sky was black in the west, and the darkness was moving in very fast—

How fast, she didn't quite realize, until lightning hit the top of a pine just ahead of her, startling Hellsbane into shying and bucking, and half-blinding her rider. The thunder that came with it *did* deafen her rider.

And the downpour that followed in the next breath damned near *drowned* her rider.

It was like standing under a waterfall; she couldn't see more than a few feet in front of her. She dismounted and automatically peered through the curtain of rain back down the trail behind her—

Just in time to see it disappear, melting beneath the pounding rain. She stared in complete disbelief as the trail literally vanished, leaving her pursuers no clue as to where she had gone, or where she was going.

In fact, the part of the trail she and the mare were standing on was showing signs of possible disintegration. . . .

Taking the hint, she took Hellsbane's reins in hand and began leading her through the torrent of water. Streams poured down the side of the hill and crossed the trail;

the water was ankle-deep, and carried sizable rocks in its churning currents. She found that out the hard way, as one of them hit her ankle with a *crack* that she felt, rather than heard.

She went down on one knee, eyes filling with tears at the pain—but this was not the time or the place to stop, no matter how much it hurt. She forced herself to go on, while icy water poured from the sky and she grew so numb and chilled that she couldn't even shiver.

And grateful for the rescue; too grateful even to curse that errant rock. *This—thing—came up so fast*—she thought, peering at the little she could see of the footing ahead of her, leading Hellsbane step by painful step. *It—could almost be—supernatural.*

In fact, a suspicion lurked in the back of her mind perhaps Need had had something to do with it. There was no way of telling, and it *could* all be just sheer coincidence.

Still, there was no doubt that it had saved her.

Always provided she could find some shelter before it washed her away.

And wouldn't that be ironic, she found herself thinking wryly. *Saved from the Karsites only to drown in the storm! Whoever says the gods don't have a sense of humor.* . . .

Fifteen

I'm glad Hellsbane can see, because I can't. Kerowyn's eyelids were practically glued shut with fatigue. She rode into the Skybolts' camp in a fog of weariness so deep that she could hardly do more than stick to Hellsbane's saddle. The mare wasn't in much better case; she shambled, rather than walked, with her head and tail down, and Kero could feel ribs under her knee instead of the firm flesh that should be there.

She rode in with the rain, rain that had followed her all the way from beyond the Karsite Border. Or maybe she had been chasing a storm the entire time; she wasn't sure. All she did know was that the rain had saved her, and continued to save her as she traveled—washing out her tracks as soon as she made them, for one thing. It also seemed as if it was keeping those supernatural spies of the Karsites from taking to the air, for another; at any rate she hadn't felt those "eyes" on her from the moment the rain started to come down. And last of all, the mud and rain had completely exhausted her pursuers' horses, who had none of Hellsbane's stamina.

From the exact instant when the first storm hit, she'd been able to make her soggy way across Karse virtually unhindered. She hadn't been *comfortable,* in fact, she spent most of the time wet to the skin and numb with cold, but she hadn't had to worry about becoming a guest in a Karsite prison.

Her only real regret: she'd had to ride Hellsbane after the first storm slackened; that rock hadn't broken her ankle, but it had done some damage. A bone-bruise, she thought. She wasn't precisely a Healer, but that was what it felt like. She'd hated putting that much extra strain on the mare, but there was no help for it.

Luck or the sword or some benign godlet had brought

her across the border at one of the rare Menmellith bor-
derposts. She'd introduced herself and showed her Mercenary Guild tag, and her Skybolt badge; she'd hoped for
a warm meal and a dry place to sleep, but found cold
comfort among the army regulars.

*They damn near picked me up and threw me out. Bas-
tards. They could at least have given me a chance to dry
off.*

At least they'd told her where the Skybolts had gone
to ground; she'd ridden two days through more heavy
rains to get there, so numb that she wasn't even thinking
about what she was likely to find.

The camp didn't seem much smaller; she'd feared the
worst, that half or three-fourths of the Skybolts were
gone. But it was much shabbier; the tents were make do
and secondhand, and the banner at the sentry post was
clumsily sewn with a base of what *looked* like had once
been someone's cloak.

The rain slacked off as they reached the perimeter of
the camp itself. Hellsbane halted automatically at the
sentry post; the sentry was a youngster Kero didn't recognize, probably a new recruit. He seemed very young
to Kero.

So new he hasn't got the shiny rubbed off him yet.

And he looked eager and a little apprehensive as he
eyed her.

*Probably because I look like I just dragged through the
ninth hell.*

She dragged out her Skybolt badge and waved it at
him. "Scout Kerowyn," she croaked, days and nights of
being cold and wet having left her with a cough and a
raspy throat. "Reporting back from the Menmellith Border."

Before the boy could answer, there was a screech from
beyond the first row of tents, and a black-clad wraith shot
across the camp toward her, vaulting tent ropes and the
tarp-covered piles of wood beside each tent.

"Kero!" Shallan screamed again, and heads popped
out of some of the tents nearest the sentry post. Hellsbane was so weary she didn't even shy; she just flicked
an ear as Shallan reached them and grabbed Kero's boot.
"Kero, you're *alive!*"

"Of course I'm alive," Kero coughed, slowly getting herself out of the saddle. "I feel too rotten to be dead."

By now more than heads were popping out of the tents and she and Shallan had acquired a small mob, all familiar faces Kero hadn't realized she missed until now. They crowded around her, shoving the poor young sentry out of their way, all of them laughing (some with tears in their eyes), shouting, trying to get to Kero to hug her or kiss her—it was a homecoming, the kind she'd never had.

She looked around in surprise, some of her tiredness fading before their outpouring of welcome. She hadn't known so many people felt that strongly about her, and to her embarrassment, she found herself crying, too, as she returned the embraces, the infrequent kisses, the more common back-poundings and well-meant curses. *They're family. They're my family, more than my own blood is. This is what Tarma was trying to tell me, the way it is in a good Company; this is what makes Lerryn a good Captain.*

"I have to report!" she shouted over the bedlam. Shallan nodded her blonde head, and seized her elbow, wriggling with determination through the press of people. Gies showed up at Hellsbane's bridle and waved to her before leading the mare off to the picket line.

She knows him—yes, she's going. she'll be fine.

Word began to pass, and the rest parted for her when they realized what she'd said; a merc unit didn't stand on much protocol, but what it did, it took seriously. Somewhere in the confusion someone got the bright idea that they should all meet at the mess tent; the entire mob headed in that direction, while Shallan took Kero off in the direction of the Captain's tent.

"I've got the legendary good news and bad news." They slogged through mud up to their ankles, and Kero blessed Lerryn's insistence on camp hygiene. In a morass like this, fevers and dysentery were deadly serious prospects unless a camp was kept under strict sanitary conditions. The blonde looked up as the gray sky began dripping again, scowling in distaste. "So what do you want first?"

"The bad, and make it the casualties." Kero sighed and braced herself to hear how many friends were dead or hurt beyond mending; this was the last thing she wanted to hear, but the very first she needed to to know.

Who am I going to be mourning tonight? she asked herself, the thought weighing down her heart the way the sticky clay weighed down her steps.

"Right." Shallan grimaced. "That's the worst of the bad, because number one was Lerryn and number two was his second, Icolan. In fact, most of the officers didn't make it out. It's like every one of them had a great big target painted on his back; I've never seen anything like it." She glanced over to see how Kero was taking the news—and Kero didn't know quite what to say or do. It was just too much to take all at once.

She felt stunned, as if someone had just hit her in the stomach and it hadn't begun to hurt quite yet. *Lerryn? Dear Agnetha—* it didn't seem possible; Lerryn was everything a good Captain had to be. There was no way he should be dead. . . . "He? His?" she said sharply, as the sense of what she'd just heard penetrated. Shallan never worded anything by accident. "Does that mean—"

Shallan's head bobbed, her short hair plastered to her scalp by the rain. "Both the women made it. The only problem is that the higher-ranked one is—"

"Ardana Flinteyes." Kero took in a deep breath and held it. That was bad news for the Company, or so Kero judged, and she was fairly certain Shallan felt the same way. Ardana should by rights never have risen above the rank she'd held before the rout. *She's a good fighter, but she's got no head for strategy, she blows up over the least little thing and stays hot for months, and—I don't like her ethics. No, that's not true. I don't like the fact that she doesn't seem to have many.* "So Ardana's a topranker? Not over—"

"Worse," Shallan said grimly, then looked significantly at the Captain's tent, with its tattered standard flying overhead. It wasn't the crossed swords anymore. It was flint and steel striking and casting a lightning bolt.

"She's the Captain?" Kero whispered, appalled by the prospect.

Shallan nodded, once.

Kero took a deep breath. The Company had to go to someone. At least Ardana had experience, and with *this* Company. It was better than disbanding. Well, it was *probably* better than disbanding. She stopped where she was and stared at the new standard, oblivious to the rain pouring down on her. After all, she was already soaked.

"The good news is that all the scouts made it," Shallan said hurriedly, as if to get her mind off the uneasy prospect of Ardana as Captain. "And I've got a tent, a whole one; it fits four and there's only me and Relli. You can come on in with us, we don't mind."

Kero sighed; she'd rather not have shared with anyone, but she doubted there was a choice. It was shelter, and the company was good. She'd rather have her own—but maybe she could manage that in the next couple of days. Obviously the Company had lost all of the equipment left behind during the rout.

"I'll take you up on that," she said, surprised at the gratitude she heard in her voice beneath the weariness. She straightened her back and squared her shoulders. "Might as well get this over with while I can still stand."

She smoothed back her soaked hair with both hands, and smiled slightly at the younger woman. Shallan patted her shoulder encouragingly, and led the way.

Kero stared up at the stained and mildew-spotted canvas overhead. It wasn't *her* tent, but it was waterproof, and Shallan and Relli had gotten the mildew stink out of it somehow. She was happy just to be lying down, and dry, and warm. Granted that the bedroll was looted from who knew where, smelled of horse, and had seen better days; that didn't matter. Dry and warm counted for a lot right now.

The interview with Ardana had not proved the ordeal Kero feared it might be. *Except that she ignored half of what I said about the Karsites, where Lerryn would have had me in there till I fell over, taking notes.* That was disturbing; more disturbing was that Ardana really didn't seem interested in the things she *had* asked about. It was as if she was going through the motions, as if she had some other opponent in mind than the Karsites.

But just about everyone had deduced from Hellsbane's condition what Kero's must be like; when Ardana let her go, they'd sent Shallan over to bring her to the mess tent—but *then* they sat her down and got her fed, and didn't ask too many questions. Then someone had brought in a spare shirt, and someone else produced breeches and socks, and a third party a heavy woolen sweater—

They'd stripped her to the skin right there in the mess tent, amid a lot of laughter and rude jokes about how it would be more fun to bed her sword than her, right now.

"So change that!" she'd retorted. "You can all start buying me steaks!" Meanwhile she had been pulling on the first warm, dry clothing she'd had in a week.

Then they ran her over to Shallan's tent under a pilfered tarp, so she wouldn't get wet again. It had all been a demonstration of caring that had left her a little breathless.

Maybe that was why she was having trouble falling asleep.

I was right, she thought, staring at the mottled ceiling, listening to the rain drum on it. *I was right to come back. This is where I belong. I could never fit in with Eldan, with his friends, no more than I could have with Daren and the Court. I'd have only made both of us miserable trying.*

Her eyes burned; she sniffed, and rubbed them with her sleeve, glad that Shallan and Relli were off somewhere else. Probably in the mess tent; they were both passable fletchers, and the Skybolts had lost a lot of arrows. . . .

A lot of other things, too. Kero thankfully shifted her thoughts to the general troubles. The Company was in trouble. Equipment lost, officers decimated, about a third of the roster gone and another third on the wounded list— and Menmellith had declined to pay them more than half their fee, on the grounds that they hadn't stopped the "bandits," and they hadn't come up with real proof that they were operating with more than the Karsite blessing. The Guild, when appealed to, had reluctantly ruled in Menmellith's favor.

It could always be worse. The Wolflings are going to have to find another Company to combine with. There's hardly enough of them left to fill out one rank.

Dearest goddess, I'm going to miss Lerryn.

There were a lot of people she was going to miss. And right on the top of the list was Eldan.

Her throat closed again, and she choked down a sob. *I love him, and it would never have worked. I love him,*

*and I'm never going to see him again. He probably thinks
I deserted him under fire or something.*

She'd been hoping for some kind of message from him
when she reached the camp; he knew what her Company
was, and messages moved swiftly through the aegis of
the Guild. But there had been nothing.

*He probably got back to Valdemar and came to his
senses. He's probably sitting with friends now, with pretty
little Court ladies all around him, thinking what a lucky
escape he had, that he could have been stuck with this
barbarian merc with a figure like a sword and a face like
a piece of granite.* She blinked, and a couple of hot tears
spilled down her temples into her hair. *He's probably so
grateful I left that he's burning incense to the gods. He's
probably even making jokes about me. Like, "how many
mercs does it take to change a candle—"*

More tears followed the first. *It doesn't matter. I love
him anyway. I'll always love him.*

And I'm better off alone. We both are.

She turned over on her side and faced the canvas wall,
with one of the blankets pulled up over her head so they'd
think she was asleep if anyone came in. She muffled her
face in her sleeve, and cried as quietly as she could manage, with hardly even a quiver of her shoulders to betray
her; only the occasional sniff and the steady creeping of
tears down into her pillow. And somehow she managed
to cry herself to sleep.

When she woke, the tent was dark, and there was
breathing on the other side of it. The steady breathing of
sleep; somehow Shallan and Relli had come in and settled down without her being aware of it.

She didn't wake very thoroughly; just enough to reg-
ister that she wasn't alone, and remember who it was.

I'm not alone. Somehow that was a comforting
thought. *I have friends. I can live without him.* That was
another. Holding those thoughts warmed her; and
warmed, she fell back asleep.

It was raining again. A half-dozen of them were in the
mess tent, attaching heads and feathers to grooved arrow
shafts. Kero reckoned up the weeks in her head, and
came to a nasty total.

"This is the winter rains, isn't it?" Kero asked Shal-

lan, as they reached for feathers at the same moment.
"We've gone over into winter, haven't we?"

Shallan's studious inspection of the arrow fletchings
didn't fool Kero a bit. "Come on," she said warningly.
"I'm going to find out sooner or later. Cough it up."

"We've hit the winter rainy season, yes," Shallan replied, glancing uneasily over her shoulder at Kero. "It
did come awfully early, but—"

"But nothing. If this is winter, why aren't we in winter
quarters?" Kero lowered her voice, after a warning look
from Relli. "What are we doing still out in the field?"
she hissed.

"Well," Shallan said unhappily, taking a great deal of
time over setting her feather. "You know we didn't get
paid enough. And we lost a lot of manpower and material—"

"And? So?" Kero had a feeling she knew what was
coming up, and she wasn't going to like it. "That's what
the reserves are for, Right?"

"Well—uh—" Shallan floundered.

Finally Relli came to her partner's rescue. "We aren't
going to use the reserves," she said tersely. "Ardana has
a line on a job."

That was what I was afraid of. "In winter."

Shallan nodded. "In winter. It's south of here—"

Kero just snorted. "I *come* from south of here. We're
going to be fighting in cold rain *if we're lucky.* If we're
not—snow, up to our asses, for the next three months.
And ice. I trained in weather like that, but most of the
rest of you didn't. Think what it's going to do to the horses,
if you won't think of yourself!"

"It's not that bad," Relli said sturdily, though she
wouldn't look Kero in the face. "It's in Seejay. Flat as
your hand, and not more than a couple of inches of snow
all winter. And it's not supposed to be a hard job—it's a
merchant's guild thing. Economic. One side or the other
is going to get tired of paying, and we can go home.
Frankly, it's better to fight there in winter than summer—
summer you're like to cook in your armor."

*So instead we drown—provided we don't die of ex-
haustion on a forced march down through Ruvan.*

"So is this just a rumor, or have you got something
more substantial?" she asked.

"I'm pretty sure it's going down," Relli told her. "I got it from Willi."

Since Willi was the Company accountant, it was a pretty fair bet that the bid was in. Kero sighed.

"I suppose it could always be worse—"

Three months later, she found herself wishing for that hip-deep snow.

She cleaned mud off her equipment and Shallan's, scouring savagely at the rust underneath on Shallan's scale-mail. Rain dribbled down on the roof of her tent, and down the *inside* of the shabby walls. Practically anything would have been better than the bog that was Seejay in winter.

A *cold* bog. One that froze overnight and thawed by midday, only to freeze again as soon as the sun set.

And they were the only Company that had been hired. *That should have told us something from the start,* she told herself, for the thousandth time. *We should have walked before we took this one.*

Fighting beside them were the cheapest of free-lancers, one step up from prison scum; drunks and madmen, vicious alley rats who'd knife an ally quick as an enemy. No point in depending on them—and no turning your back on them. The sentries caught the bastards sneaking around camp every night and most days, and everyone had *something* missing.

Facing them were more prison-scum and a "company" of non-Guild conscripts; old men too damned stubborn to quit fighting, and bewildered farmers hauled in after the harvest.

That was the reason for holding this "war" in winter in the first place: it was after harvest and trading season. *No money-making opportunities lost to combat,* she thought cynically. *As witness the little "bazaar" just outside camp. Everything they think a merc could want; from flea-ridden whores to watered wine.*

This entire setup had Kero completely disgusted. Ardana's "deal"—such as it was—had been for half pay and half resupply. *First of all, she should have known never to trust them on that. Secondly, she should have gotten the resupply in advance.*

The total had come to half their usual fee, which Ar-

dana covered, stridently defensive, by pointing out that
they were undermanned, and she couldn't ask the full fee
for what was effectively half a Company. Then the "resupply" train had shown up—late—and there was nothing Ardana could say that would defend what came in
with *that*.

*We got tents, all right—old enough to have served the
Sunhawks in Grandmother's fighting days; patched, and rotting. We got armor—cheap and rusted. We got weapons—
and I practiced with better under Tarma; dull pot-metal
that wouldn't hold an edge if you got a gods'-blessing on
it. And food—stale journey-rations that could have given
the Karsites lessons in tasteless, barrels of meat too salty
to eat, flour full of weevils. And as for the horses—* Kero
shuddered. They'd had to shoot half of them, and half of
the ones they'd shot had been so disease- and parasite-
riddled they couldn't even be eaten.

By then it was too late. They'd given their bond. If
they defaulted, the Skybolts' reputation—already suffering from the defeat in Menmellith—would be decimated.

We should have defaulted, Kero thought angrily, cursing under her breath as the metal scales on Shallan's
armor came off in her hands. *We should have defaulted
anyway. Anything is better than this. The Guild would
back us, once they heard about the "supplies."*

The "war" had turned out to be waged *within* a House;
two factions of the same merchants' guild. Kero wasn't
sure what it was about—mines, or some other kind of
raw material, she thought—and she wasn't sure she cared.
Neither side gave a rat's ass about the welfare of the
troops they'd hired—the Skybolts were just so many
warm, weapon-wielding bodies to them, and if they
thought about it at all, they probably assumed that the
Company members *welcomed* a certain number of losses,
as it made for fewer to split the pay at the end.

Kero had been made the officer over the scouts, and
that made it all the worse for her. *She* was the one who
had to take Ardana's stupid orders—distilled from the
even stupider orders of their employers—and try and
make something of them that stood any kind of chance
of working.

Kero dug into her kit for some of the half-cured horse-
hide that was all they had been able to salvage from those

poor, slaughtered nags, and laboriously patched it into the back of Shallan's mail-coat. Then she stitched the scales that had come off back into *that,* cursing when the holes broke where they'd rusted through.

Fewer and fewer of her friends came back after each foray; she'd managed to keep most of the scouts alive, but as for the rest—

It was pretty demoralizing. Ardana didn't *have* any strategy worth the name. The merchants dictated, and she followed their orders, directing the Skybolts—skirmishers all—to fight like a Company of light cavalry. They'd been cut down to two-thirds normal strength by the Menmel-lith affair—now they were down to half of that. Mostly wounded, thank the gods, and not dead—but definitely out of the action.

She shook the corselet and growled under her breath. Like the situation with her command, it was so tempting to just do what she could and leave the rest to the gods—but—*Damned if I'm going to leave my friend half-protected.* She cut the stitching on the faulty scales, took a rock from her hearth to use as a hammer, a bit of wood to use as an anvil and a nail for a awl, and punched new holes below the old ones, *then* stitched them back on.

Miserable cheap bastards. If I'd gone with Eldan, who'd be doing this for her?

If she'd gone with Eldan—the thought occurred a dozen times a day, and it didn't hurt any the less for repetition.

I didn't go with Eldan. I came back to my people. If Ardana won't take care of them, I have to do what I can to make up for that.

And part of that was making sure her scouts stayed well-protected.

She held up the corselet and shook it, frowning at it, just as Shallan burst through the tent door, ripping one of the tie-cords loose as she did so.

"We're being hit!" she cried, as a fire-arrow lodged in the canvas of the tent wall. Kero lurched to her feet, just as something large and panicked crashed into the tent wall.

Kero came to lying on her back, with her left arm and shoulder on fire. Literally; there was a fire-arrow lodged in her arm.

She screamed, as much from shock as pain, and rolled over into the mud. She put out the fire, but she broke the arrow off and drove the head deep into her shoulder, and passed out again from the pain.

The next time she woke, she wished she hadn't. She couldn't believe how much she hurt. Without opening her eyes, she took slow, deep breaths the way Tarma had taught her, hoping it would make the pain ebb a little.

If I—just had Need—

She had never been wounded before without having the sword with her—and now she realized just what a difference that made. She forced her eyes open, and blinked away tears of pain until she could see.

Canvas.

She turned her head to the left, since turning it to the right only made things hurt worse. Evidently she wasn't the only victim of the camp raid; there were a dozen others laid out in various stages of injury within easy reach.

Someone stood up just beyond the last one; the Company Healer, Eren. She tried to move a little too far, and gasped; he jumped as if *he* was the one who'd been shot, and somehow turned in midair so that he came down facing her.

He didn't say a word; just moved while her eyes blurred, and seemed to materialize beside her.

"What is it?" he asked, resting his hand lightly on her bandaged shoulder. The pain ebbed enough for her to speak.

"I need that damned sword," she whispered. "It's—I need it, that's all."

To her relief, since she hadn't told *anyone* about everything the blade could do, he just nodded. "If you have it, can I get rid of you?" She nodded, and he narrowed his eyes in thought for a moment. "Anything that saves my strength is a bonus. I'll send somebody off for it."

He took his hand away, and the pain surged over her in a wave. She just endured for half an eternity—then, with no warning at all, the pain was gone.

She gasped again, but this time with relief, and opened her eyes slowly. Shallan knelt beside her, with one hand over Kero's right, which in turn she was holding clasped to Need's hilt.

"What happened?" she asked, only now able to think of anything besides her own pain.

"The last straw." Shallan looked like she hadn't slept in a while. "Or rather, several last straws. First we got hit by the natives. They're tired of having their farms trampled, their houses looted, and their daughters raped."

"But we didn't—" she stopped at the look Shallan gave her.

"Much," Shallan amended. "You officers haven't been told everything. No rape, anyway; the lads know us women'd have them singing a permanent soprano when we found out about it. But when we're hungry and cold and mad as hell, things happen. Anyway, mostly it hasn't been us, they just didn't give a damn about who it was."

"What happened, then?" Kero asked, shamed past blushing. *Have we come that low so fast?*

"You were about the only real casualty in that particular raid. We lost a couple of horses, couple of tents, but mostly it looked worse than it was. All these—" she waved her hand at the wounded lying beyond Kero "—were from the guerrilla ambushes they've been laying for *both* sides. You've been out of things for about four days. They're whittling us down by ones and twos is what they're doing. Caught one, the other day. Twelve-year-old kid. Said they're trying to make life miserable for us, the Skybolts, so we'll pack up and leave. He said their leader figures when we leave, the fight's over."

"I—can't fault his reasoning." This was not why she'd gotten into fighting, to destroy the lives of ordinary people.

Shallan shrugged. "No more can I," she admitted. "Well, the absolute last straw just showed up today. The merchant-men. Demanding to know why we haven't won this thing for them, since we're supposed to be so good."

Outrage filled her and died just as quickly. These fat, complacent sideline-sitters didn't know fighting, and didn't care. They probably worked their beasts the same—use them up, throw them away. *After all, we're only mercs. No one is going to miss us. . . .*

"Ardana's called a meeting," Shallan concluded, the shrewd and calculating expression on her face telling Kero that she'd read every thought as clearly as if she'd

had Kero's Thoughtsensing ability. "Think you're up to
it?"

Kero attempted to sit. And succeeded. And for the first
time in a long time felt unleavened gratitude for Need.
"Give me a hand up, and a shoulder to lean on, and I'm
up to it," she asserted, though her head swam for a moment. Her shoulder didn't hurt, it itched, itched horribly,
which made her think that the sword was making up for
the four days it had been away from her, all at once. With
every moment she felt stronger, and as Shallan helped
her to her feet, she was able to ignore what pain there
was and keep herself upright with a minimum of help.

*Which is just as well. I have the feeling I'm not going
to like this meeting.*

By the time they reached the mess tent, only iron will
kept her from tearing the bandage from her shoulder and
scratching the wound bloody. She ground her teeth with
the effort it took to leave the thing alone.

Shallan found a place for them by dint of glaring at a
couple of the skirmishers until they gave up their seats
on the splintery half-log benches. A few more arrived
after they did; not many, though, and when Kero looked
around, she realized with a start that the Company was
down to *less* than half the strength they'd had when they
rode in here. Ardana's incompetence had decimated them
that badly. But worse than the numbers was the fact that
many of the mercs wouldn't meet her eyes, or looked
away after a moment.

There was no sense of unity as there had been whenever Lerryn held a meeting. Only unhappiness and unease, and a feeling of resignation, as if they all knew the
orders would be bad, and no longer cared.

Ardana finally showed up, with one of the merchants
following like a fat shadow, stalking to the front of the
tent with a jerky, stiff-legged gait that reminded Kero of
a half-mad, half-starved dog she'd seen once that was
trying to face down a much bigger animal over a bone.
Outmatched, but too crazy to admit it.

Ardana's scowl, which had become as much a part of
her face as her flint-hard eyes, didn't do anything to
change that assessment. *She knows she can't handle this,
but she can't give it up,* Kero thought wonderingly. *She's
so eaten up with the importance of being Captain that*

she won't step down even though she's killing off her own Company. What is wrong with the woman? Did she get hit over the head when we weren't looking? What turned her into this monster?

The Captain tugged at the hem of her tunic constantly, trying to pull out wrinkles that weren't there. Like the scowl, it was a nervous habit that had emerged after her elevation to Captain.

"Our employers aren't happy with our progress," the woman said, into the sullen silence that followed her entrance. "They say they have reason to believe that we're slacking off."

A few months ago, that pronouncement would have been met with angry shouts. Now—a low rumbling, a weary growl, was all the Captain got as a response. *They don't care anymore. Not about our reputation, not about pride—they're like saddle-galled horses, still going only because they're being prodded and quitting hurts more.*

Ardana's lips tightened in what Kero read as satisfaction when no one said anything. "I told them we're going to end this now. Tomorrow I want every one of you up and ready to ride—"

And the orders she outlined were nothing less than suicide. A straight charge, right up onto the line, when they had nothing backing them and their opponents had holed themselves up in the ruins of a village. The place was a maze of half-ruined buildings; ideal for defense, and impossible for cavalry. And that was if the Skybolts actually *were* cavalry.

Kero listened with her mouth agape, unable to believe the monumental stupidity of such a plan. *It's them, the merchants*, she thought, slowly, putting what she was hearing together with what she was not hearing, but sensing from the merchant. She opened her mind to him, and was sickened by what she found there. *Dearest gods. I should have read their thoughts when they were here the first time. I should have—*

Because what she read was worse than anything she had imagined. These men had no intention of paying the rest of their fee—but they were going to solve the problem by making certain there was no Company left to be paid.

So far as they were concerned, this final charge would solve all their problems very neatly. Most of the Skybolts would die; the rest would drift away, leaderless—six months ago, that would have been unthinkable, but demoralized as they were now, it was not only possible, it was probable. And the suicidal charge would also decimate the enemy ranks enough that the free-lancers could mop them up, and would probably be only too willing for the sake of the looting involved.

I'm on the wounded list—I won't be going out there— that had been her first reaction, when Ardana had outlined the "battle plan." Now she blushed with shame at her own reaction. *Even I've sunk that low, thinking only of myself. How can I fault the others?*

But the fact that she was on the wounded list gave her a weapon this fat merchant could never have anticipated. She would sacrifice her career—but better that, than to see the last of her friends going down to physical and moral death.

By Guild rules, anyone on the wounded list could sever his contract, though hardly anyone ever did.

Maybe if she walked, now, she'd wake them up, force them to see what they were being lured into.

It was worth a try.

She stood up, and suddenly every eye in the room was on her. Even Ardana stopped in mid-sentence, and stared at her in mild surprise.

"I've never heard such a crock of shit in my life," Kero said, loudly and bluntly. She pointed an accusatory finger at the merchant. "*He* is going to get every one of us killed." She pointed at Ardana, "And *you* are going to let him get away with it. Lerryn has to be spinning in his grave like an express-wagon axle."

Ardana's mouth dropped open; beside her, the fat merchant registered equal shock. He wasn't thinking; just reacting. Surprise that any of these "stupid mercenaries" had seen what the "master plan" was, and outrage that the same stupid mercenary would have the audacity to challenge him on it.

Kero looked around her, slowly and deliberately. "In fact, I don't see *anyone* here I'd be willing to call a Skybolt." She turned back to Ardana, ripped the badge off her sleeve, and threw it at the Captain's feet. "I'm severing my contract. Go hire some of that scum outside the camp to take my place. *If* you can find one stupid enough to go along with this."

She turned and started to shove her way through the crowd. Behind her, Ardana suddenly woke up, and stridently ordered her to halt.

She ignored the order—as she ignored those that followed, each more hysterical and shrill than the last. Finally orders were issued to someone else—to stop and arrest her for court-martial.

That was when Kero turned back and stared her former Captain in the eyes, putting hand to hilt. "I wouldn't try that," she said, mildly, into the deathly quiet that followed the simple action. "I really wouldn't. You won't like the result."

And she drew about an inch of blade.

Ardana went red, then white. And her hand crept to her own hilt.

That was when a half-dozen of the scouts leapt to their feet, and tore their own badges off, throwing them beside Kero's. Then ten more, then twenty, until the air was full of the sound of tearing cloth, and there were too many people between them for Kero to even see Ardana, though she could still hear her, stridently shouting for order.

Order which she was never going to be able to command again.

Kero turned and shoved her way past the remaining Skybolts, suddenly terrified of what she'd done.

She still has a couple of loyal followers. She has people that merchant has bought. She can order them to get me, make an example of me—it's the only way she'll get anybody to fall into line now—

She half fell across someone's feet as she stumbled out toward her tent, to grab whatever she could and make for the road north while Ardana was still too confused to think. The tent was not too far away, and while she was winded by her weakness and her run, thanks to Need's work she was fully capable of riding. And Hellsbane could easily outdistance any other horse in the Skybolts' picket line, especially now.

She flung herself into the tent, and tore open her saddlebags.

Blessed Agnira, she prayed, fervently, while she stuffed belongings into the top. *Blessed Agnetha—only keep her confused. Just give me that head start—*

Sixteen

Hellsbane regarded the pile of dead and wilted grass under her nose with uniquely equine doubt. She gave Kero a sorrowful look, one as filled with entreaty as any spaniel could have managed, and pawed the hard-packed snow.

"Sorry girl," Kero told her wearily, all too conscious of her own hunger, and of the cold that made her feet and hands numb. "That's all there is. And you should be glad you can eat grass; you're doing better than I am."

She doubted that the warsteed understood any of that, but the mare was at least someone to talk to. And talking kept her mind off of how tired she was.

She'd avoided settlements since she began this run back up north, figuring that whatever Ardana had decided to do about her, it wasn't going to be to Kero's advantage. They'd ridden from dawn to sunset every day since she'd left the Skybolts' camp, while the rain became sleet, then real snow, and the snow-cover grew thicker all the time. She'd been grateful then for all of Tarma's training, for without it she'd never have been able to live off the land in late winter.

She and Hellsbane were both in sad condition, but they were at least alive and still able to travel if they had to. The hard run was almost over now; by nightfall she'd be at the Skybolts' winter quarters; she'd collect her gear and get on out of there. Once she had her gear, which included her Mercenary Guild identification, she'd be in a position to take her case to the Guild itself.

She looked up at the leaden sky, and thought bitterly that it was too bad that Ardana would never be called to account for her blundering. Kero had no hope that Ardana would be punished in any way—after all, there was no point in punishing someone for being stupid—but at least there'd be that much warning in the Guild for any-one thinking of joining the Skybolts. And Kero would get her name and record clear of any charges Ardana levied against her.

Then I can go free-lance, she thought, chewing on some nourishing (if tasteless) cattail roots she'd grubbed up for herself out of a half-frozen stream. Her teeth hurt from the cold, and her hands ached as much as her teeth. *Damn that bitch. I'm guiltless. She's the one who should get it in the teeth, but I'm the one who's going to suffer. With a record of insubordination, even if it was legal and justified, no bonded Company is ever going to be willing to take a chance on me again. I've got a brand of "trou-blemaker" on me for all time. But better that than dead.*

She waited until Hellsbane had eaten her own rations down to the last strand of grass, tightened the girth, and remounted, the ache of her feet only partially relieved by tucking them in close to the mare's warm body. *Riding your horse just after she's eaten isn't exactly good horse-manship. Sorry Hellsbane, I don't have much of a choice. I'd spare you if I could.*

The mare shook herself, and snorted, but settled to the pace willingly enough. They rode on at a fast walk under lowering skies just as they had for days past counting, long, dull days that meant nothing more than so many leagues toward their goal. But Kero's calculations had been right on the money; sunset saw her riding up to the village that supported the Skybolts' winter quarters, a kind of snow-capped, stockaded heart in the midst of a cluster of buildings. Kero looked up and saw it in the distance, and felt the same kind of rush of relief and "homecoming" she'd felt on riding up to the Skybolts' camp. She quickly repressed it, but not without a lump in her throat. This wasn't and would never again be home. Not for her.

The village was made up of fairly unusual buildings, if one supposed this to be an ordinary village. Three inns, a blacksmith, an armorer, and several other, less identifiable places that were obviously businesses of some sort. No sign of a village market, no signs of craftsmen or farmers.

The one aspect that dominated everything was that stockade at the heart of the place.

Every town that served as winter quarters to a Company looked like this, more or less. The Company would build or buy an appropriate establishment; several buildings were needed for a Company of any size. Barracks for one thing, and you could add armory, training-ground, stables, and administrative office at the least. Once the place was up and tenanted and past its first year of occupancy, the rest would follow. The only craftsmen that would establish themselves would be smiths and armorers; for the rest, members of the Merchants' and Traders' Guilds would take care of anything material the wintering troops needed to spend money on. And for their nonmaterial needs, the innkeepers would take care of anything they might desire. The Skybolts hadn't been established long enough to acquire an entire town about their walls as old members retired and chose to stay nearby and raise families. Hawksnest, the Sunhawks' wintering quarters, supported a thriving population of noncombatants.

A token force stayed behind even during fighting season, to train new recruits, and see to the upkeep of the place. Those were usually members of the Company that were no longer fit for field duty, but couldn't or wouldn't retire. If the Captain judged them fit enough, and if there were positions open, they could become caretakers and trainers, especially if they'd been officers. There was no sense in wasting resources.

Evidently word of her defection hadn't preceded her, for the guard at the front entrance to the stockade, a taciturn one-eyed fellow she knew only vaguely, welcomed her in through the gates with no comments, opening the smaller, side gate for her rather than forcing the great gates open against the piled-up snow. She was mortally glad he was the one on duty; he seldom spoke more than three words in a row, and then only if spoken to first. She didn't want to have to answer questions, and she most especially didn't want to have to lie. She feigned a weariness only a little greater than she felt; she knew she and the mare were thin and worn, and those things evidently were all the excuse she needed for silence.

The snow-covered training-ground was silent and looked curiously unused as she rode past; she thought perhaps all the new recruits were eating dinner, but when she dismounted and brought the mare into the darkened, redolent stables, and saw how few horses there were there, she realized that, for the first time in her knowledge, there *were* no new recruits.

Evidently, since the Skybolts weren't going to be there to train them, the riders recruited and rough-trained during the summer months had been sent down south to join the rest of the Company.

Which meant that in order to take any kind of job in the normal fighting season, what was left of the Company would have to accept green recruits or free-lancers who'd never been with a Company before, and put them right into the front lines with the rest.

That was just more evidence of the kind of shortsighted thinking Ardana had been displaying all along. While it was true that the Skybolts had only accepted seasoned fighters, without proper drilling and practice, new recruits were twice as likely to die as old hands. And that was in a nonspecialist Company; in a Company of skirmishers, Kero wouldn't have given a new recruit a rat's chance of surviving the first fight.

But that certainly explained where all the new faces had come from while she'd been across the Karsite border. And it would give Ardana a fine excuse for why the casualty figures were so high if the Guild made inquiries.

She left Hellsbane under saddle; just backed her into the nearest empty stall and gave her a good feed, then went off to the empty barracks to retrieve her gear.

There wasn't much of it, but there were warm winter clothes to replace her threadbare garments, some weaponry to replace things lost or left behind. And as for the personal gear, every little bit would help. She'd undoubtedly have to sell the semiprecious gems she'd stored to carve into little figurines this winter. The carving equipment itself wasn't worth much, and didn't take up a great deal of room; she'd keep it a while, on the chance that she would one day be able to carve again.

The barracks were dark, with most of the windows shuttered. Her footsteps echoed hollowly and her breath showed white in the gloom, telling her that the place hadn't been heated at all this winter.

Somehow the very emptiness oppressed her more than the entire trip back. Maybe it had something to do with actually seeing the place that should have been full of people standing deserted.

She didn't bother with pulling off her worn gloves or cloak; it was too cold. She had no intention of sleeping here; if she found herself with enough breathing space, she'd draw on the little credit she had at the Woolly Ram and spend the night there. She felt her way across the building and climbed the creaking stairs to the veterans' floor, and sought her own little niche in the barracks.

Cold penetrated her cloak, and depression weighed heavily on her shoulders. She threw open the shutter to get the last of the light. Beside her bare bunk was her armor-stand with her spare suit of chain, which could be sold easily enough. At the foot of the bunk was the locked chest where she kept the smaller objects she didn't want to carry with her on campaign, and under the bunk was the clothespress that held the rest of her wardrobe.

Winter clothing, all of it, and she bundled it all up and bound it into a pack with a spare blanket. She unlocked the chest and looted it just as thoroughly, though there was considerably less in it. Knives, her jewel-carving supplies, a couple of pieces she'd finished, various odds and ends. Some were too bulky to take with her; some impractical. It was only after she'd made it all up into packs that she saw the letter lying on the shelf above her bed, with the odd bits and carvings she'd picked up over the years, the sentimental things she could not take with her.

Who would send me a letter? My brother? But the seal was unfamiliar, and the handwriting on the outside none she'd seen before. She picked the folded parchment up, her hands trembling for no reason that she could think of, and opened it, breaking the strange blue-and-silver seal.

It contained two pieces of paper. The first was a simple note of two lines and a name.

"I kept the letter of our agreement, but you can't fault me for arranging the terms to suit myself," it read. *"If you want to redeem this, you'll have to come here, and you'll have to see me."*

And it was signed, simply, "Eldan."

The other paper was a draft, in Valdemaran scrip, for

the amount of the Herald's ransom. She would have to go to Valdemar in person to cash it in.

More specifically, she would have to go to the capital of Haven, as the draft had been written on a Crown account there. And it had to be countersigned by the issuer, which in this case was Eldan himself.

To claim her reward, she would have to confront him on his own ground, and deal with him and all her tangled feelings about him.

It was a bitter sort of salvation he offered. If she went to him, to Valdemar, her troubles would be over, temporarily at least. She would have ready cash to tide her over until she managed to land a free-lance position. She might even be able to get a position within Valdemar. Surely they needed bodyguards, personal guards, and caravan guards even there.

But if she went, Eldan would undoubtedly try to persuade her to stay with him, perhaps even teaching at that Collegium of his as he had suggested. And right now she had no better prospects than to give in to that persuasion. But if she did give in, she'd be right back in the situation she had fled from in the first place, first from Lordan's keeping, then from his. The idea of being completely dependent on someone else made her feel as if she was being stifled. If she did that, she wouldn't have proved anything, not even to herself.

But she'd be with the one man she'd ever been able to love, to give herself completely to, heart and mind and soul—because he had given himself to her in the same way.

She stood there, staring at the blank wall above the shelf, unaware that she had crushed both papers in her hand until a clamor from beyond the gates of the stockade woke her out of her trance.

There was no mistaking that kind of noise; friendly shouts, whinnies, someone pounding on the gate. All the sounds indicating a crowd of riders wanted entrance.

She stuffed the papers into her belt-pouch hastily. She could decide what to do about them later. Right now she needed to get out of there and quickly. *Ardana's messengers must have been right behind me*, she thought, shutting out panic. *I have to get to the Guild before they throw me in detention!*

She had no doubt that Ardana would court-martial her if the Captain ever got her hands on her. If Ardana had her way, Kero would never even see a Guild Arbitrator.

She grabbed up her packs and bolted down the stairs just as she heard, from the open window behind her, the sound of the great gates being forced open, groaning against the load of snow pressed up against them.

She thought about her possible exits as she ran down the stairs and out the side door of the barracks. There was a back postern-gate that self-locked right behind the barracks. Kero waited for a moment until she was certain that no one was in a position to see her, then dashed across the open space between the buildings into the stables. She fumbled open the stall door and grabbed Hellsbane's reins to lead her out. Now she heard people and horses milling around just inside the gates; at least twenty if not more. It would take them a few more moments to get organized, then they would have to explain their mission to the guard and the guard would have to remember what direction she'd taken.

That would all take time, precious time, time she could use to make her escape.

She threw the packs over Hellsbane's rump without fastening them, and led Hellsbane in back of the stables, past the odorous manure pile, to the back of the stockade itself. There was the postern gate; narrow, scarcely tall enough for a led horse, not tall enough for a rider, and a real test of a rider's ability to get his horse to pass through something the animal judged to be too small.

But the mare would follow wherever Kero led; such was her training and breeding, and the trust they had built together. Kero had to pull the packs off and pitch them into drifts beside the gate to get her through, but the mare gave no trouble with squeezing through the gate, even though the saddle scraped on the stockade walls on either side of her.

The counter-weighted gate swung shut behind her horse's tail, and the lock clicked. Hellsbane flicked her ears at the sound and whickered nervously.

Kero pulled the packs out of the snow and swung them back up behind the saddle, fastening them as best she could to the lean packs that were already there.

She mounted as soon as the packs were in place; every

heartbeat counted at this point. *I had no idea they were so close behind me,* she thought worriedly. *I know we didn't make the best time, because we had to keep back-tracking to avoid the towns—and I know Hellsbane wasn't in the best shape, either, but I thought we were farther ahead of them than that.*

There was another possibility as well. If Ardana had wanted her badly enough to mount up the freshest horses and the best riders in the Company to go after her, with enough money to permit them to change horses at every posting-house, they could have caught up with her quite easily. And that made getting to a town with a strong representation of the Mercenary's Guild all the more important.

Even if it meant riding all night.

It had meant more than riding all night, it had meant riding past dawn. Kero had never known a person could be so tired, so deep-down exhausted, and still be standing. She stifled a yawn as she recited her story for the third time before the representatives of the Guild.

Each time, she had faced a different set of people. The first time was right after she'd come through the city gates. She wanted bed and food, but with Ardana's flunkies out there looking for her, she knew she didn't dare stop for either.

She'd breathed a whole lot easier after she passed the door of the Guild, a sturdy stone edifice that didn't look a great deal different from the Guildhall of any other Guild. Once inside, she asked for directions to the Arbitrators. She had been sent up a flight of worn wooden stairs to a tiny office, where she'd told a shortened version to a stone-faced secretary of some kind.

He gave her a chair when she'd finished, and went off somewhere. When he came back, his stonelike demeanor had thawed a little, and he took her to another office. That was where she had told the story a second time, to a much friendlier and sympathetic official—one who seemed to strive to make her feel comfortable, and to convince her that she could trust him. She did—but mostly because she was convinced she was in the right, and she was only trying to protect herself and her standing within the Guild. She could see how someone with a falsified tale could easily get himself in deep trouble with this man; he had asked many careful questions, all designed to make her incriminate herself or uncover flaws in her story that would reveal it to be a fabrication.

That had taken the better part of the morning, and she was dizzy with fatigue when he was finished with her. She didn't try to touch his thoughts, but she had a very real sense that everything he said was part of a carefully prepared script, and that he wasn't about to deviate from it except in the most extreme circumstances.

She couldn't help but wonder how many cases the Arbitrators saw that never got beyond this man. Probably quite a few, judging by his reactions to her. Although he didn't actually say anything that (probably) fell outside his prepared speeches, she got the distinct impression that he was warming to her—outside of the "hail-fellow-well-met" facade he presented.

Once again she was sent off to wait, this time in a little room with three other people, all as silent as she, and two of them looking considerably more harried. The third was black and blue, with splints on one arm. She got the feeling that this man was desperate, under the fog of his pain-killers. If the Arbitrators denied him his perceived justice, he might well do something, something excessive.

He was the first called, and she didn't see him again. Evidently, petitioners did not leave by the same door they came in, because the other petitioner was called a few moments later, and when Kero was summoned into the room, there was no sign of either of them.

She found herself in a large, well-lit, barren room, empty of everything except a long table with three chairs behind it. In those chairs sat the Arbitrators, two men and a woman, all three of them the very image of the perfect soldier. All three sat as erect as if this was a parade ground, all three wore identical long-sleeved tunics of brown leather, and all three wore their graying hair close-cropped.

This third and final time she recited her entire story to the panel of three Guild Arbitrators, who all remained as impassive and unemotional as statues. She thought that was probably a good sign. This town of Selina was completely outside Ardana's immediate reach, and had a strong town council of its own. And the administrative branch of the Guild here was well known for fair play. Their completely impartial attitudes let her know they would be weighing not only everything she said, but how she said it.

By now she was exhausted, and she greatly envied Hellsbane, safely and warmly installed in the Guild stables, fed and groomed and probably now asleep.

She tried to tell things simply and clearly, with as little emotional weight as possible; tried to act as impassive and neutral as her judges seemed to be. But she heard herself slurring words as if she was drunk; and so she was, but with weariness, not wine.

It wasn't hard to sound impassive after all. As she did her best to make sure she kept all her facts straight, she discovered that right at this moment she didn't care much about anything; all she was really aware of was her acute need to sleep and the hollow emptiness of her stomach. Too late, she thought perhaps that her approach was all wrong; maybe she should have been passionate and full of righteous anger—maybe she wasn't convincing them. Maybe they read her stoicism as the facade of someone who was making everything up.

But it was too late to change now, and besides, she was too tired. It was all she could do to keep her narrative clear, and answer their questions with some semblance of intelligence.

Finally she came to the end of her story, and the Arbitrators came to the end of their questions.

They sent her out through a second door on the opposite side of the room, where she found a small chamber identical to the one she'd waited in before her "audience."

It was a tiny, windowless box of a room, stuffy, and airless. There were three chairs, all empty, all equally uncomfortable, which was just as well. She wouldn't have been able to resist the implied comfort of a padded chair, and once settled into something like that, she'd have fallen asleep for certain.

She took her seat to await their decision in the middle of the three chairs, a high-backed, unyielding piece, so tired that only the deep ache of hunger kept her awake.

That, and the fact that her imagination began to run wild. Being alone like this, with nothing to think about except her performance and possible fate, only made her worry more.

What if they don't believe a word I said? What if they think I'm lying? There had been no way to tell what they were thinking while she was talking; if they hadn't been breathing occasionally, she would have taken them for corpses. *But what possible motive could I have for lying? Ambition? I was promoted under Ardana. Revenge? She never did anything to me directly.* But that might not make any difference. People had mutinied against their leaders with no apparent reason before this. She worried the fear until the edges were frayed, but she couldn't dismiss it. It seemed to be taking forever for the Arbitrators to make their decision.

She got up and paced the floor, hands clasped tightly behind her back, trying to walk softly, but unable to keep her boots quiet against the hard wooden floor. *What if Ardana's flunkies went here first, instead of the winter quarters? What if they told Ardana's version, and the Arbitrators believe her?*

It was possible. If they had changed horses, and gone by the trade roads, they could have beaten her here easily. *But she can't argue away the casualty rate. She can't argue away her lack of strategy.*

There were plenty of excuses Ardana *could* make for those things, though, and Kero's imagination was quick to supply them. Illness, inexperience, treachery on the part of their allies, unfamiliar territory, a chain of command fundamentally new to their positions. . . .

She had managed to work herself up to such a pitch that when the door opened behind her, she jumped and uttered a muffled (and undignified) squeak of alarm. She was so rattled that she turned and just stood there staring at the newcomer, heart pounding, unable to speak for a moment.

Standing framed in the doorway was her second questioner, the friendly middle-aged man who had cross-examined her so skillfully. He stared at her for a moment, obviously taken aback by her nervous response to the simple act of a door opening behind her.

"I—I'm sorry," she stammered. "I'm kind of—jumpy. I'm letting my nerves get the better of me."

He recovered his aplomb, and smiled, and this time

she had the feeling it was a genuine smile and not the facade he'd worn for her the first time they'd met. "I'm the one who should apologize," he said. "I knew very well what you'd been through, and I didn't make allowances for it. I'm lucky all you did was jump—with that poor fellow whose case was heard first, I might have found myself on the floor with a knife at my throat."

She smiled wanly, and he waved her through the door. "The Arbitrators have decided in your favor, Kerowyn," he continued, tugging his leather tunic straight with a gesture that seemed to be habit. "But they want you to hear it from them. Even though this is a decision for you, it may not be everything you were hoping for."

All of the tension drained out of her, leaving her limp and ready to accept just about anything. She obeyed his direction, and found herself back in front of the table, facing the three granite-faced Arbitrators.

Now that she knew they'd decided for her, she looked at them a little more closely. All three of them were older than she'd first thought; old enough to be grandparents, though she had no doubt that any of the three could challenge her at their chosen forms of combat and quite probably beat her. They all had that indefinable air of the professional mercenary; cool, calm, unruffled, and quite able to take on whatever needs doing.

Two men, and one woman; all three had probably worked themselves up from the ranks. She smiled a little to herself. If they *had* come up from the ranks, they weren't going to appreciate what the Skybolts' Captain had done to her people. Ardana was going to get short shrift from them, if she hadn't already.

The woman spoke; she had the seat on Kero's left, and looked a little older than the other two. "We've decided in your favor, Kerowyn," she said, her voice surprisingly soft and melodic. "We agree that you had every right and every reason to sever your contract, and that you did so legally."

That was all she had ever wanted to hear. "Thank you—" she started to say, but the woman interrupted her with an upraised hand.

"Your Captain was and is a fool," she said, "but there's nothing in the Guild Code preventing fools from being in command, or from getting their people hurt or killed. We aren't in the business of telling Captains how to command; we only deal with violations of the Code. The Guild allows only one kind of retribution for Captains of her sort—the kind you took. Severing contracts neatly and legally until she is in command of nothing. Do you understand me?''

Kero put a lock on her reaction of disappointment and nodded. "What you're saying is pretty much what I'd expected," she replied, trying not to think of those friends still trapped under Ardana's command until the end of the Company contract. Only then could they sever *their* relations with her.

Of course, they would have one advantage over Kero. There would be no record of insubordination in their files.

The woman smiled ever so slightly; the barest hint of a curve to her weathered lips. "Unfortunately, no matter what we put in your record, it is unlikely that any bonded Company will ever accept you again. I hope you realized that, if not when you severed, at least when you'd had a chance to think all this out. Mercenaries who sever contracts in the field, even under extreme provocation such as you experienced, tend to be viewed with a jaundiced eye by other commanders. After all, by their way of thinking, if you do it once, what's to stop you from doing it again? To them, it's just another form of desertion under fire.''

Well, that was what I thought, although I'd rather she hadn't said it. Kero sighed. "I understand that, sir," she said, rocking a little back and forth to ease her aching feet.

"But I wonder if you really know what that means in terms of the immediate present," the woman persisted. "This is the lean season. The only places hiring right now are Companies. I understand that you have very little in the way of savings. You are going to find it all but impossible to find work here in Selina, and you won't have the wherewithal to go elsewhere.''

Kero blinked. "But—what about going bonded free-lance?'' she asked, wondering what on earth she was missing. "I thought bonded free-lancers were always in demand. All anyone is going to check is whether or not I *am* bonded—''

"If you can find work," the woman told her. "You

have no experience outside of a Company. This is winter. No caravans, no warfare, no hunting where someone might need a tracker who is also a fighter, no work as a city guard and damned near no bodyguard work. Nothing's moving. No one is going anywhere. I can promise you that there is *no* work in Sclina for someone of your talents.''

Kero swallowed. *I never had any idea it was going to be this bad. But groveling isn't going to help. I have to put a good face on this. Falling apart is not going to earn me anything, certainly not their respect. I think I have that now. I don't want to lose it.*

She stiffened her back and raised her chin. "I'll have to manage," she replied. "I have other skills. I can handle horses, or train them, no matter how difficult they are. I can work a tavern if I have to. I even have some experience with medicine. Tarma—my teacher told me to learn other things, because I might have to fall back on them.''

The other two nodded, although the woman looked dubious. "Even if you get free-lance work, you've never worked anywhere except within a Company,'' she persisted. "You have no idea what it's like to work free-lance. It's hard enough for a man, but for a woman—"

"I'll manage," Kero replied. "I'm tougher than I look. Thank you for your judgment in my favor. I had heard that the Guild was fair, and I will be very happy to confirm that.''

The woman shook her head, but said nothing more. Kero bowed slightly, and turned. The friendly man was still standing beside the second door; he beckoned a little, and she followed him out of it.

"You're entitled to three days here in the Guildhall,'' he told her. "Three days, bed and board, for you and your beast.''

She sighed. That was one worry out of the way. Three days of grace, three days where she wouldn't have to fret about where she was going to lay her head. "I'll take you up on that," she told him. "Because right now I couldn't find my way to an inn, even if I could afford to pay for it.''

"I thought as much," he replied, with real, unfeigned sympathy. "I took the liberty of having your things taken to one of the rooms. The food is nothing to boast about, and the room isn't fancy, but it's safe, and it has a bed.''

''And right now, that's all I need,'' she said wearily. ''I'll work on solutions for my problems when I've got a mind to work with. Maybe I'm being too optimistic, but I can't believe that someone with my skills can't find work.''

After a day and a night of solid slumber, and half a day of hunting, she came to the conclusion that the woman Arbitrator was right. There was no work in Selina for a merc of any kind, much less a female.

That left other options. First, before the day was over, she sold everything she didn't actually need; that left her with one suit of armor, her weapons, her clothing, and Hellsbane and her tack.

The Guild gave her a decent price for the armor and weaponry—decent by the standards of a town in midwinter, at any rate. Decent, considering that her second-best suit of chain was now her best, and the suit she was willing to sell had been immersed in a river, drenched with rain, covered with mud, and generally abused.

What she wound up with would pay for room and board for her and Hellsbane for a fortnight.

She counted the pitiful little pile of coins carefully, but they didn't multiply, and the numbers didn't change.

She started to put them back in her belt-pouch, and her hand encountered something that crackled. She pulled it out, puzzled for a moment, then felt the blood drain from her face as she recognized Eldan's letter and voucher.

It would be the easy answer. Her fortnight's worth of coin, if augmented by living off the land, would take her to Valdemar.

I don't have to do anything, she thought reluctantly. *All I have to do is go. I can just collect my money, and leave. I don't have to listen to anything he says.*

She was lying to herself, and she knew it. She shoved the parchment back into the pouch and dropped the coins on top of them with a little groan. She lay back on the bed and rubbed her aching temples. *I'll go up there, and he'll tell me how much he loves me, and he'll offer me some sinecure—and I'll take it, I know I will. Then I'll*

be trapped. Because it'll be his *job, and probably it'll be
no more than a token, a pretense-job, to make me feel
less like he's giving me everything. And gods, I do love
him, it'd be so easy to accept that. . . .*

But love wasn't enough, not for her. She had to have
freedom, too. She had to know that she was *earning* her
way, not just playing someone else's shadow.

No. She gritted her teeth stubbornly. *No. Not unless
there's no choice. I'll go to the Plains, first, and become
a nomad like my crazy cousins. And I haven't exhausted
all my options. I still have two more days.*

As it happened, it wasn't until sunset of her third grace-
day that she found work. It wasn't what she had expected; she was looking for work as a groom. She'd tried
all the places mercs frequented, then the places that were
the haunts of the city guard, and finally started trying
tradesmen's inns. No one had a place for her, not even
after she demonstrated her ability with a couple of surly,
troublemaking beasts.

One of the last places on her mental list was a peddler's inn; a cheap place mostly used by traveling ped-
dlers and minor traders. It wasn't a place where she would
have worked if she'd had a choice; but the fact was, she
didn't have a choice. She walked into the stable yard and
right into a fight.

The conflict was complicated by the involuntary in-
volvement of a donkey and a pony, both kicking and
protesting at the tops of their lungs.

Kero was tempted to wade straight in, but years of
tavern brawling had taught her not to get involved in an
ongoing fight without reinforcements. There were an assortment of servants and stablehands gawking at the fra-
cas. She grabbed them all and formed them into an
assault force, which she led into the fray.

When the pony and donkey were on opposite sides of
the yard, several heads had been knocked together, and
calm had been restored, she turned to what she thought
was the head groom who now sported an impressive black
eye.

"I need work," she said shortly. "I'm a bonded free-
lance merc, but I'm willing to do just about anything.

Especially if it has something to do with horses. Think your master could find a place in the stables for me?"

The man squinted against the light of the setting sun, holding a handful of snow against his eye. "There's nothin' open in the stables," he said with what sounded like mixed admiration and regret. She turned to go, without waiting to hear what else he would say, the bitter taste of disappointment in her mouth once again.

"Wait!" she heard behind her. She *almost* hurried her steps, not wanting to listen to another offer of a meal, or worse, an offer that she whore for the owner. But this time something stopped her. Perhaps it had been the honest admiration in the man's voice; perhaps it was her own desperation. She stopped, and slowly turned.

"We don' need anyone in th' stables," the man said, limping toward her. "But we sure's fire need a hand like you i' th' taproom."

"I don't whore," she said shortly, knowing that *this* inn's serving-girls were expected to do just that.

"Whore?" the man seemed genuinely surprised. "Hellfires, no! Ye'd be wasted as a whore! Need i' th' taproom's fer a peacekeeper."

"A what?" She raised both eyebrows, trying not to laugh.

"Peacekeeper. Break up fights, throw them as makes too much trouble out on th' ear." The man seemed earnest enough, and Kero kept a straight face. "Ye unnerstand, men won' reckon on pickin' fights wi' a wench, see? Big hulkin' brute, they kick up dust just t' challenge 'im. Wench, they don' see as worth makin' trouble with. Then, trouble *does* start, they won' be lookin' t' a wench t' stop it. See?"

Oddly enough, Kero could see the sense of it. "How did you figure this out?" she asked.

The man sighed. "Had a wench 's peacekeeper fer years. Lost 'er t' th' Wolflings. That's 'cause all we c'n give is room'n'board. Been hopin' t' replace 'er, but ain't seen nobody I'd trust, much less a bonded, that'd work fer that."

Kero was still skeptical, but her time was running out, and she needed somewhere to go. This was the only decent offer she'd had. "And how do I know your master will go along with this?" she asked.

The man grinned. " 'Cause th' master's *me*. An' ye're hired, 'f ye'll take just room'n'board. Startin' t'night."

It was better than she'd feared, but no place to rest or recover. Hellsbane had to winter in the corral since the stable was reserved for paying customers. She had to sleep on the floor with the rest of the help—with the exception of the serving girls, who spent the nights with customers. The floor was packed dirt, and cold, and half-healed wounds ached at night. She could understand his reasoning—he only *had* three sleeping rooms upstairs. But that didn't make her position any easier.

The food was fresh and filling, and she could eat all she could hold, but it was poor stuff. Thin soup and coarse bread for the most part. She never felt quite right, and never regained her lost weight even though she was stuffing herself at every meal.

The innmaster, a cheerful little squirrel of a man, was fair and decent to her and backed her on every decision she made. He was all right, but the rest of the staff avoided her, especially after she brained a peddler who caught her out in the stable and tried to rape her.

She lost track of the days; she was exhausted by the time the inn closed, and never seemed to get enough rest. Each day blurred into the next, and she was never able to get up enough energy to go out and hunt down other jobs as she had intended to. Her little store of coins steadily dribbled away as she had to replace clothing that wore out, and repair armor and tack.

Even the sword seemed to have given up on her; she never felt so much as a prod from it anymore.

She leaned up against the bar, carefully positioning herself in the shadows, and surveyed the crowd. There was a larger group than usual here tonight, which had Rudi bouncing with joy, but didn't exactly make her feel like singing. More people meant more chances of fighting, and more people meant that some of them would likely buy places on the floor. Paying customers got the places nearest the fire, leaving the help to shiver in their blankets. A cold night meant aches in the morning.

Maybe I can talk Rudi out of some something hot to drink, she thought, rubbing one thumb along Need's grip. *Or maybe wine. Then I can at least fall asleep quickly.*

Goddess, I'm tired. I wish I could have a bed for just one night. There was a little eddy of raucousness over by the door; she wasn't sure who or what was causing it, and she decided to keep a sharp eye on it.

The disturbance moved nearer; laughing and cursing in equal amounts marked the trail of one customer as he made his way toward the bar. Finally the cause of the commotion got close enough for Kero to see him, and she grimaced as she realized why no one was willing to take exception to his behavior.

It was a city guardsman, drunk as a lord, and throwing his weight and rank around. No one here wanted to touch him and risk arrest, and he was taking full advantage of the fact.

Her heart sank when she saw him peering around as if he was looking for something, then grin when he finally spotted her.

He shoved a couple of drovers aside, and shouldered a potter out of his place next to her. "Well-a-day," he said nastily. " 'F it isn' Rudi's li'l she-man. Watcha still doin' here, sweetheart? Ain' never foun' a man t' take ye outa them britches an' put ye in a skirt?"

She ignored him.

At first, he didn't seem to notice that she was staring off into the crowd with a completely bored expression on her face. She'd learned long ago that the worst thing she could do would be to respond at all to bullies like this one. Her only possible defense was to do nothing. Eventually they tended to get bored and go away.

This one was remarkably persistent, though. And he got in one or two shots that came too damn near the bone and made her blood boil. But Tarma hadn't taught her control in vain; she kept a tight rein on her temper and continued to ignore him, even though a crowd was collecting around them, waiting to see if he could goad her into a fight.

He was drunk, but only enough to make him belligerent, not enough to slow him down or fox his reactions. She'd be a fool to give him the fight he wanted. Twice a fool, since it was against the law to lay a hand on a city guardsman.

So she kept silent, and finally he *did* seem to get bored with his game. He started to lean close, and she saw what was coming; the old ploy of "accidentally" spilling liquor on someone—her, to be specific. She decided she'd had enough.

Just a heartbeat before the guardsman moved, she reached out and pulled one of the watchers into her place, then slipped into the mob before the guardsman could stop her. Since she was shorter than most of the patrons, it wasn't hard to keep herself hidden long enough to get into the safe haven of the kitchen.

The kitchen staff stared at her as she passed through and out the rear door, but they didn't say anything. She waited just inside the kitchen door for a moment, making sure the kitchen yard outside was clear.

There wasn't so much as a cat moving out there. She closed the door behind her and rubbed her eyes with the back of her hand. They felt gritty and sore from all the smoke, and she wondered just how long it was going to be before Rudi closed up.

Dear gods, I'm tired. Even though her stomach was full, she *felt* empty, without any energy. *That guardsman—I hope he leaves. I don't want to have to take him on. I don't think Rudi could protect me from the town law if I had to hit him. I'm not sure the Guild could, and I'm not sure they'd be willing to, either.*

She walked slowly across the uneven kitchen yard, treacherous where snow had melted and refrozen in ruts. The moon was in its last quarter, and cast thin light that did little to help her in seeing her way. *Might as well check on the stable. Maybe by the time I get back, that drunk will have gotten tired of looking for me. Or maybe he'll get so drunk he'll pass out. Either will do.*

There were only two horses in the stable tonight, and both were asleep. One of the stableboys dozed beside the door, but leapt to his feet when she passed him. She patted his shoulder, suppressing a tired smile. "Good lad," she said calmly and with reassurance, as she would to a dog. "Just checking on things." He stared at her with wide, half-frightened eyes, and she felt the sting of rejection. She turned away without saying anything more.

She knew there were several other animals in the paddock with Hellsbane, but she seldom bothered to check them; the mare herself was more than enough guard. She stopped by the fence, suddenly lonely for any kind of a

friendly face, even a horse's. But Hellsbane was asleep,
and Kero decided on reflection not to wake her. What
would be the use, after all? The warsteed was only a
horse, not an intelligent creature like a Companion.
Hellsbane couldn't talk to her, and probably wouldn't
even know how unhappy her mistress was.

She turned her back on the paddock and began the long
walk back to the inn.

Just as she passed the stable, something jumped out of
the shadows of the stable door. Her reactions, numbed
by weariness and inadequate food, were not what they
had been. Before she could turn to meet her attacker, he
was on top of her, and hit her in the back with a scab-
barded blade.

She saw stars of pain and went down, breath driven
out of her. The unknown grabbed her arm before she had
a chance to recover, and hauled her to her feet.

She tried to make her arms and legs move, but they
wouldn't obey her. She was hauled around to face her
attacker, and he seized a handful of her tunic and pulled
her nose-to-nose with him. His ale-sour breath made her
cough; and even in the dim light she had no trouble rec-
ognizing him or his uniform. It was the guardsman; still
drunk, and obviously ale-crazed.

"Thought ye'd slip out on me, she-man?" he snarled.
"Couldn' face a real man? 'M minded t' gi' ye a lesson
i' th' way a wench *should* mind 'erself."

A hand as massive as the business end of a club holding a sword hilt connected with the side of her face so
hard her teeth rattled. That was a mistake, for the blow
managed to knock her out of the stunned daze she had
been in. She brought up her knee—not into his crotch,
which he was expecting, but in order to stamp down hard
on his instep.

She was wearing riding boots with a hard heel—they
were the only foot-covering she had; he was wearing soft
town-shoes. Something cracked under her heel. He
screeched, and let go of her.

But only for a moment. He'd taken in so much ale—or
possibly other things—that the pain was only temporary.
While she was still trying to get her breath and to clear
her eyes of the tears of pain, he swung out and bashed
her in the side of the head with his still-sheathed blade.

She cried out, and grabbed automatically for the hilt of her own sword as she went down to one knee—

And Need took over.

Even while her mind was still reeling, her body jumped to its feet, unsheathed blade in hands, driving straight for the guardsman. He parried clumsily with his weapon; Need came in over the top of his blade and only by slipping and falling on an ice patch did he escape a heart-thrust. He scrambled back up to his feet (if anything, more enraged than before), while Kero slipped on another bit of ice. The blade's control faltered for a moment; still half-stunned, she tried to get control of her own body back, as Need reasserted control and forced her to attack again and again while the guardsman scrambled backward. After the second attack, he seemed to have gotten the idea that he was in imminent danger of being killed; now he was only trying to get away from her.

Finally, the guardsman fetched up against the wall of the stable. There were lights and shouts behind Kero now, but she paid no attention to them; she was far too busy trying to get the upper hand before the blade killed the man.

Need caught the man's blade in a bind and disarmed him. Kero thought for a moment that the sword would release her then, but it held her as tightly as ever. Evidently the man's crimes against women were such that the blade had no intention of letting him get away. The guardsman's eyes were wide with fear, reflecting the torchlight behind her, and he flung up both his hands in a futile attempt to ward her off, as Need drove toward his throat.

And at the last moment. Kero got just enough control back to reverse the blade and punch the man in the chin with the pommel.

As he slumped to the ground, and the blade's control over her vanished, hands seized her from behind.

Kero lay on her stomach on the hard wooden shelf that served as a bed in her damp, unheated cell. It hurt too much to lie on either her back or her side. She hadn't been treated badly; they'd brought her food and water, earlier, but stabbing pains ran down both legs every time she tried to move, so she ignored both. Her back hurt so much she was afraid that the guardsman might have broken something.

Not that it mattered. Drawing steel on a city guardsman was an offense punishable by a flogging and exile from the city, stripped of all possessions. Which, in her circumstances, was tantamount to a sentence of death. Right now she couldn't have moved to save herself even with Need in her hand and in full control.

They'd taken the sword away from her, of course, which meant she was without its Healing and pain-blocking powers again. She'd collapsed in agony the moment it had left her hand, but it wasn't likely anyone had made the connection. Probably they'd assumed she'd been in the same kind of berserk rage as the guardsman. Certainly they wouldn't have left it with her even if they had known she was injured.

She didn't expect anyone to speak for her. Most city guardsmen had one or more influential friends. Rudi wouldn't dare go against anyone who could close down his inn. The Guild had already told her not to expect help if she caused trouble.

And even if he dares to speak for me, he'll have to fire me. Which will put me right back in the same situation, only inside the city gates. In fact, it probably would take less time for someone to find me and kill me. I don't think even Need can fix this back in a few moments.

Worst of all, she was more alone than she'd ever been in her life. There was no one in all this city who would be willing to stand by her or take her in—or even offer a friendly word. Her entire "family" was somewhere in the south—assuming that even *they* still felt kindly toward her, which might be assuming a lot after what she'd done.

At least if they convict me, anyone who tries to take Hellsbane is going to see a lot of hoof, she thought, between the stabs of pain from her back. *I hope it's that bastard who tried to beat me. Serve him right to get his brains bashed in by a mare.*

She knew she should be trying to think of a way out of her trap, but she couldn't muster the energy to think at all, much less to plan a defense. All she could do was try and lie as quietly as possible, and endure the pain of her back and bruised and swollen face.

Slow, hot tears trickled down and pooled under her cheek, as she listened to heavy footsteps passing outside the door of her cell. It sounded like a regular patrol. She had no idea how long she'd been in here, and the windowless cell gave no clues either. The fellow with the food and water had come in once—which might mean a day, or only a few hours. The sound of those boots on the stone only made her more acutely aware of her own isolation.

Faced away from the door as she was, her only warning that some of those footsteps were for her was the rattle of the key in her lock. She tensed herself against seizure, and gasped as her back sent rivers of fire down her legs. For a moment she couldn't think of anything but the pain.

"Guildsman Kerowyn?" said a strange, masculine voice. "Please don't move."

Please don't move? She had expected to be hauled summarily to her feet; the request came as such a surprise that she probably couldn't have moved if she'd wanted to.

A gentle hand touched her back—awaking agony beside which the previous several hours had simply held common aches. She yelped once, and passed out.

When she came to again, most of the pain was gone, subsided to a dull, but bearable, level. Whoever had touched her back was gone, but she sensed that there was still someone in the cell with her, by the little sounds she heard beside the door. She levered herself up and turned toward the sounds. Another city guardsman stood there, a real giant of a man, a good two heads taller than anyone Kero had ever seen before. Kero gawked up at him, a tiny, idle part of her mind wondering how on earth he ever found uniforms to fit him.

"Guildsman Kerowyn," the man said, in a surprisingly soft voice, "Several witnesses have come forward to testify that Guardsman Dane provoked you and you took no action in the inn. The stableboy has come forward to testify that the Guardsman struck the first blow. Your Guild has said that you are a sober and reliable professional with no history of troublemaking. Based on

all these testimonies, it has been determined that you
acted only in your own defense, although we strongly
recommend that in the future you choose a weapon other
than an unsheathed blade within the city walls.''

She blinked at him, feeling more than usually stupid.

''Because he provoked the fight,'' the guardsman continued, ''Guardsman Dane has been fined and the pro-
ceeds used to pay for a Healer's services, which you just
received.'' The giant paused and seemed to be waiting
for her to say something, and finally she managed to get
her mind and mouth working enough to string a couple
of words together.

''So that means what?'' she asked.

''Your injuries have been treated. You're being released,'' he explained patiently, and stood aside.

The door behind him was wide open, and she rose
shakily to her feet, to stumble out of it.

The guardsman took her arm to help her—she had no
doubt that if he wanted to, he could have picked her up
like a loaf of bread and carried her off, but he limited
his aid to only what was necessary. They stopped at the
room at the end of the long, stone corridor, and he took
her weapons from the guard stationed inside and gave
them to her with his own hands. As she buckled Need
back on, she felt a hundred times better. The remaining
pain vanished. That Healer had been good—but Need
was better.

She was still numb with surprise, though, as the
guardsman led her up the stairs to the wooden building
above the jail cells and opened the door, for her to walk
out. *Rudi spoke for me—and the stableboy—and the
Guild? Is this more of Need's magic, or is it something
I've done? And if it's me, what on earth did I do to make
them speak for me?*

But that surprise was nothing to the one waiting for
her outside the prison gates.

There was a crowd waiting there; a crowd wearing the
silver and gray tabards *she* used to sport, with a device
of crossed lighting-bolts on the sleeve. A crowd that
cheered the moment she came stumbling out into the
sunlight, squinting against the sudden glare.

''What?'' she stuttered. ''Wh–what?''

Someone took her arm; she turned at a flash of familiar

golden hair. Shallan stood right at her elbow, grinning
like a fool.

"You sure do get yourself in messes, don't you, Captain?" she said.

Several hours later, she finally had a glimmer of the
story, but only after putting together all the bits and
pieces of it that had been flung at her during the long
ride back to the Skybolts' winter quarters.

And it took a good meal, a sleep from dawn to dawn,
and another good meal before she was ready to try to
make sense of it all.

She called a half-dozen of her old friends together in
the outer room of the Captain's quarters. *That*, she still
had trouble with. She didn't feel like a Captain. And no
matter how often someone called her that, she kept looking over her shoulder to see who they were talking to.

She ordered hot tea all around from the orderly, feeling
very uneasy about doing so, even though the one-armed
twenty-year veteran who had served Lerryn seemed equally
content to serve her. "Let me see if I've got this straight,"
she said, as the others nursed their mugs in hands that
looked fully as thin as hers. "When I walked, you lot kept
Ardana from sending her hounds after me. Then you called
a *vote?*"

"It's an old law, part of the oldest part of the Code
that goes right back to the Oathbreaking ceremony," Tre
said solemnly. "Nobody uses it much, but nobody's ever
revoked it. What it 'mounts to, is any Company that's
lost more'n half its officers an' a third of the rest can call
the Captaincy to vote from the ranks. Me an' Shallan,
we'd been talkin' 'bout that since you'd got hurt. Lot of
the rest was thinkin' it was a good notion, but nobody
wanted t' start it." He took a sip of his tea, and smiled
ruefully. "Not even me."

"But when you walked like that, an' Ardana was gonna
haul you back in chains for takin' your rights, well, it
made everybody mad." Shallan ran her hands through
her short hair, and scratched at a new scar. "So since
we *knew* everybody'd been told about vote-right, we
started hollerin' for it. Next thing you know, Ardana's
out. Out of Captain, and out of the Company."

Tre took up the thread again. "So we needed a Cap-

tain, and the only person ev'body could agree on was
you.''

"Blessed Agnira.'' She covered her face with both
hands. "This isn't something I'm ready for—''

But who is? asked a little voice in the back of her
mind.

The Guild representative that had come with them
spoke for the first time. "Neither Tre nor Kynan are
trained in tactics, logistics, and supply the way you are,
Kerowyn. Their expertise stops at groups larger than a
squad. And neither of them care for mages.''

Which is a definite liability, she though, reluctantly.
*One thing this Company needs badly is a couple of com-
petent hedge-wizards.*

"How do you know I'll be any better?'' she asked,
dropping her hands.''

"You can't be worse,'' Shallan replied emphatically.

"You've seen for yourself how vulnerable a Company
is to bad leadership,'' the Guildsman said solemnly. "We
think that judging by your past performance, you would
step down rather than cause the Company harm.''

She stared at his impassive face; he was cut of the
same cloth as the Arbitrators, if a great deal younger.
You know *I would,* she thought at him, as if he could
hear her. *These are my friends, my family. It would be
hell on earth to spend the rest of my life leading them
into situations where some of them are going to get
killed. . . .*

*. . . but it would be worse watching someone well-
meaning but incompetent or untrained double those
deaths. And worse to ride off on my own, knowing it was
going to happen.*

*I haven't a choice. They're my people, and my respon-
sibility.*

And in that moment, she suddenly understood Eldan,
and the way he felt about his duty and his own people. His "Company'' was simply very much larger than
hers.

She tightened her jaw, and raised her chin a little. "All
right,'' she told them all. "You've convinced me.''

Shallan let out a whoop, and the others started to con-
gratulate her, but she held up a hand to forestall them.
"Let's first find out if we actually *have* a Company left.''

She turned to the Company accountant and quartermaster. "Scratcher, how bad is it?"

The man she queried did not much resemble a scholar; he was as lean and hard as any of the rest of the Skybolts, but there was a shrewd mind behind those enigmatic eyes. He chewed the end of his pen, studied the open book before him, and muttered to himself a little. Finally he looked up.

"With all the losses we took in people and supplies, Captain, we're going to exhaust the bank just replacing them. We aren't going to have enough to take us out again in the spring. We may not have enough to last the winter."

The Guild representative stirred a little, and Kero took the chance to read his thoughts.

We could—should—extend them a loan. But I don't have the authority—

She ground her teeth silently. *Take a loan that would be years in repayment? And what if we have a bad year, or a bad run of years. What, then?* She shifted her weight, and a crackle of parchment in her belt pouch made her frown.

What in—

Then she remembered. Eldan's ransom. Which *she* couldn't get. But the Guild?

She smiled slowly, and pulled it out, leaving the letter within. "Here," she said, handing it to the Guildsman. "This is from the Herald I pulled out of the fire. I think you can see he's played fast and loose with the conditions. Think the Guild can do something about that?"

The flat-faced mercenary took the parchment from her, opened it, and his lips pursed in a soundless whistle. "All that for a *mere* Herald? Are you certain he wasn't a prince?"

She shrugged. "All I care about is that right now that little piece of paper can make us if we can redeem it."

The Guildsman scrutinized the writing carefully, then suddenly, unexpectedly, smiled. "It specifies that the *holder* of the note is the one who has to redeem it in person," he pointed out. "If you signed it over to us, in return for an immediate sum minus—oh—ten percent, *our* representative would be the holder."

He'll never forgive me. "Done," she said, reaching

for Scratcher's pen. "Send it half in supplies and weapons. The *Guild* I trust."

The rest was over quickly, leaving Kero alone in the wardroom, her hand clenched around the letter still in her otherwise empty pouch. Slowly, she drew it out.

She stared at it for a long moment, her mind tired and blank. Then, she folded it and tore it into precise halves, then quarters, then repeated herself until there was no piece larger than the nail of her little finger.

She stared at the pile of pieces, stirring them a little with her forefinger. A noise from outside made her look up and through the window that gave out on the practice grounds.

Shallan was running a new recruit against the archery-target, at the trot. He jounced painfully and his arrows went everywhere except in the straw dummy. Her own buttocks ached in sympathy.

She looked down at the collection of tiny white scraps, then abruptly swept them into her hand and cast them into the fire.

She stood up, and strode to the door. Her orderly was waiting for her with her cape in his hands, as if her thoughts had summoned him. She paused just long enough for him to flick it over her back and settle it across her shoulders, before striding out onto the practice grounds.

Her practice grounds. *Her* recruits.

Her mouth opened, and the words came without her even having to think about them, as Shallan saw her and snapped to attention, the recruits following her raggedly.

"So, these are the new ones." She nodded, as she remembered Lerryn doing. "Very promising, Sergeant. Carry on."

BOOK THREE

The Price of
Command

Seventeen

Kero rubbed her eyes; they burned, though whether from the smoke from her dimming lantern, or from the late hour, she didn't know and didn't really care. "Maps," she muttered under her breath, the irritation in her voice plain even to *her* ears. "Bloody maps. I *hate* maps. If I see one more tactical map or *gashkana* supply list, I'll throw myself off a gods-be-damned cliff. Happily."

The command tent was as hot as all of the nine hells combined, but the dead-still air outside was no better, and full of biting insects to boot. At least whatever Healer-apprentice Hovan had put in the lamp oil that made it smoke so badly was keeping the bugs out of the tent. Shadows danced a slow pavane against the parchment-colored walls as the lamp flame wavered.

She stared at the minute details and tiny, claw-track notations of her terrain-map until her eyes watered, and she still couldn't see any better plan than the one she'd already made. She snarled at the blue line of the stream, which obstinately refused to shift its position to oblige her strategy, and slowly straightened in her chair.

Her neck and shoulders were tight and stiff. She ran a hand through hair that was damp at the roots from sweat, and she wished she'd brought Raslir, her orderly, along. One-armed he might be, but he had a way with muscles and a little bit of leather-oil. . . .

But he was also old enough to be her grandfather, and the battlefield was no place for him. He might find himself tempted beyond endurance to engage in one *little* fray—and that would be the end of him.

The wine flask set just within her reach looked very inviting, with water forming little crystal beads along its sides, and the cot beyond the folding table beckoned as well. She hadn't yet availed herself of either. She

stretched, as Warrl had taught her; slow, and easy, a fiber
at a time. A vertebra in her neck popped, and her right
shoulder-joint, and some of the strain in her neck eased.
*Either I'm getting old, or the damp is getting to me.
Maybe both.*

The lamp set up a puff of smoke, and she waved it
away, coughing, as she reached for the wine flask. And
despite her earlier vow to throw herself off a cliff if she
had to look at another list, she glanced at the tally sheet.
And smiled. She could smile, still, before the battle, before she actually had to send anyone out on the lines, to
kill and be killed. *If only I never had to send them out
to fight in anything but the kind of bloodless contests we
had last year. Then I could be entirely content.*

But a year like the last, where all they had to do was
show themselves, was the exception rather than the usual,
and she well knew it.

Still the tally sheet was impressive. *Not bad, if I do
say so myself.* It had been ten years since she'd been
made Captain, and there had been no serious complaints
from any Skybolt *or* from their clients or the Guild in all
that time. And from the beaten force that had come up
from Seejay, tails between their legs, she had built the
foundations for a specialist-Company that now tallied
twice the number Lerryn had commanded.

And in many ways, it was four Companies, not one,
each with its own pair of Lieutenants. For some reason
that she could not fathom, shared command had always
worked well for the Skybolts, though no one else could
ever succeed with it. The largest group was the light cavalry; next came the horse-archers. Those two groups
made up two-thirds of their forces. The remaining third
was divided equally between the scouts and the true specialists.

Those specialists included messengers, on the fastest
beasts Kero's Shin'a'in cousins would sell her; experts in
sabotage; and the nonfighters—two full Healers, and their
four assistants, and three mages and *their* six appren-
tices. The chief of those mages, and the jewel Kero frequently gloated over, was White Winds Master-class
mage Quenten, a mercurial, lean and incurably cheerful
carrot-top sent as a Journeyman straight to the Skybolts
by Kero's uncle.

He will tell you that he wants (gods help him), adventure, the young mage's letter of introduction had read. And for a moment, Kero had hesitated, knowing that a lust for "adventure" had been the death of plenty of mercenary recruits, and the disenchantment of plenty more. But then she had read on. *Don't mistake me, niece. He is as patient as even I could want, with a mind capable of dealing with the tedious as well as the exciting. What he calls "adventure," I would call challenge. There isn't enough outside of the magics of warfare to sharpen his skills as quickly as they can be sharpened. So although we are a school of peace, I send Quenten to you, knowing you will both be the wealthier for the association.*

So it had proved; she'd never known her uncle to be mistaken, so she took the young man on, and rapidly discovered what a prize she had been gifted with. He had, over the course of the years, managed to convince Need to extend her power of protection-against-magics to cover all of the Company. When she asked him how he had done it, he grinned triumphantly. "I did something to make it look as if you were the Company and the Company was you," he said, a light in his eyes that Kero had responded to with a smile of her own.

And if Need was aware that her magic had been tampered with, she hadn't bothered to do anything about it. Now the Skybolts were in the unique position of having mages whose concentrated efforts could be directed to things other than defensive magics. No one else could enjoy that kind of advantage. It made their three mages capable of doing the work of six. Only the armies of nations could afford that many mages deployed with a group the size of a Company. Most Companies couldn't even afford to field more than one mage, and the Skybolts used that advantage mercilessly.

After all these years, Kero still wasn't certain of how aware the sword was of the things that went on around her. In her first years as Captain, it had still occasionally tried to wrest control away from her, yet she had the impression that the blade wasn't really "awake" when it made these periodic trials. She sometimes thought that it reacted to her self-assertion the way a sleeping person would to an irritating insect.

When was *the last time it tested me?* She pondered, taking a long slow sip from the wine flask. The water slicking the sides of the pewter flask cooled the palm of her hand, and the chill liquid slid down her throat and eased the tickle in the back of it. She closed her eyes and savored it. *About five years ago. And I know I got the feeling that it wasn't going to try again. Gods, I hope not. Not now, anyway. Damned thing is likely to decide for the enemy!*

That was because the current campaign was against her old enemies, the Karsites. And *that* recollection made her smile with bitter pleasure. She had quite a debt to collect from the Karsites, and this was the first time in ten years that she'd had a chance to do so. The Skybolts were fighting beside the Rethwellan regular army on behalf of the *male* monarch of Rethwellan, against the self-styled *female* Prophet of Vkandis, and that could bring trouble from Need, if the sword noticed. Kero recalled only too well the time the blade had refused to fight against one of the Karsite priestesses. She didn't relish the idea of it turning on her again.

"If there's one thing I can't stand besides maps," she muttered to herself, "It's a holy war. These religious fanatics are so damned—*unprofessional.*"

Messy, that was what it was. *Seems like the moment religion enters into a question, people's brains turn to mush. Messy wars and messy thinking. Messy thinking* causing *messy wars.*

The Karsites had been causing trouble since long before the disaster in Menmellith, and had continued to do so afterward. But this was the first time that the followers of the Sunlord had ever actually moved openly against Rethwellan. The so-called Prophet, claiming to be the *original* Prophet, reborn into a female body to prove the Oneness of the deity, had managed to raise a good-sized army on the strength of her charisma and the "miracles" she performed. She had moved that army into the province south of Menmellith during the winter, while travel was hard and news moved slowly. By spring she had taken it over and sealed it off.

The King of Rethwellan made no secret of the fact that he suspected collusion on the part of the provincial governor. Kero was fairly sure, from *her* sources of infor-

mation within the Guild, that he was right. The governor
was an old man, a man who had suffered through a series
of serious illnesses. Kero had seen his kind before, and
sniffed cynically as she thought about him. *Odds are he's
figured out that he's as mortal as the rest of us for the
first time in his life, and he's been looking frantically for
someone, anyone, who'll promise him a quick and easy
route into some kind of paradise when he kicks over the
traces.*

She sipped again at her wine; carefully, it wouldn't do
to have a head in the morning. But wine was the only
thing that kept the dreams away.

She resolutely turned her mind away from those
dreams. Not because they were unpleasant; quite the
contrary, they were *too* pleasant. Seductively so. The
trouble was, they featured Eldan, and he was a subject
she was determined to forget.

*He can't have forgiven me for sending the Guild up to
collect that ransom instead of going myself. Either that,
or else by now he's completely forgotten me, assuming
he's even still alive.*

She'd dreamed of him often . . . far too often for her
own comfort. The dreams had come frequently, in those
first years, when she was unsure in her command, and
unhappy—and lonely. Sometimes in those night-visions
they hadn't done more than talk, and she'd come away
with answers she desperately needed.

But sometimes, especially lately, they'd done a great
deal more than talk. Since she was half-convinced that
her dreams were simply fantasies conjured up by her
sleeping mind, those dreams were a cruel reflection on
her current state of isolation, and while those incorporeal
rolls in the hay might be what she *wanted,* they didn't
make waking up any easier of a morning.

She told herself, over and over, that her self-imposed
loneliness didn't matter. Look at what she had built in
the past few years! Most *male* mercenaries never made
Captain, most male Captains had not achieved their rank
until well into their late forties. That it had cost her little
more than hard work, sleepless nights, and a lack of amorous company was hardly something to complain about.
And she knew very well the reasons *why* she needed to
keep herself free from amorous entanglements. Tarma

had explained that aspect of command to her in intimate detail, with plenty of examples of what not to do.

A Captain of a Company did not take lovers from the ranks; that was the quickest way in the world for suspicions of favoritism to start—and *that* let in factionalism and divisiveness. A Captain always remained the Captain, even among old friends.

The hired charms of the camp-followers were not at all to Kero's taste—and her peers either regarded her (rightly) as possible competition, or at best, a rival and equal power. But there was more to it than that, though most of Kero's peers would have laughed (if uneasily) if she'd told them her chief reason. It was asking for trouble to take someone into your bed with whom you might well find yourself crossing swords one day. *You never know who's going to be hired to come up against you. Having someone on the other side who had that kind of knowledge of me—in no way am I going to take that kind of risk.*

She put the flask down, and traced little patterns on the table with her wet forefinger. *That's the one thing Tarma never warned me about,* she reflected, waving away another puff of sharp-scented smoke. *She never told me that rank and holding yourself apart makes for lonely nights. She always had Grandmother for friendship—and she never* wanted *a lover thanks to that vow of hers. Gods know being Swordsworn would be easier than overhearing some of what goes on in the tents after dark. She could ignore it; I try, but can't always.*

Being Captain didn't necessarily mean an empty bed, even if you didn't much care for whores. More than a few of her fellow Captains went through wenches the way a ram goes through a flock of ewes. They tended to pick up country girls bedazzled by the glamour and danger, and abandon them when their lovers got a little too possessive. Kero had never been able to bring herself to just lure off some wide-eyed farmboy as if she was some kind of mate-devouring spider. And besides, more than half the men she met these days seemed overwhelmed by her.

I've been awfully circumspect, she thought, with perverse pride, looking back over the years. *There were three—no, four minstrels. That worked. All four of them were too cocky to be intimidated by me. The only problem*

*was, while the Skybolts make good song-fodder, they
don't offer much more to a rhymester. So I lost all four
of them to soft jobs in noble houses. There were a couple
of merchants, but that didn't last past a couple of nights.
And there was that Healer. But every time I went out he
was in knots by the time I came back, figuring it would
be me that got carried in for him to fix—that alliance was
doomed from the start. It's been cold beds for the past
two years now.* Unlike *Daren.*

She had to smile at that, because this campaign against
the Karsites had brought her back into personal contact
with "the boy," as she had continued to think of him.
Meeting him again had forced her to change that memory, drastically. He'd matured; not his face, which was
still boyishly handsome, if a bit more weathered, but in
the expression around the eyes and mouth. Not such a
boy anymore—

They hadn't renewed their affair; it would have been a
stupid thing to do in the middle of a war for one thing,
and for another, while they found themselves better
friends than ever, they discovered at that first meeting
that they were no longer attracted to each other.

Daren had achieved his dream of becoming the Lord
Martial of his brother's standing army. One thing about
him had not changed; he still worshiped his older brother.
Kero toyed with the flask, holding its cool surface to her
forehead for a moment, and wondered if the King knew
what a completely and selflessly loyal treasure he had in
his sibling. She hoped so; over the past several years
she'd learned that loyalty in the high ranks was hardly
something to be taken for granted.

Daren was as randy as Kero was discreet. He hopped
in and out of beds as casually as any of the Captains she
knew, and there'd even been rumors of betrothal once or
twice, but nothing ever came of it.

We're too much alike. She smiled, thinking about how
even their battle plans still meshed after all these years.
*Far too much alike to ever be lovers again. Just as well, I
suppose. He just makes me feel too sisterly to want him.*

"Captain?" Her aide-de-camp stuck his head just inside the flap of the tent. "Shallan and Geyr to see you."

Gods. I forgot I sent for them. Must be the heat. She
stifled a yawn. "Good; send them in." She made certain

two special bits of cloth were at hand, and fished one particular map out of the pile and smoothed it out on the table.

"Captain?" Shallan said doubtfully.

"Come on in," she replied easily. "No formality."

Her old friend—whom Kero wanted to make Lieutenant of the specialist corps—slipped inside, followed by the man Kero intended to make Shallan's co-commander.

A year ago Shallan had lost Relli to a chance arrow, and for a while Kero was afraid they were going to lose the surviving partner to melancholy or madness. But given the responsibility of command of a squad, Shallan had made a remarkable recovery. She and Geyr had never actually worked together; Kero had a shrewd notion they'd do fine, not the least because they were both *she'chorne*. They looked like total opposites; Shallan still a golden blonde as ageless as the mysterious Hawkbrothers, and Geyr, a native of some land so far to the south Kero had never even heard of it before he told her his story, a true *black* man from his hair to his feet.

The two of them stood a little awkwardly in front of her table. She stayed seated; even though she had said "no formality," she intended to keep that much distance between them. They were friends, yes—but they had to be Captain and underling first, even now.

"How's Bel?" Shallan asked immediately. The scout-lieutenant had been taken victim, not by wounds, but by the killer that fighters feared more than battle—fever. That same fever had already struck down one of the co-commanders of the horse-archers.

"I had to send him back, like Dende," Kero replied regretfully. "The Healers think he'll be all right, but only if we get him up into the mountains where it's cool and dry. That's why I wanted you here. I want to buck Losh over to command the horse-archers, and put you two in charge of the specialists."

Shallan's mouth fell open; Geyr looked as if he thought he hadn't rightly understood what she'd said. He scratched his curly head, as Shallan took a deep breath.

She waited for them to recover; Shallan managed first. "But—but—"

"You've earned it, both of you," she said. "I've been shorthanded with the horse-archers, and that's really where Losh belongs. The troops know you, and you've both been handling squads up until now with no complaints. I think you'll do fine.''

"What about the dogs?" Geyr asked slowly, the whites of his eyes shining starkly against his dark skin. "Do I keep on running the dogs?"

"Damn bet you do," Kero told him. "The only difference this command will make in that, is that now *you and I* will be the only ones deciding when to run them, and when it's too dangerous. I know you and Losh didn't always agree on that.''

Geyr grinned, showing the gold patterns inlaid in his front teeth. *"Khala il rede he, Ishuna,"* he replied, in the tongue that he alone knew. "Blessings follow and luck precede you, liege-lady. I and mine thank you."

"You're welcome," she said, with a little weary amusement. She had *yet* to get Geyr to understand the difference between Mercenary's Oath and swearing fealty. Maybe in his land there *were* no differences. She turned to Shallan. "What have you to say, Lieutenant?"

"I—" Shallan swallowed hard and tried again, her eyes dilated wide in the lamplight. "Thank you, Captain. I accept.'' She glanced out of the corner of her eye at Geyr, and Kero saw her face grow thoughtful, her expression speculative. "This isn't an accident, is it?" she stated, rather than asked. "You picked us both because we're *she'chorne,* and we'll be able to work together without sex getting into it.''

Kero chuckled. "One reason out of many, yes," she admitted. "And by seeing that, I think I can safely say you're starting to think like an officer. Good.'' She rolled up the map in front of her, and passed it across the table to them. Shallan took it. "This is the initial battle line for tomorrow. I want you two to study it, and come back to me if you have any changes you'd like to make. Otherwise, that is all I have to say to you for now.''

She picked up the two Lieutenant's badges that had been hidden under the pile of papers at the side of the table. Both her new officers took them gravely, saluted her with clean precision, and took themselves out. The tent flapped closed behind them, letting in a breeze that was a little fresher, but no cooler.

It's going to be impossible to sleep tonight without some

help. Kero sighed, reached once more for the wine flask, and downed the rest of the contents in a single gulp. *Better risk a bit of a headache than no sleep.*

She peeled herself out of her clothing before the wine could fuddle her, and left the uniform in a heap for her aide to pick up, falling onto the cot as a flush of light-headedness overtook her.

Maybe it's a good thing I don't have a lover, she thought muzzily as she allowed sleep to take her. *Between battle plans and supply lists, I'd never see him unless he disguised himself as a gods-be-damned map.*

"What are you trying to do, work yourself into an early grave?" Eldan crossed his arms over his chest and glared at her. "Or are you planning on drinking yourself there first?"

Kero matched him, glare for glare, anger and shame burning her cheeks. She knew very well she'd been hitting the wine flask a little too hard, and she didn't like being reminded of the fact. "I don't drink that much. Just enough to put me out for the night. And you ought to be thanking me for working this hard—it's the enemies of your precious Valdemar I'm up against this time."

Inside she was quaking, a cold fear clutching at her heart. She'd had her wine. She shouldn't be having this dream. Drinking had always kept the dreams away before—

"Oh, you're up against one faction of Karse, all right. One minor faction of Karse—and meanwhile the real power in Karse is free to—"

"What? Free to what? Nobody's made a move in Karse since the Prophet started her power play. So what's the big problem here?" She turned her back on him, and spoke to the vague, gray mist that always surrounded them in her dreams, hoping he wouldn't see how her shoulders were shaking. She wasn't sure of anything. She was terrified he'd touch her—and she wanted him to touch her, so badly, so very badly. . . .

"You know what I think?" she said before he could form a reply. "I think the big problem is that I'm fighting for money. That just sticks in your throat, doesn't it? And it sticks in your throat that I'm good at it, that I could probably teach your people a trick or two, that—"

A hand touched her shoulder, and the words froze in her throat. "Kero—" he said, humbly. "I'm sorry. I shouldn't have—I worry about you. You do work too hard."

"I don't have much of a choice," she reminded him tartly, without turning around. She was afraid if she did, she'd never be able to stay under control. *"There are people depending on me—and you know what's really bothering you. It's that I do this for money."*

Eldan stepped slowly and soundlessly around her, so that he was looking into her eyes. She averted hers, looking down at her feet. *This is only a dream,* she kept telling herself. *It doesn't mean anything.*

"That does bother me," he said earnestly. *"I think it's wrong. There are other things you could be fighting for. You could be killed, and is money worth dying for? Honor—"*

That word again. That stupid, suicidal word. It made her cheeks flame, this time with unmingled anger. *"Honor won't put food on my troopers' table, or pay in their pockets,"* she snapped. *"Honor won't pay for much of anything. It's all very well to prate about honor, when you're on a first-name basis with a Queen, but my people rely on me to see that they get the means to live!"*

"But—" he began.

"More stupid wars have been fought over honor than I care to think about," she continued inexorably, raising her eyes just enough to stare angrily at the middle of his chest. *"Seems to me that honor is a word that gets used to cover a lot of other things. Things like greed and ambition, hatred, and bigotry. It's honorable to attack someone who doesn't believe in the same things you do. It's honorable to fight someone over a strip of land you covet. It's honorable—"*

She looked up at his uncomprehending face, and threw her hands up in the air. *"I don't know why I bother! At least I'm honest about my killing. I do it for money. I try to pick the side that was attacked, not the attackers. Most of the rest of the world wages war to support one lie or another—"*

"Not here," he said, softly. *"Not us."*

She would have rather he argued with her. She would

*much rather he'd shouted. Instead, this hurt expression—
the look in his eyes, pleading with her to believe him.*

"I only know what I've seen," she said gruffly. "And
what I've seen says that most of what people call 'honor'
is no more than self-deception. Maybe you people in Valdemar are different."

"We are," he said. "Please, Kero, you know me—you
know what I'm like. You've been inside my mind—"

"Right," she interrupted hastily. "All right, you are
different. Maybe all you Heralds are. That doesn't make
what I do any less valid. The rest of the world isn't like
you. And if there are going to be people out there making
war on other people, don't you think it's a good idea for
some of those people to at least follow a code of ethics?
Not 'honor,' but something you can pin down and be sure
of, something with the same rules for everybody. That's
what we're doing. And if we do it for money, so be it. At
least someone is doing it at all."

She looked back up, to see he was smiling, ruefully.
"You have a point," he said, with a sigh. "Kero, that
wasn't why I came here—"

Before she knew what she was doing, she had responded to that smile, to the invitation in his eyes, and
was locked in a mutual embrace with him.

Part of her was in terror. This was real—too real.
Eldan's arms felt too solid; his body too warm against
hers. I'm going crazy, I must be! Being alone—

But the rest of her welcomed his embrace, the warmth
of his lips on her forehead. The only intimate human
touch she had—

Even if it wasn't real.

"I didn't want to argue with you," he said in her ear.
"I am worried about you. You're trying to do too much.
You take to much on yourself. And you bottle up your
own feelings, never let anything out. You're going to destroy yourself this way—you can't be everything to everyone."

"I thought you said you didn't come here to argue with
me," she heard herself saying. "Keep that up and you'll
start another one."

"Oh, Kero," he shook his head, and she looked up
into his eyes. "Kero, what am I going to do with you?"

"You might try—"

He stopped the words with a kiss, a kiss that led to more kisses, and then to something more intimate than mere kisses—

Hands warm on skin, illusory clothing vanishing as they touched each other in wonder and pleasure and joy—

"Blessed Agnira!"

Kero woke up with a start, and the moment she was actually *awake*, she began to shake with terror.

The wine hadn't worked. The dreams were back, more vivid than ever, and the wine hadn't helped. This one— it had been *real*. Too real, too close to home. Part of her had *wanted* it, that was the worst thing; part of her had welcomed not only the dream, but the fantasy lovemaking.

She flung off the light blanket, and sat up on the edge of the cot, shaking. *I'm going mad. I'm truly going mad. It's all been too much for me.*

Easy to believe she was going mad, Easier than to believe that she had created the dream because she missed Eldan, and wanted him so much. . . .

Before she realized it, tears began to burn her eyes, and her throat closed. She buried her face in her hands. *It wasn't a mistake. It never could have worked. We— Oh, gods. Oh, Eldan—*

Seizing the flask of water that stood beside her bed, she drank it dry, hoping to drown the tears. Instead, they only fell faster, and she was helpless to stop them.

As helpless as she was to stop the loneliness that was the price of command. . . .

She seized her tunic, groped for her cloak, and went out into the cool night, hoping to pace away the doubts, the fears, and most of all, the memories.

This place had been pretty, before warfare had scarred the land; low, rolling hills covered in grass, tree lines that marked streambeds and river bottoms. Now the grass was trampled, and dust rose above the scuffling armies like smoke. Sun burned down onto the battlefield like Vkandis' own curse. Kero stood beside her old friend, magnificent in his scarlet cloak of the Lord Martial, and squinted into the distance. Beside her, Geyr stood as impassively as a black stone statue. She could not imagine how he was able to stand there and look so cool and unmoved.

Maybe he doesn't feel the heat. Maybe this isn't that bad to him. If that's so, I don't think I ever want to visit his homeland.

Up until now, the Prophet had held several groups of infantry in reserve. It looked as if those last groups on the Prophet's side had finally joined the battle. "This is it," Daren said quietly, confirming her observation. "The Prophet just committed herself entirely. And so have I. If we don't win this one—"

"You'll lose the war, the province, and a hell of a lot of face," Kero finished for him, wiping her sweaty face with a rag she kept tucked into her belt. "But that won't be the worst of it. If you lose, *she'll* have a power base, and you'll have to fight her every time you turn around, or you'll lose the country to her a furlong at a time." She scowled, though not at him, but rather at the thought.

Beside them, a handsome—and very young—noble assigned as Daren's aide looked puzzled. "Why is that, m'lord?" he asked. "Won't she be content with what she's won?"

Daren snorted, and wiped his own face with a rag no cleaner or fancier than Kero's. "Not too damned likely. If we don't eliminate her now, it'll prove that her god really *is* on her side, and we'll be fighting religious fanatics all over Rethwellan. This kind of 'holy war' is like gangrene—if you don't get rid of it, it poisons the whole body. If we can't burn it out, it'll kill us all."

The young aide gave Kero a sideways glance, as if asking her to confirm what Daren had said. She'd already discovered that she had a formidable reputation among Daren's highborn young fire-eaters; she was using that reputation to reinforce *his* authority. There could only be *one* Commander of all the forces, just as there could only be *one* Captain of a Company.

"You're dead right about that, my lord," she said, answering the boy's glance without speaking to him directly. "I can't think of anything worse than fighting a religious fanatic, especially one that's sure he's going to some kind of paradise if he dies for his god. That kind'll charge your lines, run right up your blade, and kill himself in order to take your head off."

She peered through the sun, the heat-haze, and the dust, and cursed again under her breath, resolutely shaking off the weariness that was the legacy of her sleepless night. It was pretty obvious that both armies had stalemated each other. *Her* people were out of it, for now; they'd done what they could early this morning, and now they were behind the lines, taking what rest they could, and awaiting further orders. *And with only a handful of dead and twice that wounded. New recruits, mostly, and no one I really knew well. Gods pass their souls.*

For once, she wasn't having to prove herself and her Company to anyone. Daren had made her pretty well autonomous; he trusted her judgment and her battle sense. He knew she had twice the actual combat experience he or any of his commanders had. He knew that if she saw an opening where the Skybolts could do some good, she'd send them. That was more trust than Kero had gotten from any other Commander, and she wondered if he treated all mercenary Captains like that, or only her, because he knew her.

Right now, the action was all afoot, and hand-to-hand, and there was no place for a mounted force to go—except for the heavy cavalry, who kept trying to plow through the enemy lines without getting trapped behind them.

A glitter of sun-reflection caught her eye and she grimaced at the shrine of Vkandis anchoring the left flank. *The damn thing is the rallying point for the entire line,* she thought angrily. *Every time those idiots haul it forward a couple of paces, the whole left flank follows it.*

It was pulled on clumsy rollers by nearly a hundred of the most manic of the Prophet's followers. Every day now they'd added captured booty and ornamentation to it, making it more impressive, more elaborate, and doubtless making it heavier as well. The latest trick had been to gild the roof; that was what had caught her eye, the shine of sun on gold-leaf. She wondered how many poor peasants had been starved to pay for the ornamentation.

Another blur of motion caught her eye, and one more familiar—the yellow-gray streak that marked the passage of one of Geyr's messenger-dogs behind the lines. The poor beasts looked like nothing more than bags of bones, but they moved like lightning incarnate. Geyr had brought them with him when he'd joined; Kero gathered that in his country, men raced the pups the way the folk of the north raced horses. He had the notion that they could be used as messengers, but only Kero had been willing to take a chance on his idea. They were amazingly intelligent for their size; once they knew that a particular human carried a horn full of lumps of suet or balls of butter on his belt, they had that person's name and scent locked in memory for all time, and anyone could put a message in their collars and tell them to find that person, and they would. No matter what stood in their way. The scrawny little beasts would literally race through fire for a bit of fat. Geyr had once said, laughingly, that if you buttered a brick, they'd eat it.

The little dog evaded people and horses with equal ease, then stopped dead for a moment. Before Kero had a chance to ask Geyr what was wrong with it, the beast was off again, this time streaking in *their* direction, so low to the ground that his chest must be scraping the earth.

"Meant for me, which means you, Captain," Geyr muttered, as the dog dove fearlessly among the hooves of the Skybolts' horses and out the other side of the picket lines. She recognized it now by the scarlet collar—it was the one they'd sent with Shallan's scouts.

It flung itself through the air, landing in Geyr's waiting arms; panting, but not with exhaustion. This punishing heat was no more bother to Geyr's dogs than to Geyr himself.

The black Lieutenant gave the little animal his reward, and passed the message cylinder from its collar to Kero. She opened it, and scanned the short scrawl with a sinking heart. Shallan had seen something important, and had dutifully reported it. And Daren would most certainly see the way to break the deadlock that Shallan's observation opened up. She knew how he thought, and it was the only logical course of action—only now it was no longer counters on a sand-table they put at risk, it was her men's and women's lives. But something had to be done, or they'd risk more Karsite intervention before they had neutralized the Prophet.

Even it meant *her* people would die.

And if by some chance he doesn't see it, I'll have to point it out to him. Gods have mercy. . . .

Her throat closed. She passed him the note without comment; his brows creased as he puzzled out Shallan's crabbed and half-literate printing. Then he looked up into her eyes.

"She says there's a way to get to the shrine, coming up the bed of the stream."

Kero nodded, and cleared her throat discreetly. *They know what they're getting paid to do.* "But if you sent foot, they'd see you coming in time and reinforce the lines there."

"But if I sent horse-archers with fire-arrows . . . they'd move too quickly for the Prophet's commanders to see what we were up to and maneuver foot into place. And if the shrine goes, the whole army will panic."

Kero closed her eyes for a moment to think. There might yet be a way to spare her people. "We've tried this before," she reminded him. "Getting the shrine was one of the first things we thought of, and we couldn't even touch it."

"But not using the horse-archers," he retorted. "We didn't have a clear shot at it with the archers before; we tried for it using magic. It's shielded against magic, but I'd be willing to bet it isn't shielded against plain old fire-arrows. It wasn't shielded against that ballista shot that took off a corner of the roof. If it can be hit, it can be burned."

Dear gods, there's no hope for it. Either they go in, impossible odds and all, or we lose. Her stomach knotted, and her throat ached with sorrow for the slaughter to come. Bad enough to send her people into an ordinary battle, where the odds were in their favor because of their strike-and-run tactics. But this—

She swallowed, stared off into the distance, and tried to think of them as markers on a table. Running the tactic straight—she'd lose about half of those that went in.

But she had the only force that *could* get in, get the job done, and get out.

It's a suicide mission! half of her cried in agony.

It's necessary, said the other half, coldly, logically.

She took a deep breath, lowered her eyes, and looked straight back into Daren's. And saw that he didn't like the odds any better than she did. He hated the cost of this as much as she. She saw the same pain she felt in the back of *his* eyes, and it steadied her.

"All right," she said. "Give me time to set this up, right to requisition what I might need from your quartermaster, then get us an escort in and out. Leave the rest to us. Geyr, on me."

She turned on her heel, and walked off without another word. *How can I even up the odds? There has to be a way.* The black man whistled to his dog and followed after her, as she strode down toward the picket line, and the rows of horses drowsing in the sun, oblivious to the battle beyond.

"Get me Quenten," she called as she reached the lines and lounging fighters jumped to their feet. She scanned them, looking for the bright white of Lieutenants' badges. She spotted one, and providentially, it was exactly the person she needed most. "Losh," she ordered, not slacking her pace in the least, as she kept straight on through the lines. "Get the horse-archers to the Healers' tent. The rest of you, at ease."

A third of the Skybolts went back to their scraps of shade, veterans enough to know and follow the maxim that a fighter rests whenever he can. The rest left their beasts in the care of friends and followed after her to the Healers' tent.

Quenten turned up just as she got there, popping out of the Healers' tent so suddenly he seemed to appear out of the air, like one of his illusions. And seeing that started an idea in the back of her mind.

She left it there to simmer a while, as she gathered her troops around her, and explained the mission. The horse-archers sat or stood, each according to his nature, but all with one thing in common; absolute attention and complete silence.

As Kero drew a rough map in the dust and laid out the plan, she couldn't help but notice how appallingly young the gathered faces were. One and all, they were veterans, yes, without a doubt—but none was over the age of twenty-five. Most were under twenty. *Young enough to believe in their own immortality and invulnerability. Too young to really understand what bad odds mean, or really care if they do know. Each and every one of them thinks he can beat the odds and the omens, however un-favorable.* She felt sickened; as if she was somehow be-traying them.

As she completed her explanation, the glimmering of an idea burst into full flower, and she turned to Quenten. "You're in on this because I want *you* to do something to make them harder to hit—maybe make them harder to see," she told him. "They're already going to be moving targets; I want you to make it so hard for the enemy to look at them that he has nothing to aim at."

He scratched his peeling nose thoughtfully; like most redheads, he sunburned at the merest hint of summer. That was probably why he had been in the Healers' tent; either sensibly avoiding injury or getting his burns seen to. "I can't make weapons bounce off 'em, Captain," he replied uneasily. "I think I know what you're thinking of, and I'm not as good as your grandmother was, I haven't got the power to pull that spell that makes 'em look like they're a little off where they really are. And I sure's hell can't make 'em invisible."

"That wasn't what I had in mind," she said, impatient with herself for not knowing how to explain clearly what she *did* want. "You're damned good at illusion. There's a lot of sun out there today—hellfires, the way it comes off that shrine roof, you get spots in front of your eyes trying to look at it. What about if I get real shiny armor issued for everybody—can you do something to make it brighter?"

Quenten brightened immediately. "Now *that* I can do!" he enthused. "I can double the light reflecting off of it, at least—maybe triple it."

"Good man." She slapped him lightly on the back, and he grinned like a boy. "You work on that while I see what I can do about armor."

In the end, she scrounged shiny breastplates and hel-mets from Daren's stores for all of her horse-archers, and Geyr had the clever notion of fixing mirrors to the top of every nose-guard and the nose-band of every bridle. Quenten worked a miracle in the short time she gave him; not only did he concoct the spell, creating it liter-ally from nothing but the light-gathering cantrip mages used when working in a dimly-lit area, but he managed to cast it so that the Skybolts themselves were immune to its effects.

"That's the best I can do," he said, finally. Kero watched the effect on some of Daren's troopers; they winced, and squinted, and eventually had to look away. She nodded; it wasn't full protection, but it would tilt the odds farther in their favor.

Now all they have to worry about are the arrows shot at them unaimed. And hope none of the Prophets' officers get the bright idea of just letting fly en masse.

"Quenten, you've outstripped what your training says you should be able to do," she told him honestly, and gratefully, mopping her neck with her rag. "You've managed a brand new spell in less than a candlemark. I think my uncle would salute you himself."

Quenten glowed, and not just from his sunburn. Kero turned to one of the junior mages, a grave, colorless girl whose name she could never remember.

Jana. That's it.

"Jana, is the way still open to the shrine?"

Jana's eyes got the unfocused look she wore when she was using her powers to see at a distance. "Yes," she said, in a voice as flat and colorless as the rest of her. "As open as it's ever going to be."

Kero looked over Jana's head at the rest of the horse-archers. "The plan is simple enough. You with the fire-arrows, ride in the middle. The rest of you try to keep them covered and yourselves alive. Get in, and get out. We're not in this for glory or revenge, so don't take stupid chances. Got that?"

The fighters grunted, or nodded, or otherwise showed their assent. *At least the foolhardy were weeded out early,* she thought, watching them mount up with an aching heart and an impassive face. *If they wanted out of this life, they could get out.*

She saluted them as they wheeled their mounts and took off at a gallop. Losh was leading them in a feint toward the center of the left flank. Only at the last moment would they turn and rush up the watercourse. By then they would be out of unaided sight, and she would not have to watch them fall and die. . . .

They'd do this if I wasn't Captain, she told herself for the hundredth time. *This is what they're good at; it's their choice. And if I didn't lead them, someone else would. Someone with less care for them, maybe, or less imagination.*

And as always, as she waited for the survivors to return, the words comforted her not at all.

Eighteen

Daren finished the last of his dispatches, and slumped at the folding desk in his tent, very glad that he'd brought an aide who knew massage. Right now, he was torn equally between a tired elation and a sense of deep and guilty loss.

When the horse-archers had moved in, the shrine went up in a glorious gout of flames, just as he and Kerowyn had planned. And exactly as he and Kero had known it would, the Prophet's line collapsed in a panic. The only thing they had not predicted was how *total* the rout would be. But now that he thought about it, the reaction only made sense—Vkandis Sunlord was a god of the sun—hence, fire—and when his *own shrine* went up in flames, it must have seemed to the Prophet's followers that the god himself had turned against them.

After that it had been so easy to defeat them that an army of raw recruits could have handled the job. The worst casualties were from men who had gotten between the fleeing Karsites and the Eastern border.

He'd heard that Kerowyn's people got in and out with about a twenty-five percent loss, which was excellent for such a risky undertaking.

Excellent—except that these aren't just numbers we're talking about, or the counters we used to plan strategy with. Those numbers represented people. Kero's people. Fighters that she's recruited and trained with, and promised to lead intelligently. He stared at the papers on his desk without really seeing them, knowing how she must be feeling. It wasn't quite so bad for him, now that he was Lord Martial of the entire army. He didn't, couldn't know every man in his forces the way Kero knew every fighter in hers. But he remembered very well how it had felt to lose even *one* man, back when his commands were smaller.

He stood abruptly. *I'll go see her. It helped me to have old Lord Vaul to unburden myself on. Maybe I can do the same for her. I'm supposed to see if she's willing to come talk to my brother, anyway. And I can bring her horsearchers a bonus at the same time; gods know they've earned it. My coffers are plump enough, I can afford it.*

"Binn!" he said, not quite shouting, but loud enough for his orderly to hear. The grizzled veteran of a dozen tiny wars slid out of the shadows at the back of the tent, coming from behind the screen that kept his sleeping area private.

The man saluted smartly. "Sir," he said, and waited for orders. They were not long in coming.

"Saddle my palfrey, and get me—hmm—two gold per head for those horse-archers Captain Kerowyn sent in."

The orderly nodded, and saluted again. "Sir, general funds, or your private coffer?"

"Private, Binn. This is between me and the Captain. If my brother decides on an extra bonus, that'll be a Crown decision."

"Sir. Begging the Lord Martial's pardon, but—they deserve it. Don't generally see mercs with that kind of guts." The man's face remained expressionless, but Daren fancied he caught a gleam of admiration in his eyes. That in itself was a bit of a surprise. Binn seldom unbent enough to praise anyone, and never a mercenary, not to Daren's recollection.

"No pardon needed. As it happens, I agree with you." He straightened his papers, and locked them away in the desk, as the orderly moved off briskly to see to his orders.

He mounted up and rode off as the first torches were lit along the rows of tents. He had left his scarlet cloak back in the tent, so there was nothing to distinguish him from any other mounted officer, and the men paid him no particular heed as they went about their business.

The dead had been collected and burned; the wounded were treated and would either live or die. The survivors tended to themselves, now—either celebrating or mourning. Mostly celebrating; even those who mourned could be coaxed into forgetting their losses for an hour or two over the strong distilled wine he had ordered distributed. They'd have wicked heads in the morning, those who were foolish enough to overindulge, but that was all right. If their heads ached enough, it would distract them from the aches of wounds, bruises, and hearts.

He passed over the invisible dividing line between the camp of the army and that of the mercenaries, and was, as ever, impressed by the discipline that *still* held there, victory or no. Kero's people still had sentries posted, and he was challenged three times before he reached the camp itself. The Skybolts had lanterns instead of torches, an innovation he noted and made up his mind to copy. Torches were useless in a rainstorm—lanterns could be used regardless of the weather. And lanterns, once set, didn't need the kind of watching torches did. It was just the kind of detail that set the Skybolts apart from the average mercenary Company.

By the time he reached the actual bounds of the camp itself, word of his coming and who he was had somehow, in that mysterious way known only to soldiers, preceded him. Since he was not in "uniform," he was hailed only as "m'lord Daren"—but it was obvious from the covert looks at his bulging saddlebag and the grins of satisfaction (or envy, from those who were *not* archers), that these men knew of his penchant for delivering bonuses, and knew who those bonuses were due.

He asked after Kerowyn, and was directed to the command tent. All about him were the sounds of the same kind of celebration as back in his own camp, but more subdued, and there were fewer bonfires, and nothing like some of the wildness he'd left back there.

He dismounted at Kero's tent and handed the reins of his horse to one of the two sentries posted there, taking the saddlebag with him. When he pushed back the flap, and looked inside, Kero was bent over a folding table identical to his own, going over lists. The lantern beside her seemed unusually smoky, and the pungent odor it emitted made him sneeze. She looked up, smiled wanly, and nodded at a stool beside the table before going back to her task. Her eyes were dark-rimmed, and red; her cheekbones starkly prominent.

Dear gods, she looks like hell. Worse than I expected. He got a good look at those lists before he sat down;

lists of names, and he had a feeling that they were the lists of the dead. *He* had always left that task till last, and he didn't think she'd be any different.

She was writing little notations after each name; most looked like other names, which made him think she was probably noting who inherited the dead fighter's possessions. Before a very few of those names, she made a little mark—

Those must be the ones with relatives, the ones she has to write the letter for. He craned his neck a little, shamelessly curious. That was the single task he had hated the most. Still *did* hate, since he still had to write letters for the families of his officers, from Lieutenant upward.

There don't seem to be a lot of those. He grimaced a little. *Dear gods. What a sad life they must lead, that so many of them live and die with no one to mourn their loss except their fellows. . . .*

Kero sighed, and reached for a scrap of cloth to clean her pen. "Well, that's done," she said, tossing her long blonde braid over her shoulder. "All but the letters. Damn." For a moment she was silent, chewing absently on the end of her pen, and he couldn't help but notice that her nails had been chewed down to nothing. "At least most of my people don't have anyone outside of the Company, and a damned good thing, too."

Daren couldn't help himself; he was so surprised to hear her voice an opinion so exactly opposite his that he blurted out the first thing that came into his mind. *"Good?"* he exclaimed. "You say that's *good?* Demonfire, Kero, how can you say something like that?"

He could have bitten his tongue, and waited in the next instant for her to snap some kind of angry reply. When she didn't, when she only gave him a raised eyebrow eloquent with unspoken irony, he was just as amazed as he had been by her initial bald statement. *She's changed,* he thought numbly. *She's really changed, in deep ways, that don't show . . . maybe that's what's wrong. She feels things even more now—*

But there seemed to be a deeper trouble there; something more personal.

"If you're going to make your living by selling your sword," she pointed out dryly, pointing her pen at him like one of his old tutors used to, "it's a pretty stupid

idea to burden yourself with a lot of dependents who
don't—or won't—understand that you're basically gambling with your life, betting on the odds that you *won't*
be killed.''

"But—'' he started to object.

"No 'buts,' my friend,'' she said emphatically. "My
people, by the time they've seen one whole season, know
exactly what they're getting into. To tell you the truth,
it's *your* people I feel sorry for. You have all these farm-
boys and merchant sons, minor nobles and conscripts
swept up off the streets—all of them burdened with parents and sibs, friends and lovers. And when *they* become
just another target, how do you explain to *those* people
that their precious, immortal child is embracing the
Shadow-Lover, hmm?''

He hung his head, unable to answer, because he'd never
been able to find a way that convinced even himself. *War
is a waste. It's my job to keep it from wasting as little as
possible. . . .*

"At least my people and *their* people know what
they're getting into,'' she said, her voice going dull with
weariness—and perhaps with emotion that she refused to
display. "And if it so happens that they find someone
who makes them think again about laying their life on
the line for nothing but cash, they tend to get *out* before
it ever comes to the letter. Your people don't have that
luxury. They're in it until you let them go, or they're
dead.''

He squirmed on his stool; her words had cut much too
close to the bone.

*Trust Kero not to be polite about it. And maybe she's
right. If we're going to have fighting, maybe the only ones
who should do it are the ones willing to fight for pay. I
don't know. Right now I'm just glad it's over for us.* He
quickly changed the subject. *And it's a good thing I have
a new subject right here with me.* He dropped the saddlebag on the table, and Kero smiled knowingly at the
chink it made as it fell. "Bonus for the archers?'' she
asked, and at his nod, picked it up and dropped it into a
little chest beside her table. "I'll hand it out in the morning, and I hope you'll accept my thanks for them. That
kind of appreciation means a lot to us.''

He nodded, embarrassed to be equating the kind of

bravery that last charge had taken with the sum of two paltry gold pieces. *Then again—that's their job, isn't it? The laborer is worth the hire.* "Where are you going now?" he asked. "We finished this a lot faster than I'd thought we would; it's barely past Midsummer. Have you got another job lined up?"

She shook her head, which surprised him a little. "We'll go straight to winter quarters," she said. "Remember, you hired us before Vernal Equinox because the Prophet had stolen a march on you in the winter; it's been plenty long enough for us. We don't need to take another job this season, and we haven't needed to take winter jobs since the second year I was Captain. Ending early in the season will give us a head start on training the green recruits, schooling new horses, healing up—" She noted his surprise, and chuckled. "That's right—Tarma never taught you all that, did she? Winter quarters is what makes a good Company stronger. When we can winter up, we get a chance to learn without killing anybody, we get a chance to get everything Healed *right*. There's another side of it, too; wintering is where we become— well—a kind of family, if that doesn't sound too impossible to you. And since the Skybolts don't *need* to take the extra jobs anymore, I'll be damned if I cheat them out of that rest time."

She fixed him with a sharp glance, a look that told him that if he'd been considering offering them hire for the winter, he'd better change his mind.

But since that wasn't what he'd had on his mind at all, he smiled right back at her, and her expression softened and relaxed. "Is there any reason why you can't leave them for a month or two?" he asked, innocently.

"Well, no," she replied, obviously wondering why he would ask that particular question. She waited for a reply, but he simply smiled at her, until she said, impatiently, "All right! Why do you want to know *that?*"

"Because my brother wants to meet you, and this seems like a good time." He grinned at her blank stare, and continued. "Tarma trained the lot of us, remember? But she trained us a little differently than the way she trained you—she knew you were going to end up a hiresword, so she gave you things she never gave us. My brother wants to pick your brain."

"On what?" she asked, with a hint of suspicion.

"Nothing you wouldn't be willing to tell us," Daren assured her. "He wants to know about all the bonded Companies doing business, for one thing; things the Guild won't tell us, like who can't work with whom, what weaknesses each Captain has. You're the best, Kero—everybody says so. We want to know why. We want to know if it's something we can copy. We know you'll be honest with us. And we'll make it worth your while—"

"I don't take bribes," she replied harshly. "You won't get me to tell you Guild secrets."

"We don't care about Guild secrets, and it's not a bribe," he said quickly. "Just a bonus for the information. Free run through the Royal armory, your choice, whatever you can carry away in three wagon-loads with two-horse teams. We've got a lot of good horse-gear in storage, because we don't have a lot of mounted fighters. Besides, I want to catch up on what's happened to you the last fifteen years."

She started to answer, then gave him a careful, measuring look, and hesitated. "Daren," she said slowly, and a little sadly, "I hope this isn't a try at reviving the old romance. That's *dead*, lad, and there's no mage with a spell strong enough to resurrect it."

He stared at her for a moment, at the expression on her face that reminded him irresistibly of someone sitting on a tack, then relieved her by bursting into honest laughter.

"Romance?" he squeaked, unable to get his breath. "Romance? With the Fire-Mare herself? The woman who thinks a seductive garment is one that doesn't have armor plating on it? With the Captain *my own people* look to before they trust *my* strategy?"

Kero stiffened—then, as he continued to howl, began to unbend a little. "Well—"

"Kero, you're a handsome woman, but gods help me—I don't fancy sharing my bed-space with you *and* that—" He pointed, and she turned to see that her sword was lying across her cot with the hilt resting on her pillow as if it were a person. She stared for a moment, then started laughing, too. That set him off again, and after a moment, both of them were so convulsed that they had tears running down their faces.

He recovered enough to wipe his eyes, and handed her the goblet of watered wine on her table so that she could take a drink and get herself under control.

"Goddess, Kero—I never thought you saw me as *that* much of a romantic!" He chuckled again, and stole the goblet from her for a sip. "No, I promise you—I *like* you, but you're the last woman I'd want to have a liaison with. You're too damned—outrageous."

She took another sip, and made a face at him. "I did warn you, all those years ago. Still, I've learned a few things since then. I can be a lady for a couple of months if—"

"Oh, no," he interrupted her. "I want you to be yourself; in fact, the wilder, the better. My brother's looking forward to it. He wants you to shake up his Court a little. He says they could do with some shaking up."

She threw her head back and laughed whole-heartedly. "All right, then, I'll take you up on this. I'll be there before the end of summer, as soon as I get things arranged so I can leave. This may work out really well, actually; the cousins bring horses up every summer, and I always miss them. This time I won't. I was afraid that when the second batch came up in the fall, my people would still be in the field."

"Perfect," he replied happily. "Just send word ahead, so we can give you the proper reception." She covered a yawn, then, but not before he caught it. "You're tired," he said, rising. "I'll let you get some sleep."

"I'd be polite, but I'm too exhausted," she admitted, as he opened the tent flap. "And—thanks for everything."

"You're welcome, Captain," he said, hesitated a moment more. She still looked—haunted. And he didn't think it had anything to do with this last battle.

"Kero," he said, as he held open the tent flap, "I—I don't know how to ask this discreetly, so I'll be blunt. Is there something wrong? Something I can help you with? Something personal?"

She stared at him for a moment, her eyes shadow-laden, and looked as if she was about to say something. But then a clot of her troopers passed by the tent, talking in the slightly-too-loud voices of those who are just drunk enough to be convinced that they're sober. She jumped, and smiled, with a kind of false brightness.

"Nothing that a few days of rest and a few nights of solid sleep won't cure," she said, and waved him away. "Thanks for the concern; I wish all my employers were that interested in my well-being."

That was a dismissal if ever he heard one. He shrugged and grinned, as he let the entrance flap fall.

He mounted his horse, still being held by the patient sentry, and turned the palfrey's nose back toward his own camp.

It's funny. We have become so different in the little things—which is where we used to agree. But in the important things, where we didn't agree before, now we think exactly the same—responsibility, caring about your people—making sure they get treated right—holding to a personal code—it's amazing. We're more alike than ever. And I suspect she figured that out within half a candle-mark after we met again.

The Skybolts' camp had settled; he heard singing, softly, over by one of the fires, and the murmur of conversation somewhere nearby, but there was nothing like the riotous celebrating still going on ahead of him.

She's really changed in other ways, too. She seems completely comfortable and stable—even happy—being entirely alone. Even if she does push herself too hard, trying to be everywhere and everything at once. And I still feel like there's someone out there, somewhere, another person who could be my complement and partner. And that's what I want, now. I don't want a "lady," I don't want someone to show off for. I want a woman who will back me when I need backing, fight at my side, and take me down a notch when I need that, and who wants me to do the same for her. A real partner.

He let the palfrey amble on at his own pace, saluting the sentry who stood beside the entrance to his own camp. *I don't know where on the face of this earth I'm going to find someone like that, though. It'd take a miracle. . . .* Then he chuckled. *But at least I know one thing. If she exists, whoever she is, she isn't Kero!*

The sunlight that had been such punishment on the battlefield now poured over Bolthaven like golden syrup, balm instead of bane. Kero stood at the open window of her office, and smiled. Five years ago, when she'd ordered the new watchtower built onto the barracks, she'd had a new office and her own quarters incorporated into the plans. The old office Lerryn had used was over in the warehouse building—not a bad place for it, except when you had to get to it on winter mornings when no one sane went out of doors. This office had the triple advantages of convenience, proximity to the barracks, and the best view outside of the platform above her. Any day that the weather was decent, she flung open the shutters to all four windows, and enjoyed an unobstructed panorama of her little domain.

Beyond the gates, the town of Bolthaven spread out in the sun like a prosperous, basking cat asleep atop the fortress-crowned plateau. Beyond the town, acres of tended fields alternating with fenced pasture stretched eastward, and acres of grassland dotted with white patches of grazing sheep went westward. Here on the southwestern border of Rethwellan, so close to the Pelagir Hills, no farmers settled land without having protection nearby.

The town itself was less than ten years old, and she would never had anticipated its birth or growth when she'd returned to the winter quarters as the Skybolts' new Captain. Besides the ransom, the single thing that had most contributed to the salvation of the Skybolts the first year of her Captaincy had been her own relatives. And not her brother, either—her Shin'a'in cousins, who'd heard, by some mysterious means, of her need. They had brought their entire herd of sale-horses up through the Pelagiris Forest to the winter quarters that fall, camped at the gate, and informed her that they had told the world that *she* was having a Shin'a'in horse-fair.

That, in other words, they'd just made her their agent.

They settled back and let *her* do all the bargaining for them. When the dust had settled and the last of the purchases had been escorted off, she found herself in possession of enough coin to bring the Company back up to full strength and equipage, the sum representing half of the difference between what the cousins would have gotten at their regular venue at Kata'shin'a'in and what she'd won for them, this far north.

Then, as if that wasn't enough, they'd brought out the horses they'd saved for her Company, the replacement mounts her people couldn't afford.

By the next year, when they appeared again, a small army of merchants had begun the town of Bolthaven. By the third year it was a *real* town, supporting farmers who sold their produce to the fort, and shepherds providing meat for their tables and wool for a new contingent from the craft guilds. And now the Bolthaven Horse Fair was the talk of Rethwellan, attracting far more than just horse merchants—and more horse-traders than just her cousins.

By the fifth year, Bolthaven was so prosperous that whole families of craftsmen were in residence. That was the sign of a really good bonded Company; that ordinary people were willing to come settle beside their winter quarters. A town like Hawksnest or Bolthaven meant that the troops were reliable, steady, and stable even when idle, the Captain could be relied upon to keep order, and that there was money to be had.

So Kero smiled at the town, and at the brightly-colored tents springing up at the edge of the town like so many odd-colored mushrooms. Her cousins had arrived on schedule, and had been surprised and delighted to see her Company back so soon.

Eldan had commented on it last—

She resolutely shoved the false memory away, along with the memory of his sitting in this very window, with moonlight shining down on him instead of sunlight.

Rest. That's what I need. And distraction. The cousins can take care of that. As soon as they get things settled, we'll have a chance to talk, she thought. *I need to replace Hellsbane soon.* Kero's current mount was actually the second "Hellsbane" she'd ridden; following Tarma's example, she'd simply kept the same name for the new mount; it was less confusing for her and her horse. *She's too good not to send back to breed, and there should be a mare from Number One's foaling ready for me by now. I'm glad they have the training of her; I don't have time to school my own horses anymore.*

That thought sent her to the east window, looking down on the arenas and the stables, where she checked up on the current batch of new recruits.

She was just in time to see a rangy gelding with a lot

of Plains' pony in him blunder into a barrel at full gallop. He managed to pull himself up, but the impact sent his rider somersaulting over his left shoulder as he stumbled. Kero caught her breath—even the best rider can take a bad fall—but the recruit kept right on rolling, in a perfectly controlled tumble, and jumped to his feet.

She let out the breath she'd been holding. The gelding didn't bolt; he stayed obediently where he'd stopped; the rider planted hands on hips and read him a description of his parentage that didn't once mention ponies.

Kero chuckled, as the gelding lowered ears, then head, in a gesture of submission and conciliation; horses were generally not the brightest of beasts, but this one was evidently smart enough to figure out he'd done something wrong.

The recruit finished his recitation, limped up to his horse's side, and remounted. He called something to one of the other recruits, backing the gelding up and evidently checking his action for signs of injury, before finishing the rest of the course. The Skybolts simply did not accept recruits that couldn't ride well—which saved them a great deal of trouble when starry-eyed shepherds' daughters and plowboys showed up at the gate. They generally took one look at what the *recruits* were doing, blanched, and went back to their sheep, their plows or to another Company—unless, of course, it so happened that besides tending sheep, they were superb riders.

Most recruits brought at least one mount with them, but their beasts generally weren't up to Skybolt standards. The gelding just completing the course was an exception. He was tough, strong, and smart, and he would probably be accepted, but for those with beasts that weren't, there was a simple solution.

Every Skybolt, without exception, received a Shin'a'in-bred saddle-beast, hand-picked by the cousins. That included the recruits. But Shin'a'in-bred horses were *not* cheap—they amounted to half a year's pay for a recruit. That meant that for the first six months a recruit was in the Skybolts, he only got half shares—and once in the field and getting battle-pay, got only three-fourths of it for the remaining six months. Every would-be recruit knew this before he or she signed on—which tended to weed out the ones who thought being with the Skybolts meant glamour and easy money. Already this year, four would-be fighters had choked on the idea that they weren't going to get full pay and gone to find a Company with less exacting standards.

Kero noted with approval that the fellow who'd been spilled *also* had a Shin'a'in remount on the side. As soon as his gelding had completed the course, he switched to the other horse, leading the gelding down to the farrier's end of the stables to be checked over. From what she could see of him, she thought he might be from Ruvan— which meant the gelding might be a Shin'a'in cross with a Plains' pony. That was a good outcrossing, excellent for working the herds of half-wild cattle down there. And from the way the rider held himself, he might be one of those mounted herdsman. Which meant he could use a bow.

If he can shoot as well as he can ride, and use a sword with the care he takes with his beasts, he'll do. He obviously had *not* objected to paying what seemed to the untutored to be an outlandish amount for a horse when he already had a good one.

In point of fact, every veteran had two horses, and often took an entire string on campaign. Veterans knew there was never a problem with paying for remounts— not when there were bonuses to be had, like the bonus Daren had paid the horse-archers, and the cash from permissible looting.

There was a lot of looting when the Prophet went down, she thought suddenly. *Some of it good stuff, from the Prophet and her priests, and from that shrine. I had the stuff I knew about checked, but the troops may have traded with Daren's people, and who knows what they got. Besides, religious magic isn't always like secular magic. I'd better tell everybody to bring their booty in before trading it, and I'll have Quenten and the shaman check trade-goods for curses.*

Intensive training and the very best mounts and equipment were what made the Skybolts in demand. Horse-units were expensive to maintain; most standing armies didn't bother. That meant that there was always work for them—and very little competition.

Twoblades had taken the long view, and Kero continued his philosophy; given the access to excellent horses, it was worth the time, mounts, and training it took to keep the Skybolts' corner on their little piece of the war-market. Not everyone could manage that long view—even the Sunhawks had gone back to being a Company of foot after Idra's death, with only the scouts and other specialists going mounted.

That sent Kero back to the north window, and she strained her eyes to estimate the number of horses the cousins had brought up with them this year. They were out in temporary corrals, ten to an enclosure, sorted as to age and sex. She grinned a little; this was going to be a *very* profitable Fair. They'd told her that they had managed to talk Liha'irden into making Kero *their* outside agent, pointing out their high profits, and the security of trading here in Bolthaven. Here, under Kero's eye, not only would they need only enough Clansmen to see the horses safely to the Fair, if anyone so much as cheated them of a copper, the Skybolts would descend as a group to enforce the fair-trade laws. And Kero always, *always* sent a squad back with them, to see them safely to the Plains with their trade-goods and their profits.

She moved automatically to the west window—that many horses needed a lot of fodder. . . .

But the hay and grain wagons were rolling in, too, right on schedule—not like last year, when they'd been late, and every recruit in the fortress had taken his turn out mowing grass for the hungry horses.

I don't think there's a single Clansman that really enjoys the conventional horse-fairs. They worry about security for their horses when they arrive, they're constantly on guard and frequently harassed on the way there. And none of them have ever forgotten what happened to Tale'sedrin. They're at a disadvantage in bargaining, and there's no one out here willing to protect their interests.

Except, of course, me.

The haywagons stopped at a very special checkpoint before they were ever let inside the grounds of the Fair, an inspection point manned by more recruits. Each wagon was inspected from the ground up—and the recruits themselves had been very carefully instructed and frightened to within an inch of their lives by Geyr.

Quite an impressive little talk he gave them. "If any of you let anything *past that either harms the horses or*

breeches our security, I'll hamstring you myself.'' And
him standing there slapping a gelding-knife into his glove,
over and over. . . .

And this year, Geyr had a new twist on the inspec-
tions—a set of enormous mastiffs as tall as a child's first
pony. Geyr claimed they had noses "keen enough to track
the West Wind." He'd acquired them on the march home
last year, but had been looking for something like them
ever since a load of poisoned grain killed two horses on
campaign.

He wanted to use them as additional camp-guards and
on scouting runs. Kero was a bit doubtful of the latter—
she couldn't see how Geyr would keep them from bark-
ing, for one thing—but she had agreed to try them out as
wagon inspectors. Their sense of smell was certainly as
good as Geyr claimed, and they could be trained to recognize any scent and alert their handler to it. And their
sheer size had the wagoners as terrified of *them* as the
recruits were of Geyr.

*I suppose now the other Companies are going to start
calling us "the dog-and-pony show,"* she thought with a
sigh. *I could keep those little messengers out of sight, but
I'm never going to be able to hide* those *monsters.*

On the other hand, Warrl had been damned useful to
the Sunhawks. What these mastiffs lacked in intelligence, they might make up for in strength, size and numbers.

I wonder where he got them. She still suspected they
were from the Pelagirs. He had spent quite a bit of time
in the company of Kra'heera, the cousin that just happened to be an apprentice shaman. What the shaman
didn't know about the Pelagirs, the Hawkbrothers *did*,
and the Hawkbrothers and shaman were probably talking
more than most people guessed.

*We were coming up through Ruvan, along the Pelagiris
Forest; we met up with a couple of the cousins on the
way, after I'd left word of our route with one of the Outriders. I remember that he and Kra'heera vanished about
the same time, telling me he'd get back to the fort on his
own—then in he comes, just before the first snow, with
the bitch and her half-grown litter of fourteen. That kind
of fertility all by itself is suspicious, and smacks of the
Pelagirs.*

The Shin'a'in didn't use dogs much, except for herding sheep and goats—but the Hawkbrothers might well have been able to produce something like Geyr's dogs on very short notice.

She watched them checking out the wagons, one on each side, and it did not escape her notice that they performed their duty with a brisk efficiency that reminded her of her own veterans. Certainly there was an odd look of intelligence in their eyes—unlike Geyr's little messenger-dogs, who had brains that would shame a bird, or at least acted like it. They knew three things only— eat, run, and be petted.

I tried Mindtouch, but—all I got was images, not the kind of real speech I got from Warrl or Eldan's Companion.

Damn. Thinking of the Companion always made her think of Eldan—and she'd had another dream last night. She caught herself caressing the smooth fabric of her sleeve at the mere thought, and clenched her fist. *Damn him. You'd think after ten years I could forget the man.*

Maybe Kra'heera could suggest something to make the dreams stop. Though she'd have to tell him *why* she wanted them to stop. And that could be—embarrassing. Her Shin'a'in cousins had much the same dry sense of humor as Tarma, but they occasionally got a bit odd even for Kero, and the Shin'a'in notion of what was funny didn't always match hers.

It was amazing how fast the Clan had grown, once the children that had elected to take Clan membership were of an age to claim it. They'd had as many young adults join them as they could provide tents for. Part of it had to be the glamour, the mystique of the "Clan that could not die"—certainly orphans and "extra" children had flocked to the Tale'sedrin banner once it was raised again.

But part of it, no doubt, had to do with my cousins' sheer good looks. They're all damned attractive, and with Grandmother's green eyes and Grandfather's blond hair, they must have been as exotic and fascinating to the Shin'a'in suitors as the Shin'a'in are to us.

None of them had lacked for potential partners, and in the end, all but one had taken up multiple marriages. *Like queen bees with entourages, or stags with harems. No, I don't think I'll tell Kra'heera about the dreams of*

Eldan. He'll only give me a hard time about it, and ask me why I didn't just knock the man in the head and carry him off with me like a sack of loot. Besides, he's young enough to be my own child; I just can't confess something like that to a person who looks like he's waiting for me to tell him a story. Gods, they make me feel ancient.

Though still small, the Tale'sedrin Clan was as thriving as any on the Plains, boasting no less than three shaman, a Healer, and even a Kal'enedral—

The last was Swordsworn by choice, rather than because of the kind of circumstances that forced Tarma to her vow. Kero liked him the best of all of them. He never turned her away when she asked for lessons, and his sense of humor was a little less mordant than the rest of her cousins.

Her thought of them might have summoned them; they made no noise on the stairs with their soft boots, but she heard their distinctive chatter echoing up the shaft of the staircase long before she saw them.

"Heyla, cousin!" Istren, one of the two horse-trainers along this year and the only one of the three who was actually related to her by blood, sprang into the room as if he were taking it by storm. He was followed at a more sedate pace by the other trainer, Sa'dassan, and the shaman-in-training, Kra'heera. Where Istren boasted the dusky-gold skin of his Shin'a'in father, and his father's black hair, his mother's startling green eyes flashed at Kero with excitement.

"Second cousin, to be precise," Sa'dassan said mildly, her Shin'a'in blue eyes as tranquil as a cloudless sky. "And both a Captain of the Company and your elder. A little more respect, youngling."

Istren ignored her; when a normally reserved Shin'a'in became excited, it was pretty hard to get them calmed down. "Have you heard, Cousin Kero? Have you seen? What do you know about these North men, these Valdemar men?"

For one startled moment, Kero thought he was talking about her dream and Eldan, and her tongue seemed glued to the roof of her mouth. But Kra'heera solved her dilemma for her, by snorting, "What, do you think she is a mage, like our uncle? She can't possibly know anything—these Valdemar men have only just arrived."

She shook herself out of her paralysis. "What Valdemar men?" she asked.

"We have *heard,* heard only, that there are men from the North come to buy all that we will sell them," Sa'dassan said, with a fine precision of speech. "We wish you to come and look at these men. You can speak their tongue and say the things that will call the thoughts that we wish to read to the surface of their minds like little fish to crumbs on the stream. Kra'heera can then judge of their thoughts. And, perhaps, you also, for you had converse with one of their kind before, not so?"

"I did," she said, slowly. "The man that I knew, if he is a good representative of his people, was a good and honest man, and one who would treat your *jel'sutho'edrin* as children of his own heart and hearth. But he was only one man."

"Exactly so," Sa'dassan replied. "Will you come with us, cousin?"

"I think I had better," Kero replied, catching up her weapons-belt from the back of her chair, and buckling it on. "There's a saying among the mercs, you know— 'When the wind blows folk out of Valdemar, prepare for heavy weather.' They tend not to stray too far from their borders."

Whatever brought them here, it's going to affect us all, she thought, with a shiver of premonition. *And the sooner prepared we are, the better off we'll be. . . .*

Nineteen

"Captain!" One of the recruits came pelting up to her and skidded to a halt. He was all out of breath, but that didn't stop him from saluting crisply. "Message, Captain!" he gasped, as a trickle of sweat ran down his cheek.

He must be first year; he hasn't learned to pace himself yet. She nodded, he gasped it out, trying not to seem as if he was winded. *Definitely new; second year on, they'd get their breath before reciting a message.* "People at the North Gate, Captain. From Valdemar. Official papers in order, Scratcher says. Want to see you. Shallan sent 'em to the guest house. Says to tell you that makin' em go to the inn didn't seem right, even if the inn wasn't already full."

"Good. Thank you. Is Shallan still with them?"

The youngster shook his head. "Put Laker on them; he knows Valdemaran pretty well."

She nodded. *I always thought Shallan had good sense. If they have anything to say, Laker will overhear it.* "Fine, tell Laker I'll be there shortly, and that he should go ahead and tell these people that. Tell him to use tradetongue; no use letting them know we're multilingual. Have you seen them?"

He shook his head. *Pity. Oh, well.*

"Go run that message to Laker," she said. "Then go on up to the North Gate and let Shallan know where I'll be." The young man saluted again, turned, and ran off like a rabbit. Kero envied him his energy, but not the way he was going to feel in a moment after running that much in this heat. *I'd give a lot to know if these are Heralds or not in advance of seeing them.* She turned her steps toward the guest house inside the fortress walls, followed silently by the three Shin'a'in.

"Have any of *you* seen these people?" she asked. "Can you tell me what they're wearing?"

"They are not Heralds, cousin," Sa'dassan said, surprising her with her easy use of the term in its correct context. "Not even Heralds in disguise. Such a one would not be able to conceal his nature from Kra'-heera, even without his Companion to betray him for what he was. Had a Herald ridden into this place, Kra'heera would know without seeing him with the Outer eyes."

"Oh, really?" That was news to her.

Kra'heera had the grace to blush. "It is only what I was born with," he said disparagingly. "It is no great virtue, or ability earned by study."

"It may not be a virtue, but it's nothing to be discounted, either," she replied. *Thank you for once again pulling an egg out of your ear, cousin. Or rather, Kra'heera's ear.* "So what *do* they look like? Do you know?"

Istren spoke up as they turned the corner of the barracks and came into view of the guest house. "I had heard they were all in dark blue and silver, sober, like a kind of Kal'enedral. That there are two with much silver who speak with authority, two with a little who speak only to the first, and four with none who speak not at all."

Dark blue and silver. That would be the Royal Army. What in the gods' names are Royal Valdemaran Guards doing down here?

"Just on that alone, I'd say you were safe to sell to them," she said, as in the distance, the noise of the fair carried over the walls. "But I think we ought to check them out, anyway. If there's something going on up north that sends them down here, we had all better know about it."

Kra'heera nodded. "It is said that war respects no one's boundaries that are not guarded, and I can think of nothing that would bring those secret folk to us except war."

Pot calling kettle black—a Shin'a'in calling someone else secretive! She hid her amusement, as they reached the door of the guest house, and the sentry (posted there any time there were guests) saluted her and opened it for them.

The guest house included a small common room, and there they found the first four of their visitors, seated at the table there. Somehow they had managed the seating so that no one had his back to the door. All four were sitting with military stiffness that they couldn't seem to drop, even over four flagons of chilled ale.

They rose slowly to their feet, looking from her to the Shin'a'in and back with uncertainty; obviously, since she had no uniform or insignia they'd recognize, they had no idea who or what she was nor how to treat her. And the Shin'a'in, in their brightly embroidered vests and trappings of barbaric splendor had them severely puzzled. She ended their suspense, though not after a struggle with temptation. "I'm Captain Kerowyn," she said in their own tongue, and accepted their belated attention and salutes with a nod. "These are my Shin'a'in cousins; I am the agent for their horses. What can we do for you?"

She watched them work that through—a mercenary Captain, who knew their language, *related* to the purportedly unfriendly Shin'a'in, who was also acting as a *merchant-agent* for those same unfriendly Shin'a'in, who were standing beside her with undisguised curiosity eating them alive. That was at least two outright contradictions and three real surprises.

"We're here on behalf of Queen Selenay," said the one with the most silver braid on his sleeves, a man about a decade older than the other three, and "military" from his teeth to his toenails. "We need cavalry mounts, good ones, horses we can depend on with very little training; while we normally wouldn't seek this far for them, word has come as far as Valdemar of this fair. Everyone knows about the quality of the beasts the Shin'a'in breed, and it seemed more than worth our time to come here. While we ordinarily might not trust that these horses for sale were full Shin'a'in-bloods, the H—our information is that you are very honest and that the fair and the beasts are what rumor claims them. Our query with the Mercenary Guild supported that."

She hadn't missed his slip—he'd been about to say "the Heralds," or even "the Herald Eldan." She translated quickly for her cousins, trying to ignore the little thrill of elation that Eldan at least still thought well enough of her to call her "honest and fair."

"Ask them how many they want," Sa'dassan said, coming straight to the point.

"All you have," one of the younger Guards said eagerly, when she repeated the question. "We saw them as we were coming in—the mounts your people were training with. Wonderful! We'll take everything!"

The older man looked at him oddly, but didn't contradict or reprimand him for speaking out of turn.

So that's the one who holds the purse strings. The older one is in nominal command, but this is the important one. Hmm. Noble, younger son would be my guess. the other two are probably breeders or trainers, brought along as consultants. Right, now I know who's what.

She explained her observations to her cousins, then turned back to the visitors. "This is where I put on my merchant hat," she said, "Only it's an odd sort of merchant hat, because I am *not* going to urge you to buy everything with legs in sight. First of all, only about half the horses here are Shin'a'in-blood, and of those, not all of them are going to be suitable for cavalry mounts. Yes, they've all been broken and given some training that involves fighting, but it may not be what you want. The Shin'a'in feel very strongly about their beasts; the name they call them means 'younger sibs.' If they think you're going to put *one* horse to a task for which it isn't suited, they won't sell you *any.*"

Purse-holder opened and shut his mouth twice, without saying anything. The One In Charge blinked, as if he was so surprised by her response that he wasn't certain he'd heard it right.

"And in any event, these are light beasts; good for skirmishers, horse-archers and light cavalry. So, has Valdemar ever run any troops like that before so that you know what to look for?" She waited for a response; the One In Charge gave it.

"Not in the standing army, no," he admitted. "Some of the nobles on the Border have private troops like that; no one else. That's why we came here for the mounts."

She nodded, and translated. Kra'heera put in his own

discoveries. "I have been watching their minds, cousin. The one who speaks out of turn is a wealthy man of highborn, who breeds the Ashkevron hunters and heavy horses. The ones who do not speak are trainers of skir- mishers. The one who speaks much is a warleader. It is as he has said—and these are fighters they wish now to have. He has not told you why. There is to be fighting upon their eastern border, and soon, he thinks. Very, very serious fighting."

Kero nodded; there had been rumors about conflict between Valdemar and Hardorn, but since Karse was be- tween Hardorn and any potential client, and Valdemar never hired mercenaries, she hadn't paid much attention to the rumors.

This might involve more j̇ s than just selling horses. If Hardorn is starting a major war and wins, they'll be on Rethwellan's border, and that means we get involved. Another thought occurred to her. *Just because Valdemar hasn't hired mercs in the past, that doesn't mean they won't start.*

"Troops like that aren't trained in a day," she warned. "It took us ten years to get where we are. Most standing armies don't bother—but if you're sure of the need—?"

Purse-holder nodded, and he wasn't entirely happy about the need being there, either.

"Well, if you'll trust my judgment on what beasts will suit you," she told him, "I think we can come to the bargaining table."

Purse-holder tapped One In Charge on the shoulder, and they spent a moment in huddled conference. One In Charge finally turned back toward her and nodded.

"Is this all right with you?" she asked her cousins. They looked at each other, then Sa'dassan shrugged. "We had rather our younger-sibs did not go to war, but if they go to hands that will care for them, they are as safe as may be in this world. It is well."

"All right, gentlemen," she said, waving to the cous- ins to precede her. "If you'll follow me, we can expedite this transaction as quickly as even you might want."

Sa'dassan weighed the first of three heavy pouches in her hand as she held the other two in the crook of one arm. She smiled, watching as the last of the Valdemaran horse-handlers urged a straggler to catch up with the rest of the herd and out past the corrals. Kero coughed at the dust they raised, and quirked her eyebrow at the Shin'a'in trainer. "Well, they certainly paid enough. Are you content, cousin?"

"More than content," Sa'dassan said with certainty. "Kra'heera has kept watch on their minds. Their ruler is a good one; this, their Queen, has sold some of her wedding gifts to give to these men, that they might purchase the best mounts they could find. She thinks first of her people, their lands, and their beasts, and only then of herself."

"That's what I'd heard from El—from a Herald I knew," Kero said, hastily avoiding Eldan's name. "I didn't know whether to believe it or not, frankly. You know, if all monarchs took care of their people that way, there might be fewer wars."

"Perhaps." Sa'dassan put the pouch with the others, cradled like a baby. "Perhaps. We, we do not place much store in Kings and the like. You have a good one in this year—who is to say that the one that follows him will be as good?"

"Nothing, unless you have a system like the Rethwellans have, with the sword that chooses the King." She shrugged. "And then, of course, you could lose the sword, or someone enchants it, or puts in a substitute. Besides, if there were fewer wars, I'd be out of work. So, what do you plan to do now? You've sold most of your string all at once."

Sa'dassan glanced toward the temporary corrals. "It has been a good three years," she observed. "Our mares bred widely, and many foaled twins. And the first of the young ones are coming upon the market—we had a fear to glut it and bring prices down."

Kero laughed to hear the Shin'a'in—reputed to be the most ruthless fighters in the world—talking like a merchant. "Which was one reason, no doubt, why Liha'irden sent their string with ours."

Kero raised her eyebrow a little higher. "So what did you have in mind?"

"That I shall intercept those Clans going to the An-

duras Fair in Jkatha and send them here. It is not so far
from here, a week's ride, and they were going out behind
us. Some Clans drew lots to send their beasts abroad
beyond Kata'shin'a'in, and that was one of the places.
They were to wait for us and your armed escort before
returning to the Plains.''

The last time that the Shin'a'in had gone to Anduras
Fair was when Tale'sedrin had been ambushed on the
way home, and only Tarma left as a survivor. Kero
clamped her teeth on her first reaction; that the fear of
glut must have been very great to send horses again to a
place so ill-omened.

''As I said, they set out after us; and Anduras is not
so great a distance that we cannot coax the buyers here
to wait, I think.'' Sa'dassan smiled slyly, and Kero
chuckled.

''And in return for that coaxing, you will, of course,
get a percentage of *their* profits.'' She shook her head.

Sa'dassan spread her hands wide. ''Value for value,
and reward for the deserving—that is how the Clans have
always been, cousin. And lest you hold up to me that
first fair, and the horses we brought you—let me point
out that you are Clan by blood, and we only delivered to
you your own share that had been unclaimed.''

Kero shrugged. ''I won't argue with you, if that's the
way you see it—but look, will you trust me and mine
with your earnings in return? You're going to lose time
going down and back and the best is going to be gone by
the time you return; if you'll leave your needs and your
coin with Scratcher, I think he can get everything you
want at the price you want.''

Sa'dassan thought the idea over with her head tilted to
the side, then nodded. ''He provisions your people;
doubtless he has the skill and the contacts. Done, then,
and that is a kinly offer.''

I think they're going to get a pleasant surprise, Kero
thought, leading Sa'dassan back to the accounting office
and Scratcher's domain. *They're good—but he's better!
He hasn't lost a bargaining session once that I ever heard
of!*

With that settled, the Shin'a'in saw no reason to lin-
ger; they left their tents, but gathered up their belongings

and headed south with a speed and efficiency that Kero could only envy. She saw them off, then made her rounds of town and fortress—

Only to discover that everything was running perfectly smoothly. By nightfall she had inspected every aspect of fair and training and provisioning, and concluded that *she* might as well not even be there.

She sat down on her bed, pulled off her boots, and looked out of her window as a cool breeze stirred her hair. The fortress was quiet—the recruits and veterans alike were kept too busy by training and the fair to carouse much in the barracks after the sun went down. Besides, why carry on at home, when there were both the old familiar haunts of the town and the new amusements of the fair to tempt you out of the gates each night?

Lights burned out beyond the walls and the sounds of music and voices drifted toward the barracks on the breeze; both the town and the fair kept late hours. She found herself wondering where on the road those Valdemar men were tonight. They had been in such a hurry that they hadn't even *looked* at the fair.

And that made her think, think ahead. Tarma had taught her to think in terms of the greater picture as well as her own little part of it. You never knew when something happening hundreds of leagues away would affect you. *If I were a Queen looking to strengthen my forces, what would I do? Assuming that I have a stupid prejudice against hiring mercs.*

For a moment, as she stared out at the lights of the fair, and the colored shapes of the tents lit up from within, like fire-flowers, she thought she heard Eldan's voice, faint and far off, protesting, "That's not fair!"

She ignored that imagined voice. *You're not real, and you aren't here, and anyway, you aren't interested in me anymore,* she thought sternly, to exorcise the persistent ghost.

There were no more outbursts from her overheated imagination.

Well, as far as *she,* a strategist, was concerned, it was a stupid prejudice. Merc Companies had, more than once, won wars. People who refused to hire them had, more than once, lost those wars.

The young and idealistic fight for medals and honor, she thought cynically. *The experienced and worldly-wise fight for money. You see a lot more retired mercs than old farmers with a chest full of medals.* That was, after all, the goal of a successful merc; to live long enough and collect enough to retire, usually on one's own land. Many mercs came out of multichild families without a chance for land of their own, and this was their only way to earn it.

But that was a digression. If Kero were this Queen, what would she do?

Conscript those private troops the Guardsman talked about. Get them equipped with the best. While they're in place, start calling up volunteers, and if you can't get enough volunteers, start conscription. Rush those troops through training. And start calling in any debts my allies owe me.

She had a mental map of everything as far north as the mountains above Valdemar, and as far south as the Bitter Sea; west to the Pelagirs and the Plains, east to the High Kingdom of Brendan. And the only allies she could think of that Valdemar might possibly have in this conflict would be Iftel and Rethwellan.

Iftel would be logical, but—dear gods, they are strange there. The Shin'a'in Warrior doesn't intervene half as often as the Wind Lords. I can't see Iftel mixing up in this unless they're threatened. Which leaves Rethwellan. Now, Karse is between Rethwellan and Hardorn, but they might be able to persuade King Faramentha that Hardorn could threaten Rethwellan if they overran southern Valdemar. Which means the next logical step will be for the Queen to send an envoy to the Rethwellan Court.

The fair really interested her very little, these days. Most of her entertainment came from acting as her cousins' agent. She used to help train the new recruits, but that was back in the days when they were shorthanded. There were others that were better trainers, and she knew when to get the hell out of the way. Basically, all she did in winter quarters, was keep herself in training, study strategy, keep the books straight, get familiar with the strengths and weaknesses of the recruits, study the political situation with an eye to offers in the spring, and carve her little gemstones. Of all of them, Scratcher could keep the books by himself, the new recruits wouldn't be showing anything distinct for another couple of months, the gemstones could wait—and the rest could be done elsewhere.

Furthermore, right now, living here at the Fortress was—painful. She kept looking for faces that wouldn't be here anymore. It happened every year, certainly, and it took her a couple of months to get over it—but they'd never made it home this early before, and she kept seeing the backs of head that looked familiar—until the owner turned, and it was a new recruit. It would be a relief to get away until the pain faded with time, the pain that always came when she sent someone out who didn't come back again.

It will be a relief to sleep in a strange bed. Maybe the dreams won't find me there.

And yet, part of her wanted them so badly—

No.

Before she realized it, she'd made up her mind to leave. And that trip to Rethwellan seemed a bit more important than it had before.

Lord Baron Dudlyn had plainly just begun his diatribe. Daren jabbed his heel into the side of his hunter, making the gelding jump and dance in surprise, and giving him an excuse to concentrate on the horse.

Because if he didn't, he was going to laugh in Lord Baron Dudlyn's face. *The hunt's hardly started, and already he's complaining. Too bad we're at a walk. I wish the dogs would scent something besides rabbits; once we take off, he'll be left behind.*

The old man moved his fat old palfrey out of the way of the gelding's path, and actually shook his finger up at Daren. "I tell you, I don't know what this Court is coming to!" he shouted querulously. "It's a disgrace, I tell you! You brother is King of this land, and he can't go accepting barbarian mercenaries that are no better than bandits as equals to members of his Court and ambassadors from other realms! That mercenary female, that so-called Captain, is making a mockery of all of us! I haven't seen such a disgraceful display since that wild

Shin'a'in female showed up, back in your blessed father's day—''

Daren decided to end the lecture by dancing his gelding out of the Lord Baron's vocal range. Not that the Lord Baron didn't *try* to increase his volume—

But aged lungs can only produce so much wind.

He grinned as he spurred his gelding to catch up with the front of the hunting party. His brother was up there, as the King *had* to be, which had left Daren to be polite to the old dotards, show-offs, and those with more bravado than sense in the rear. For a while, anyway. Depending on what the hounds turned up next, at least half of the party might well be left behind or turn back voluntarily, as they had during the morning hunt.

I haven't had so much fun in a year, he thought with glee, as the gelding spotted his stable mate and put on an extra burst of speed to catch up with him. *It's a good thing that Kero and Faram hit it off so well, though. Otherwise the Lord Baron might not be the only one complaining. And it would be damned hard to keep the peace around here.*

Just as he reached the two of them, Kero on her ugly gray warsteed, and Faram on his pure Shin'a'in-bred chestnut, one of the hounds flushed a pheasant. Two bows came up at the same time; two bowstrings hummed at once—but when the retrievers brought the bird back, and the huntsman took it from the dog's gentle mouth to present it to the King, it was obvious that Faram's arrow had gone wide of the mark, and Kero had outshot him once again.

And for at least the twentieth time this morning, the courtiers were scandalized. There was a hum of comment behind Daren, and he heard the Lord Baron's voice rising unpleasantly above the rest, though he couldn't make out the words.

''You've beaten me again, Captain,'' Faram said ruefully, handing the bird to the gamekeepers to stow with the rest. ''I'm not exactly a bad shot, but I find myself very glad now that you turned down my offer to wager on the outcome of this contest.'' He looked back over his shoulder, past Daren, and the corners of his eyes crinkled as he suppressed a grin. ''I am afraid that my courtiers don't approve of your manner, however. No subject is supposed to outshoot the King.''

Kero chuckled as Daren pulled up next to Kero, putting her in between himself and his brother. ''My Lord,'' she replied, ''I may live in your Kingdom, but I've seen the Mercenary Guild Charter for Rethwellan. I'm a Freeholder by that Charter, and no subject of anyone's.''

''An excellent point, and it seems that you are as much lawyer as fighter.'' The King looked across Kero at his brother. ''You did warn me, didn't you, Daren?''

''I did. About her scholarship *and* her skills. I said that Tarma called her a 'natural' when we were learning together. I said I didn't think she'd let any of her skills slip just because she was a Captain. And you kept saying I was exaggerating.'' Daren shrugged expansively. ''Will you believe me when I tell you something now?''

''I suppose I'll have to. You keep telling me 'I told you so' at every opportunity.'' Faram turned his attention back to Kero, as his horse shook his head. ''What I would really like to know is how you learned to shoot so well—we both had the same teacher, but you never seem to miss. I'd suspect you of magic if you weren't so entirely unmagical.''

Kero bit her lip as if she was trying to keep from laughing, and replied, ''My lord, the fact is that you have never been either on the front line or dependent entirely on your own skill to keep your belly full. I think you'd find that the two harshest teachers in the world are survival and hunger. I've had both, and trust me, they make a difference.''

''On the whole,'' Faram admitted, ''I think I'd prefer to skip that sort of lessoning. I'm too old for those teachers.''

''You're too fond of your comforts, brother,'' Daren jibed. Faram was about to retort—but at exactly that moment, the head of the boar-pack belled, and the entire pack started off. Daren's mount lurched from a walk into a gallop, and as he passed the huntsmen who were whistling in the retrievers, he grinned.

This was a hunt meant to supply the Court with meat for the Sovvan Feast tonight. If Sovvan hunt-luck meant luck for the rest of the winter, as the old folks said it did, the winter would be a prosperous and easy one. Already they'd brought down a half-dozen deer this morning—several bachelor bucks and a couple of does that everyone agreed were past their bearing prime. That was enough venison that Faram had sent back the deerhounds and brought up the boar-hounds. The Queen and her ladies were coursing the woods and meadows nearer the Palace, taking their hawks out after birds and hare.

Most of the ladies, that is—

He looked back over *his* shoulder, to see that the handful of women who'd ridden out with the King's party were still there, keeping up valiantly, and already outdistancing the likes of the Lord Baron.

Last year there hadn't been any women with the King's party, but since Kero's arrival—and example—there were a respectable number of ladies exchanging their skirts for full-cut breeches, and riding neck-and-knee with the men. And some of those ladies were *not* young; Lady Sarnedelia, who had a formidable reputation as a rider on her own estate, had hailed Kero's "innovation" with relief and enthusiasm. She was right up there beside the best of the riders, proving rumor to be truth—and she was fifty if she was a day.

I can't help but wonder how many others would have joined us, but weren't willing to risk losing suitors or enraging husbands. I know the Lord Baron's daughter looked as if she'd rather have been with us. His granddaughter is, and I'll bet that's what kicked off that tirade about "disgrace." Of course, she's safely wedded to young Randel, and she can snap her fingers at what her grandfather thinks, since her loving spouse thinks that everything she does is wonderful. And if I could find a lady that suited me as well as she suits him, I'd probably think the same. Huh. Wonder whatever happened to that little prig Daren, who was horrified at the notion of "Lady Kerowyn" riding to hunt exactly like this? Maybe he grew up.

He leaned forward into his horse's neck, ducking a low-hanging tree limb. He saw a fallen trunk just ahead of them, and braced himself for the jump.

. The gelding took it, but stumbled; he recovered quickly, but not before he'd made Daren's teeth rattle.

They broke through a screening of bushes into a clearing, and ahead of him Daren saw Kero's big, ugly mare sail over another fallen tree-giant with a twinge of envy. The Shin'a'in-blood was taking rough ground with a contemptuous ease that left most of the other horses faltering or outright refusing. About the only ones that were keeping up with her were himself, the King, and the huntsmen.

And probably only because we have Shin'a'in-breds, too. Though not like that. No wonder people would kill to get a warsteed.

This boar was leading the hounds a merry chase; he was obviously fast and canny. *I hope he's the one they wanted us to go after; he's surely acting as if he was the bad one.* The local farmers had reported some trouble with an unusually large and evil-tempered boar to the King's huntsmen—a boar who had already killed one swineherd and wounded others, stealing their herds of pigs for his harem when they took the beasts into the forest after fallen acorns. That was why they'd hunted stag this morning; to give the horses a chance to run off any skittishness before going after such a dangerous beast as a boar.

That's the one time I've seen Kero back down from something, he thought, as the trail wound deeper into the forest, and the horses were forced to slow their headlong gallop. *When she said she'd stay a-horse, even Faram was surprised. But then she's never fought on foot, and she didn't even bring a proper boar-spear with her, just that saddle-quiver full of lances.*

Curious weapons, those; Daren had never seen anything like them. She had told him that they were used by the Shin'a'in, and it was obvious that they were *not* intended for game—those were man-killing weapons, with narrow, razor-barbed metal heads as long as Daren's hand.

Well, maybe if it runs, she can sting it with one of those and turn it for us.

The pack was belling ahead of them, and the huntsman sounding the "brought to cover" call on his horn. The horses emerged into a tiny clearing before a covert; that was obviously where the boar had holed up, and now they were going to have to flush him into the open.

While Kero stayed on horseback as she'd pledged, the rest dismounted and went ahead on foot. The pack was still ahead of them, and the huntsman sounded the "broken cover" call. Daren broke into a trot; he heard Kero's horse behind him, eeling through dense brush that even he was having trouble with, afoot.

The sound of the pack changed, just as the huntsman sounded "brought to bay."

Daren vaulted a tangle of roots, and burst out into a clearing. The boar was standing off the pack; he was an enormous brute, with a wide, scarred back. *Not* a wild boar at all, but a domestic beast gone feral.

That made him all the more dangerous. Daren pulled himself up before charging into the fray, and looked at his brother.

Faram read the plan in Daren's look and nod—they'd hunted boar together for years now, and needed only a glance to determine what the other intended. This time Daren would be the bait.

The huntsmen pulled the pack back at his command, and while Faram moved quietly around the edge of the clearing, Daren shouted at the boar, getting ready to drop to his knee or dodge aside at any moment. The success of this tactic lay in the fact that once a boar this big began a charge, it had trouble changing direction quickly, and its poor eyesight interfered with its ability to follow anything moving in a way it didn't expect. You only had to avoid those slashing tusks—

Only. "Hey!" he yelled at it, stamping one foot. "Hey!"

It waved its head from side to side, nose up in the air, seeking a scent that the musk of the dogs covered—then saw him, and charged perfectly down the center of the clearing.

He leapt aside at the last possible moment; saw the flash of a tusk as it made a strike for him. Then he leapt back before it had a chance to change direction, jabbing down at the heart with his boar-spear, knocked off balance for a moment, as Faram ran in from the side a heartbeat later to plunge his own spear into the boar's back.

It shrieked in pain and anger, and struggled forward, tearing up the soft earth in deep furrows with its cloven hooves. But the two of them had it pinned between them; another moment, and its legs collapsed from under it, and it died, as one spear or both found the heart.

He started to look up, a grin of congratulation spreading across his face, when a human scream rang across the clearing, cutting across the cheer started by the huntsmen.

Movement and a flash of red caught his eyes—

One huntsman was down, his leg savaged, and standing above him, with her tushes dripping red, was a sow—a wild sow, as big as the boar they'd just brought down.

My gods. It had a mate. . . .

She squealed once, trampled the huntsman, and then whirled to face them all.

And the first thing she saw was Faram.

She squealed again with rage, and charged.

Daren tugged futilely at his spear, but it was stuck fast in the boar, lodged as it was intended to do, and wouldn't come free. Faram was on his knees, and struggling to get up, but it was obvious he was never going to get out of the way in time.

Suddenly, there was a blur of gray, *flying* between the King and the charging sow.

The pig screamed, and turned aside; whirled and charged this new target, her eye streaming blood. The gray warsteed pivoted on a single hoof, and lashed out with her hind feet, sending the sow flying through the air. Two flashes of metal followed it, and the sow hit the ground and lay there, thrashing, two of Kero's lances sticking out of its sides.

The mare whirled again, but on seeing that the "enemy" was no longer a threat, snorted once and tossed her head. Kero dismounted, walked cautiously toward the convulsing beast with her knife in her hand, then dived in and slit the sow's throat with one perfectly timed stroke.

The beast shuddered and died.

Kero rose from the carcass, and wiped her knife carefully on the sow's hide. Only then did she look over to where Daren and his brother were sprawled beside the body of the boar.

"Survival, my lord," she said mildly. "has taught me to always leave a mobile scout to the rear."

Then she walked over to her mare, and mounted, leaving the huntsmen to deal with the carcass.

Twenty

Kero sipped at her watered wine, turned to the woman at her said, and said, "Honestly, it was mostly Hells-bane. I've never hunted boar before, and I didn't know what to expect. That was why I stayed mounted."

Lady 'Delia nodded. "A good horse is worth twenty armsmen, or so it seems to me. I've never seen a horse quite as well trained as yours, though. She follows and obeys you more like a dog than a horse."

"So I've noticed," Kero told her, without elaborating. *Let her wonder. She seems nice enough, but the less people know about warsteeds, the better off I'll be. Whether people overestimate or underestimate Hellsbane, I win.*

"She's really the second horse of her line that I've had from the cousins," she continued, which allowed Lady 'Delia to elaborate on her own horses' lines, and ask which of the King's Shin'a'in-bloods it would be best to breed her hunters to.

Kero answered with only half of her mind occupied by the conversation; the rest monitored the feast and the peoples' reactions to her, a response as automatic as breathing. She couldn't help but contrast the reaction of the Rethwellan Court to that of her brother's. Despite the similarity of the circumstances—that she had personally rescued both Dierna and King Faram—in her brother's home she had honor without admiration. Here she had both; an embarrassment of admiration, in fact. Some of the young ladies of the Court, those in the hero-worshipping early teens, had even taken to *dressing* like her. Predictably, Daren found this very funny.

But better that than fear; she was as much feared as admired by many of the Court. King Faram's people had seen her in action and knew what she could do, now, where her brother's people saw her successes as being mostly luck.

On the other hand, fear didn't bother her as much as it used to. *I guess I've gotten thicker-skinned. As long as the babies don't run screaming from me, I think I can handle a little fear.*

King Faram impressed her as much as she had evidently impressed him. *I can see why Daren loves his brother,* she thought, watching the relaxed and easy manner they had between them, sharing jokes or admiring a particularly toothsome lady. *It would have been very easy for Faram to resent what I did for him, but there's absolutely no sign of any such thing.*

In fact, he had ordered the sow's head prepared and served alongside the boar's head, and presented to her with a full retelling of the story. The Court Bard was a good one; with very little warning he'd done the tale up with bangles and bells, making her sigh, and wonder if *this* song was going to make the rounds the way "Kerowyn's Ride" had. He had promised her a boon when the song was over; right now she had no idea what she'd ask for, but something like that was worth taking time to think about.

The feast was a bit more than she was comfortable with, anyway. Her people ate well, but nothing like this. She didn't recognize half of what was served, and even though she did no more than nibble at what she did recognize, she was ready to end the meal when it was only half over.

Probably that was as much reaction as anything else, though. As always, she got her battle-nerves *after* the fact, when everything was over and done with. *If I was standing, my knees would be knocking together. And I never, ever would have been able to pull that one off without Hellsbane.*

The sow had burst cover at the boar's death-squeal; Kero happened to be looking right at the spot, and watched in horror as she savaged the huntsman before Kero or anyone else realized that she was going to attack. She had known that pigs were notoriously short-sighted; she'd spurred Hellsbane straight for the sow, inspired by the thought that only a horse was going to be big enough to distract the pig or make her pause. The lance in the

eye had been a purely lucky—or gods-sent—hit; she'd
hoped only to score the sow's tender snout and distract
her.

Then, as she'd passed, she'd signaled Hellsbane to
kick, hoping to keep the pig's teeth away from the mare's
hamstrings. She'd forgotten that Hellsbane had been
taught a low kick as well as a high, meant to take out
men on the ground who might have strength enough to
hurt her. Hellsbane had made her own judgment, and had
used the low kick, connecting solidly, and sending the
sow flying *before* she could charge.

Then Hellsbane had wheeled, allowing Kero to launch
another lance. And that, too, had connected solidly, as
had the third.

It had been as close a call as any she had ever had on
the battlefield, and she hadn't been entirely sure her legs
would hold her when she dismounted. She'd said as much
to Daren, who had been just as shaken as she was.

As soon as this feast is over, she promised herself, *I'm
going to have a nice hot bath, in my room, with a good
fire going, and only one candle for light. And tea, not
wine.*

The noise and the mingled odors of food and perfume
were beginning to give her a headache. Though it was
no bad thing to have the King's gratitude demonstrated
so openly, she rather wished she'd be able to get away
from the crowd some time soon. She wasn't used to people like this; undisciplined, so wildly different, and yet
so much the same, with such—to her, at least—trivial
interests.

She blinked to clear her eyes as the glitter and color
swam before them for a moment. Thousands of jewels
winked at her in the light from hundreds of candles; fab-
rics she couldn't even name made pools of rich color all
down the tables. The candles were scented, the people
were scented, the drink perfumed with flower petals, the
food spiced. On one side of the room, the Court Bard
held forth; on the other, a consort of recorders, and near
the low table, an acrobat. It was too much, a surfeit of
luxury.

The door at the far end of the room opened, and a man
in a black tabard embroidered with Faram's arms slipped
inside. He rapped three times on the floor with his staff,

and somehow the sound penetrated the babble. A hush
descended for a moment; the King's herald rapped on the
floor with his staff again to ensure the silence. Heads
turned toward him with surprise, including the King's;
Faram had been so deep in conversation that he had not
noticed the herald's entrance.

"Your majesty," the herald said, in a rich, baritone
voice that was nothing like Kero's own parade-ground
bellow, but seemed to carry as well and as far, "An
envoy from Queen Selenay of Valdemar asks permission
to approach."

Kero sat up straighter, suddenly much more alert. *From
Valdemar? But what are they doing here now? Why don't
they wait until formal Court in the morning?* She looked
back at Daren and his brother, only to see from their
expressions that they were just as baffled as she was.

"Let them approach," the King said, after a whispered conference with Daren and his Seneschal. The herald turned and left, to return into expectant silence,
escorting two people.

One was a tall, raw-boned, blond man, with an attrac-
tively homely face; a man who looked like a farmboy
and moved like an assassin. The other was a small,
slightly built woman, with a sweet, heart-shaped face,
who limped slightly. That was what they looked like, but
even Kero recognized them for what they *were;* Heralds
out of Valdemar, in the white uniform of their calling.
And the sight of that uniform sent a pang through her
heart that she hadn't expected. For a moment she couldn't
even think.

"Queen's Own Herald Talia, and Herald Dirk," the
King's herald announced. And did Kero only imagine it,
or did even he seem to feel the portent hanging heavy in
his words? One thing she did know—this Talia was no
ordinary Herald, and no ordinary envoy, either. The
"Queen's Own" was the most important Herald in the
Kingdom, second only to the Monarch, and often exercising the power of the Monarch when needed. That was
what Eldan had explained, anyway, ten years ago.

The two approached the head table, and bowed slightly.
The man stayed about a half pace behind the woman;
interesting positioning. *No doubt that's partially because
she's the ranking officer—but it's also partially because*

he's guarding her back. Wonder if anyone else will notice that.

The young woman began to speak; she had a wonderful, musical contralto, and she knew how to use it to gain her listener's attention. Kero listened closely and carefully as Talia explained what had brought them. The girl's Rethwellan wasn't bad, but her accent and occasional odd turn of phrase made it very clear that she didn't have complete mastery of the language yet.

". . . and so my Queen has sent me here, directly, rather than to speak through her embassy. You will have heard, your majesty, of the events in Hardorn these past two years?" the young woman asked. Faram nodded, and she clasped her hands behind her. Only Kero was near enough to see that those hands were white-knuckled with tension. *She's scared to death,* Kero realized with surprise. *She's nowhere near as casual as she seems about this; it's a life-and-death situation, and she knows it. But she's not going to give that away.* She felt herself warming to the young woman, for no apparent reason other than a feeling that she was going to like this Talia.

"Ancar of Hardorn is friend to no man, and no nation," Talia continued flatly, and there was something in her lack of expression that sent off vague feelings of alarm in Kero. After a moment she realized what it was. Severely traumatized veterans would speak in that flat, expressionless tone, about the battle experiences that had broken them.

What on earth could King Ancar have done to the Queen's Own Herald? And how did he happen to get hold of her? And why? Something terrible had happened to this young woman at Ancar's hands, she was as certain of that as she was of her own name.

And so was Need. For the first time in years, Kero felt the blade stirring.

"Ancar is guilty of regicide and patricide," Talia continued. "He has visited terrors that no sane man would countenance on his own people, and he has turned to dark powers to grant him his desires. I have proofs of this with me, if you would care to see them."

Faram shook his head, and indicated that she should go on.

"We stopped him once, we of Valdemar," she said.

"We held him at our Border and turned him back. Now he amasses a new army, one of men and steel rather than magic, and he marches again on our Border."

"So what is it you want?" Faram asked, leaning back in his chair so that his face was in shadow and could not be read.

"Your aid," Talia said simply. "We simply don't have enough armed men to hold him back this time."

As the Queen's Own Herald continued to speak, Kero grew more and more puzzled. *I don't understand this. Grandmother must have told me the story of the way she and Tarma got rid of Leslac the Bard a dozen times—and every single time she told it, she mentioned the pledge King Stefansen gave to Herald-Prince Roald; that Rethwellan owed Valdemar a favor equal to that of putting a King on his rightful throne. And how Valdemar had never redeemed that favor.* She watched as Talia's hands clenched tighter and tighter behind her back, the only outward sign of the young woman's increasing desperation. *I know for a fact that Valdemar hasn't cashed in the pledge since Grandmother told me the story. So why is she pleading for help when she could demand it?*

She glanced back at King Faram—and saw that *he* was just as tense as the Herald, and a swift appraisal of Daren, whom she knew better than she knew his brother, convinced her that they were mentally torn—

For some reason, she decided at last, *Queen Selenay purely and simply does not know about the pledge. Faram knows about it, though, and Daren—they've figured out that Selenay doesn't know of the pledge, and as people, they want to help. But as the King, Faram has to be reluctant to get Rethwellan involved in a war with someone who isn't even on his border, who isn't any kind of a threat to him.*

So he is not going to remind anyone about the pledge, if it's been forgotten.

In a way, Kero could understand that kind of attitude—except that it was ruinously short-sighted. *Half of their trade is with Valdemar, and that trade is going to vanish if Valdemar's involved in a losing war. And if Ancar wins—he will be on the border, and he doesn't sound to me like the kind of neighbor I'd welcome. And if Faram can't see that—*

Thanks to Eldan, Kero knew a bit about Heralds and their country, and what she knew—even if only half of it were true—she liked.

And besides that, all through the young woman's speech, Need had been rousing, putting a slowly increasing pressure on the back of her mind. It was pretty nebulous, confined to a vague feeling of *help her!*, but it was certainly getting stronger. By the time this Talia had come to the end of her speech, the sword was all but screaming in Kero's ear.

She waited for a moment to see what Faram would do; it was always possible that he'd surprise her and offer Talia his help. But he didn't; he spoke of the necessity of remaining neutral, of the problems with Karse and the need to guard his own border. He temporized, and said in polite, diplomatic terms that he wasn't *going* to help, as the man's face fell and the woman grew as rigid as a statue of ice. Kero felt their anguish as if it was her own. Clearly, this had been their last hope.

I can't take this anymore. Kero sighed, hoped Daren would forgive her, and stood up.

All eyes in the room swung toward her, and even the King stopped in mid-sentence as her chair scraped across the amber marble of the floor.

"Majesty," she said, slowly and distinctly, with every ounce of dignity and authority she could muster. "You said in this very hall as the feast began, that I could crave a boon of you in return for my actions at the hunt this afternoon."

She saw Daren clutch the table just out of the corner of her eye, his expression pleading with her *not* to say what he was sure she intended to say. She ignored him. Even if Need hadn't been goading her, the nagging of her own conscience would have forced this on her.

"This is what I ask, Majesty," she told him, fixing her gaze directly into his eyes. "And I think it is no more than what all our honor demands. As not only the one who is owed a boon, but as my Grandmother Kethry's granddaughter, I ask: *hold to the pledge your grandfather Stefansen made to Selenay's grandfather Roald in the library of this very castle.*"

The Heralds' faces were equally comic studies in bafflement. Daren buried his face in his hands. She waited for the King's anger to break out.

But although he winced, he gave no sign of anger. Instead, he only sighed, and shook his head, then looked back into her eyes and spoke softly, directly to her. "I never thought that it would be a mercenary Captain that would act as my conscience," he said ruefully. "Well, since the cat is well and truly escaped from the bag—"

He raised his voice. "My lords, my ladies, we have some private business to attend to—but let the feast continue. We shall return to you when we may."

A hum of conversation rose when he had finished and stood up. "Daren, Captain—come with me, if you will. I have need of both of you." He gestured, and Kero took her place at his side, though not without a certain trepidation. She could only remember the old saying: be careful what you ask for, you might get it.

I just asked for him to remember his grandfather's promise. He may well ask me to remember who and what I am.

He directed the two Heralds to follow him, and led the little procession out a small door behind the head table, down a warmly lit hallway, and into a room Kero had not seen before.

And there was no doubt *what* room this was, either, not when it was lined in books, floor to ceiling. This was the famous library. The King waved at the various chairs available, all of them worn shabby and comfortable-looking, and Kero sat gingerly on the edge of one, not entirely certain that she wanted to be here.

The King waited until all four of them were seated, before speaking. "You," he said, pointing at Kero in a way that made her want to sink into the chair and hide, "are both a most welcome and a most inconvenient guest, Captain. I am extremely grateful that you were with us on this afternoon's hunt, but I could wish your excellent memory to the Shin'a'in hell. Perhaps it is not to my credit, but I would have preferred not to have my country involved in a war that poses us no danger."

She stayed silent, since she couldn't think of any way to respond to his words that wasn't undiplomatic at best. He dropped his hand, and shrugged. "But you reminded me of an unredeemed pledge and saved my honor, if not my country. I suppose I should be grateful for that, even if, like medicine, this is not what I would have chosen."

The man—Herald Dirk—raised his hand tentatively. "Your pardon, Majesty," he said, when Faram responded to the movement by pivoting to face him, "but we haven't got the faintest idea of what you have been talking about. Just what is this pledge?"

Faram turned back to Kero. "Well, Captain," he said smiling a little crookedly. "It *began* with your grandmother and your Clanmother. Would you care to start?"

Kero cleared her throat, swallowed to give herself a moment to think, and began. "It all started—for my grandmother, at least—when she and her blood-oath sister Tarma joined Idra's Sunhawks. . . ."

In the end, she and Daren and Faram took turns explaining the entire story to the Heralds. It was Faram who ended the tale, saying, "—so as you can see, Rethwellan owes you what you came to beg of us. I have to admit that if the Captain hadn't made the question moot, I don't know whether I would actually have continued to allow you to remain in ignorance of that debt. I've been corresponding with my niece Elspeth, and she's a charming child—but joining my country to yours in a war is not a step to make based on how charming one's niece is."

"But—" Talia began, when Faram held up his hand to interrupt her.

"My conscience, at least, is much happier with the secret out in the open, even if my coldly practical side is not. The real problem, my lady, is that the Rethwellan army is composed mainly of foot. That is why we hire mercenary Companies when we need other forces. Even if I could muster them, and start them off for Valdemar immediately, they couldn't possibly be there before. . . ."

He looked to Daren for his answer, and got it. "Spring Equinox, assuming we started on the road tomorrow," Daren said promptly. And the Heralds' faces fell again. "And there's no way we can get them mustered and on the march for at least a fortnight, so they'll arrive later than that. But—"

"But?" said three voices together, as the King raised an eyebrow.

"The Skybolts are mounted—and really, that's exactly the kind of troops you of Valdemar need for the initial encounters. Skirmishers, experts in ambush and strike-and-run, anything to throw Ancar's army off-balance and keep them that way. Kero knows warfare like—like no one except her Clanmother."

He made a little bow in her direction, as she unaccountably blushed. *Dear gods, blushing, and at my age! And not for a pretty little compliment, but because he says that I'm a better tactician than anyone but Tarma! Certainly shows where* my *priorities have gone!*

"She may even surpass Tarma by now; it wouldn't surprise me. Between the Skybolts, the Valdemar forces, and Kero's knowledge of tactics, she can distract Ancar for long enough that we'd have a chance to come in to take Ancar's rear. In fact, if I were the Captain, I'd lead them chasing wild hares all over the countryside and have them exhaust themselves to no purpose."

Kero ran the basic plan in her head, and found that she liked it. "Huh," she said thoughtfully. "I think it would work. Especially if we let them get just inside the Border enough so they think they're winning, then lead them up along it. Frankly, Heralds, you're better off with us; we get paid whether we win or lose, and we don't have any national pride tied up with *appearing* to lose. You might have a hard time convincing your own troops to look like cowards, but my people have done it before, and accept it as good tactics. Daren, if you let me run them ragged, you'd probably make it to us at exactly the right moment. And he won't be expecting you; he'll probably be completely off-guard. I've only got one question—*we* didn't make any pledges. My lords, my lady, we're mercenaries, and we don't work for free. Who's paying our way?"

"We are," said Talia and the King at exactly the same moment. They looked at each other, and laughed weakly.

"Split the fee," Kero advised. "This is going to be a winter march for us, and winter marches don't come cheaply."

Talia nodded, somewhat to Kero's surprise. "I've done my share of winter marches," she said wryly. "I think I can guess what it will be like, going over mountains in a full Company in winter. We were told about you, Captain, and advised and authorized to hire you. That was our next job; to find you and negotiate. I hope you realize how rare that is.''

Eldan? Probably. How can I miss a man so much, when I spent so little time with him, so long ago? Well, whatever, he's getting his wish; he's got me coming up to Valdemar now. I'm just as glad the troops don't know about him, or they'd be placing bets on the outcome of our first meeting. Blessed Agnira, I never thought becoming Captain would mean anything like that!

''I do understand, and I appreciate that this shows your confidence in me and mine,'' she said, hoping her voice sounded businesslike and didn't betray how shaky she felt.

Nods all around the table, and she found herself vowing silently that she *would not* let these people down. ''First things first, since you trust my skill—let's see if we can't work out the actual logistics of this thing. . . .''

''I can't believe this,'' Kero said out loud, watching from Hellsbane's back as the troops rode past, out of the big double gates of Bolthaven and up the road to Valdemar. She shifted in her saddle, and Hellsbane shifted to match her. It was a good day for leaving; not too cold, under a bright-blue, cloudless sky. Good weather was a good omen, and soldiers are as superstitious as any man.

The Skybolts rode in march-formation; two abreast, which made for a long line, but as long as they were in friendly territory, it didn't matter. It was quite an impressive sight, and the Company looked far larger than it actually was. Every one of them had at least one spare riding animal on a lead-rope behind him, plus his own packhorse. Those with longer strings rode at the head of the column; they'd be breaking the trail, and being able to switch to a fresh horse every time the ones they were riding got tired would keep the column slogging on at a much faster pace than anyone other than Kero guessed. That was one of the Skybolts' tricks; they had more. A lot more. And in this campaign, they'd probably need every one of them.

''You don't believe what, Captain?'' Shallan asked,

her breath puffing out of her hood in a white cloud. She and Geyr waited patiently beside Kero for the last of the column to move out. The other Lieutenants were spaced at roughly equal intervals along the column, so that there would never be an officer out of effective range to handle an emergency.

"I don't believe *them,*" she said, pointing her chin at the last of the column, passing out of the gates. Now the quartermaster and his pack-strings moved out. Ten years ago, Kero had made the decision that the Skybolts would have *no* wagons with them. If something couldn't be carried horseback, it wouldn't come with them. Some ingenious, lightweight substitutions had been arrived at, due to the quartermaster's ingenuity. The tents, for instance, that could be packed twenty to a horse. New poles had to be cut each night, but it was worth it.

"There's not near enough bitching and moaning," Kero continued. "Here I am, hauling them out of cozy winter quarters for a midwinter march, a march across all of Rethwellan and over the mountains, and hardly a complaint out of them. What's wrong?"

"They're bored, Captain," said Geyr. "Campaign ended early, they got all their resting out of the way—and half the winter yet to go. They wanted something to do. Besides, the money on this is worth a winter march, and it's not like we're having to cross enemy territory."

"Well, it isn't going to be a Midsummer picnic, either," Kero replied, as the last of the supply-strings moved out. "The Comb isn't a bad range, but I'd rather not cross any mountains in winter. Well, that's the last of them. I'll see you when we camp."

Both Lieutenants saluted, so wrapped up in wool and furs that except for Geyr's black face, Kero couldn't tell them apart. Every trooper in the lot had a new, fur-lined wool cloak for this campaign; normally clothing was their own responsibility, but Kero knew soldiers, and she didn't want to lose a badly-needed fighter to frostbite just because the fool gambled away his cloak the night before. Orders were that the cloaks were Company property, like tents and standard weapons; anyone found using them for gambling stakes would find himself shoveling manure, scrubbing pots, and taking the worst of the night-watches. Anyone *accepting* them would get worse than that.

Kero nodded permission to go, and they spurred their horses onto the side of the road, to canter up past the pack-lines. Shallan would be riding just in front of the quartermaster, Geyr halfway down the line. Tomorrow, the two that had ridden first would move back here, and the other officers would all move up a notch, in strict rotation. Except for Kero, who would ride at the very tail. Winter or summer, tailmost was the worst position on the march, which was why she always took it. That was one of the little things that gave her the respect of her troops, as well as their obedience.

She gave Hellsbane a little nudge, and the mare took her accustomed place, so used to it now that she didn't even sigh. As the gates closed behind them, leaving the skeleton training staff and the new recruits deemed still too green to fight in this campaign, Kero settled comfortably into her saddle, and went over everything she had learned once more.

The one advantage they all had, and one Kero had *never* been able to count on before, was that all of Selenay's knowledge of their enemy was actually *fore-*knowledge. Evidently some of these Heralds were able to actively, consistently, see the future. They knew when he would strike, and where.

Mostly. And at least for the next six moons or so. After that, according to Talia, they were seeing "different futures." The Herald had tried to explain that to Kero, something about how what they did now to alter things would affect what had been seen and make different outcomes possible—it had all been too much for Kero. She'd always thought the future was like the past; a path that started somewhere and ended somewhere else, solid, immutable. It was disconcerting to hear otherwise. She wasn't sure she liked the idea of the future being so nebulous and fluid.

It was a pity that they couldn't see what was happening *now* as well; it would have been useful to know where this army of Ancar's was forming up. If Kero had known *that,* she could have arranged for a little exercise of the Skybolts' other specialty, the one she didn't talk about.

A few careful assassinations, some sabotage, some

*meddling with supplies; that was what helped cut the
Prophet campaign so short, and let us get her cornered.
That, and the strikes from behind, ambushes, and traps
until she had to find somewhere she considered safe to
make a stand. If you can ruin your enemy's morale, and
make him think everyone and everything is after him, it
doesn't do your side any harm. . . . Oh, well, we'll do
what we can with what we have.*

They had Guild blessing on this one, too, which was
no bad thing. She'd checked with the Guild, as required,
to find out if Ancar had hired on either Guild free-lancers
or Companies, and had gotten a delightful surprise. Ancar had actually had the gall to chase the Guild out of his
country and deny them access to Guild members still
inside his borders. So as far as the Guild was concerned,
it was no-holds-barred, and anything the Skybolts did to
Ancar's troops or on his side of the Border was all right
with them.

That was really phenomenally stupid, she reflected.
*Not even Karse or Valdemar have ever thrown the Guild
out. They may not be welcome, but they're tolerated,
because sooner or later, everyone comes to us. Even Valdemar.*

She shook her head over Ancar's foolishness.

*But I'd better watch my strategy with him. A fool can
kill you just as dead as a wise man, and is unpredictable
enough to do so.*

She saw something bright in the packs of the horse
ahead of her, and recognized some of the paraphernalia
strapped to the pack of the final horse in the train as an
object belonging to Quenten, a remarkable leather-
covered box he kept his books in, that had survived
floods, fires, and even being struck by lightning.

That turned her thoughts toward her chief mage. *He
should be just about ready for Master-status,* she thought.
*Maybe he can figure out my puzzle for me, why there are
no mages in Valdemar.*

For Talia had confided to Kerowyn, with an unmistak-
able tone of fear and bewilderment, that Ancar had mages
in his employ. She'd looked at Kero as if she expected
the Captain to challenge that statement, and had been
even more bewildered when Kero had simply nodded.

Bewilderment was a pretty odd reaction to magic, especially when the Heralds had magic of their own—mind-magic that was, from all Kero had ever learned from Eldan, equal in strength and refinement to the powers of any Master of any school Kero had ever met. And probably there were those who were the equal of any Adept as well.

Then again, he didn't seem to recognize real magic when he saw it, even when the Karsites were working it on us and calling it the hand of their god. And I think I remember that it was kind of hard even to talk to him about magic, as if I was saying one thing, but he was hearing something else.

The box swayed from side to side, hypnotically. Hellsbane had already gotten into her "march pace;" a steady, head-bowed walk, an easy motion to match.

Though not what I'd choose if I had a hangover or a twitchy stomach. . . . I wonder if magic doesn't work inside Valdemar? I think Grandmother said something about that, once. But if that's true, why is Ancar using mages against them? Unless it is true, but he either doesn't know it, or has a way to counteract whatever it is.

Kero gave up speculation as a bad job, and turned her mind toward the immediate future. Instead of supplies, the quartermaster carried cash. Since they would be traveling through exclusively friendly territory and harvests had been good this year, they were going to buy every bit of food they needed, for horse and human alike, except for what they needed to get them over the mountains. That was going to keep them light enough to travel at a good speed, and ensure the locals were always happy to see them.

We should meet Daren and the army about halfway between Petras and the Valdemar border, she figured, making rough calculations in her head. *And may the gods watch over* them. *Foot-slogging in winter is as bad as anything I can think of. I bet they'll be glad we broke the trail for them. Let's see; about a moon to the Valdemar border, then at least a fortnight to get across the mountains if I figure on bad weather all the way. Then another moon to get to the capital. Not bad. Better than any other Company I ever heard of, including the Sunhawks. Of course, without the cousins to help me with packhorse breeding, we'd be pulling wagons through this muck, and making the same kind of time as anybody else.*

And I don't even want to think about taking wagons over the mountains in the dead of winter.

Hellsbane's eyes were half-closed; Kero suspected she was dozing. Although the road was churned-up muck, it wasn't really too bad, since it was too warm for the stuff to freeze before the hooves of the tailmost horse went through it. Later though, it would be bad.

Let her doze, Kero thought, settling. *This is the easy part. Anything from here on is gong to be worse.*

Pray gods, not as bad as I fear.

Pray gods, the dreams don't follow me. . . .

Twenty-one

Snow swirled around Hellsbane's hocks, as the wind made Kero's feet ache with cold. Kerowyn huddled as much of herself inside her cloak as she could, and kept her face set in a reasonable approximation of a pleasant expression.

She would not dismount until her tent was set up. Her tent would not be set up until the rest of the camp was in order. The troops could look up from their own camp tasks at any time, and see her, still in the saddle, still out in the weather, for as long as it took for all of them to have their shelters put together.

Wonderful discoveries, these little dome-shaped, felt-lined tents. The wind just went around them; they never blew over, or collapsed, and instead of needing rigid tent-poles, you only needed to find a willow-grove, and cut eight of the flexible branches to thread through the eight channels sewn into the tents. You wouldn't even damage the trees; willows actually responded well to being cut back, and the Company had passed groves they'd trimmed in the past, whose trees were more luxuriant than before they'd been cut.

The hard part, especially in midwinter, was pounding the eight tent stakes into the rock-hard ground to pin the tents in place. Without those eight stakes, the tents could and had blown away, like down puffs on the wind. That was what took time, lots of time, and each pair of troopers was sweating long before the stakes were secure.

And meanwhile, the Captain got to sit on her horse and look impressive, while in reality she wanted to thump every one of her troopers who looked up at her for taking even a half-breath to do so, forcing her to be out in the cold that much longer. She'd *rather* have been pounding stakes herself; she used to help with setup, before she realized that helping could be construed as a sign of favoritism. Then she set up her own tent, before her own orderlies told her in distress that it wasn't "appropriate."

So she sat, like a guardian-statue, turning into a giant icicle, a sodden pile of wet leather, or a well-broiled piece of jerky, as the season determined.

The sun just touched the horizon, glaring an angry red beneath the low-hanging clouds. No snow—yet. It was on the way; Kero knew snow-scent when she caught it.

A wonderful aroma of roasting meat wafted on the icy breeze, making her mouth water and her stomach growl. In that much, at least, being Captain had its privileges. When she finally *could* crawl down off Hellsbane's back, her tent would be waiting, warmed by a clever charcoal brazier no larger than a dish, and her dinner would be sitting beside it. She sniffed again, and identified the scent as pork.

Good. The past three weeks it's been mutton, and I'm beginning to dislike the sight of sheep. Then she had to smile; when she'd last been this far north, she'd have sold her soul for a slice of mutton. In fact, most merc Companies would be making do with what they'd brought in the way of dried meat, eked out with anything the scouts brought in. This business of buying fresh food every time they halted had its advantages. Given the opportunity of making twice an animal's normal price, in midwinter when there was no possibility of other money coming in, most farmers and herders could manage to find an extra male, or a female past bearing. Just before they'd gotten into the Comb, in fact, they'd found a fellow with a herd of half-wild, woolly cattle who had been overjoyed to part with a pair of troublemaking beasts at the price the quartermaster had offered.

"Them's mean 'uns," he'd said laconically, as he delivered the hobbled, bellowing, head-tossing creatures to the cooks. The smile on his face when he accepted a slice of roast, and the tale her quartermaster told later of putting the cattle down, convinced her that they had done the man a favor.

The last tent went up, and Geyr, currently in charge of the crew digging the jakes, hove into view from the other side of the camp, and waved his hand. Kero sighed with relief, and dismounted.

Slowly. She was having a hard time feeling her feet. Hellsbane let out a tremendous sigh as Kero pulled her left foot out of the stirrup and the youngster assigned as the officer's groom came trotting up with his mittened hands tucked up into his armpits. He took the reins shyly from Kero, and led the mare off to the picket lines at a fast walk.

Kero made her way toward her tent at a *slow* walk; first of all, it wouldn't do for the troops to see the Captain scurrying for her tent like any green recruit on her first winter campaign. And second, she didn't trust her footing when she couldn't feel anything out of her feet but cold and pain.

The command tent was easily three times the size of the others, but that was because the troops' tents only had to hold two fighters and their belongings. Hers had to hold the map-table, and take several people standing up inside it, besides. That was the disadvantage of the little dome-shaped tents, and the reason she had a separate packhorse for her own traditional tent.

Her orderly held the tent flap open just enough for her to squeeze inside without letting too much of the precious heat out. And the first thing she did, once in the privacy of her quarters, was peel her boots off and stick her half-frozen, white feet into the sheepskin slippers he'd left warming beside the brazier for her.

As life returned to her extremities, she thanked the gods that she had made it through another day on the march without losing something to frostbite.

"There has to be a way to keep your feet from turning into chunks of ice the moment the wind picks up," she said crossly to her orderly. "It's fine when there's no wind; the horse keeps your feet warm enough—but once there's a wind, you might as well be barefoot."

Her orderly, a wiry little fellow from the very mountains they'd just crossed, frowned a little. " 'Tis them boots, Cap'n," he said solemnly. " 'Tis nothin' betwixt the foot an' the wind but a thin bit'a leather. 'Tis not what we do."

She took an experimental sip of the contents of her wooden mug. It was tea tonight, which was fine. She hadn't had any more of those dreams of Eldan since crossing the Comb, which left her with mixed feelings, indeed, and wine was not what she wanted tonight, even mulled. She didn't want to go all maudlin in her cups, mourning the loss of those illusionary lovemaking sessions.

Whatever was wrong with me is cured, she though resolutely. *I should be thankful. I'm back to being myself. But—come to think of it, Need's been as silent as a stone,* she realized, with a moment of alarm. *Nothing. Not even a "feel" at the back of my mind. She might just as well be ordinary metal!*

Dear gods, what if she won't Heal me anymore?

I'll deal with it, that's what. It's too late to turn back now. Think about something else. "Enlighten me, Holard. What do your people do?"

"Sheepskin boots, Cap'n," he replied promptly, "An' wool socks, double pairs. Only trouble is, 'tis bulky, an' has no heel. We don't use stirrups, ye ken."

She shook her head. "That won't do, not for us. I guess I'll just have to suffer—"

At that moment, the guard outside her tent knocked his dagger hilt against the pole supporting the door canopy, and let someone in with a swirl of snow.

Quenten, and Kero had a feeling she wasn't going to like what he was about to say the moment he came fully into the light from her lantern. He was haggard and nervous, two states she'd *never* seen Quenten in—and the mages had been conspicuous by their absence since they'd crossed the Comb. There was something up, and whatever it was, it was coming to her now because they couldn't handle it themselves.

"Captain," said Quenten, and his voice cracked on the second syllable. She waited for him to try again. "Captain," he repeated, with a little more success this time. "We have a problem. . . ."

Gods. Need, and now the mages?

"I'd already gathered that, Quenten, since you look like a day-old corpse, and I haven't seen so much as a mage's sleeve for a fortnight. Is it just you, or do all the mages look like you?"

"All of us," Quenten replied unhappily. "We'd like permission to turn back, Captain. It isn't you, or the Company, or the job. We think it's Valdemar itself.

There's something strange going on here, and it's driving us mad.''

He waited for a moment, obviously to see if she believed him. She just nodded. ''Go on,'' she told him, figuring she was about to have her little puzzle of mages and Valdemar solved, at least in part.

''I remembered what you told me, about how the Heralds seemed surprised by magic, and you never heard of a mage up in Valdemar. I thought maybe it was coincidence or something.'' His hands twisted the hem of his sleeve nervously. ''Well, it isn't. The moment we got across the border, we all felt something.''

''What?'' she asked, impatiently. ''What is it? If there's something around that's costing me the use of my mages, I want to know about it.''

Quenten ground his teeth in frustration. ''I don't *know*,'' he said, around a clenched jaw. ''I really don't know! It was like there was somebody watching us, all the time. At first, it was just an annoyance; we figured there was just some Talented youngling out there, thinking he could spy on us. But we never caught anybody, and after a while, it started getting on our nerves. It was like having somebody staring, staring right at you, *all the time*. It goes on day and night, waking and sleeping, and it's like nothing any of us have ever seen or heard of before. We couldn't get rid of it, we couldn't shield against it, and its been getting worse every day. I can't even sleep anymore. Please, Captain, give us permission to go back. We'll wait for you at winter quarters.''

Now if it had been one of the others who asked that of her, with a nebulous story like that, she'd have suspected fakery, slacking, or at least exaggeration. But it was Quenten, as trustworthy as they came, and not prone to exaggerate anything. And he did look awful.

And if all this was true, even if she kept them, they wouldn't do her any good. *You can't take time to aim when you have to keep ducking, and that's obviously the way they feel right now.*

''Are the Healers being affected?'' she asked anxiously. ''Or is it only you?''

''The Healers are fine, Captain,'' Quenten reported, with a certain hangdog expression, as if he felt he was somehow responsible for the mages being singled out.

Then with luck, Need will still be able to Heal me. And with none, she's still a good sword. Besides, a sword probably wouldn't care about being stared at. "All right," she said unhappily. "You can go. You go back on noncombatant status, though, and we can't spare anyone to get you back home."

"That's all right," Quenten replied, nearly faint with relief. "Once we're across the border we'll be fine. Thank you, Captain. I think if I'd had to go two more days, I'd have killed someone. We've already had to restrain Arnod twice; he tried to run off into the snow last night with nothing on but a shirt."

"Oh," Kero replied, wishing that they'd told her about this earlier. Then, it might have been possible to get Quenten to fiddle with Need again, to extend the protections over the mages. . . .

Then again, maybe not. Need never had protected mages from magic. They were all probably better off this way. And besides, Need was silent. Who knew if she was actually working or not?

She told her orderly to go with Quenten and see that the quartermaster gave them what supplies he could.

Something watching you all the time, she thought, bemused, as she settled down to the remains of her dinner. *Now that I think of it, that is something that would drive you crazy. Especially if you were already unbalanced. Which mages are, a lot of times, and with good reason.*

No wonder there are no mages in Valdemar. They're either mad, or fled. Clever defense. End of puzzle.

Except I hope my blade is still working. Things could get sticky if it isn't.

Halfway to the Valdemar capital of Haven, it seemed that their purpose and reputation had preceded them. People came out of the towns along the way to watch them pass; reservedly friendly, but cautious, as if they didn't quite know what to expect of a mercenary Company. Kero ordered her troopers to respond to positive overtures, but ignore negative ones. And there were negative responses; old men and women who remembered the Tedrel Wars, and had decided that all mercs were like the Tedrels had been. At least once every time they halted, someone would shout an insult (which more than half the troopers couldn't understand anyway), someone else would half-apologize for "granther," and Kero or one of her Lieutenants would carefully explain the difference between Guild and non-Guild mercs. It got to be so much of a commonplace, that the troops began laying bets on who the troublemaker would be the moment they entered a town. Privately, Kero was relieved that the Tedrel Wars had been so very long ago—years tended to bring forgetfulness, especially in the light of this new enemy. It didn't matter so much anymore that the Karsites had hired fighters calling themselves mercenaries—those hired fighters had been just like the Karsites who hired them; they fought with steel like anyone else, and could be killed with that same steel. *Ancar* had hired mages, about which there were only tales, and every childhood bogeyman came leaping out of the closet to become the adult's worst nightmare.

So, for the most part, the people of Valdemar came out to see these hired fighters—hired to fight on *their* side—and came away comforted. These were tough, seasoned veterans, on fast, slim horses like these farmers had never seen before—but they smiled at children, offered bits of candy, and let toddlers ride on a led horse. They had faced mages and won. When someone managed to find a Skybolt who knew either trade-tongue or had a sketchy grasp of Valdemaran, and managed to ask through the medium of painfully slow pantomime about fighting against mages, the answer always surprised the the questioner, for it was invariably a shrug, and a reply of, "they die."

Kero finally reduced it to a few simple sentences she had the officers teach the troops. "Tell them 'mages are human. They bleed if you cut them, die if you strike them right. They need to eat, and they get tired if they work magic for too long. And there are things to stop them and things their magic can't work on—' " And then would follow the list of all the little tricks every Guild merc knew; salt and herbs, holy talismans, disrupting the mage's concentration, spellbreaking by interfering with the components, sneaking up and taking the mage from behind, even overwhelming the mage with a rush of ar-

rows or bodies so that he couldn't counter every one before he was taken down.

These farmer-folk and tradesmen, crafters and herders, were ordinary people. They'd heard all the old tales,
and nothing they heard gave them any confidence that
they could do anything to protect themselves. The power
of a mage seemed enormous and unstoppable, like a
thunderstorm. To be told, by those who had faced them
and won, that mages were just another kind of fighter,
with weapons that determination could counter, gave the
common people courage they hadn't had before, and a
new trust in these foreign soldiers.

All of which was all to the good, so far as Kero was
concerned. *A friendly civilian populace is the best ally a
merc can have;* that was one of Tarma's maxims—and
Ardana had certainly proved what kind of enemy an *unfriendly* civilian populace could become, down in Seejay.
The Skybolts knew the maxim, and the drill, and even
here, where half of them didn't even know the language
well enough to ask for the jakes, they were leaving allies
on the road behind them.

This kind of behavior was so ingrained in Kero and
her troops that when Heralds Talia and Dirk rode in,
about a week out of Haven, Kero was more than a little
surprised by the broad grin of approval the latter sported.

They arrived just after camp had been set up, and Kero
was huddling over her brazier. The wind was particularly
bitter, and seemed to find every weak point in the tent;
the walls alternately flapped and belled, and Kero was
hoping to get her cold bones into her bed where she at
least had a chance of getting them warm. She'd been
expecting the arrival of an escort at any point, so when
a runner brought her word of the Heralds' arrival, she
grumbled a little, threw a little more charcoal on the
brazier, kicked loose belongings under the cot, and went
back to trying to soak up a bit more heat until her orderly
brought them to the tent, both of them muffled up in thick
white cloaks, like walking snowdrifts.

But when they entered and Kero invited them to join
her in hot tea, Dirk's open friendliness came as something of a shock. Back in Rethwellan both the Heralds
had been close-mouthed, but Dirk had been practically

mute, with an overtone of suspicion. Now he acted like she was a long-lost cousin, his homely face made handsome by his genuine smile.

Now what on earth caused that? she wondered. They made some small talk, and as soon as the tea arrived, Kero asked, cautiously, "So, now that we're within a week of Haven, how do your Queen and her Lord Marshal feel about our arrival? Is there anything we should expect?"

Dirk laughed, and shook his head. "If you're expecting a cool reception, you aren't going to get it, Captain. You and your Skybolts have handled yourselves exceptionally well on the march up; she's very pleased with your diplomacy and restraint and—"

"Diplomacy?" Kero said, too annoyed to be polite. "Restraint? What did she think we were going to do, ride down little children, rape the sheep, and wreck the taverns?"

"Well—" Dirk looked embarrassed.

That's exactly what they expected. Which we knew, really. "Herald, we are professionals," she said tiredly. "We fight for a living. This does not make us animals. In fact, on the whole, I think you'll find that my troopers, male and female, are less likely to cause trouble in a town than your average lot of spoiled-rotten highborn brats."

Dirk flushed, a deep crimson. "All we have to go on are stories—"

"Yes, well, you should hear some of the stories down south about Shin'a'in in warsteeds, or Heralds. The latter are demons and the former are basically ugly Companions," she said, mustering up a frank smile. "Now, one man's demon is another man's angel, and since the lads calling you lot 'demonic' were thieves and scum that would rather do anything than work, I'll withhold my judgment on that. But I ride a warsteed, and while she's a *very* intelligent beast, specially bred for what she does, she's nothing like a Companion. So—"

"So we shouldn't have been so quick to give credence to stories," Talia chuckled, bending a little closer to the fire. "A well-deserved rebuke. But I have to tell you, Captain, that I think we were rightfully surprised at the way you've made friends for yourselves coming up the road. We were expecting to have to do a lot of calming of nerves on your behalf; our people aren't used to the concept of mercenaries, and what they know about them is mostly bad. But you've done all our work for us."

Kero shrugged, secretly pleased, and put another scoop of charcoal on the fire. "Well, one of my Clanmother's Shin'a'in sayings is, 'A slighted friend is more dangerous than an enemy.' We try to operate by that in friendly territory, and really, it isn't that hard unless the people really have a bad attitude toward mercs in general. In fact, there was only one problem I had—and it seems to be in the family tradition—"

"Oh?" Dirk said, he and Talia both looking puzzled.

She sighed. "All their lives, my grandmother and her *she'enedra* were plagued by the songs of a particular minstrel. The things he told about them were half-true at best, and led to all kinds of problems about what people expected from them. Well, when I was young and foolish and very full of—myself—someone wrote a song about *me*. It's called 'Kerowyn's Ride,' and to my utter disgust, it seems to have penetrated language barriers."

Dirk looked as if he was having a hard time keeping from laughing. So did Talia. "I know the song," the woman said, her face full of mirth. "In fact, I've sung it."

"I was afraid of that. Do I dare hope no one in your Court knows it's about me?"

Talia smiled. "As far as I know, they don't. But it's a very popular song."

Kerowyn sipped her tea, wondering for a moment if there was anyone in the world who *hadn't* heard the song. "My troopers are ridiculously proud of that, and I can't get them to stop telling people that I'm *that* Kerowyn. And as soon as your villagers would find that out, I'd wind up having to listen to whatever unholy rendition of it someone had come up with in *this* village. And I don't even *like* most music," she concluded plaintively.

Dirk was red-faced with the effort of holding in laughter. Kero glowered at him, but that only seemed to make it worse. "*You* should have had to sit through some of those performances," she growled. "The Revenie Temple children's choir, the oldest fart in Thornton accompanying himself on hurdy-gurdy, a pair of religious sopranos who seemed to think the thing was a dialogue between the Crone and the Maiden—and at least a dozen would-be Bards with out-of-tune harps. Minstrels. I'd like to strangle the entire breed.''

That did it; Dirk couldn't restrain himself any longer. He excused himself in a choking voice, and fled outside. Once there, his bellows of laughter were just as clear as they would have been if he'd been inside the tent's four walls.

"Oh, well," Kero said with resignation. "At least he didn't laugh in my face.''

Talia was a little better at controlling herself. "I can see where it would get tiresome, especially if you don't care for music.''

"I don't like vocal music," Kero explained forlornly. "And the reason I don't like it is because every damn fool that can tell one note from another thinks he rates right up there with Master Bards. I have perfect pitch, Herald—nothing else, *I* certainly am no performer—but I do have perfect pitch, and my relative pitch is just as good. Out-of-tune amateurs make my skin crawl, like fingernails on slate. And it's no great benefit to have had a song written about you, either—just you wait, one of these days it'll happen to you, and then that tall fellow out there won't find it so funny to hear it every night for a fortnight straight, and only once in all that time will it be sung well.''

"You're right, Captain," Dirk said contritely from the door flap. "I apologize. But I wish you could have seen your own expression.''

"I'm glad I couldn't. Listen, there's something I need to tell you people about. I didn't mention this before, but I had mages with this troop. Real mages, practicing real magic.'' She watched them carefully to see what their reactions to this would be. "Most merc Companies do, if they can afford them, and we can.''

"Had?" Dirk replied, after a long moment of silence. "Does that mean you didn't bring them with you?''

She couldn't read anything from either of them—and this was not the time to try prying into anyone's mind.

Especially not a Herald, who might catch her at it. "No," she said, honestly, "I *tried* to bring them with me, but they were stopped at the Border. By what, they couldn't tell me—only that it felt as if something was watching them, waking and sleeping. It finally got so bad they begged me to send them home before they went mad. That is evidently the reason why you don't have real mages here in Valdemar. Something doesn't want them here, and stares at them until they go away."

Like the time with Eldan, she was having to fight something to get every word out, and she spoke slowly so that the effort wouldn't be noticed. *It doesn't explain why something around here doesn't want you even knowing about magic, but that's not my problem. As long as it doesn't freeze the words in my throat, I don't care. Need's been awfully quiet, but it really doesn't feel like the sword's being tampered with, it's beginning to feel as if Need doesn't want to draw attention to itself. Which is fine with me. It means she* is *still working.*

The wind howled around the corners of the tent, and Talia pulled her white cloak closer. "It certainly does explain a lot," she said, slowly. "Though I'm not sure what it means or where it comes from."

"It would probably take a very powerful mage to get around something like that," Dirk put in. "Maybe by somehow disguising his nature?"

Kero shrugged. "You could be right, but other than the fact that I've lost the use of my mages, it really doesn't matter. And if I were you, I wouldn't count on this effect saving Valdemar from mages in the future. My grandmother always said that every spell ever cast could be broken, and if Ancar has a strong enough mage in his back pocket, he can take the thing down altogether. Since I *have* lost the mages, I'm going to have to talk with more of you Heralds to find out what you can do. I'm pretty certain you can make up for them, but I'll have to know what your limits are. One other thing—you might let the Queen know that having worked pretty closely with all my mages and having watched my grandmother at work, I would say I'm a fair hand at judging mage-powers and what they can and cannot do."

"That's easily enough done, Captain," Dirk said, standing up. "Is there anything else we can do for you?"

"No, not until we get to Haven and we can get into a real barracks building and I can get warm again." Kero remained seated when Dirk waved her down. "Unless you can conjure me up a tent that's tighter than this one. I'm looking forward to meeting Queen Selenay."

"Well, she's looking forward to meeting you," Talia said with a smile, as she smiled back over her shoulder. "I think you're going to like each other a great deal."

Queen Selenay was the sister Kero would have chosen if she'd been given the power to make that choice; Kero knew it the moment their eyes met, blue to blue-green. They could easily have been sisters, too; Kero judged herself to be Selenay's senior by no more than two or three years.

"Captain Kerowyn," the Queen said, rising from behind her desk, and holding out her hand with no formality at all. "I'm very glad to finally meet you, and equally glad that the years have brought you the kind of fortune Eldan said you deserved. Please, sit down."

The mention of Eldan's name startled her; she swallowed with difficulty, and she searched the Queen's face carefully before accepting her hand. "That could be considered faint praise, your Majesty," she replied cautiously, as she took a chair. "There's a Shin'a'in curse considered to be very potent: 'May you get exactly what you deserve.'"

Selenay laughed, a velvety laugh with no sign of malice in it. "I'm sure neither of us meant it that way—and I am not 'your Majesty' among my commanders. On the field, the Lord Marshal ranks me, so I'm just plain 'Selenay.'"

There was nothing in the Queen's appearance to suggest that her statement was either coy or false modesty. She was dressed almost identically to Talia, who now stood at her side, in the uniform Kero had learned was called "Herald's Whites." Here in Valdemar, it seemed, Heralds dressed all in white, Bards in scarlet, and Healers in green. Kero rather liked that last; it would make finding the Healers much easier in battlefield conditions. On the other hand, on that same battlefield, as she had once pointed out to Eldan, those white uniforms must surely shout "I'm a target! Hit me!"

The only difference between Talia's and Selenay's uniforms was that Talia openly carried a long knife, and wore breeches, and Selenay wore a kind of divided riding skirt that gave the appearance of a little more formality without sacrificing too much in the way of mobility. The Queen's thick, shoulder-length blonde hair was confined by a simple gold circlet—there was no other outward sign of her rank. Even this office, the first room of the Royal Suite, was furnished quite plainly. There were two old tapestries on the wall, a few chairs chosen more for comfort than looks, and a dark wooden desk cluttered with papers; there was no indication anywhere that this room was used by anyone with any kind of rank.

"We're under wartime conditions here, Captain," Selenay continued, accepting Kero's scrutiny serenely. "I don't know what you were anticipating, but I am expecting a certain amount of work out of your troops until we take the field."

Hmm. Better make some things plain—like we aren't miracle workers. "I'll tell you this honestly, your—Selenay," Kero replied. "If you're expecting us to turn to and help with everything except training green recruits, we'll be able to do what you want. But if you thought we could take plowboys and make specialist cavalry out of them in less than a fortnight, you might as well just send us straight out to where you expect Ancar, because we can't do it. Nobody can."

Selenay nodded quickly, as if that was what she had expected Kero would say. "I realize that. What I'd like your people to do is work with the mounted troops we've gotten from some of the highborn, privately recruited, maintained, and trained. I expect some of them will be dreadful; I'd like the dreadful ones weeded out and put somewhere harmless. Some will be marginal, and those we'll put with the mounted Guard units, the ones I had out chasing bandits. The good ones I'd like you to train as much as you can, so that they'll work together without charging into each other."

"Which is what they're doing at the moment," Talia added from behind the Queen. "If the situation wasn't so bad, I'd advise keeping them around for entertainment."

Kero managed to keep her face straight.

Selenay's mouth quirked up at one corner, but she did likewise. "Keep the Lord Marshal appraised on a daily basis; I've appointed a liaison for you."

Kerowyn was impressed and relieved, both. Selenay had a good grasp of what was possible and what was not, and was willing to settle for the possible. That made *her* job that much easier.

"Can do," she replied, relaxing. "Who's my liaison to the Lord Marshal?"

"My daughter, Elspeth," Selenay said, and Kero's heart sank. *Just what I need, a know-everything princess at my heels. I wonder if I can convince Anders to charm her and get her of my way—with those big, brown eyes, the beautiful body, and all the rest of it, he should—*

A rap on the door to the Queen's quarters interrupted them, and as Kero turned, startled, another slim young woman in Whites slipped inside, a brown-haired, brown-eyed girl with a startling resemblance to Faram. "Mother, I'm sorry I'm late, but there was a—" she stopped instantly as Selenay held up her hand.

"You're here now, and you can tell me what delayed you later. Elspeth, this is Captain Kerowyn. Captain, your liaison, my daughter."

The girl's eyes went round with surprise, and she crossed the room quickly, to take Kero's hand in as firm a clasp as her mother had.

"I'm dreadfully sorry, Captain," she said in accentless Rethwellan. "If I'd known you were arriving today, I'd have arranged things differently. We Heralds have to spend our first year or two acting as arbitrators and judges under the supervision of a senior Herald—normally that's outside Haven, where we can't run home to mama when a thunderstorm hits, but since I'm the Heir, they won't let me do that. Go out in the Field, I mean, not run home to mama."

Kero blinked. *Well, this is amazing. First highborn child I've ever met who wasn't either spoiled or convinced rank alone conferred wisdom.* "I can understand the constraints," she replied, in Elspeth's tongue. "All it would take would be one stray arrow."

Elspeth sighed. "I know, but the problem is that since

I'm *not* out of reach, the Weaponsmaster seems to think I have all the time I need for lessoning and practice, and Herald Presen keeps assigning me to *another* city court and I *still* have all the Council meetings as Heir—and Mother, Teren said to tell you that—''

"I have the War Council, I know. So do you, and I'm bringing the Captain along." Selenay smiled fondly on her offspring, and Kero didn't blame her. Kero echoed the smile. There wasn't going to be any trouble in working with this one.

Then, out of nowhere, Need roused, for the first time since crossing the Border—focused on Elspeth—

And for one moment, sang.

Kero felt as if someone had dropped her inside a metal bell, then hit the outside with a hammer. She and the sword vibrated together for what seemed like forever, with everything, *everything*, focused on Elspeth, who seemed entirely unaware that anything was going on. She kept right on with her conversation with her mother, while Kero tried to regain her scattered wits.

There was no doubt in her mind that Need had found the person she wanted to be passed on to.

But—now?

She thought that question at the sword as hard as she could, but the blade was entirely quiescent once more, as if nothing had happened.

Blessed Agnira, Kero thought, mortally glad that Selenay and her daughter were still deep in conversation. *Is that what the thing did to Grandmother the first time I showed up on her doorstep? No, it couldn't have. For one thing, she wasn't wearing it at the time. But I'd be willing to bet this is how that old fighter that passed it to her felt.*

Well, at least the stupid thing wasn't going to insist on being handed over immediately. Maybe it sensed that Kero was going to require its power in the not-too-distant future. And surely it knew—if it was aware—that she'd fight it on that point until this war was over.

Fine, she decided, as Selenay turned away from her daughter, and gestured that the two of them should followed her out the door. *I'll worry about it later. We all have other things to worry about—and I'll be damned if*

I'll give this thing to a perfectly nice child like Elspeth with no warning of what it can do to her!

And she thought straight at the blade—*So don't you go trying your tricks on her—or I'll see that she drops you down a well!*

Twenty-two

Spring is a lousy time to fight, Kero thought, peering through the drizzle, as droplets condensed and ran down her nose and into her eyes. She wiped them away in bleak misery. *And if that fool is going to attack, you'd think he'd pick better weather than this. Fog* and *rain, what a slimy mess.*

She stood beside the mare on the only significant elevation in the area. Though it stood well above the surrounding countryside, it wasn't doing her any good. This miasma had reduced visibility to a few lengths, and the only way she was going to find anything out was through the scouts and outriders.

Hellsbane shivered her skin to shed collected water droplets. Kero wished she could do the same. If Selenay's people hadn't insisted that *here* and *now* was where Ancar was going to make his first attempt, expecting no resistance, she'd have gone right back to the tent where it was warm. Her hands ached with cold, and there was a leaky place in her rain cloak just above her right shoulder.

But the tent was already packed up, and the Heralds with the Gift of ForeSight hadn't been wrong so far.

The only troops on the field today were the Skybolts in Valdemar colors. To them would fall the task of harrying Ancar for the first couple of engagements, of wearing him out before he ever encountered real Valdemar troops, and of confusing him with tactics he wouldn't have expected out of regular army troopers.

They'd staged their defense with an eye to making him lose his more mobile fighters early on. The troops Ancar would meet for the next several days were all mounted; the foot troops would meet up with them farther north. At that point, hopefully, his foot soldiers would be exhausted from trying to keep up with the horse, while their foot would still be fresh.

Kero's plan was to make every inch of ground Ancar gained into an expensive mistake, and to lure him northward with the illusion of success, when all the time he was only moving along his own border.

When Kero had explained, as delicately as possible, her Company's other specialty, Selenay had given her another pleasant surprise. "You mean you're saboteurs?" she'd exclaimed with delight. "A whole *Company* of dirty tricksters? Bright Astera, why didn't you say that before? For Haven's sake, if anyone questions your tactics, send them to me, I'll back you!"

So now Kero and the Skybolts had carte blanche to do whatever they needed to. Which was just as well, really, since they would have done so anyway.

I thought some of the things we'd run into before were odd, but this is stranger than snake feet, she thought, recalling her presentation to the War Council once she'd finally worked out a general plan based on the tentative one she'd put together with Daren. *First, the "watchers," whatever they were—then the fact that it's like driving nails into stone to talk to people around here about magic—but then there's the business with Iftel. It's like the country was invisible from inside Valdemar. It's on the map, but their eyes slide right by it. . . .*

"We basically have to get Ancar in a pincer, and leave him with only one avenue of escape. Our best bet right now is to get him right up against the Iftel border, and trap him there," she'd said to the War Council.

And they had, to a man and woman, looked absolutely blank.

Finally, "Iftel?" faltered Talia, as if she had trouble even saying the name. "Why Iftel?"

"Because of what I've been told by the Guild," Kero had said to them all. "That Iftel protects itself—by making you forget it exists, and keeping you out if it doesn't want you in. I think you've just confirmed the first, which makes me think the second is true, too."

"Iftel is—strange," Selenay admitted. "I do have an ambassador there, a non-Herald. They—how odd, they didn't want a Herald there at all. Yet they have never, ever threatened us in all our history, and they have signed some fairly binding treaties that they never will. From all accounts, though, the country is just as strange as the Pelagirs, and that is very strange indeed.''

That matched with what Kero had been told by the Guild. *They* didn't have a representative there, but it wasn't because they'd been barred from the place. It was because every time they'd sent someone in, he'd nearly died of boredom. Iftel had no bandits. Iftel had its own standing militia, organized at the county level. Iftel hired no mercenaries—because Iftel needed no mercenaries. Occasionally young folk got restless enough to leave, but that was the only time the Guild ever got members from Iftel, and *they* never went back home.

Iftel took care of itself, thank you.

Well, that made it a good place to take a stand; Ancar's forces would be squeezed against the Iftel border to the north, Valdemar's forces would be to the west, and Rethwellan's—hopefully—would be coming up from the south.

Kero wiped rain out of her eyes, without doing much good. She still couldn't see past the bottom of the hill. But somewhere out beyond in the fog, the specialists had been at work, and if the Foreseers were right, in the next candlemark or so, Ancar's forward troops would run right into something nasty that wasn't supposed to be there.

The skirmishers stirred restlessly below her, waiting for their chance. Today was likely to be the only easy day of the campaign, which was why Kero had wanted only her Company in on it. *They* knew that a war is neither lost nor won in the first battle, and they knew very well that one easy day is the exception, not the rule. But if Selenay's greener forces were in on this, when the going got rougher and rougher, they might see every day after the easy one as a constant series of defeats, and lose heart. In fact, Kero hoped she wouldn't lose a single fighter this first day, but she knew as well as anyone on the field that engagements like that came once in a career and never again.

So we're due one.

The sound of muffled hoofbeats came through the fog; years of practice had enabled Kero to pinpoint where sound was really coming from on days of rotten visibility.

It's from the ambush site. I think we're about to get

some action. One of the scouts materialized out of the drizzle and pelted up the hillside, his horse mired to the belly. "They're coming on, Captain, straight for the trap."

Her heartbeat quickened, in spite of years of experience. "Good," she replied, and the Herald beside her silently relayed that on to the rest of his kind—which included Selenay and Elspeth. "Tell the rest that if it looks like he's straying, tease him into it."

"Sir." The scout saluted, and pelted off again, vanishing back into the mist like a ghost.

The "trap" was a swamp—a swamp that hadn't been there a week ago. But last month Kero's experts had diverted a small river from its bed, several leagues away, and had confined its waters behind an earthen dam just above the flat, grassy meadow the ForeSeers said Ancar was aiming for. Then, two nights ago, they had broken the dam.

Now the place was two and three feet deep in water and mud, all covered by the long grass growing there and the luxuriant, green, mosslike scum floating on the top. One of Kero's Healers had a remarkable ability with plants . . . and, much to everyone's surprise and delight, the Heralds were able to feed him energy. Between the scum they'd cultured with tender care on the temporary lake for the past month, and the accelerated growth of the past two nights, they now had the kind of cover that normally took half the summer to grow. It looked just like solid land—until you tried to walk on it.

Now was when Kero missed her mages the most. *They* would have been able to create illusions of solid land— and phantoms of Valdemar forces along with those illusions. That would have lured Ancar's people into a charge right into the worst of the muck. And once the charge had started, the momentum of the troops behind the front line would have driven the rest even deeper. Whole wars had been won with blunders like that.

Instead, she could only wait for his front line to wander into the swamp, and bring her skirmishers around to harry him deeper into the mire. Supposedly there was a Herald out there also diverting water from a nearby spring to come up behind him, so that he'd have muck on three sides, but she wasn't counting on that.

Hoofbeats again in the mist, but this time the scout didn't bother to gallop up the hillside; he just waved, and turned back. That was the signal Kero had been waiting for. She vaulted into her saddle, and whistled.

Below her, the skirmishers moved out at a careful walk, so that every part of the line stayed in contact with the part next to it. Fighting in conditions like these was hellish—and it was appallingly easy to fire on some vague shape out there, only to discover that it was one of your own.

"Friendly fire isn't." That was one of Tarma's Shin'a'in sayings, succinct, and to the point. *We haven't lost a Skybolt to friendly fire yet,* she thought, as she sent her horse carefully picking her way down the slick, grassy slope. *I don't want to start now.*

The Herald and his Companion followed her, silent as a pair of ghosts, and hardly more substantial in the mist. For once that white uniform was an advantage. She urged Hellsbane into a brief trot at the bottom of the hill, then reined the warsteed in once they caught up with the skirmishers. She was anchoring the westernmost portion of the line, the place where Ancar's men might get around them if they weren't vigilant.

They sure as hell can't go south.

Another reason not to have Valdemar regulars on this action: most of the ground to the south was boobytrapped, and Kero didn't want the green troops to wander into it. Any place horses or foot could get through was thick with trip-wires, pit-traps—and gopher-holes. One of the Heralds, it seemed, had a Gift of "speaking" to animals, and he must have called in every mole and gopher for leagues around to undermine those fields. No horse could *ever* get safely across those fields, and it was even risking a broken ankle to try if you were afoot. Regulars might forget that. The Skybolts would sooner forget their pay.

So the south was booby-trapped, then came the swamp on the west. The only "safe" ground was to the north, which was exactly where they *wanted* Ancar to go. That was the side they'd contest, and they were going to have to make it look as if they'd come upon Ancar by accident.

If he thought they were a small force of Selenay's Guard—

Which we are, small that is—
—backed by nobody—
Which we aren't—

—depending mostly on the treacherous terrain to protect this section of the Border, he'd be on them like a hound on a hare. Meanwhile, they'd try and stay just out of his range (*"If the enemy is within firing range, so are you,"* Tarma's voice croaked in her mind), and pick as many of his men off as they could before he extracted them from the mire. That was the heart and soul of Kero's strategy in this first engagement.

Up ahead in the mist, and far to her right, Kero heard a wild horn call; it sounded *exactly* like a young bugler in a panic, and she mentally congratulated Geyr on his imitation fear. That was the signal that the right flank was up even with the edge of the swamp, and the enemy was in sight. She took Hellsbane up to a fast walk, and the rest followed her lead.

Then the mare planted all four feet and snorted; she whistled, and the line stopped moving. They'd planted the edge of the bad ground with wild onions, and the moment Hellsbane had smelled one, she'd known to stop. Right at this point, it wasn't marsh, but it was waterlogged and soft, and not what any of them wanted to take a horse through.

Besides, in a few moments, the enemy would come to *them*.

The mist muffled noise, but as Kero strained to hear past the sounds of her own people, she made out faint cries and things that sounded like shouted orders and curses, off to her right and ahead. And they were coming closer with every moment. She whistled again; the signal was repeated up and down the line, and as if they were reflections of a single man, every Skybolt slipped his short horse-bow or crossbow from its oiled case, strung or cocked it, set one arrow on the string, and put another between his teeth or behind his ear.

Their range with these weapons was far longer than their current range of visibility. There would be one ideal moment, when *they* knew the enemy was coming, but he didn't know the Skybolts were there, when they would have the best chance of trimming down some of the front ranks. It was the best opportunity that they'd likely ever

get during the march north; the point where the enemy
forces would be just barely visible as vague shapes moving through the mist.

No one aimed yet. Kero strained her eyes for the first
sign of the enemy, knowing that every one of her people
was doing the same. The skirmishers knew to fire as soon
as they thought they saw *anything,* and never mind bothering about targets; the mist would be too deceptive to
allow for accurate shooting anyway, and the more arrows
that sped toward the enemy lines, the likelier the chances
of actually hitting someone. Any injury is a nuisance; in
a swamp, any injury could be fatal.

She heard splashing, and thought she saw something—
hesitated a moment. *There, to the right—was that—yes!*
The thought actually followed on the act of aiming, firing, and nocking a second arrow and firing again. Nor
was she alone; virtually all of the fighters in her immediate vicinity had done the same, and the shouts and
screams from the billowing fog were all the reward any
of them could have asked for.

The enemy surged forward; became, for a moment,
more than just shapes. Now they were targets, and the
hail of shafts became more deadly-accurate. The Skybolts fired, and fired again, while Ancar's forces tried in
vain to get their own archers into position, and lost man
after man to the wicked little arrows. Half of the skirmishers fired Shin'a'in bows; powerful out of all proportion to their size, made of laminated wood, horn, and
sinew. The little arrows couldn't penetrate good armor,
but they could and did find the joints, the neck, the helm-
slits, all the small but numerous weak spots in a common
soldier's war-gear. The other half of the Skybolts used
heavy horse-crossbows—which *could* penetrate armor,
and often entire bodies, though the short-bowmen got off
four shots for every single crossbow bolt. The trade was
worth it, since they made a devastating combination.

Hellsbane stood as steady as a statue under her, ignoring the screams and the whirring of arrows all around
her. Ancar's forces floundered in the mud for long enough
to lose plenty of men, before the armored officers that
weren't dropped by the crossbows pulled them back into
the cover of the mist. A few moments later, Kero heard
the whistled signal farther up the line, then the whir of

arrows and the shouts and cries of pain started all over again, off beyond the wall of fog.

We probably aren't doing more than nibble away at him, she thought, trying to judge the size of the army from the sounds in the murk. *But right now I'll bet the front rank isn't a very popular place to be.*

But the sun began to break through the clouds, and the drizzle lessened. Whether Ancar had weather-working mages with him, or whether it was just the time for the weather to clear, Kero couldn't tell. *It looks natural enough,* she decided, as the sun became a visible disk through the overcast. *Well, no streak of luck runs forever.*

Ancar's officers had figured out what was happening, too; the sounds from out of the mist quieted, except for the moaning of those unfortunates wounded and left behind in the muck as their comrades retreated. Kero whistled another signal, also passed up the line—Geyr sounded his bugle again, still in character as a frightened youngster. As soon as the mist broke and the enemy could see them clearly, she expected a charge, and she wanted the Skybolts ready to move just before it came.

The sun broke through the clouds, and the fog lifted in a rush, as if frightened away by the light. That was when the Skybolts saw the true size of the force facing them.

The sun blazed down on the field, as if to make up for the fact that it had hidden all morning. Kero hadn't known what size of army to expect, and had planned for the worst, but hoped for the best. In that fleeting instant between when the enemy officers sighted them, and their trumpeters sounded a charge, Kero had time first to curse, then to be very thankful that the only troops here were hers. The veteran Skybolts would fake a panic and turn tail, just as the plan dictated. If Selenay's green forces had been faced with this sight, the panicked flight might well have been real. She couldn't imagine unseasoned fighters being able to hold against something like this.

There seemed no end to them; they filled the valley, and spilled out over the hills beyond. She couldn't imagine where Ancar had gotten so many men—and they were *all* men, all that she could see, anyway. That in itself was ominous; why *not* have female fighters, archers at least?

Bloody hell. Better get out of range, quick! She gave Hellsbane her cue, and the mare reared as if spurred, screamed and slewed around on her hindquarters, and lurched into a gallop. The rest of her fighters weren't far behind her. She bent over Hellsbane's neck and looked back over her shoulder.

As she had expected, Ancar's officers reacted to that apparent stampede by frantically signaling a charge. But they didn't know the ground, and Kero and her native guides did.

Their mounted troops were on tired beasts that had just spent the last candlemark struggling through mire. And the poor things weren't Shin'a'in-bred. They did their best, but before they'd even gotten to firm ground, the Skybolts were well out of range of even the heaviest crossbow. Once on firm ground, they still weren't a match for Shin'a'in-bred speed and stamina. The lead continued to open. She grinned, ferally. *Never reckoned on that, did you, m'lord Ancar?*

Kero halfway expected them to give up and turn back, but they didn't; that meant it was time to give them another goading. She wheeled Hellsbane at the top of the slope, and raised her hand; a heartbeat later, the rest of the Skybolts joined her on the ridge, already readying another flight of arrows, and as she brought her hand down, they rained missiles down on the cavalry struggling up the slope toward them. Horses and riders alike fell screaming in pain, and as the front rank went down, they tripped the ranks behind, bringing the charge to chaos. She hated to do it, but horses were harder to replace than fighters, so horses were fair targets.

This time she only allowed time for one crossbow volley before signaling that it was time to run again.

She thought that surely they'd turn back now—but when she looked back over her shoulder as the Skybolts pounded down the other side of the hill, she saw the first of them, silhouetted against the sky, still coming.

What in hell is driving these men? What could be so bad behind them that they'd rather face this?

She debated stopping a second time and letting off another volley, but something deep inside her told her that might not be wise. In another moment, she was very glad she'd made that decision, for riding at the head of the

BY THE SWORD   443

charge, on a strange, horned creature that was *not* a
horse, was an unarmored man dressed in brilliant scarlet.

A mage. She made a split-second decision. Need would
protect her—but she didn't know if it could still protect
the rest of her troops without Quenten there to make sure
of the extension of the spell. As always, Hellsbane was
in the lead, whether in retreat or in the charge; she waved
to her Lieutenants to go on without her, and pulled the
mare up, reining her around, and readying her own bow.

This one had better count—

She raised the bow, arrow pulled to her ear; saw the
mage raise his hands—gesture, a throwing motion—

—felt a tingle all over her body, like the pins-and-
needles of a limb waking from being benumbed—

And heard, in the back of her mind, an angry humming, as if she'd roused a hive full of enraged bees.

Need? What's the damned thing doing this time?

She was too far away to see the mage's face—he was
really at the extreme of her best range—but he raised his
hands again as she loosed her arrow, and his abrupt
movement seemed to speak of anger and puzzlement.

She never even saw the arrow in flight; neither did he,
or he might have been able to deflect it arcanely. But as
the tingle increased, so did the humming, until it seemed
to be actually in her ears. And not two lengths from him,
the arrow she had loosed suddenly incandesced, and
flared to an intolerable brightness as it hit him squarely
in the chest, burying itself right to the feathers.

He froze for a moment in mid-gesture, then slowly
toppled from his mount, which turned—of all unlikely
things—into a milch-cow. An exhausted, gaunt cow, that
wandered two or three steps, then fell over on its side,
unable to rise again.

The humming stopped, and Kero was not about to wait
around to see if her action stopped the pursuit. She turned
Hellsbane in a pivot on her two rear hooves, and continued her flight, giving the mare her head until the warsteed caught up with the rest of the troops. She didn't
look back. *If there's anything more back there, I don't
want to know about it.*

Hellsbane was no longer running easily; sweat foamed
on her neck, and Kero felt her sides heave under her legs.
Finally the laboring of their horses forced them to slow—

and this time, when they slowed to a walk and looked back, there was no one in sight. The horses drooped, gasping great gulps of air, coats sodden with sweat. She felt guilty for having had to push them so much.

And she was profoundly grateful that she wasn't going to have to push them any more. It looked as if Ancar didn't have any more mages to spare.

Gods be praised. I don't think I'll get to pull that off a second time. They weren't expecting Need—now they'll be doubly careful. And damned if I know what it was she did to my arrow. She's never done anything like that before.

Then again, we've never fought in service of a female monarch against a male enemy before, an enemy who wants the monarch's hide for a rug, and that's just for a beginning.

The Herald gave her a peculiar look when she took Hellsbane in beside him, but he didn't say anything. She wondered how much of the exchange with the mage he had seen, then decided that it really didn't matter. "I don't see any reason to alter the plan yet," she told him. "Tell Selenay to bring up her light cavalry behind us—I don't think we'll be seeing any more action today, but I didn't think they'd follow us over that first ridge, either. We need a rear guard, at least for the moment."

He nodded, and went off into his little trance, and his Companion gave her one of those blue-eyed stares that Eldan's Companion Ratha had sometimes fixed her with. She nudged the mare with her heel, and moved Hellsbane ahead of them, suddenly uneasy with the penetrating intelligence behind those eyes. She had the feeling that even if the Herald had missed the mage's attack and defeat, his Companion hadn't.

He doesn't know what to make of me, either. He's giving me one of those looks, like he had thought I was just a grunt-fighter, and now he's not so sure.

It was a most unnerving feeling, and she began to have an idea how Quenten and the others had felt, before they'd quit Valdemar and headed home.

It felt as if she was being weighed and tested against some unknown standard. And what was more, she didn't like it.

Finally she couldn't take any more of it. She dropped

Hellsbane back, and deliberately made eye contact with the Companion. His Herald was still off in the clouds somewhere, communing with his brethren, which left the field safe for what she intended to do—

Which was to drop shields, and think directly at the creature, *:Look, I don't tell you how to do your job. I'm doing what I pledged Selenay I'd do, and what's more, I'm doing a damned good piece of work so far. You keep your prejudices to yourself and stay the hell out of my way and my head so I can keep doing it!:*

The Companion started and jerked his head up, his eyes wide, as if she'd stung him with a pebble in the hindquarters. She slammed her shields shut again, and sent Hellsbane into a tired canter that took her to the front of the troop.

And when next she looked back, the Companion met her gaze with a wary respect—and nothing more.

She couldn't help herself; she wore a smug little smile all the way back to the camp. *"Don't make judgment calls; you might find yourself on the other end of one."* That's another one of Tarma's sayings. And right now, I'm as guilty of it as that Companion is.

But damn if that didn't feel good.

Camp was a cold camp; no fires, and trail rations. Tents stayed packed up; until they figured out the pattern Ancar's troops had, Kero wasn't going to give him any vulnerable points to hit—like a camp. Even with experienced fighters like hers, "camp" meant "safe" in the back of their minds, and right now she didn't want anyone thinking "safe."

They'd bivouacked in a grove of hezelnut bushes, tucking bedrolls out of sight under the bushes themselves, helping out nature's own camouflage with artfully placed branches. From a distance, no one would ever guess there was an entire Company of fighters and their horses in here; it looked like any deserted orchard. What with the three rings of perimeter guards, no one would get close enough to find out any differently.

And that tentlessness included Kero. It was good for morale—and it made her less of a target. She *did* have one of the better bushes, a clump of them, actually, with thick, drooping branches, but room on the inside for three or four; and she had it alone—but there were a few advantages to being Captain.

The Herald vanished after they'd tucked themselves up, established perimeters and set watches, and sent the specialists off to make Ancar's life interesting. She settled down on her bedroll with a piece of jerky in one hand and a tiny, shielded dark-lantern focused on the detailed map spread over her knees. At some point during her study her orderly brought her a battered tin cup full of water, and said—rather too calmly—that the Herald who'd been with her this morning was being replaced.

She looked up, sharply, and saw the corners of his mouth twitching. "Ah," she said, and left it at that.

Made himself unwelcome, did he? Maybe I did a little judging, but it sounds like he did a lot more.

She fell asleep with a clear conscience, and a resolve not to let the replacement get on her officers' nerves as the first Herald had.

In the morning, as soon as she'd gotten the reports from her scouts, she gathered her officers together inside the heart of the grove, to lay out her next plan of action. While she gave each Lieutenant his orders, she caught sight of something white moving up, just out of the corner of her eye.

So our first liaison couldn't handle the job. A little late, my friend, she thought to herself, *and I hope you're a bit more flexible than your predecessor.* But she otherwise ignored him until she'd finished briefing her officers. Only then did she turn to see who—or what—Selenay had sent to her this time.

And felt as if someone had just poleaxed her.

"Oh," she said, faintly.

"I'm—uh—the replacement," Eldan said with hesitation, playing with the ends of his Companion's reins. "Selenay thought you'd be less likely to frighten us off. At least, on purpose."

"I wouldn't count on that if I were her," Kero replied, around a funny feeling in her chest, still staring at him. He looked wonderful; he hadn't aged to speak of, her dream Eldan become substantial. "You've never ridden with my troops. We're a nasty lot, and what we meet up with tends to be just as vicious as we are."

"That wasn't what she meant." Eldan dropped his eyes

before she did, which gave her a chance to give him a quick once-over before he looked up again. He hadn't changed much, either; maybe the white streaks in his hair were a little wider, and there were a couple of smile-lines around his mouth and eyes, but otherwise he was the same. She wondered how she looked to him. "It doesn't have to be me. If you don't want—I mean—"

"I *don't,*" she interrupted him fiercely, fairly sure what he was going to say, and not wanting to hear it. "I can't afford a liability, not here, not now. I can't permit you to distract me from my people. If you can do your job and leave it at that, *fine.* Otherwise, find me someone else. And make sure it's someone with guts and a sense of humor this time. We're perilous short of both."

"I'd noticed," Eldan muttered with a flash of resentment and irritation, not quite under his breath.

"You—you *what?*" She stared at him for a moment, torn between wanting to laugh, and wanting to rip his face off for that.

Laughter won.

She leaned up against Hellsbane's saddle, then shook with silent laughter, until her knees were weak and tears ran down her face. Eldan just stood there, looking a little puzzled, but otherwise keeping his mouth shut.

"Oh, gods," she said, or rather, gasped. "Oh, dear *gods.* I had that coming." She pushed away from the mare, and wiped her eyes with the back of her hand.

"You certainly did," Eldan said agreeably. Then he widened his eyes, and his tone grew wheedling. "Come on, Kero, you need me along just to keep you humble."

"I do *not,*" she retorted, stung. "And I don't need you pulling any 'mama, may I' acts on me. But as long as you're here, you might as well tag along anyway." She was tempted to jump into the saddle without using the stirrups—

But that's a youngster's show-off trick. Besides, it wouldn't impress him.

:I wouldn't leap into the saddle like a young hero if I were you,: said the familiar voice in her head. *:I'd have to match you, and I'm too old and tired for that.:*

:Sure you are.: She'd answered him the same way without realizing it until she'd done so. For the first time in her life, Mindspeech felt as natural as audible speech.

Even with Warrl it had been an effort, and seemed *wrong,* like trying to walk on her hands and eat with her feet.

She should have been alarmed by that; she should have been unhappy to be reminded that she had the Gift. The youngster training with Tarma would have been ready to gut him. The Kero of ten years ago would have ordered him out of her Company. But now—all that fuss seemed pretty stupid, and awfully paranoid. It was an ability, like her perfect pitch—and a lot more useful. Now talking by Mindspeech felt as if she'd been doing it for years. *:Besides, it's about time you found out what military discipline is like. It'll do you good. And while we're in the field, it's* Captain. *Not Kero, not Captain Kero.* Captain. *Got that?:*

He nodded, swinging up into his Companion's saddle. *:Sorry, Captain. And I think I understand. This is a military command, and you need a different kind of attitude from everybody connected with your troops, right? Otherwise discipline breaks down. Heralds do things differently; we encourage familiarity, but we almost never get it.:*

:Heralds don't have to command a few hundred hot-blooded, hard-headed fighters, each of whom is at some time or other convinced he could Captain the Company better than you.: She sent Hellsbane out through the bushes to the field on the other side where the Skybolts were mustering. Eldan kept right at her side, as if they'd been doing this together for years.

:You haven't had that particular problem for the past six fighting seasons,: he retorted, *:Your people follow you the way no other Captain could command. Right now your only problem is that they are so confident in you that you're afraid they* won't *come to you when they think there's something wrong with your strategy. So don't start feeling sorry for yourself.:*

Since that was exactly what she'd been confiding in the dream-Eldan in the last dream she'd had about him, she was understandably startled.

She reined Hellsbane in so fast that the horse reared a little, snorting, as she whipped around in the saddle to face him. *"How did you know that?"* she blurted, flushing and chilling in turn. "I haven't said anything to anyone about that—"

:Except in dreams.: He had gone a little pale, himself. *:But they weren't dreams, were they?:*

Hellsbane reacted to her unconscious signals, and backed up, one slow step at a time. "I thought they were," she said, and her voice shook. "I thought you were. I thought I was going crazy. I thought it didn't matter. If I hadn't, I'd never have said—done—half of what I did—"

"Why not?" he demanded, his Companion Ratha matching Hellsbane's every step. The mare flattened her ears and snapped; the Companion ignored her. "Weren't we friends, at least? *I* thought we were. Oh, I admit it, that was a dirty trick I played on you with the ransom, but I had no idea how desperate your situation was, I thought your Company and Captain were pretty much intact. If I'd known, I'd have had Selenay send you double, with no strings attached, and not because I felt sorry for you, no, but because we were—*are*—friends, and friends help each other. But after that—the dreams—I thought I'd made amends. I needed to talk with you, needed to be with you. I couldn't let you just walk out of my life like that. Kero—I—I love you. I'll take any thing I can get with you."

She forced herself to think rationally—after all, this wasn't much different from the way he was Mindspeaking her now—and slowly relaxed. "I got you back with the ransom," she reminded him, as she loosed her hands on the reins, and Hellsbane stopped backing.

He grinned at that, and nodded. *:You certainly did, and cleverly, too. And I wish you'd been there to see the old goat they sent as the Guild proxy. He just gave me one look, and made me feel like a small boy who's been caught trying to look up little girls' dresses.:*

She chuckled at the image he sent her; it was a Guild representative she barely recognized, but knew by reputation, which was formidable.

:But that's not the point,: he continued. *:The reason I kept coming to you is that I'm your friend before I'm anything else, Kero. Friends help each other; friends bring their troubles to each other, especially if they can't take them anywhere else. And I confided a good share in you, didn't I?:*

She nodded reluctantly, once he'd called up the memory. "Did you really want to strangle that idiot that much?"

"Yes," Eldan replied. "He made me angry, then made me look like a fool in front of a lot of people because I acted out of anger before I thought. I wanted to strangle him. You managed to persuade me that the best way to deal with him was to ignore him. But you know—I *still* want to strangle him."

She laughed, silently, and shook her head. All she'd done with him was talk mind-to-mind—which was probably why she was no longer so awkward at it—and take and give advice. The same kind she'd have taken and given if they'd been talking face-to-face. That wasn't so bad. . . .

In fact, she'd enjoyed it.

I probably should be angry at him, but I can't be. "Are you sure you're up to this job?" she asked, after a long pause. "You don't have to be my liaison. I'm not the easiest person in the world to get along with. And I wasn't joking about calling me 'Captain,' at least in public."

:I have my share of warts. I'll call you anything you want. And you could *do without me, you know. You're just as good at Mindspeech as I am.:*

"Not a chance," she snorted. "Come on, tagalong. I've got a war to run."

Then, shyly—

:I love you, too. But you knew that, didn't you. I told you before. In dreams.:

:You did,: he replied promptly. *:I can't promise it won't color things. But I can and do promise if it starts causing problems for either of us, I'll get Selenay to assign you someone else. She—she knows about us. This was her idea.:*

That put a whole new complexion on things.

:I'm a Captain first, and a lover second. But—there just might be room for the lover, now.:

:Only if it doesn't interfere.: He was adamant.

So was she. *:Only if it doesn't interfere. So far it hasn't. Let's ride this out.:*

He smiled. *:Captain, you've got yourself a bargain. And a recruit.:*

* * *

Today the plan called for her Company and Selenay's cavalry to combine, and give Ancar just enough of a taste of combat to make him think that they really were trying to keep him out of Valdemar. Then they were to pretend panic, and run for the next set of Guards, posted farther north.

The trouble was, that little taste turned into a rather large and painful bite.

They spent most of the day leading the enemy overland, keeping just out of range, exhausting his horses while they changed off on their remounts at noon, and had fresh beasts to his tired ones. Then, just before sunset, they pretended to make a stand, teased Ancar's men into a charge, and retreated, under covering fire.

The spot for their stand had been carefully chosen; a rocky hillside with plenty of cover, and too many boulders for Ancar's cavalry to charge. Kero watched with a critical eye, carefully gauging the weariness of Ancar's fighters. She let three successive waves approach her position, and be driven back—waiting for Ancar's officers to call in the tired men for the night.

Instead, they kept coming; a fourth wave, and as the sun set, a fifth.

And under torchlight, a sixth.

They were running out of ammunition, energy—and still the enemy kept coming, though he left his dead and wounded in heaps at the foot of their stony shelter.

After the eighth wave had retreated, Kero put down her bow and sagged against her boulder with exhaustion. Her arms were like a pair of lead bars; her legs shook with weariness. And she was in relatively good shape. Selenay's people, far more inclined than hers to risk themselves for a good shot, had managed to populate the rude shelter the Healers had assembled with their wounded. Not too many Skybolts wore bandages yet, but if this kept up. . . .

She watched the torches bobbing and dancing out beyond firing range and longed fiercely for her mages. It looked—dear gods!—like they were massing for attack-wave number nine.

"I don't believe this," she muttered, staring at Ancar's lines.

"I don't either," said Shallan from the other side of

the boulder, in a voice fogged with fatigue. "They're not human."

"Or they're *driven* by something that isn't human," Eldan said grimly. "The bastard has some kind of hold over them. They'd rather face our arrows than what he's got over there."

Kero turned around and looked over her shoulder. "Is that a guess, or information?"

Eldan looked like the rest of them; his white uniform was smudged and filthy, there was dirt in his hair, and sweat-streaked dust on his face. "A guess," he said, staring past her at the enemy. "I'm not an Empath, like Talia. And they have some kind of shield over them that prevents me from reading their thoughts. But I think it's a pretty good guess."

"Seeing as they had one mage with them that was willing to charge right in after us, you're probably right," Kero said, turning back to look at the enemy herself.

"If they have mages, why haven't they used magic on us?" Eldan wondered aloud. Kero gave him a sharp look out of the corner of her eye, but it didn't look as if he was being sarcastic *or* asking a pointed question; merely as if he really was puzzled.

She shrugged. "Maybe because we're inside Valdemar," she said. "Maybe he only had the one mage. Maybe because he's saving the mages for when he has a target worth their while." She watched the milling of the enemy troops for a moment more, then made her decision.

"Tell Selenay and the rest that I've just changed the plan," she told Eldan. "Get the foot troops out first, then Selenay's horse, then we'll play rearguard. We've got the advantage of knowing this country in the dark; they don't. I don't think *they* plan on stopping until every last one of us is dead, and I think we'd better get our rumps out of here while we have the cover of darkness."

"Yes, Captain," Eldan said—he didn't wander off in a trance when he MindSpoke with someone like his fellow Herald had, he simply frowned a little, as if he was concentrating. "Selenay and the Lord Marshal agree," he said after a moment. "The foot is already moving out."

"Fine," She turned to Shallan. "Pass the order. The retreat is for real."

And dear gods of my childhood, help us. Because we're in dire need of it.

Twenty-three

It was a retreat, not a rout—but only because no one panicked. That retreat didn't end with morning, either.

When dawn broke, Kero sent scouts back, more because she believed in being too cautious than because she really expected anything.

She knew there was trouble when they returned too quickly.

The first one in saluted her, his face gray with exhaustion. "They're right behind us, Captain," he croaked, as she handed him her own water skin. He gulped down a mouthful and poured the rest on his head. "I swear by Apponel, there's no way they can be behind us, and they are anyway. Some of 'em are dropping like whipped dogs, but the rest are still on their feet and it don't look like they plan on giving up any time soon."

She swore and gathered the officers; hers, and Selenay's and together they goaded their weary troopers into another push.

That set the pattern for succeeding days—and sometimes nights—as they retreated farther north, and deeper into Valdemar itself. Every step westward galled Kero like spurs in her side. Never before had she hated to give up land so much. Always before it had been a matter of indifference; what mattered was the final outcome, not whether a few farmers were overrun and burned out. But this time was different. The farmers pressed everything Selenay's forces needed on them as they passed, then abandoned their farms with unshed tears making their eyes bright. She knew these farmers as people, however briefly they'd met, and it made her seethe with rage to see smoke rising in their rear and know what Ancar's troops were doing to the abandoned properties.

Every time she took provisioning from another farmer,

and watched him drive off into the west with family and whatever he could transport piled up onto pitiful little wagons with his stock herded behind him, the rage grew.

It's so damned unfair, she told herself, *And I know that life's unfair, but these people never did anything to earn losses like these.* She'd never felt quite so powerless to help, before.

And she had never hated any foe other than the Karsites with the fierce hatred she developed for Ancar.

The fool drove his men as if they were mindless machines. She couldn't imagine why they weren't deserting in droves—unless the mages were somehow controlling them, either directly or through fear. That might explain why the mages hadn't attacked Selenay's army—they were too busy keeping Ancar's own troops in line. She was a good leader—and she couldn't hate men who were being forced the way these were. But she certainly could hate the kind of man who forced them.

Or the kind of man who tortured for the sheer pleasure of it. Eldan told her what he'd done to Talia—and she'd felt Need waking during the tale, with that deep, gut-fire rage that was so hard to control. But Ancar wasn't within reach, so the blade subsided; though for once, Kero agreed with it.

But most important of all, one of the other officers in Selenay's army who had once lived in Hardorn told her what he had done to his father and his people, and why they had left. Kero had encountered tyrants before, but never one who so abused his powers as this one. The way he drove his men was a fair example of the way he treated his people as a whole. Worse than cattle, for a good farmer sees his cattle cared for.

She finally called her Company together one night when they dared have a fire, and told them everything she'd learned, figuring that they should know what would happen to them if they ever fell into Ancar's hands.

They listened, quietly. Then Shallan made a single, flat statement for all of them. "He's an oathbreaker," she said, her mouth set in a grim line. "And he's just lucky we haven't a mage with us, or I'd set the full Outcasting on him."

Kero looked from one fire-gilded face to another, and saw no sign of disagreement. Several, in fact, were nodding. The Guild was full of people with disparate and sometimes mutually antagonistic beliefs. The one thing every mercenary in the Guild commonly held sacred was an oath. They reserved terrible punishment for an oath-breaker in their own ranks. For rulers and priests there was another form of retribution—the Outcasting. Kings were bound by oaths to protect their lands and men, usually from the time they were old enough to swear to the pledges, and Ancar had broken his oaths—as surely, and as dreadfully, as had the late, unmourned, King Raschar of Rethwellan, the monarch Tarma and Kethry had helped to unseat. Kero learned that night that she was not alone in her hatred of Ancar—as her troops had heard more tales from the Hardorn refugees, one and all, they came to share her cold rage.

It gave them an extra edge they'd never had before. But rage was not enough, not when confronted with the desperate strength of Ancar's men.

They were worn thin by running alone, and when you added the steady losses, manpower that wasn't being replaced, you had another kind of drain on them.

Of course, Ancar was losing an equal number of men in those encounters, but Ancar could afford to lose them. Selenay's army couldn't.

Kero tried an ambush at one point, splitting her forces on either side of a river hoping to catch him with a good part of his men still in the water. But she'd discovered, only through the vigilance of the scouts, that he had outflanked *her.*

He brought his foot in to surround the ambush-party on his bank and only years of experience had enabled her to get them out again. Those years of experience had taught her to always have an escape route—in this case, an unlikely one, the river itself. Profiting from her escape by water, she'd engineered a more controlled version of the same, by making sure the ambushers were all strong and experienced swimmers, with horses capable of pulling the trick off.

Even so, the escape had been a narrow one, and their luck ran down from there.

Every day meant a succession of tricks and guerrilla tactics, just to keep Ancar from closing with the entire force and finishing the job. With the Heralds acting as links between them, they split their forces by day, pecking away at the edges of the massive army, and rejoined by night. The individual groups, some as small as Kero's original scout group, could dart in and out to whittle away at Ancar's more cumbersome foot—but to offset that mobility, they were a great deal more vulnerable. Quite a few of those little groups vanished, Herald and all, when Ancar's troops could surround or entrap them.

Every loss meant far more to them than a comparable loss meant to Ancar—if, in fact, the losses meant anything to him at all, other than the drop in manpower.

"I can't believe this," she muttered to Eldan, as she shaded her eyes and stared at Ancar's army, a dark carpet of them covering the fields below her vantage point, trampling the fields of new grain into mud. They should have been ready to drop; they'd been marching at a steady pace all day, and any sane commander would have them making camp now. Yet here they were, pressing on though sunset painted the sky a bloody red. "I thought I'd planned for everything, including the very worst possible case, but these people aren't human. No one can follow the pace we've set—"

"You did," Eldan pointed out. "You set it."

She glared sideways at him; she had a headache from wearing her helmet all day, and she was in no mood for quibbling. "Semantics. We're on home ground; we have the advantage of local support and supply, and we know the territory. He doesn't have any of that. He shouldn't be able to keep up with us, much less attack every chance he gets. But he's doing it, and I'll be damned if I know how."

"Because he's willing to sacrifice everything to get you—or rather, Selenay," Eldan said flatly. "Everything is expendable if he gets her. He's perfectly willing to burn out every man he has to achieve that single goal."

She shook her head, and pounded her fist on the tree trunk beside her in anger and frustration, gashing the bark with her armored gauntlet. "That's insane. I can't predict what a madman is going to do next! How can I plan against someone like that?"

Eldan sighed. "I don't know, Captain. Strategy was never anything I was good at." Then he smiled weakly.

"But you'll think of something, I'm sure. We all believe in you."

That was cold comfort. *They believe in me. Just what I needed to hear.*

Especially when she was exercising all of her ingenuity just to keep them alive a little bit longer. They'd lost track of Daren a while back, and not even the FarSeers could find him. In fact, other than the Mindspeakers, the Heralds' powers had been frustrated or limited by Ancar's mages. There was some kind of shield over the army that the FarSeers couldn't break through, and the ForeSeers reported only "too many possibilities."

There were only three possibilities that made any difference to Kero; that Daren was still on schedule, that Daren had been turned back by more of Ancar's forces, or that Daren had run afoul of those same forces and was late. No other "possibilities" mattered.

And right now, anyway, all that really mattered was staying alive.

The question haunted her as the Skybolts stopped to salt a ford with flint shards after everyone else had passed it. The little fragments were heavy enough to stay where they were without washing downstream, small and sharp enough to lodge in hooves and slash boots and feet to ribbons. " 'Be careful what you ask for,' " she quoted to herself. " 'You might get it.' I wanted Ancar to follow us. Now I can't shake him off our trail." When she'd consulted the Lord Marshal through the agency of Eldan and the Lord Marshal's Herald, he hadn't had any suggestions either. *I feel like I'm letting them down,* she thought grimly, as the last of the flint-strewers returned to the saddle, and the Company moved out again. *They think I'm going to pull something brilliant out of my sleeve and save everyone. Not even Ardana got herself into a situation like this one.*

And while he lasted, Lerryn was so lucky he'd fall into a cesspit and come up with a handful of gold.

She looked back over her shoulder, checking for strays, although technically Shallan and Geyr were supposed to be in charge of that. It didn't look as if any of her people had dropped out of the march—though if they hadn't been mounting Shin'a'in-breds, they would have been by now. Even the Companions were beginning to look tired. *So*

*far the only luck we've had was that Ancar hasn't used
a mage since I took out the first one.*

She pushed her helm up and rubbed a spot on her forehead where it pressed uncomfortably. *That might not have
been luck, though; it might have been that Need was shel-
tering the whole army, and it might also have been that
the mages Ancar has left are required to keep his own
people disciplined.* She wished she knew which it was;
or even if it was a combination.

The Skybolts caught up with the rearguard of Selenay's
troops, and became the rearguard themselves. Shallan and
Geyr sent back outriders, while the rest spread themselves along the rear, resting their horses by staying at
the pace set by the foot in front of them. Kero hoped the
outriders would bring back word that Ancar had camped
soon. Those poor souls ahead of her looked as though
they were on their last gasp of energy.

*All that work to get the entire army together, and we're
too small to do anything but run. He must outnumber us
ten to one, and that's after losses. About the only advantage we have is the Heralds. We're too large and without
the proper training to use as a specialist force, and too
small to actually take a stand against him.*

It was maddening, and soon enough they'd run up
against the Iftel border, which would leave them with
nowhere to go except into Valdemar. Was Daren back
there behind them? If not—and she had to plan for the
worst—if they retreated, would Selenay be able to raise
enough of the common people to make a difference
against trained fighters? It *could* be done, what had happened to the Skybolts in Seejay was proof enough of
that—but it was expensive in terms of casualties, the people had to be committed to it wholeheartedly.

*If only we could get him to divide his army up some-
how, and arrange things so that we could deal with each
segment alone.*

A foot soldier in front of her stumbled and fell, saw
Hellsbane practically on top of him, and blanched,
scrambling onto his feet and back to his place in the
wavering lines. The mare's behavior in battle had earned
her the reputation of a mankilling horse, and no one but
the Skybolts wanted to be within range of those teeth and
hooves.

What have we got ahead of us? I wonder if there's some way I can force him to commit too many of his people on too many fronts? Can we use the terrain somehow?

No, that was a stupid idea. The only thing they had ahead of them was farmland and rolling hills.

She pulled off her helm and hung it on the saddlebow, and wiped the sweat out of them. It didn't help. She'd never been so tired, not even when running from Karsite priestesses and Karsite demons.

If only my riders weren't forced to stay with the foot. . . .

Then again, maybe they weren't.

If we take the Skybolts and the cavalry and circle around behind them, I wonder if we could make them think we were reinforcements . . . make them think we were Daren's lot.

The she gave herself a mental kick for idiocy. *How in hell can I think that? It would leave them without support. And even if he fell for it, that would get him going in the wrong direction. That won't work. We don't want him going south, and we certainly don't want him going west.*

Every new idea seemed to have less chance of succeeding than the last. And none of them were going to work if they didn't get a chance to rest!

I feel like a hunted stag, she thought—then froze as she realized that she wasn't far wrong with that image.

She made a quick mental review of everything Ancar had done since that first encounter, and realized with a sinking heart that they had been doing exactly what he wanted them to do. Run. Run themselves into exhaustion. . . .

"What's wrong?" Eldan had ridden up beside her without her even noticing his arrival.

"I just realized we made a monumental mistake," she replied slowly, as her spine chilled. "We all thought we were leading him. We haven't been. He's been herding *us*, like stags being herded by beaters." She looked around for one of the scout Lieutenants, and spotted Shallan's blonde cap of hair. "Shallan!" she called sharply; the scout-leader looked back, and reined her horse around, sending him loping wearily toward them.

"I want you to send out scouts west and east," she said as soon as Shallan was within easy speaking distance. "Send them out about a half a day's ride, on their freshest horses. Have them take Heralds; if what I think is out there really is, I want to know immediately."

Shallan looked thoughtful for a moment—then blanched. "We've been bracketed?" she asked, as her horse stood listlessly, saving his energy.

Kero nodded, and looked back over her shoulder, feeling as if she half-expected the enemy to come into view. "I think so. I couldn't figure out where his cavalry was, and I'd just about decided he didn't have any. But if I had his resources, why would I field only foot fighters with less than a Company of cavalry? Now I think I know where he sent them—to bracket us in either the east or the west. I'd bet east, but I want you to check inside Valdemar just to be sure. In all the confusion caused by evacuation he could have slipped someone in."

"Astera help us, if you're right," Eldan said grimly as Shallan rode off to pick her scouts and send them on their way. He, too, looked back over his shoulder, with a grimace. "He'll have us where we planned to have him—pinned between him and the Iftel Border."

"I know," she replied, watching as two small groups of Skybolts broke off from the main body and rode off east and west. "Believe me, I know. I'd give my arm to know where Daren is right now—and my leg to have him close enough to help."

We must be halfway to Iftel by now. Gods, I don't know how much more of this dying territory there is— Daren flexed cramped fingers, wiping the nervous sweat from his face with his sleeve, and stared up at the sun. He reined his gelding in a little to drop back beside one of the few unarmored riders in the group. "How far past the Valdemar Border would you say we are?" he asked young Quenten, who frowned a little, and unfocused his eyes. "Last thing I want is for Ancar's toadies to scent us."

"Far enough," the mage replied after a moment. "We're out of range of whatever it is in Valdemar, and Ancar's mages are too busy keeping the troops under control to try looking for us. That's devilish clever of him, keeping his mages just this side of the Border; I don't know what that guardian is, m'lord, but it's cursed literal-minded. Your magic can cross the Border all you like, so long as you *don't*. And I 'spect that if you didn't ever do anything magical, once you *were* inside, it'd leave you alone.''

"I suspect you're right," Daren replied. *Quenten's a good lad. Wish I knew how Kero managed to recruit him.* "And I'm damned glad you went looking for us on your way back to your winter quarters. If we'd followed along the short route, we'd have lost *our* mages, too.''

"I didn't want to leave them in the first place, m'lord," Quenten said absently. "Let the gods witness it, I'd have stayed if I could! It only seemed right to track you down and warn you, and maybe come with you if you figured a way around the magic problem.'' His gentle little mare glided along beside Daren's tall hunter, the only horse he'd ever seen besides his own that could trot without jolting her rider. Daren kept silent, wrestling with the problem of how to make up the days lost in crossing over to Hardorn, sneaking through the passes and hoping the Karsites would choose to ignore this little invasion of their borders.

He'd had double his usual complement of mages to cloak their movements, but who knew what the Karsite priests could and could not do.

Perhaps they had their own troubles to occupy them. Since the defeat of the Prophet there had been no more trouble from Karse; only rumors that the Temple was engaging in a war of intrigue within itself, and more rumors that the Chief Priest of the Sunlord was being challenged for his place by a woman.

That was heresy enough, but further rumor had it that this woman affected the robes and false beard of a man, and styled herself the "True-born *Son* of the Sun.''

If even half those rumors were true, small wonder Karse paid no attention to the army of her old enemy, when it was plainly going elsewhere.

But once across the border into Hardorn, Daren had been tempted to turn right around and take his chances with Valdemar and this mysterious "guardian" that drove mages mad. For from the border to a distance of three leagues within Hardorn, the land was blighted and empty.

Bad enough that entire villages lay empty and abandoned; worse came when his men poked cautiously through the tumbled-down buildings.

The places had been looted, then demolished. But in the wreckage, Daren's men found the remains of women and children—and *only* women and children, and only those younger than three, and (presumably) older than thirty.

Daren had thought at first that it might have been the work of bandits—but then they had encountered another village, smaller than the first, that had fared the same. Then another, and another.

After the fourth such discovery, Daren forbade his men to even go near the places. They had no priest with them, but the mages, Quenten in particular, had felt an odd uneasiness there, and the Healers had refused, in a hysterical body, to set foot inside the perimeters.

And the land itself looked drained and ill. The rank weeds that had taken over the fields were pale, with thin, weak stems. The leaves of the trees were discolored. The only birds to be seen were an occasional crow, and so far Daren hadn't spotted so much as a rabbit moving. It had been getting worse since the first village, and now the countryside looked to his eyes like a beautiful woman lying ravaged by plague. He couldn't imagine how his men could bear it—many of them were of farm stock, and intended to retire to little pension-farms of their own, and to see good land like this must be making them ill.

"What do you think happened here?" he asked Quenten, as they crossed a muddy, rust-colored stream. "Is it safe to be riding on this land, do you think?"

"It's safe enough, m'lord," Quenten said, but only after the mage gave him a peculiar look. "Why do you ask?"

Daren looked around at the withered limbs of the trees, at the yellow grass, at the diseased cankers spotting the leaves, and shuddered. "Because the place looks poisoned, that's why. What happened at the villages was easy enough to read—that bastard conscripted the men, took the useful women and little ones and slaughtered the rest as an example—but I don't understand this . . . and I don't see how the men can accept it as easily as they do."

Quenten shook his head in wonder. "M'lord, they don't see what you see. To them it looks perfectly ordinary, except that there's not much in the way of birds and beasts." He looked pointedly about them, at the men marching calmly up the road in front of them, and tilted his shaggy, dust-dulled head to one side, as if waiting for a response.

Daren cast a sharp glance at him, but the young mage's expression was entirely sober. "A glamour? An illusion?"

Again the mage shook his head, but this time he stared into Daren's face searchingly before replying. "I don't think so, m'lord. Is there mage-blood in your family?"

"Some, not much," he said after a moment of thought. "Of course Grandmother's family's been sprouting Healers every so often, and Mother's line was supposed to be some kind of earth-priestess—"

"Ah," Quenten said in satisfaction. "That would be it; you have the earth-sense. Many folk with the blood of the old earth-priestesses in them have it. What you're seeing is the land revealed to you by the earth-sense, you see what lies *under* the surface everyone else sees with his outer eyes. This land *is* sick; there's been blood-magic practiced here, too much of it for the land to absorb without harm. That was the real horror back at those villages; it wasn't just the slaughter itself—it's that it was done to invoke the powers of blood-magic and death-magic."

Daren remembered all the rumors he'd heard about Ancar, and suddenly they began making sense. "Blood-magic to control the minds of the ones he took?" he asked shrewdly, "Blood-magic to create a reservoir of power he can feed off?" And Quenten's eyes widened. "Blood-magic so that the land keeps *him* healthy and young, at its own expense?"

"There's not one highborn in ten that would know that," the mage whispered. "Keep it to yourself, m'lord. There's some that would say that *knowing* is a short step away from *wanting*. I don't hold by that, but even the mage-schools have their fanatics." He resumed his normal tone. "Probably, m'lord, and it's more than the land can bear. That's why it looks sick to you. Trust your earth-sense, m'lord. If you learn to use it, it'll tell you more than just this."

It was Daren's turn to shake his head. The land cried out to him in a way—and he couldn't help it, any more than he could bring back those poor slaughtered innocents. He wanted to beg its pardon for not healing it—to beg theirs for not being there. It was foolish—but it was very real. He understood the Heralds of Valdemar far better than his brother did. He understood how it was to care for *people,* even if those people were not bound to you, personally, in any way. Faram would die for *his* people—but not those of Valdemar. He would feel badly about the slaughters here, but he would not *feel* them personally, the way Daren did.

And he also understood duty and pledges. "Right now all I care about is whether this land is safe to travel through—which you say it is—and whether or not Ancar has any mages likely to detect us here."

"We're working to prevent that, m'lord," Quenten replied dryly. "And—" he looked up, sharply.

"What is it?" Daren said, reining in his horse as Quenten's mount stopped dead.

The mage raised one hand to his forehead, his eyes focusing elsewhere. He looked for all the world as if he was listening to something. "Quenten?" Daren persisted. "Quenten?"

The mage's eyes refocused on *him.* "Ancar has a reserve force just ahead," he said vaguely. "Several mages, and three companies of cavalry. And—Daren, m'lord, they're mostly from here, this barren zone."

"Controlled, then. There's no other way he could make farmers into cavalry that quickly" He caught the attention of his officers, who halted the march. "Quenten, how far ahead is 'just ahead'?"

"Half a day's march, maybe less. Not much less." Quenten didn't seem to notice Daren' sigh of relief.

"What are they doing there?" he persisted. "We haven't seen a sign of Ancar's army. What are *reserves* doing out here?"

"I don't—they're—I need my bowl." Without warning, the mage scrambled off his mare's back to dig into her packs. He emerged with a completely black bowl, shiny, made of black glass, or something very like it. He poured water from his own water skin into the bottom of it, sat right down in the dust of the road, and stared into it.

Daren had been around enough mages to know when to keep his mouth shut. He waited, patiently, in sunlight too thin to even warm him. The army waited, just as patiently, glad for a chance to sit by the roadside and rest. Daren watched his men sprawling ungracefully against their packs, and wished he hadn't had to push them so hard. They'd had a lot of time to make up, once they'd gotten down out of the hills. He had been weary at the end of the day, and *he* was riding. He hated to think what the foot soldiers felt like.

"They're waiting," Quenten said, in a thin, disinterested voice, an eerie echo of his own thoughts "They are half of the claw that will capture Selenay and crush Valdemar."

"What?" Daren snapped, startled.

Quenten looked up, blinking, then picked up the bowl and spilled the water out in the dust. "Ancar has these reserves out here, pacing him, waiting for when he has Selenay's forces worn down enough to trap," the mage said in a more normal tone of voice. "Then he'll have this lot sweep in from the side and above while he cuts his main force in from below."

"I don't think so," Daren replied, in a kind of grim satisfaction at finally having something to fight.

"Well, that's not all, m'lord," Quenten added as he got up, shook the dust from his robes and stowed his bowl carefully away. "It's *who* these reserves are—or rather, where they're from. Like I said, before, here. Tied into obedience by the blood of their own kin. Now, *you* have the earth-sense; you could tell me which mage is controlling them, because the earth hereabouts would tell you. It hates him, and it's bound to him, and you'll see him as it sees him."

"And what will happen when you break him?" Daren asked, leaning forward in his saddle and clutching the pommel with one hand. "How do I do see these things, anyway? What do you need to teach me, and have we the time to spare?"

Quenten paused to remount, and turned to look back at Daren only when firmly in his seat. "You have the earth-sense," Quenten repeated. "It's a matter of instinct rather than learning. Break the controlling mage and you not only free the victims—but it's altogether possible the earth hereabouts would rise up in revolt. And it would listen to you, follow some of your directions, if you made them simple enough.''

''It would?''

Quenten nodded. Daren thought about those heaps of pitiful bones and rags—looked around him at the dying land. And thought of Kero and Selenay's army, and pledges. And just maybe a god somewhere had just gifted him with the chance to satisfy all of them.

''Quenten, you're in charge of the magic-folk; get your mages. Find out everything you can, and keep us cloaked.'' Daren turned his horse and rode off in search of the scouts before he had a chance to hear Quenten's eager assent.

All right, Ancar, you bastard, he couldn't help thinking, with a kind of fierce exultation. *I am about to visit a little retribution on you and yours.*

Ancar's reserves were pathetically unaware of any danger—but after all, they were deep inside their own territory, and had no reason to suspect any threat. Daren himself went out with the scouts to the river-valley where they camped to get a good look at enemy, and at the way they were conducting themselves.

What he saw fit in very well with Quenten's theory of mind-control. Only about a quarter of the men down there were moving about or acting in any kind of a normal fashion. The rest might as well have been puppets; in fact, watching them was rather disturbing. They moved listlessly, when they moved at all, and none of them were idle—yet they wasted no time on their chores, picking up one task, carrying it to the end, picking up another. And all without exchanging a single word with anyone, or taking a single step out of the way. Nothing was cooked, except at the camps of the officers; a small group of men handed out the tasteless ration-bread Rethwellan no longer used because of complaints from the men. These fighters took the bread, ate it methodically, and went back to their chores.

By nightfall, the camp was utterly quiet. No socializing around campfires, no idle games of chance—nothing.

The men simply rolled up in their blankets, and went to sleep; except for the officers and mages, who had tents, and were presumably doing things inside them.

It was an entirely unnerving sight to someone who knew what a camp *should* look and sound like, because of the complete unnaturalness of it—although Daren had to admit to himself that there were times when he'd wished his men would—

He stopped the thought before he could complete it, chillingly aware of how close he'd come to thinking that he'd wanted his men to be like this. Was that what those mages meant, when they said it was a short step from *knowing* to *wanting*?

Horrible thought. . . .

He closed his eyes on the too-quiet camp below him for a moment, then opened them. *No,* he deliberately decided. *I've never wanted that. It's worse than slavery; at least a slave has his own thoughts. These poor creatures don't even have that much. It's as bad to destroy or enslave a mind as it is to kill a body. Maybe worse, if the mind is aware of what has happened to it.*

The scout tugged at his sleeve, and he crawled away with the rest of them, avoiding the slack-jawed perimeter guard. They made it back to the rest of his troops without further incident, and he and his officers spent the hours until midnight charting the next day's course.

Dawn of the next day saw the Rethwellan troops poised just above the camp. It had been impossible to keep the movement of so large a group secret, but by splitting his troops in two and cutting off Ancar's fighters from their easy escape by river, Daren had forced Ancar's reserves to meet him instead of running to join the larger force, or escaping into the interior of Hardorn.

Daren waited at the command post with Quenten, the other mages, and his under-officers; far from being even as comfortable as a tent, the site basically had only two things to recommend it. The unobstructed view, and a very tall shade tree.

"Can you tell who he is, yet?" Quenten asked in an undertone as the officers scattered off to take their places with their men.

Daren shook his head. There was a kind of sink of

"bad feeling" a little to the right of center, but no one mage stood out. They were assuming that Ancar's mages were too strong for any single one of Daren's mages to take. They would have to wait for their one best opportunity, and all hit him at once, in order to break him.

One of Daren's mages was effectively out of the picture; he was preventing the enemy from calling for help, at least magically. And that was *all* he was good for; they'd left him in trance in the Healer's tent, and there he would stay even after this was over, recovering. Or not; there was always the possibility he might die, either from exhausting himself, or being drained or killed by the enemy mages. And if Daren's force lost, he would almost certainly die. Mages were harder to control than captured fighters; the enemy usually did not even bother to try.

Daren gave the signal to advance, no point in a charge; mind-controlled men would not be unnerved by a charge or a battle cry. They'd simply fight until they dropped, and others took their places. Daren had given his officers careful instructions: keep the men in formation, no hero-tactics, fight as carefully as if it was all a drill. The one advantage to fighting mind-controlled men was that they *were* slower; it was the difference between knowing what to do and being told what to do—between learned reflex, and something that hasn't been absorbed bone-deep yet.

The battle was, as a result, curiously, grimly dull. No flag waving, no shouts except for exclamations of pain, no charges—the only sounds being those calls and the clash of weapons, the cries of horses, the scuffling of hundreds of feet and hooves—the men might as well have been those little counters he and Kero used to practice maneuvers with. Except for the blood, the wounded, the fallen. *Those* made it real, and made the fighting itself all the more unreal.

Daren concentrated on the mages, clustered near the officers' command post, and visible because of the dull colors of their robes, which were bright compared with the brown and buff leathers of the fighters and officers. But the more he concentrated, the less he seemed to see. He started to get angry and frustrated—*my people are* dying *down there*—but then he stopped himself, before he stormed off to harangue Quenten.

This is my problem, not his. I should be able to figure it out. Quenten said this earth-sense works like instinct, he thought, finally. *So—maybe if I* don't *concentrate. . . .*

I used to wonder what on earth good those meditation exercises Tarma insisted we both learn would do me. I thought if there was anything more useless—

I can almost hear her now. "Surprise, youngling. Nothing's ever wasted."

He closed his eyes and dredged the exercise out of deepest memory. It wasn't as hard as he'd thought it was going to be, for in moments he was relaxed. He centered himself in the earth beneath his feet, as Tarma had taught him, and when he felt as if he was truly an extension of it, opened his eyes—

And nearly choked. He'd never, ever seen anything like this before—and if it hadn't been that he felt fine, and had shared the same rations as everyone else this morning, he'd have suspected sickness or drugs. Superimposed over the fighting, the battlefield was divided into fields of glowing, healthy green, and dull, dead, leprous white, with edges of scarlet and vermilion where they met. Outside the area of fighting, the landscape was the same as it had been all the way north—sickly greens, poisoned yellows.

Except for one spot, behind the lines, in the ranks of the mages and commanders—one spot of black, auraed by angry red.

"Get Quenten," he told his aide. "We've got them."

Eleven of the twelve mages materialized beside him so quickly he suspected they'd conjured themselves there. "Where is he?" Quenten said—then shook his head as Daren started to open his mouth to explain that he couldn't *tell* him. "Never mind, I know, I'm being stupid. Hadli, would—"

A dark-haired, plump girl reached up and touched both his temples before he could say or do anything. "Got him, Quenten," she said in satisfaction. "If you want to feed through me, I'm not much use for anything else right now."

"What are you going to do?" Daren asked anxiously. "I mean, I don't want you to go blasting at him and hit *our* people."

"Not a chance. Kero likes things subtle. We figured out last night that we get the same effect by killing or wounding him physically—he'll still lose his hold on the magic and on the minds he's controlling."

"So I'm going to give them the way to identify him," Hadli said. "Quenten will bowl-cast a FarSeeing spell, and Gem and Myrqan will find a weapon to hit him with, while the rest distract him and keep his defenses all facing forward."

Daren turned; Quenten was already kneeling on the ground with his bowl of water in front of him—but this time there was a picture forming in it that even he could see.

Hadli and two others knelt beside him, and Daren found that he could still see over their heads. What he saw was the backs of several people in robes, with coruscating colors and strange shapes appearing just beyond them. His eyes went to one in a dull blue robe, and he saw, faintly, the same overlay of black and scarlet auras he'd "seen" before.

"That's him," Hadli said. "The one in the blue, with the copper belt and the serpent-glyph on his sleeve."

"Daren," Quenten called, without taking his attention from the bowl, "When we strike him, you'll feel it in the earth. There's going to be a moment of recoil, and then a hesitation. *That* is when you need to concentrate on what, exactly, you want to happen. There's a lot of power there; think of it as a flash flood about to roll down the river. Once you get it started, you won't be able to get it to stop or even change directions. If you don't know what to do—*don't think of anything.*"

Daren refrained from making a sarcastic answer. In the bowl, a light, ornamental dagger was elevating from a table behind the mages. Before he had a chance to ask what that meant, the thing snapped forward as if it had been thrown, and buried itself to the hilt in Blue-robe's back.

Daren had been in an earthquake, once. The feeling was similar. For a moment, the earth seemed to drop out beneath him, and he was left hanging in space, with a sense that something huge and ponderous was poised over him, like a wave, waiting to break.

Belatedly, he recalled Quenten's orders, and realized

the impossibility of not thinking anything. *Make it simple. Dear gods, it's going to let go—and I don't know what to tell it—*

Make it simple.

Put everything back the way it was!

The wave broke. He swayed, and started to fall, when his aide caught him. And suddenly, there was noise out on the battlefield.

The sound of several thousand enraged, half-mad men, turning on their officers and tearing them to pieces.

Twenty-four

Bodies pressed in on all sides of her. *Gods. Blessed Agnira. I got them into this. They trust me to get them out of it. How do I tell them that I can't?* The camp was unusually silent; somewhere on the Valdemar side, Selenay, too, was breaking the bad news to her troops. The regulars, that is; the Heralds already knew about it, of course. Kero wanted to look away from all those eyes staring at her with perfect confidence, to gaze up at the sky or down at the ground—anywhere but back at them. *They depended on me, and I fouled up. Now what do I say? "I'm sorry?"*

Instead, she gazed directly back at them all, trying to meet each pair of eyes before she spoke to them. "I haven't got any good news," she told them, finally. "Ancar's fighters have managed to force us east enough for his southernmost troops to divide and get in west of us. They're doing that now, and we haven't been able to stop them. He's had cavalry to the east in his own lands that has probably moved in north as well. We've been bracketed, and now we're surrounded."

She waited for a moment for that to sink in, then continued, rubbing the back of her neck. "They outnumber us by a goodly amount. Selenay's troops tried this morning to prevent the southern forces from coming west, but there were too many for them, and the farmers just aren't a match for trained fighters, not in pitched battles. It looks like the big confrontation is coming tomorrow; he has us right where he wants us, and no getting around it."

She listened to them breathe for a moment. "Where's Lord Daren?" asked a voice from the rear. Kero looked up, above the heads of those nearest her, and attempted to find the questioner.

"We lost track of him about the time he was going to cross over into the Valdemar side of the Comb, somewhere in the mountains. We don't know what happened to him. There's been no word of him coming up through Valdemar like he was supposed to. He could be on the way. He could have been turned back. He could have been defeated by Ancar down in the mountains. We just don't know, so we can't count on him being here."

Much less being here in time. That's the way ballads end, not real battles. They'd been in trouble before, but never this badly, and never while under her command. The weight of responsibility made her ache.

"Now, here's what we can do," she continued. "We're mounted, and we're the best hit-and-hide specialists in the business. We can break out, leave this mess behind, and head back down home. There isn't a soul outside Valdemar that would blame us for doing that. We're not in this for glory, or for patriotism, or because we're fanatics." She looked around again, and saw heads nodding. "We're in this for the money, purely and simply, and our Guild Charter and our contract allows for this sort of thing. Ancar threw the Guild out; we know he isn't going to accept a Code surrender from us. *Probably* what he'd do if we tried is kill us out of hand. He might even stick to killing the officers only, and mind-controlling you troops. I don't think I have to go any further into that."

She noticed one or two nearest her shuddering at the idea, and nodded to herself.

"As I said, the Code and the Charter allow for that. We can break out and go home; this is a no-win, hopeless situation. However—we won't be able to take any wounded with us, and anyone who goes down on the way out stays behind. My guess is we'll lose about half of our troops—the ones that are left—getting out. It's not going to be easy, but staying here means worse odds, so far as I can tell."

"What are the Heralds doing?" asked one of the Lieutenants. "They're mounted, and they're as good as we are, most of 'em."

"Good question," Kero replied. "They're going to break Selenay out, if they can. It's by no means certain; Ancar wants her hide, and if he finds out they're breaking her loose, he'll bring everything to bear that he has. We can use that as a diversion, of course, which makes our chances better.''

"Then what?" asked the same voice as before.

"Then they're going to turn back and rejoin the fight,'' she replied, as neutrally as she could. "All but an escort force to get Selenay to safe ground.''

A murmur of surprise and admiration rose from the troopers. Some of the Heralds—Eldan, for instance—had made themselves very popular; others, like the one Eldan had replaced, were considered nuisances. But the Sky-bolts could not help but admire anyone with the kind of guts it took to break free of a suicide-situation, then turn and go back into it.

"That has little or nothing to do with us," Kero reminded them forcefully. "We're mercenaries. They aren't. They have oaths to fulfill, and duties that they won't renege on. We're in this for pay. Now, the Skybolts have never been an ordinary Company, and I've never been an ordinary Captain. That's why I've called you all here. I'm not going to make a decision like this one alone, or even with my officers. Do we try to go, or do we stay? And do I stay your Captain—"

The shouts of disapproval that met *that* question made her feel terribly self-conscious. "All right," she bellowed at last, holding up her hands for silence. "All right, if you want me that badly, you've got me. But the other question—break out, or stay and do what we can? You know the drill; dark-colored pebble for 'go,' light or white for 'stay.' And no maybe-colored rocks, either—I don't want any maybes on this one. Geyr will collect your votes.''

She turned and sat down, waiting for the results of the vote, keeping her mind tightly sealed against their thoughts. She didn't want to know what they were thinking, and she didn't want to influence it, either.

She tried not to think of anything, really. As Geyr moved out with the basket into the massed fighters someone else called out a question. "What about you?''

"I'll be going with you, since you'll have me," she said. "And I'll stay with you as far as Bolthaven; I intend to call another vote then, and see if you still want me when this is over. I have my responsibilities as much as these Heralds have, and my oaths have been made to you. I don't intend to break them.''

She heard the murmurs, saw the looks, and knew what they were thinking as well as if she *had* opened her mind to them. They all knew about Eldan—quite a few of them knew about their first meeting, ten years ago. They knew what she would be sacrificing by leading them if they voted to break out, or at least they thought they did.

She ignored the murmurs, and kept her expression schooled into serenity. *I made my oaths, I have my responsibilities. He knows that. It doesn't hurt any less—but there's no choice. Vows are made to be kept, and he would be the first one to agree.*

Finally Geyr brought the basket around to her, and she steeled herself against the inevitable. How could they *not* vote to save themselves? Only a fool would stay here and die. *So, I'm a fool. But it isn't just Eldan. . . .* True, the odds were only fifty-fifty that any of them would make it out in the clear, and those weren't good odds—but when had a youngster ever thought he couldn't beat the odds?

Then Geyr turned the basket upside-down on the table—

And she felt her mouth dropping open in shock.

A pile—a tiny mountain of white. Pale sandstone pebbles trickled down off the top with a gentle clicking sound. She spread the pebbles out on the table with a shaking hand. No dark pebbles, none at all.

They'd stay, fighting beside the Valdemar folk. No dissenting votes.

She looked up at them, searched each face she could see, and found nothing there but determination. "You're mad," she said, flatly. "You're all of you mad. We haven't a chance if we stay."

Shallan stood up, awkwardly, as if she'd been appointed as spokesperson for the entire Company. "We don't think so, beggin' your pardon, Captain. 'Sides, what's the odds of a merc livin' long enough to collect his pension from the Guild, eh? We all got to talking about this last night. General feeling is, these people here deserve help. Merc's likely to go down any time—but if we got a choice in goin' down, I'd rather do it for somebody that deserves a hand, than in fightin' for some pig-merchant workin' out a fight over territory with some other hog, an' doin' it with my sword an' my life.''

There was a murmur of agreement from the rest, and an ''Aye, that!'' or two from the veterans old enough in service to remember Ardana and the Seejay debacle.

Kero rose slowly to her feet, and to Shallan's immense surprise, embraced her. She kept one arm around her old friend, as she scanned their faces again, this time with her eyes burning with the effort of holding back tears. ''You're all fools, thank the gods,'' she said huskily. ''Every one of you. As much fools as me—if you'd voted me out, I'd have stayed myself. All right, Skybolts. We stay. And tomorrow, we show Ancar what it means to take on the finest Company in the Guild!''

The cheers could probably have been heard in Haven.

And no one would ever guess, she thought, with a mixture of pride and sorrow, *that they're cheering their own deaths. Poor, brave fools.*

This will probably be our last battle. It's ten to one it'll be mine. May the gods help us all.

Daren stared into the stranger's flat, dead eyes, and asked in frustration, ''So what am I *supposed* to do with you?''

The tent was hot and felt stuffy, yet every time Daren looked at this man, he got a chill down the back of his neck. *Better dead, he'd have been better off dead. Poor bastard.*

''Lead us, m'lor','' replied the nameless man, who until a year ago had been a simple farmer, with no cares of who ruled and who did not. ''Lead us. We got nothin', now. Our families is dead, or as good as. Our homes is gone. Our fields is weeds an' wild things. Lead us.''

''Thrice-dead Horneth,'' Daren muttered under his breath. *Lead them, he says. Farmers on horseback. Whatever cavalry skills they had vanished when the mage controlling them died. And here I am, with a horde of undisciplined, half-mad farmers with no memory of what to do with swords and lances.*

And yet—they *were* half-mad, and had nothing to lose. Ancar had stolen everything from them, including their names, for none of them remembered exactly who he was. All they had left were the memories of what had been done to them, and to their loved ones, memories so hedged about in rage that nothing the mages could do would erase them, and so those memories had been blocked off until Daren had given the fateful, desperate command to the earth—*put everything back the way it was*.

Some things, of course, were impossible; the dead could not be brought back to life, nor memories that had been destroyed be regained. But the troops' minds had been given back to them, and the land was already beginning to heal, free of Ancar's bondage.

"Professionals are predictable," ran one of Tarma's proverbs. *"But the world is full of amateurs."* So long as he kept *his* troops out of their way, where was the harm in taking these men with him and unleashing them on Ancar's forces?

"Let me think about this," he temporized, "I'm not sure I have the right to lead you. You're not my people, and frankly, you may not like my orders. If I don't have any real hold over you, you could decide to strike out on your own, and then where would my plans be?"

"But—" the man began, when he was interrupted by the arrival of Quenten. The mage was excited, his red hair going in all directions, and he made matters worse by running his hand through it every few moments.

"My lord, we intercepted a mage-message from Ancar's commander a few moments ago," he said. "We—"

Then he noticed the nameless man sitting there, and shut his mouth with a snap.

"If you'll excuse me," Daren said to the man, who, with the intractable stubbornness of farmers everywhere, opened *his* mouth to resume his argument—or voice a protest at the interruption. "I promise I'll come back to you with an answer, but I suspect that what this man has to say will make up my mind, one way or another."

Before the farmer could say another word, Daren took Quenten's elbow and led him out of the tent, to a few paces away where they couldn't be overheard.

"Now, what was this message?" he asked, "And is there any chance that Ancar's people could know it was you that got it, and not his own mages?"

"Hildre," Quenten said in satisfaction. "She's the best there is at identifying and counterfeiting mage-auras.

Unfortunately for her, that's about all she can do—which means she's useless outside of a group. But for working within a group, she's priceless. The commander inside Valdemar sent a conventional messenger to the mages on the Border, and *they* sent the message on here—and trust me, Hildre has them convinced it went to the right person. They're attacking Selenay at dawn, my lord. He's sent half of his foot around to the west, and he expects the cavalry to come in on the east and north. Kero and the Skybolts are in the middle of that. We have to do something!''

Daren took a deep breath and stared off at a tree, reviewing all his plans and his capabilities. *My foot won't make it before the fight's over. There's no way they can make a march that's half a day's ride away in less than a day. And even if we started now, they'd be tired—*

—unless—

''Thank you, Quenten,'' he said, his plan set. ''We'll do something, all right. With luck. we'll even get there in time. Tell the mages to get packed up; we'll be on the march in a candlemark.''

He returned to his tent, and as he expected, the nameless spokesman for the farmers-turned-fighters was still there. ''M'lor—'' the man said, getting to his feet, his chest puffed out belligerently.

''How many spare horses have you?'' Daren demanded. ''And can your horses carry double? Are they in any shape for a forced march?''

The man looked bewildered by Daren's sudden demands. ''We had twice's many horses as men, m'lor,'' he replied. '' 'Spect we still got that many, an' lot fewer men. Aye, they be good for a forced march, an' go double all right.''

''Good,'' Daren replied. He looked the man in the eyes. ''I *won't* lead you, sir. But I *will* put you in a position to strike back at Ancar. Here's what we'll do. . . .''

Enemy to the west, enemy to the south. Kero stood beside Selenay on the gentle hill they'd claimed as the spot for their stand, looked out over the sea of Ancar's men, and swore under her breath.

Selenay shook her head. ''It isn't over yet, Captain,''

she replied, as she fitted her helm over her head. "In fact, it isn't even begun."

"Well, my lady," Kero replied, as she tapped her own helm to be sure her tightly coiled braids were cushioning it properly, "I won't say it's finished, but damn if I like the look of the odds."

"Daren may yet arrive," the Queen pointed out, fitting her foot into the stirrup and mounting.

And the rivers may flow backward, the moon rise in the west, and Ancar find a religious vocation. Kero said nothing, though, as she swung herself up into her own saddle. "With your permission, my lady, I'm off. You know the plan, such as it is. We'll try and cut a path for you and the Heralds, heading west."

"No," the Queen replied stubbornly. "Not yet. Not while there's still a chance we can win this—"

"Win!" Kero snorted. "We can't even hold them back! The scouts say there's a force of cavalry coming in from the east; if we go head-to-head with them, they'll win, their horses are fresher and there're more of them. The one chance we have to get you out is—"

"Captain!" One of the scouts came riding up, her horse lathered. "Captain, cavalry coming in, now—but they're riding double, and not all of them are wearing Ancar's colors."

Kero swore, and turned to Selenay. "My lady, no more arguments, or I'll have the Healers knock you out and strap you to your Companion's back with my own hands. No matter what you think, you're important to Valdemar, and—"

Kero caught lighting-fast movement out of the corner of her eye, and turned with an exclamation of recognition and astonishment. A small gray shape came hurtling through the massed enemy, then through the Valdemar cavalry, frightening horses and making them rear and dance—startling Companions, and making them snort and raise their heads. It headed straight for Kero, and flung itself through the air in a tremendous leap, landing in the arms she reflexively held out to catch it.

One of Geyr's messenger-hounds. More importantly, it was the odd-looking gray-brindle Geyr had left with Daren.

"Doolie!" Geyr hurled himself out of his saddle and

stumbled toward them. The dog wriggled with happiness, its tail beating against Kero's side like a drumstick, and it finally squirmed out of her grasp to launch itself for Geyr and his lumps of suet—though not before Kero had managed to get the message cylinder off his collar.

She opened it and took out the slip of paper with shaking hands.

"We're on the way—with friends," it read.

"Great blessed Agnira on a polka-dot mule!" she breathed. "By the seven rings of Gabora and the rock of Teylar! Someone put that bastard up for sainthood—he's pulled off a friggin' *miracle!*"

By now she was shouting, and everyone was staring at her, except for Geyr, who was crooning to his exhausted little dog.

She turned to Selenay, who had pushed her face-plate up, and was looking at her as if she had gone mad; alarmed, and a little fearful.

"That isn't Ancar's cavalry coming in from the west, my lady," she exulted, trying very hard to keep her grin from wrapping around the back of her head and splitting it in two. "At least it isn't Ancar's cavalry *now*. It's Daren, and he turned 'em. I don't know how, but the bastard turned 'em. That must be why they're riding double—that's Daren's foot up behind the cavalry-riders. I know exactly what he's doing; this is a trick we played with tokens, back when we were studying together. He'll have the cavalry come in and drop his infantry in on the southern and eastern flanks to support us, then he'll bring the cavalry in behind behind Ancar's foot, probably on the west."

Selenay's eyes widened. "We'll have *Ancar* caught in the same trap he thought he had us in!"

Kero nodded, and pulled her visor down. "That's it, my lady. That dog isn't *that* much faster than a horse. He'll be in place any moment—"

"*Captain!*" Shallan shouted, and Kero turned to see where she was pointing.

Fireworks, great splashes of color, fire-flowers against the blue, rising from three places. And Kero knew instantly why, because it was a trick the Skybolts had used before, when their mages were too exhausted or too busy to send signals—the mages were probably unable to ap-

proach the border, much less cross it, but physical
fireworks worked just fine, and didn't care about any
'guardians,'' magic or otherwise. Southeast, due south,
and southwest, the fiery fountains signaled Daren's attack
on three fronts. And already there was confusion, some
milling around, among the fighters within Kero's range
of vision. The rest of the Skybolts knew what that meant,
and let out a whoop of joy.

Kero caught Geyr's attention, and gave him a hand-
signal. He dropped the dog, sent it back to the Healer's
tent with a single command, and pulled his horn around
from behind his back. ''Prepare to charge'' rang out clear
and sweet against the growing noise from Ancar's troops.
Selenay's buglers picked it up, and echoed the command
up and down the line.

Kero waited a moment more, as the Skybolts readied
themselves. A skirmish charge was not like a regulation
charge, and she blessed the gods that her people and
Selenay's had ample opportunities to perfect their coordination these past few weeks, for this was the engagement
that would count. The Skybolts would be first in—charging
the enemy line, firing as they came, only to peel off to
right and left, continuing along the line, firing until they
ran out of arrows or line, and coming back in a wide arc.
Behind them would be the regular cavalry, lances set;
Heavy cavalry first, to hit the lines and hopefully break
through while they were still recovering from the hail of
arrows, then the light cavalry to come up through the
breech made by the heavy cavalry. Then the Skybolts
would return, this time arcing their arrows high to hit
behind the line of fighting, harass those enemy fighters
still on their feet in the front lines, and keep the enemy
from bringing foot around to engulf the cavalry.

At that point it would probably get to steel, and at that
point, Kero herself would join the affray.

The fight was still uneven—but now they had a chance.

:Don't go chasing any Shadow-Lovers, you!: said a
voice in her mind. *:I don't share with anyone!:*

She looked behind her; Eldan's Companion Ratha
shouldered Shallan's mare aside so that he could take her
place. Shallan shrugged, grinned, then made a mocking
bow and backed her mare away.

*:You'll have to keep up with me if you want a chance
to enforce that,:* she replied. *:I don't wait for anyone.:*

:Then what are you waiting for now?:

:Nothing.: She lifted her hand and signaled Geyr, who
blew the charge, and behind her, at the Healer's tent, she
heard the explosions of their own fireworks. Evidently
someone had thought quickly enough to set off their own
return signal. Whoever it was, she blessed him.

The first line of archers bore down on the lines, followed by Selenay's heavy cavalry and the Skybolts' light
mixed with Heralds and Selenay's light. Dust rose in a
blanket from beneath their horses' hooves, making a yellow haze over the battlefield, and making it hard to see
anything. Kero counted under her breath; waiting for the
archers to reappear.

At the count of one hundred, they came charging up
out of the cloud, turned their horses, and prepared to
charge again. Kero strung her bow, made sure the quiver
at her saddle-bow was full, and spurred her horse to join
them just as they made the turn.

She lost Eldan immediately as he vanished in the
chaos; she trusted to Hellsbane's sure feet to keep them
from going down. They sent arrows up over the solid
dam of milling bodies, and hoped they wouldn't hit anything friendly.

Then it was time for sword-edge, as a running line of
foot hit them from either side with a shock. Kero cut
down at a pikeman trying to hook her out of her saddle;
Hellsbane reared and bashed in the skull of another as
he hooked her neighbor, a Valdemar regular. A sword
came out of nowhere and she parried it, then kicked its
owner in the teeth.

Five men converged on her; she got two, and Hellsbane got one—but one got underneath her, because the
melee was so thick the mare couldn't maneuver. Kero
saw it coming, the same move that had gotten one of
Hellsbane's predecessors—and she could do nothing to
stop it.

The mare screamed as a sword sought her heart—then
collapsed, as the blade found it.

Kero launched herself out of the saddle as the horse
buckled under her, rolled under another set of hooves,

and came up looking for anything with four legs and no rider.

There— a flash of something pale, yellow—no saddle, but that had never mattered to her. *Must be one of ours; couple of the scouts ride bareback*— The horse seemed to sense her need; it plunged directly toward her, trampling fighters in its way, and stood still long enough for her to seize a handful of mane and drag herself up onto its back.

And just in time—

Daren stuffed the message into the cylinder, and Quenten sent the skinny little dog Kero's Lieutenant had left with them off across the field. He could hardly believe his eyes when he saw how fast the the beast moved; like a streak of gray lightning.

I hope to hell she gets that, he thought, *Quenten said one of the mages was going to put directions in the dog's head*—

Never mind. Either she gets it, or she doesn't.

"Are you ready?" he asked the putative leader of the nameless men. The man nodded curtly. "Good luck to you, then,"

" 'Tisn't luck we be lookin' for," the man replied, and rode out to the head of his troops. Daren shuddered. He hadn't liked what he'd seen in the man's eyes.

There's someone who is not coming back, and doesn't care, and the gods help whoever's in his way.

At an unspoken signal, the troops rode out, with Daren, the officers, the Rethwellan foot coming behind. Those riders would be the first thing that Ancar's men saw—and they should be assume that they were their own allies, coming up along the wrong flank. That should confuse and anger the officers, who would assume that the cavalry officers were ignoring their orders.

They passed the orchards that had screened their approach from the enemy, and as Ancar's lines came into view, Daren saw that the plan was working. The officers couldn't see what was behind the lines of horse, and they were shouting something at the lead riders.

This was what was happening at three points on Ancar's line: southeast, due south, and southwest, with Daren's foot hiding behind the eastern riders. Daren waited,

and the riders kept their beasts at a slow walk, waiting
for the signal.

It came, in a burst of colored fire overhead and to their
rear. The riders broke into a gallop, skeining away into
the west like a flock of birds, leaving behind the foot that
they'd hidden. *They* would go on to attack the western
and southern flanks, leaving the east to Daren.

Daren's trumpeter blew the charge, and while Ancar's
men were still staring in confusion, the infantry, weary
from having been carried on horseback all night, hit their
lines with a clash of metal-on-metal.

They were too tired to make it much of a charge, but
they were much better off than they would have been if
they'd come all this way on foot, instead of being carried
pillion or sharing one of the riderless horses. Daren
spurred his horse after them, intending to join his men
on the line—at odds like these, every sword was going
to make a difference.

His gelding's hooves thudded on the dry ground in time
with his pounding heart. All of the enemy nearby seemed
to be engaged, he looked around for a target. He thought
he could see a melee to his right; with horses boiling
in and out of a cloud of dust, but it was hard to tell if
it was just a confused lot of escaped horses or a real
engagement—he turned his gelding in that direction
anyway—

And a wild arrow shot his horse out from under him.

He felt the horse start to go down; tried to save himself, but the poor beast somersaulted over, throwing
him from the saddle into a bush.

He fought clear of the branches, and looked around
frantically for another set of reins, knowing he had to get
up above the foot so he could see what was going on.

There— A white horse galloped out of the dust-cloud
and headed straight for him as if he'd called it. He didn't
even stop to marvel at his good luck; he just grabbed for
the dangling reins and—

Looked up.

Met a pair of blue eyes that went on forever, with a
jolt like taking a mace to his skull—

—*oh, my*—

:*I am Jasan*,: said an imperious voice in the back of

his head. :*You are Daren. I Choose you. Now get the hell up here on my back before you get killed!*:

He didn't remember doing so, and the next thing he knew, he was up in the saddle, and looking around for some of his own people. His attention was caught by an embattled little group on the edge of the general melee.

"My lord?" someone shouted, and he turned. It was his aide, trying to get his attention. Somehow his own personal guard had managed to catch up with him; he didn't remember that, either.

He looked back to see if the group still fought. It was fairly obvious that this group held someone important; they were besieged on all sides, and most of the fighters surrounding them kept trying to pull the members of the group from their saddles, rather than trying to kill them.

Centermost was a woman; she was armored, but she'd evidently lost her helm. Her gold hair gleamed incongruously in the sunlight, confined only by—

Dear gods. That's the royal coronet.

She was giving a good account of her herself, slashing at those around her as if she'd been taking lessons in mayhem from his old teacher Tarma. But at those odds, she and her defenders weren't going to last too long.

Over my dead body. "Come on!" he shouted, and started to drive his spurs into his—

Dear gods—

His *Companion* launched himself at the Queen's position before spur could even touch flank.

:*Don't do that. Don't ever do that. Don't even think about it.*:

The wind of their passing whipped the words of apology out of his throat, but it didn't matter; they hit the enemy from behind, with Jasan doing as much fighting as Daren. For the first time Daren had an idea what it was like to have a warsteed.

:*Indeed.*: Jasan turned a man's head into red ruin with his forefeet, fastidiously dancing aside to avoid the blood. :*A warsteed. I think not.*:

:*Sorry,*: Daren replied weakly, and then he was much too busy to think, much less reply.

Then—there was no one in front of his sword, and nothing under Jasan's hooves; Selenay was sheathing her sword and looking in his direction with a thousand questions in her eyes. Jasan blew out a breath, and relaxed.

The Companion paced gracefully toward the Queen of Valdemar with his head held high and stopped just close enough for Daren to reach for her hand and kiss it properly—and there was no doubt in Daren's mind that this was what his Companion expected him to do.

He pushed back the visor of his helm, and wiped the blood from his own right hand, and started to reach—

—and met Selaney's eyes. Selaney's bright, blue, eyes. And felt the words freeze on his tongue.

:*Hmm,*: Jasan said, smugly, in his mind. :*See something you like?*:

And from the look on the Queen's face, she was having a similar tongue-tying experience.

Kero rode up beside Geyr, and slapped his arm to get his attention. "Get out there—" she shouted, waving at the lines of Ancar's fighters, who were now turning tail and running, heading for the east and even casting aside weapons and shields in order to run faster. Already some of the Skybolts, carried away by battle-fever, were spurring their tired horses to follow.

"Sound 'Assembly'!" she yelled at him "Get those fools back here before they founder!"

Geyr nodded, and cantered his horse after them. Kero sagged in her place, suddenly exhausted. It wasn't easy, riding a horse without saddle or reins—doing so in battle was doubly hard. She was just as glad now that her cousins had taught her how and drilled her in it till *she* was ready to drop.

But this had to be the most remarkable beast she'd ever sat; better than any of the Hellsbanes. It was uncanny, the way it had seemed to read her mind and act accordingly. She looked down at the back of the beast's head, so covered in yellow dust that it was impossible to say what color it was.

"Well, love," she said, patting his neck. "Hellsbane's gone to the Star-Eyed's pastures, but you seem to have been sent by the Shin'a'in Lady herself. Let's get a look at you."

She swung her leg over the horse's shoulder, and slid

down to the ground, then turned with one hand on the horse's shoulder to look into its eyes.

Its—blue—eyes.

And it was not yellow, as she saw when it shook itself and shed the dust in a cloud; it was *white*. Tall, blue-eyed, and white as the purest of summer clouds.

"Oh, my—" she said weakly, caught in those eyes, as the eyes were caught in her gaze.

:*I am Sayvel. You are my*—look out!:

But Kero only turned in time to see the mace coming at her too quickly to block—

"*Hydatha's tits!*" Daren happened to look away from Selaney's eyes just in time to see the "dead" man leap to his feet, and swing his mace down on Kero's head.

Jasan reacted faster than he did; before he managed to get out more than a simple "No!" the Companion had twisted around like a weasel and was charging Kero's attacker at a gallop.

The man saw them coming, but had no chance to do more than raise his arm ineffectually before he was under Jasan's hooves.

Not just Jasan's hooves; another Companion shouldered him aside, and began pounding the man into red dust.

Daren jumped off Jasan, with Selenay right behind him and went to his knees beside Kerowyn's body. He felt under her chin, then her wrist, for a pulse—

Dear gods, oh dear gods, she's not breathing—I can't feel a pulse—

Then *he* was shoved aside by a man in filthy, blood-flecked Whites, a man who pounded Kero's chest, then clamped his mouth over hers to force air into her lungs.

Daren still had Kero's wrist, when, suddenly, he felt the steady beat beneath his fingers, and she coughed and took a long breath. He got out of the way, as the Herald fumbled with the chin-strap of her helm while Selenay loosened her throat-guard. The other Herald was cursing the helm, and cursing her, and swearing as the tears poured down his face that if she died, he was going to kill her.

Her eyes opened just as the Herald got the helm off, and she looked straight up at him.

"That's a little extreme, isn't it, *ke'a'char?*" she said mildly, just before her eyes rolled up into her head and she passed out.

Daren decided that this was a good time to go collect Kero's troops, and take over the mopping-up.

Kero tugged at the hem of her pristine white tunic, and looked out over the grounds of the Herald's Collegium from her vantage point atop an old observation tower. She scowled as she realized what she was doing, and clasped her hands behind her back. As she did so, her hand brushed Need's hilt. She left it there for a moment, but there was no sign from the sword. She half expected the blade to demand to be passed to Elspeth when the fighting was all over, but it hadn't stirred at all since that single moment of recognition.

Well, the tradition is that the sword passes when the new bearer is about to go do something dangerous, and Elspeth's not likely to go running off on her own any time soon. But I can't say as I'd miss the damn thing too much.

Ancar—or rather, his army—had run back home to Hardorn with tails tucked between legs. Bobbed tails; those suicidal farmers Daren had brought in had done an immense amount of damage before they were cut down. Valdemar was safe for a while, at least—and there would be more tying Valdemar to Rethwellan than just a promise.

Selenay was absolutely head over heels in love with—of *all* people—Daren. And he was just as disgustingly smitten as she was. You could hardly get them apart. Eldan swore it was a lifebond.

I'll have to remember to tell her he snores when he's drunk.

Talia and that man-mountain of hers were giggling about the situation every time Kero saw them. Even Princess Elspeth seemed to find it all very amusing; Kero wondered how amusing she'd find it when she suddenly had infant sisters and brothers to tend. Selenay was no old hag, and fertility ran in Daren's family.

Oh, well, Faram is just going to have to learn to get along without the best Lord Martial he's ever had. I don't think you're going to be able to pry Daren out of Valdemar without a crowbar.

She caught herself tugging the hem of her tunic again, and scowled down at it. "How in hell can I be a Herald at *my* age?" she demanded of the air. "I've got things to do, I've got a life and responsibilities!"

But unless she wanted to give up Sayvel—*Never!*—she was going to have to stay in Valdemar.

"But what am I going to do about the Skybolts?" she asked aloud.

:I don't know, dear, the problem's never come up before.:

"That's because you idiot horses never Chose a merc Captain before," she replied acidly. "These aren't just people I order around; I've led them for ten years, they're practically my children! How can I just abandon them, put them in the hands of somebody else—somebody like Ardana, who didn't give a damn and could take them right into disaster?"

:None of your *seconds are like Ardana,:* the Companion pointed out.

"But none of my seconds have half my training, either!" She paced back and forth, just about ready to throw herself off the walls and be done with it. "They're not ready, and I'm not ready. It's either leave you, or leave them, and how can I make a decision like that?"

:You're the only one who can.:

"I told you she'd be up here." Geyr's black head peered over the edge of the observation platform. "Captain, this obsession you have with heights is damned unnatural." He climbed into view, followed by Shallan, Scratcher, and a tumble of his little dogs.

:I agree. Feet belong on the ground.:

"Captain, we voted again," Shallan said. "We figured you'd be all tied up in knots about being stuck as a Herald and you having to stay and us going back and all, so we figured we'd make up your mind for you. *We're* staying."

"You're *what?*" Kero stuttered. "How? Why?"

"Ah, it's easy enough," Scratcher said with a grin. "This Queen offered an unlimited contract, with *you* as permanent Captain, once you finish that schooling they want to give you."

"Hellfires," Kero muttered. "School. At *my* age."

"Since Quenten and the rest can't cross over the border, they're goin' back to Bolthaven and send ev'body else up here. Quenten's takin' over Bolthaven, make a school out of it.''

"Just like your grandmother's," Shallan interjected. "Town won't suffer by it, nor will the pensioners. I was talkin' with your cousins before we left; they reckoned it wouldn't be a bad thing to haul some Clan strings up here, where the market's better. So I 'spect they'll bring Tale'sedrin horses up *here,* and let another Clan take over the Bolthaven horse fair. And gods help anybody who messes with them. Quenten just made Master. No*body's* gonna try anything sharp on them, comin', goin' or in between.''

Kero turned her back on them, feeling as if she was being humored. "So you've got it all settled for me, have you?'' *They don't need me, after all. I guess I'm pretty redundant. . . .*

"Hell*fire,* Captain!" Shallan snarled, so fiercely it forced Kero to turn to look at them. "This was the only way these damn whitecoats'd let us *keep* you! You think we're gonna let you go kiting all over this heathen country by yourself? Not likely! If you're gonna find some action, *we* want a piece of it!''

"Adalnda, Captain, you've gone and landed us in the cream,'' Geyr said shrewdly. "Scratcher has not told you our hire. The Queen is *deeding* us a border town."

"Can you imagine it?'' Scratcher chuckled. "Us! Landed gentry, no less! There is no *way* we're letting you out of our sight! You took the Skybolts from half a Company to landed status—we wanta see what else you come up with! We may yet wind up dukes or something!''

"'Sides,'' Shallan growled, scuffing her boot-toe against the stone. "These folks need us. An' some of your damn morals is rubbin' off on us.''

:*High time, too.:*

:*We'll see about that. You people could use a good shaking up, Sayvel.:* Kero shook her head, and looked down at the pure white tunic. "Damn. Guess I don't have a choice, if I'm going to convert you ruffians to honest citizens.''

Geyr made a rude sound, and Shallan did her "village idiot'' imitation.

"Dear gods, what *have* I gotten myself into?''

"We're gonna shake 'em up, Captain," said Scratcher, echoing her earlier retort to Sayvel.

"They could use it," she agreed. "Gods, there's one thing I'd like to do—is there any way we can camouflage this 'oh shoot me now' uniform?"

"Could be, Captain," Scratcher said with a wink. "I'll work on it."

"I guess they're just going to have to get used to a new kind of Herald, Captain," Shallan grinned.

:High time for that, too. We're supposed to be flexible. You can keep us all on our toes, and you can start with Eldan, I think. And you should have guessed that your troopers noticed how you two feel about each other. They think this is a perfect solution for that, too. And they're taking bets on when the handfasting's going to be.:

Kero chuckled. *:Lady, you're going to get flexible like you've never seen before. And Eldan's going to get some real surprises.:* "In that case, I think this is going to work out." She saluted them, and all three returned the salute.

"Come on," she told them. "Let's go scandalize Valdemar."

"For starters," Shallan observed, "We're going to *have* to teach these whitecoats how to have a *real* party."

:As the Tayledras say, "May you live in interesting times.":

Kero threw back her head and laughed. *:You got it, horse-lady.:*

:And may you get—not what you deserve—but your heart's desire.:

:You know, lovely lady,: Kero sent back to her, as she followed her troopers down to tell the rest that she'd accepted their solution, *:I think I have. Beyond all logic and expectation, I actually think I have.:*

DAW

A note from the publishers concerning:

QUEEN'S OWN

You are invited to join "Queen's Own," an organization of readers and fans of the works of Mercedes (Misty) Lackey. This appreciation society has a worldwide membership of all ages. Nominal dues are charged.

"Queen's Own" publishes a newsletter 9 times a year, providing information about Mercedes Lackey's upcoming books, tapes, convention appearances, and more. A network of pen friends is also available for those who wish to share their enjoyment of her work.

For more information, please send a business-size SASE (self-addressed stamped envelope) to:

"Queen's Own"
P.O. Box 132
Shiloh, NJ 08353

(This notice is inserted gratis as a service to readers. DAW Books is in no way connected with this organization professionally or commercially.)

DAW

Melanie Rawn

THE DRAGON PRINCE NOVELS

☐ **DRAGON PRINCE: Book 1**   UE2450—$5.99

He was the Dragon Lord, Rohan, prince of the desert, ruler of the kingdom granted his family for as long as the Long Sands spewed fire. She was the Sunrunner Witch, Sioned, fated by Fire to be Rohan's bride. Together, they must fight desperately to save the last remaining dragons, and with them, a secret which might be the salvation of their people. . . .

☐ **THE STAR SCROLL: Book 2**   UE2349—$5.99

As Pol, prince, Sunrunner and son of High Prince Rohan, grew to manhood, other young men were being trained for a bloody battle of succession, youths descended from the former High Prince Roelstra, whom Rohan had killed. Yet not all players in these power games fought with swords. For now a foe vanquished ages ago was once again growing in strength—a foe determined to destroy Sunrunners and High Prince alike. And the only hope of defeating this foe lay concealed in the long-lost Star Scroll.

☐ **SUNRUNNER'S FIRE: Book 3**   UE2403—$5.99

It was the Star Scroll: the last repository of forgotten spells, the only surviving records of the ancient foe who had nearly destroyed the Sunrunners. Now the long-vanquished enemy is mobilizing to strike again. And soon it will be hard to tell friend from foe as spell wars to set the land ablaze, and even the dragons soar the skies, inexorably lured by magic's fiery call.

THE DRAGON STAR NOVELS

☐ **STRONGHOLD: Book 1**   UE2482—$5.99
☐ **STRONGHOLD: Book 1** HARDCOVER   UE2440—$21.95
☐ **THE DRAGON TOKEN: Book 2**   UE2542—$5.99
☐ **THE DRAGON TOKEN: Book 2** HARDCOVER   UE2493—$22.00
☐ **SKYBOWL: Book 3** HARDCOVER   UE2541—$22.00

A new cycle begins as a generation of peace is shattered by a seemingly unstoppable invasion force which even the combined powers of High Price Rohan's armies, Sunrunners' magic, and dragons' deadly fire may not be able to defeat.
